Mike Lanson for Murder

Mike Lanson for Murder

BYE–BYE, BABY!
MURDER ISN'T FUNNY
KILL ME WITH KINDNESS
IF WISHES WERE HEARSES

J. HARVEY BOND

(RUSSELL WINTERBOTHAM)

COACHWHIP PUBLICATIONS
Greenville, Ohio

Mike Lanson for Murder, by J. Harvey Bond
© 2022 Coachwhip Publications

Bye-Bye, Baby! published 1958
Murder Isn't Funny, published 1958
Kill Me with Kindness, published 1959
If Wishes were Hearses, published 1961

Russell Winterbotham, 1904-1971
CoachwhipBooks.com

ISBN 1-61646-532-8
ISBN-13 978-1-61646-532-2

BYE-BYE, BABY!

Mike Lanson
He was the kind of newshawk who would do anything to get a story—short of murder.

Clyde Guffy
A detective who had special reasons for hating reporters.

Hope Osgood
She knew her way around bachelors' apartments as well as on police carpets.

Gordon Tanner
As an army officer he'd been tough; as a publisher, he was tougher.

Herman Osgood
A crack pistol shot, he was better as a target than as a husband.

Ward Tyndall
He wanted a front-page by-line in the worst possible way.

ONE

Herman Osgood was upset one Thursday afternoon in September over the troubles the next day might bring. Whatever their nature, these problems were insignificant in comparison with the fact that he was doomed to miss tomorrow's breakfast, a possibility that he overlooked.

Very little had happened in his forty-odd years of breakfasting that brightened the ensuing days. But breakfast is a significant event, no matter how dull and uninteresting it usually is. One who eats his Crunchies, or whatever, has survived the night.

Ozzie, as we called Herman Osgood without affection, died violently Thursday evening.

Ozzie was shot. He was the second editorial executive of the *Gazette* to meet such a fate in ten years. Editors eventually die, like all other people, but they aren't shot as often as you would expect.

About five hours before somebody pulled the trigger and closed the books on Ozzie, I was shooting the breeze in the press room at Police Headquarters, across the street from City Hall. Don Hilliard, who had been with the *Gazette* only about two years to my six, had remarked how dull things were.

"But," he added sagely, "there must have been a dull afternoon during the seven days of Creation, or we wouldn't have so many of them now." It sounded very cute, but I suppose he had read it somewhere. Don was too young to be original.

Today had been so dull that we were almost glad when Lieutenant Clyde Guffy of Criminal Investigation came in and gave us a handout on the policeman's benefit ball to be held next month.

Don, a crew-cut kid whose ignorance is somewhat appalling, said, "Will tomorrow be all right, Guffy?"

Guffy fixed his blank round face on Don and replied, "Son, I've been around newspaper people long enough to know that nothing short of a disaster can get in today's paper after 3:30 p.m." He winked at me and said, "Where's your opposite number, Mike?"

Ward Tyndall, who covers the spot news and fast breaking stuff for the *Globe,* was my opposite number.

"It's a little early for him yet," I said. "He never shows up until he's at least fifteen minutes late."

"Well, give this to him. I don't want to overlook anybody." He slapped another handout down for Ward.

"One is enough for all of us, Lieutenant," said Don. "I'll write it up first thing tomorrow and a rewrite will handle it for the *Globe.*"

"I got enough for all of you," said Guffy.

"What's new on the Myler case, Guffy?" I asked.

"Nothing."

"Why don't you arrest somebody?"

Guffy threw up his hands in disgust. "There you go! Why in the hell doesn't your boss move his desk down here and run the police department from headquarters?"

"I was just asking."

The door darkened a moment and I looked up to see Ward Tyndall make his late entrance as usual. Except for signs of a hangover, which were always present on Tyndall, he was a nice-looking fellow. He was tall, wore nice clothes and kept his hair combed. On top of all this he had the manners and morals of Judas Iscariot and the disposition of a seasick gorilla.

"You're early," I said. "Only seven minutes late, instead of fifteen. But your eyes are bleeding."

"Go to hell," said red-eyed Ward Tyndall.

"Always sunny and gay," said Guffy. "Want this?" He offered the handout.

Tyndall took it. "I hate cops," he said.

"I hate reporters," said Guffy, "but I have to live with them because I'm a policeman."

"Why don't you get another job?"

"I'm happy," said Guffy. "Why don't you get one and make me happier?"

Ward snorted. "There's only one newspaper publisher in Creston. He puts out both papers. Any work but writing is degrading."

The phone rang and Don answered it; as the youngest he did all the dirty work. "Yes, he's here," said Don. He handed me the phone. "For you, Mike. Sounds like that disaster Guffy spoke of."

I spoke into the receiver. "Mike Lanson speaking."

"Mike, this is Colonel Tanner." The stentorian tones belonged to my boss, Colonel Gordon Curran Tanner. "Did Hilliard call me a disaster?"

"Heh, heh." I tried to laugh it off. "We were just telling Guffy that only a disaster could get into the paper at this hour."

"You weren't telling me, I was telling you," said Guffy.

"Heh, heh," Colonel Tanner laughed. "Very funny. You very busy, Mike?"

That's a heck of a question for the publisher of the *Gazette*, and its morning twin, the *Globe,* to ask an employee. "No. Not doing anything I can't handle tomorrow." Which meant I was doing something. Tyndall made a derisive sound with his rubbery lips.

"Fine. Drop whatever you're doing and come in. You needn't check in at the city desk. Just come up to my office. I want to talk to you."

"Yes, sir," I said. The receiver clicked and Colonel Tanner was gone. I replaced the phone and spoke to Don. "I gotta go see him. You ready to knock off, or do you want to stay and listen to Ward's misanthropical pleasantries?"

"I'll go with you," Don said. We got our hats.

"You want me to watch this till the night force comes on?" asked Guffy, pointing at Tyndall.

"Yeah. Keep him out of trouble. If he acts up, call a cop," I said.

The *Gazette* and *Globe* are housed in a big, barn-like brick building at Sixth and Cyprus. The building was constructed right after World War I and the outside hasn't been cleaned since. Soot and dirt have turned it black. Flanking the structure, on Sixth Street, is a parking lot reserved for employees. I parked my car and walked to the back door while Don ran to catch his home-bound bus. Don went to work at 7:00 a.m., and got off an hour before I did.

I walked through the mailing room, turned a corner and stopped in front of the elevators. I pressed a button and waited for a moment; then the door opened and I rode up to the fourth floor, where the Colonel's office is.

Colonel Tanner owns most of the stock in the very closed corporation, the Gazette Publishing Company, which operates the afternoon and morning newspapers. He thinks he's the most important man in Creston, and he is for me, since he pays me. If anyone else thinks differently, they don't say it to his face.

His office is at the east end of a T-shaped corridor along which the executives have their offices. At the base of the T is a large room housing the art and photography departments and photoengraving room.

Three more executive offices and a large room used by the editorial writers are at the top of the T. The one farthest to the left is Colonel Tanner's, and the third from the left is Herman Osgood's. The middle office is a sort of reception room through which you must pass to see either Colonel Tanner or his assistant, Mr. Osgood. Their secretary, Ruth Carpenter, sits in this office.

Ruth is the prettiest thing on the fourth floor, maybe the prettiest in the building. She's the kind of girl you describe by talking about her figure—forty-eighteen-thirty-eight.

As I stepped through the door, I sort of paused and admired the view. Real full was her sweater and real sweet was her smile.

"Hello, Mike," she said.

"Howdy, ma'am," I said. "They tell me out in the north forty that the ramrod wants to see me."

"He's back in the corral brandin' mavericks," she said. "Thata-way," She pointed to the door that said *Editor*. "Go on in; he's expecting you."

Osgood stuck his head out of the opposite door. "Somebody to see me, Ruth?" Then he recognized me. "Oh. I thought it was somebody important." His head disappeared.

Ozzie was a sort of dignified weasel whose main trouble was that he didn't know what he was doing himself and couldn't figure out why he did it. He had the ideal equipage of a flunky—a long, inquisitive nose which he stuck in places it had no right to be, and a perfectly blank mind that never worked unless it was doing something routine and familiar. Anything new stumped him and decisions drove him crazy.

He was about forty, and in his younger days he'd been quite a playboy. Two generations of Osgoods had manufactured steel, but they'd sort of slipped up on Ozzie. It was hard to imagine that this short, pudgy, bald little man once had been quite a boy with a polo mallet.

"Pip, pip!" I said.

Ozzie hadn't closed the door and his head came through it again. "What did you say?" he asked.

"Pip, pip!" I repeated.

"Oh," he said blankly. "That's what I thought you said." His head disappeared again and the door closed.

I went in to the Colonel's office. The minute I came through the door, I felt the editor's deep blue eyes staring at me. He sat behind his desk, which was directly across the room, with his back to the windows. His eyes were half hidden by shaggy brows, but I knew that he never missed a thing through the camouflage.

He had been reading some copy, probably editorials for tomorrow's papers, and he waved a sheet toward a chair at the right of his desk "Sit down, Mike," he said. "I'll be through in a moment."

"Yes, sir." I sat down.

The Colonel was in his early fifties, but looked as young as Ozzie. He wore glasses only when he read, and he had them on now. He was stiff and straight as a poker and there wasn't any fat in his big one-fathom height.

Once he'd been a wildcatter in the southwest. He'd struck oil and made millions. He came to Creston after the war, during which he served in the office of Strategic Services, doing jobs he would never be able to talk about. After a few years in the real estate business, he bought the Gazette Publishing Company, which was in bad financial difficulties, right after the murder of Jeff Myler, its editor. Somewhere along the line he'd married three times. I understood he had one son in Washington and a daughter in California.

When Colonel Tanner bought the *Gazette* it was priced in the neighborhood of eight million dollars, even though it was losing money. He didn't have enough capital to swing the deal and he promoted what he needed by persuading young Osgood to stop being a playboy and become a useful citizen. Strange as it may seem, the new experience of being almost top man agreed with Ozzie. He began to think of himself as on a par with his dad and grandad as a captain of industry. His job was one in which he couldn't do any harm to the business, but Tanner let him throw his weight around and do all of the nasty dirty jobs that had to be done. Like firing people.

The Colonel finished reading and looked up from his desk, which was as large as a ping-pong table. It looked larger because it was almost empty, except for a desk pen set, an ash tray and a copy spindle. He removed his glasses, then pressed a buzzer.

Ruth came through the door. "Shoot this down to composing," he said, holding out the copy.

Ruth took it and walked through the door. Both of us watched her swaying stride, and when the door closed and I looked back at the Colonel, he was smiling.

"Lousy editorials," he said. "I could do a better job myself than all three of those intellectual goons we've got penned in the corner." He jerked his thumb in the direction of the editorial writers' sanctuary on the other side of Ozzie's office.

"Mmmm," I said. After all, I don't like to run down another guy on the payroll, because he'll always have a chance to say things about my work. As far as I was concerned though, editorial writers were for the birds. Most of them were egg-heads, too old to go out and get honest news.

The Colonel leaned back in his chair and put the tips of his fingers together. "Did you handle the Myler yarn, Mike?"

He didn't mean the murder of Jeff Myler ten years ago, but the new angle on it which had cropped up this week. An anonymous sender had mailed a bullet to the police and ballistics had determined that it had been fired from the same gun that killed the *Gazette* editor ten years ago.

"Yes, sir," I said. "I handled the story."

"Anything new on it?"

"No, sir. I checked with Lieutenant Guffy this afternoon."

The Colonel beamed. "Guffy, eh? How's he doing these days?"

"Just fine. He's working his way up in Criminal Investigation."

Colonel Tanner wiggled his fingers back and forth under his nose. "Myler's murder was sort of a *Gazette* family matter, Mike," he said. "We ought to take a great deal of interest in it."

"Yes, sir," I said. "Besides, it's a pretty good story."

"It came in a little box, didn't it? The bullet, I mean."

"Yes, sir. A druggist's pillbox, only there wasn't a label on it. It was wrapped in brown paper, the ordinary wrapping kind. The address had been clipped from the telephone directory. It had an ordinary three-cent stamp and was canceled at the main post office at 6:00 p.m. last Thursday—a week ago today. The cops got it in Friday's mail, examined it Saturday, and we got the story Monday morning."

The Colonel nodded. "You're pretty good on facts, Mike," he said. "It's only when you get in the habit of unleashing that wild imagination of yours that you foul up stories. How does it happen they held up the story and didn't release it for Sunday's paper?"

"Guffy said that they didn't want to let it out at first because it might tip off Myler's killer that they were reopening the case," I told him. "Then they decided that it might do more good to get publicity on it. The murderer probably had begun to feel secure after ten years, and the new clue in the case would probably give him a scare."

"He might make a mistake, is that it?" the Colonel asked. Then he answered his own question. "Yes. He'd certainly lose some of his security. The police might be right. They ought to be right once in awhile, they're so cockeyed wrong so often." He paused. "Mike, I want you to stir up this case. Let the world know that the *Gazette* will never rest until the murderer of Jeff Myler is caught."

"I'll see if I can't dig up some new facts in the case," I said.

"You've got to. That's an order. Prod Guffy. He didn't like Myler, but he's a policeman and it's his duty to solve crimes. I'll write an editorial and that will stir up the mayor and the chief of police. We'll see if we can't catch a killer."

"Yes, sir," I said. "I will."

He pulled out his watch. "Four-thirty," he said. "Before you leave, stop by the city room and tell Hank that you'll be on a special assignment tomorrow."

"Shall I mention the Myler case?"

The Colonel looked surprise. "Of course. It's no secret. It's going to be in the paper—a lot of it."

It had been a sort of foolish question, but the Colonel had been in one of his cloak-and-dagger moods and I thought maybe he intended to surprise everybody, even the newspaper staff.

I left Colonel Tanner's office, closing the door behind me.

Ruth Carpenter was standing near the outer door, beside a filing cabinet, and I went out of my way to give her a friendly pat.

She said, "Oooo!" Then she turned around and swung at me, missing by a foot.

"Don't be angry, toots," I said. "That was a love pat."

"Fresh, you—"

She stopped suddenly as Ozzie's door opened and he came padding out. He walked past me to the outer door, where he halted, turned around and placed his right forefinger to his lips. Then he motioned for me to follow him.

I winked at Ruth and said, "So long, heart's desire," I said. "I'll see you later."

Ozzie was waiting for me when I came out. He turned without saying anything and then walked down the hallway. He kept on going until we reached the elevator. Then he stopped, turned around and faced me.

"What did he want?" he asked in a whisper.

"Just wanted me to check on a story," I said, a trifle louder than necessary perhaps.

"Sh-h! I don't want him to think I'm prying." He glanced anxiously toward the double doors which marked the entrance to the art department at the other end of the hall.

"Okay," I said in a whisper.

"Was—was it about the Myler case?" Ozzie asked.

I nodded, which made even less noise than a whisper.

"Does he want the police to catch the murderer?"

"Of course," I said. "Who doesn't?"

"Nobody, of course," said Ozzie. "Have they—the police, I mean—any further clues?"

"Nope. Not even a return address on the package they got."

"The Colonel wants you to solve it, doesn't he?"

"I suppose so, but there's a pretty big chance I won't"

"Big time reporters get to the bottom of cases like this."

I stared at him, a little hot under the collar. Maybe I'm not the greatest reporter on Earth, but I always considered myself of good average quality. Even the police admitted they were stumped on this one, so why should anybody think I was small time because I couldn't do as well as the cops?

"Thanks for calling me a newspaper bum," I said.

"Oh," Ozzie said. "I didn't mean it that way. I meant that this was your chance to do something really great. To put a feather in the *Gazette's* cap."

"I'm always glad to put a story on page one," I said, "or a feather in a pressman's hat, if it's part of earning my salary and if it's possible."

I pressed the elevator button. Ozzie hesitated a moment, as if he wanted to say something else, then he turned and tiptoed back to his office.

That was the last time I saw him alive.

TWO

The city room, and its adjacent editorial departments, shares the third floor of the building with the composing room. Twin swinging doors, one marked *In,* the other *Out,* are continually vibrating with the flow of copy boys and others going from editorial to the back shop.

Hank Newcomb, the, *Gazette* city editor, had his desk directly in front of the door leading to the elevators. He was about average build and he bore the man-killing responsibility of directing all of the reporters without having a mental breakdown. Although he was patient, he was sarcastic and he had a temper which boiled and seethed with righteous indignation whenever carelessness or stupidity got in his path, which was nearly always. Once he had nearly gotten himself fired by throwing a telephone book at a rewrite man.

However, Hank was not discriminatory. He vented his wrath on everybody and soon you got used to it. I've never heard him tell a reporter not to come back unless he got a certain story, which is a typical line for a movie city editor, but he expected everyone to do more than was humanly possible.

In the six years I'd worked under Hank, he'd fired seven men, but I had to admit he'd been justified. Once he gave me a five-dollar bonus when I risked my hide with the police when they smoked out some armed bank robbers. I'd heard a bullet whiz past my ear on that assignment.

Hank looked up at me as I came in the door. Then he glanced at the clock on the wall across the room. It was 4:30. "Cops run you out?" he asked.

I grinned. "The Colonel called me in."

Hank waved his hand to the chair beside his desk. "You interest me," he said. "Sit down. Tell me why he went over my head."

I sat down. "The Myler case," I said. "He thinks the *Gazette* should relentlessly pursue the murderer of Jeff Myler and avenge its incorporated pride."

Dwight Deems, the managing editor, was standing by the telegraph editor's desk near the allegedly sound-proofed room where the teletype machines are housed. As he turned his head, Hank beckoned and the managing editor came across the room. He was a dapper little man, about Osgood's age. Prematurely white haired, fastidious in his dress, and a good newspaperman.

"The Colonel is all for digging up the Myler case," Hank told him, when he reached the desk.

Deems looked at me. "The bullet set him off?" he asked.

I nodded. "He wants me to prod the cops."

Deems frowned. "What about that bullet, Mike? What do the cops think of it?"

I shrugged. "That somebody found the gun, had reason to think it was the Myler murder weapon, and hated to reveal his identity."

"It's been three days since we ran that story," Deems said. "About time somebody stepped forward and told what they knew."

I nodded. "It would seem that way."

"The reason they haven't is because they've got a blackmail angle," said Deems.

"Maybe."

"Good Lord, Mike, what else could be the reason for withholding evidence in a murder case? I don't think the murderer sent that bullet to the police."

"Could be the person who sent it is waiting for something else to happen."

"What, for example?"

I spread my hands. "I don't know what the motive was, but I do know that blackmail is only one of a few possibilities."

"It must be blackmail of some sort," said Hank. "What are we going to do about it, Dwight?"

"Do what the Colonel says, of course," Deems replied. "After all, he's the boss." He looked at me. "Is there anything new in the case?"

I shook my head. "Maybe one of you could be helpful," I said. "I don't even know where to start looking."

Both Deems and Hank Newcomb had worked for Myler. Hank was police reporter then and Deems was managing editor. Deems had been able to buy a little stock from the widow, and he retained both the stock and his position when the company was reorganized under Colonel Tanner.

"I can't tell you anything," said Hank. "How about you, Deems? Seems to me we covered every angle after the murder."

"No-o," said Deems. He seemed thoughtful. "There certainly wasn't much to go on then and the trail is ten years colder now. I'd suggest you read the morgue clips and rehash something. Tie it in with that bullet."

"I've read 'em," I said. "How about interviewing Mrs. Myler?"

"I wouldn't bother her," Deems said hastily. "I don't think there's much that we can turn up for ourselves. Let the police do it. We'll run a story or two on it, of course, but by next week the Colonel will have forgotten all about it and we'll let the matter drop."

This seemed to be a heck of a way for Deems to act. Usually he got enthusiastic over new angles on something old. On the other hand, I supposed he knew what he was talking about. There's not much that a lone reporter can dig up on a ten-year-old murder.

"How about theorizing a little?" I asked.

"Do you have a theory, Mike?" Deems asked.

"Sure," I said. "Like you said, the bullet didn't come from the murderer, but the fact that it came at all proves that the gun is still in somebody's possession. Likely as not, the person who has it isn't the murderer."

"How do you figure that?" Hank wanted to know.

"Since possession of a murder weapon is an incriminating bit of evidence," I said, "I don't think the murderer would want to be caught with it. Therefore, he got rid of it as soon as he could after the murder. He either threw it away and somebody found it, or he put it in a place where it wouldn't be examined or associated with the crime."

"Where would that be?" Deems asked.

"I don't know," I said. "But it turned out that the spot wasn't as secure as the murderer thought. Somebody figured out that it was the gun that killed Myler."

"After ten years?" Hank asked.

I went on. "Another thing, the person who thinks he's got the murder weapon had a darn good reason for sending that bullet anonymously to the cops. Maybe he was afraid he'd be bumped off. Maybe he didn't like to get mixed up with the cops."

"You mean crooks?"

"That's just one possibility. A lot of people don't want cops sticking their noses in their affairs."

Hank unslitted his eyes. "A lot of people had different ideas about who killed Jeff. Everybody was accused, from victims of Jeff's crusades to the cops themselves. Myler was up to his neck in politics."

"The political motive wasn't any good," Deems said. "Assassination makes a martyr out of the victim. You'll recall that Myler's reform ticket won the election after his death."

"Maybe his own party killed him." I was trying to be funny, but Deems scowled.

"It all adds up to the fact that somebody, besides the murderer, may know who killed Jeff Myler."

Hank nodded his head very slowly. "There's no such thing as a secret, Dwight. No matter what a man does, somebody always finds it out."

"Such thoughts make me shudder," I said.

"You should shudder," said Deems. "Okay, Mike. The Colonel's the boss. Dig up some kind of a story. The *Gazette* will never cease its relentless pursuit of Jeff Myler's killer. Only I wish sometimes we wouldn't be so damned relentless that we couldn't bow out of a tough story."

"Why, Dwight?" Hank asked. He seemed to think it was odd, too, coming from a man who had served under two crusading editors.

Deems shrugged. "Just a feeling I've got." He walked back to his cubby and disappeared behind the panes of frosted glass.

"Beat it," Hank said to me. "I've got work to do."

A tiny desk in one corner of the room is my home base. I'm usually at the press room in Police Headquarters because it's far away from bosses, but when I'm operating close to the deadline, I sometimes write my stories in the office.

My desk is just big enough for a typewriter, and it has a couple of drawers filled with things I need. I don't have a phone on my desk, but the one on the next desk is within arm's reach. I picked up the phone and called the press room at headquarters. Tyndall answered.

"This is Mike," I said. "Wonder if—"

"If you're wondering about me doing you any favors, go to hell," said Tyndall. "When did you ever do anything for me?"

"That's a heck of a way to talk to a man that's just about to do you a good turn," I said.

"Oh yeah? You doing anybody a good turn is about as likely as me getting a fifty-dollar bonus from the Colonel, bless his black little heart."

"Careful, sir. The king's spies are everywhere. One might be listening in on the switchboard."

"The Colonel knows his heart is black, otherwise he'd pay me what I'm worth," said Tyndall.

"Okay, okay. You're worth your weight in gold. That is why, my stalwart, I've decided you need a break. Why not be a fair-haired Rover Boy and maybe this black-hearted Colonel will give you a raise?"

"I'm listening, but I haven't said I'd do it."

"Well then, hear this. The Colonel is intrigued by the Myler case. Why don't you stick your spurs into one of those nighttime cops and dig up a new angle?"

"Hell, that case is dead and buried."

"I seem to recall there was some talk about Myler and a cop named Guffy."

"Hmm. I see you've been spending time in the morgue."

"Right. See what you can dig up."

"It doesn't sound right," said Tyndall. "Why don't you check it out yourself, instead of giving me first crack at it?"

"I want you for a friend," I said.

"The hell you do," said Tyndall. "Okay. I'll bite. I haven't been on the honor roll for so long, maybe I ought to try for it. Read about it in the *Globe* tomorrow."

"So long, chum."

"So long, you bastard."

After I put the phone back on its cradle, I felt real pleased with myself. Cuddling in the little cells of my warped brain was the idea that Guffy had a motive to murder Myler. Also, I knew, cops have access to guns which aren't theirs, and which can't be traced to any one cop. Especially cops who are in the Criminal Investigation Department. Guffy, according to clippings I'd read, had been under suspension at the time of Myler's murder. He had neglected his duty at the request of some higher-ups and had been the goat when the *Gazette* exposed the misdeeds.

Guffy said he hated newspapermen. He might have hated one enough to kill.

But if Guffy was a killer, a reporter who scratched too near the truth might wind up as Myler had. Good old Ward Tyndall, scratching in ignorance and bliss, seemed to be a much better man for this job than I was. Besides, he'd do the same thing to me, if he had the chance.

All of this Machiavellian stuff was based on the theory that Guffy had killed Myler, and I knew it probably wouldn't pan out, anyhow. I had better leads to pursue and in spite of what Deems had said, I'd go to see Mrs. Myler tomorrow.

The clock said straight-up five after I finished my plotting. The American Newspaper Guild frowns upon reporters who work past quitting time without receiving overtime pay. I got my hat from the hook near Hank's desk and started through the door. I was headed for the elevator when a soft, throaty voice called from the doorway to the Society department.

"Mike, honey."

Ruth Carpenter emerged, her hips swaying like the waves on Miami Beach. She was wearing her hat and coat.

"Huh?" I said, which was not the word that Anthony would have used to address Cleopatra.

"Would you do me a favor, sweetie?"

I knew she wanted something or she wouldn't have used those words or that voice. "You want to keep somebody's name out of the paper?"

"Oh no, lover boy! Nothing so tremendous as that," she said, "It's just that I'm late and I've got a dinner date at 6:30. Would you haul me home? I live on the North Side."

That was the way I went to get home and it wasn't a favor hard to grant, even if she lived in the other direction. Who wouldn't want to get that baby into his car as a prelude to greater times ahead? "It would be a pleasure, toots," I said. "I'd drive you to Thule and back."

"Oh, you darling, you. I'm ready. Let's go."

"I wouldn't have asked you to do this," she said as we got into the car, "but Mrs. Osgood wants me to go with her to the A.I.W.G. meeting tonight." The A.I.W.G. was the Association for the Improvement of Working Girls, which had a big project in mind if they hoped to improve Ruth.

"Why don't they let good enough alone?" I asked.

"What do you mean?"

"Improving you," I said, "would be like trying to add color to the sunset."

"How poetic. I'll tell Hope you said that. You used to run around with her, didn't you, Mike? Before she married Herman Osgood, I mean?"

I nodded. When I started to work at the *Gazette* about six years ago, Hope Smith, which was her name then, had just started being secretary to Ozzie and the Colonel, the same job Ruth held now. Hope had been a plain, almost drab-looking girl. Then, about a year later, the first Mrs. Osgood died.

Hope had suddenly blossomed into new clothes, new hairdo, new makeup, and it looked as if she'd put on new curves. The wolves began to whistle and, let's face it, I was one of them. Then, without warning, it was all over. Three years ago she eloped with Ozzie. It had been sort of a poke to my pride to be tossed over for a pussy-footer like Ozzie, but I rationalized that Ozzie had more money in his pants' pockets than I made in six months. Hope was smart to marry for security, and social position, even if her man was twenty years older than she was.

"What kind of a girl was she?" Ruth asked.

I don't know how she expected me to answer that one, but I said, "A nice kid. Very nice."

"She doesn't get along very well with Mr. Osgood now," she said.

I shrugged. "She'll make out."

"She's certainly been having her bumps since she married Mr. Osgood."

"In what way?"

"Those snobs on University Hill won't have as much to do with her as she expected. I guess they figure she just married him for his money and that she's a—well—a sort of adventuress."

"Mmm."

"I guess I'm talking too much," she said. "After all, I like Hope, even though she doesn't like me. She thinks I'm after Mr. Osgood, too."

"Are you?"

"What a thing to say! Of course not. He's a married man."

"Okay," I said. "How about seeing the town with me Saturday night?"

"Gee! I'd love to, only—"

"Only what?"

"Well, Mr. Osgood wanted me to stay after supper Saturday night. Some sort of survey we're making for an advertiser, and he wanted me to help him check."

"Okay. Some other time."

"Now listen, I want to go with you. Maybe I could get off," she said. "He asked me if I'd be busy and I told him no. Now if I tell him I've a chance to go out, I'm sure he'd arrange to do the job some other time. There's no hurry about it."

"When can you find out?"

"I'll ask him tomorrow."

She asked me to stop in front of an apartment building called the Barnum Arms, which was one of those places where all apartments are two rooms and a kitchenette and filled to the eaves with secretaries. She got out, said her thanks, and I drove off, feeling proud of myself.

A few minutes later I parked my car in the garage under the Hotel Waltham and took the elevator up to the lobby. I got my mail, all bills, and then had dinner in the coffee shop, not bothering to go up to my room first. I had chop suey because it was the cheapest thing on the menu and I had very little cash. Tomorrow was payday.

After dinner I bought a cowboy novel and read part of it downstairs. Then I took the elevator up to the sixth floor and entered Number 615, which is my room.

Number 615 is around the corner from the elevators and overlooks an alley, but it's reasonably priced and I don't stay in it very much. I took off my coat and hat, and unloosened my tie. Then I sat down on the edge of the bed, took off my shoes and turned on the reading lamp.

I read fast. I'd nearly finished the book when there was a knock at the door. I put the book down, looked at the clock on my dresser. It was a minute or two before 7:30.

"Come in," I said.

Usually my door is unlocked, as it was then, because some of the fellows on the floor, also permanent guests, like to drop in when they are broke and have nothing better to do. Sometimes one of us would have a few drinks left in a bottle.

The door opened and the light from my lamp shone on the face of Hope Osgood.

"Jeez!" I pulled myself up to a sitting position on the bed and shoved my feet into my shoes.

"Hello, Mike," she said, closing the door behind her.

I stood up.

"Are you going to kick me out, or ask me to sit down and stay awhile?" she asked.

"I've never kicked a woman out of this room," I said. I pulled a chair out from under the writing desk, but she walked past it and sat down on the edge of the bed, where I'd been sitting. I caught a faint odor of liquor on her.

I stood, facing her. "I thought you were at the A.I.W.G. meeting."

"Oh, that," she said, dismissing it with a wave of her hand. "Ruth told me you drove her home. I suppose she told you about our date."

I hardly heard her. I was thinking that this was a hell of a place for Hope Osgood. Not that I'm a Puritan. I was just wondering if she realized it. Or was she drunk?

"Sit down, Mike," she said. "Don't act as if you didn't know how to handle a situation like this."

"I'm amazed," I said. I sat down in the chair, like a crazy fool.

She put her hands on the bed and leaned back, arching her bosom like twin Capitol domes. She was still as blonde and cuddly as she had been when she came out of her drab cocoon five years ago, but now she wore much better clothes. Not flashy, but expensive.

"I've hardly had more than a couple of words with you for three years," she said.

"You got married," I said. "After all . . ."

"Yes, marriage is usually pretty final for boy friends," she said. "But this one wasn't what I expected."

"Mmm." Ruth had said about the same thing.

"I married Ozzie because I was tired of living on cornpone and hog fat," she said. "I wanted chicken and cake. Is there anything wrong with that, Mike? Men do some pretty awful things for money, and nobody condemns them. Why can't a woman?"

"I'm not condemning you."

"I offered Herman what he wanted. Don't look like that. Herman was lonesome and he wanted companionship. I had youth and health, which was more than an older woman could offer, and so I got the job of being Mrs. Osgood."

"And?"

"Herman was funny," she said. "He thought he was seducing me. He showered me with everything—jewelry, flowers, candy. He thought he was dazzling me. Then he suggested I set my vacation to coincide with the editorial convention and go there with him. It was in Chicago. He let on that everything would be very respectable. He said that it would be perfectly all right, but people might talk, so it would be better not to mention it. I had my own ideas.

"On the second day of the convention I told him, 'Now, honey lamb, you brought me all the way from Creston to Chicago. That's across State lines.' He said, 'What on earth do you mean?' As if he didn't know. And I said, 'Uncle Sam takes a dim view of such things. There's a law called the Mann Act, which says you can go to jail for taking a woman across state lines for immoral purposes.' And he said, 'But darling, think of the scandal! You wouldn't do a thing like that?' Meaning I wouldn't put him in jail, but I said I would and he got the idea. He ran out real quick and got a marriage license and we got married that same day."

I didn't know whether to laugh or not. But it was funny, and she expected me to laugh, so I did.

"When I got back to Creston," she went on, "I thought I'd be like Althea, the first Mrs. Osgood. *Althea!*" She practically hissed the word. "Nobody ever let me forget her. I thought the society women on University Hill would be nice and palsy. After all, they married their husbands for the same reason I did. What a joke! You would have thought I was a whore from the flats. They acted as if I was a kept woman. They talked about me, jeered at me. They snubbed me! And Herman didn't do a thing about it. He said, 'They're nice people, dear. You just don't understand them.' I understood them too well."

Interesting, but I was getting a little sick of the recital. "Hope," I asked. "Why did you come here? Are you drunk?"

She giggled. "Just a little loaded, sweetie-pie. I came over for a kiss."

She stretched out her arms but she forgot she was leaning on them and fell back on the bed.

She didn't try to get up. Any ideas I had, or might have had, were going down the drain. She wasn't doing anything to me.

She raised her head. "What's the matter with you, Mike?"

"Goddammit," I said, "this is dynamite. You're known around town. People right here in this hotel know you. You drive around in that flashy red-and-white Edsel and people point you out as the wife of the assistant editor of the *Gazette*. Somebody must have seen you come here. If Herman Osgood hears about it, I'm sunk."

She sat up and waggled her finger at me. "Don't you worry about old Hermie. I've got him where I want him." She giggled again. "I'm going to be free, Mike. Free as the breeze. When I'm through with him, his old bank account's gonna look half-sized. Come on, lover! Gimme a kiss."

"Hope, you're too damned drunk."

She sat up then, glaring at me. Her eyes were no longer alluring. They were filled with fury.

"Okay, you damned monk. Defend your cockeyed virtue," she said. "You newspapermen are so confounded dedicated that you've forgotten the facts of life. I'll bet you'd rather go out and dig up a story about a bullet than make love."

If I'd been a dog, my ears would have stood up. "What did you say about a bullet?"

"I didn't say anything about a bullet," she said. "I just said you were acting like a fool." She stood up. "Mike, when I get my divorce, will things be like they used to be?"

There was no use making her mad. "Maybe," I said. "But right now things aren't the same. You're married and I'm no poacher. Besides, you've been drinking."

She pushed me aside and walked to the door. She turned. "Sissy," she said. "Panty-waist."

And out she went, slamming the door behind her.

I lay down on the bed, very bothered and very confused. I could still smell her perfume. I got up. I paced. I stared out of the window into the dark alley below. I tried to finish the cowboy novel, but I had to lie down on the bed for that.

Presently I went to sleep.

The clock said 9:38 when the telephone rang and I awakened.

"Hello."

"Mike?" It was Hope Osgood's voice, no longer raspy with liquor, but shrill with fear.

"Yes," I said wearily. "What is it, Hope?"

"I—I'm sorry about the way I acted. I had too much to drink."

"Forget it," I said. "I understood."

There was a pause. "I'm in trouble, Mike. Something awful has happened."

"I know," I said. "I told you somebody would see you—"

"No. It's not that," she said. "It's Herman. He's dead. He's been murdered."

THREE

I asked her to repeat it and she said, "Herman's been shot. Murdered." Her voice expressed terror.

"Who killed him?"

"Good heavens, Mike! I don't know. I just came home and found him lying on the floor of his study."

I suspected of course that she'd done it, but if she had, she wasn't admitting it. "Don't touch anything," I said. "I'll be right over. You're sure he's dead?"

"I—yes, I'm sure."

The police should have been called, or maybe a lawyer, but I didn't suggest it. Such a thing didn't enter my mind. The only thing that did was that she'd been up here a couple of hours ago and when the cops learned about that visit, I'd be in trouble.

The elevator boy knew about her visit. He mentioned it, when he took me down to the garage. "Did the lady find your room?" he asked.

"What lady?"

"The one that asked which one was yours," he said.

"Mmm." I always said that when I didn't want to answer a question. He didn't press for an answer. He knew all right that she'd found my room.

I got my car and drove out to Clifton Road, on University Hill, where Herman Osgood had lived in a beautiful modern home.

I parked my car in front of the place. Two cars were already in the drive, but these were Ozzie's Caddy and Hope's red-and-white Edsel.

There was a light in the front room, and through the picture window I saw Hope move toward the door. I climbed three stone steps and the door opened.

Hope still wore the suit she'd had on when she came to my room. "He's in the study," she said.

I entered the house and she closed the door, then led me through a doorway to the left. It was an L-shaped hallway, but we didn't travel the length of it. Hope stopped at the first door on the left. She put her hand on the knob, and seemed to steel herself.

"Did you call the police?" I asked.

"No."

"You should have called them first."

"It's easy to second-guess," she said.

"I should have told you to call them."

"I wanted you here when they came," she said. "You don't know how deeply involved I am. Everyone knew we weren't getting along. And he didn't keep his mouth shut when it came to telling people that I tricked him into marriage. I'm sure they'll think I killed him. You don't think so, do you, Mike?"

"Of course not."

It was an overstatement. The first thing that had crossed my mind was that she'd murdered Ozzie. But on second thought, I halfway believed her. Ozzie was nettling. He got under your skin. He was nosy, exasperating and sometimes downright stupid. But he was ineffectual and, for the most part, harmless. Just somebody I didn't like.

The cops would look at it differently, though. Ozzie had money. He was the only son of a millionaire and he'd inherited his wealth before taxes got high. His first wife had left him childless and Hope was the heir presumptive to the Osgood millions. Hope was sure to gain more than anyone else by his death. Financially, anyhow. That was how the cops would see it.

"You could have thought of a thousand people before you called me," I chided.

She opened the door. I followed her into the room.

"There," she said, pointing.

The room was one Ozzie used as a study. He was on the floor between the desk and a row of bookcases, his feet toward me. A chair to my right had been overturned, indicating that there'd been a struggle.

Ozzie was lying on his side with his back against the bottom of the bookcase, which kept him from rolling over on his back. His legs were crossed, as if he'd slumped down after taking the bullet in his chest.

"Sure, you didn't touch him?" I asked Hope.

She shook her head and looked me straight in the eyes. "No."

She started to move forward, but I checked her with my hand. "Don't touch him now," I said. "Let's call the police."

I saw a phone extension on the desk. But as I reached for it, I had a sudden thought. You don't pick a cop to handle a case, of course. Cops aren't like doctors or lawyers. But sometimes, if you work it right, you can get a cop you want. I wanted Guffy. I knew him better than most of the cops in the Criminal Investigation Department, and I was already beginning to be afraid that I'd need a friend.

Instead of picking up the phone, I got a directory off one of the shelves of the bookcases near Ozzie's body. I opened the directory and stared.

The directory was open in the C's. There were lots of names beginning with C, and also firms. *The City Plumbing Company, City Laundry, City Cleaning & Dyeing,* and so on. The firm names were printed in boldface type, and there was a space where the word *City* had been clipped out; ". . . *Pharmacy.*"

And I knew that the bullet sent to the police by the party who wished to remain anonymous had been addressed with words clipped from the phone book. I thumbed the directory pages to the P's. *"Police Headquarters, Tenth and Sycamore,"* had also been clipped out.

Hope stared over my shoulder. "The police number's still there," she said.

"Who clipped it out?" I asked her.

"Herman, I suppose."

"Why?"

"We never talked about anything," she said. "Besides, I didn't even know he was playing with scissors."

I turned back to the G's and found Guffy's number. He must have been in bed, because it took him a few moments to answer.

"Clyde," I said. "This is Mike—"

"Who?"

"Mike Lanson, the reporter."

"Oh yes, Mike. What's on your mind?"

"I've got something pretty serious, Clyde. I'm at the home of Herman Osgood on Clifton Road in the University Hill section." I turned to Hope, "What's the street address?"

She told me.

"It's 4216 Clifton Road," I repeated.

"Okay," Guffy said. His voice serious. "What's up?"

"Osgood's dead."

The line was completely silent for a moment

"Somebody shot him," I said. "Can you come over?"

Another hesitant silence. "I'll send the boys out," he said. "Don't touch anything. Is he in the house?"

"Yes," I said.

"Go outside and wait. Or at least into another part of the house. Don't go tramping around till we've been over everything."

"All right," I said. "You coming?"

Another pause. "I'll probably have to work on it anyhow. But the regular crew will be there first. Do whatever they say."

"I will. Thanks, pal."

I hung up the phone for an instant; then I picked it up again and dialed the office. I got hold of Luke Taylor, the night editor. He gasped and asked a dozen questions, half of which I couldn't answer.

"I'll send Tyndall and a photographer out," he said. "Can you help Tyndall on the story, Mike?"

"Sure," I said, "unless the cops keep me too busy."

"Are you mixed up in this, Mike?"

"Not yet," I said truthfully.

"It doesn't look good, Mrs. Osgood calling you over there, Mike. You shouldn't stick your neck out."

"Yeah. You're right." I hate second-guessers, too.

"Call us soon as possible."

"Will do."

I hung up the phone and turned to Hope.

It was then that I saw the dark spot near the bottom of her skirt. She turned and saw me looking at it.

"How did you get that?" I asked.

She reached down, lifted the skirt. "It's blood," she said. She stared at it. "Yes, I remember. I must have gotten it on my skirt when I knelt down beside him." She gestured toward the irregular red stain in the thick gray carpet.

"Better change," I said. "Show the skirt to the cops when they get here. It doesn't mean anything, but it'll help convince them you're in the clear if you don't hold back anything."

She gave a sort of choking laugh.

"What's the matter?" I asked.

"You said not hold back anything. Good heavens, what I will they say if I tell them about tonight?"

"Don't take everything so literally," I growled. "You don't have to mention that to them yet."

"Do you think they'll find out?"

"They'll try to find out everything you've done since you married Ozzie. And they'll learn most of it."

She really choked then. Without another word, she turned, went out the door and hurried to her bedroom. I went out into the living room and through the front door.

I waited a few minutes and a squad car pulled up to the curb and a couple of cops got. out. They came toward me with slow, business-like deliberation. "You Mike Lanson?" the first man asked.

"Yes," I said.

"I'm Murphy and this is Sanders," said the cop. "We'll take charge till the boys get here."

"Mrs. Osgood's in her bedroom," I said.

Murphy shook his head. "I expect it's a great shock to her."

I took out a package of cigarettes, gave each of the cops one. We smoked and waited.

The phone started ringing inside the house. Murphy looked at me. "She better answer it," he said.

The phone stopped ringing. Presently Hope came to the door. She now wore a blue pleated skirt, with a tan jacket over her white blouse, "Colonel Tanner wants to speak to you on the phone, Mike," she said.

There was an extension in the kitchen and I answered there.

"Mike? This is Colonel Tanner," came the booming voice.

"Yes, sir."

"Taylor just called me from the office. What in the devil are you doing over there?"

"Mrs. Osgood called me, sir."

"Why did she call you? Why didn't she call me?"

"I don't know, sir," I said. "I suppose it's because I'm the crime reporter and she thought I could handle things."

"There isn't anything going on between you two, is there? Didn't you run around with Hope before she married Hermie?"

"No and yes," I said.

"What do you mean?"

"No to the first question, yes to the second."

"Don't get smart with me, Mike. What about Hermie?"

"I don't know anything except that he's dead. Shot, Hope says, but I didn't see the wound. Just his body and the blood."

"No clues? Anything else?"

"Not yet. The police just got here. We're waiting for the Homicide detail."

"Listen, Mike. Taylor said he's assigned Tyndall to the story. I want you to handle it. Understand? Tyndall can help you, but you're on the ground floor. You can do a better job. Do it right, understand? We'll spread it in the *Globe*. Think you'll be through in time for the two-thirty?"

"I don't know," I said. "The police may not let us go till they've talked to us several times."

"I'll call the chief. I'll tell them to hurry it up. We want complete coverage for our suburban edition if possible."

"Yes, sir."

"Taylor's got a rewrite filling in the obituary. You won't have to worry about that. You handle the crime angle. And don't let those cops push you around. Understand?"

"I understand."

The phone clicked in my ear. The Colonel never said good-bye. I hung up the phone. Murphy stood solemn and sober beside me. "He mad because we ain't arrested anybody yet?" he asked.

I grinned. "No, he's afraid we won't get it in the suburban edition."

Hope spoke to the officer. "Would you like to have me fix some coffee?"

Murphy turned toward her. "This ain't a party, Mrs. Osgood. No coffee, please." His glance was disapproving. Wives should mourn dead husbands, not fix coffee for the investigating officers.

I said to Hope, "Is there a place we can go, to wait for the other officers?"

"Downstairs in the recreation room," she said.

I glanced at Murphy, who nodded his approval. Hope led the way and we trooped back through the door. I saw Murphy glance briefly into the room where the body lay, then he followed us down the stairway to the basement.

We sat in wicker chairs around a card table.

"Did you see the gun?" I asked.

She shook her head. "No. Nothing. You know I was at the A.I.W.G. meeting tonight. I drove Ruth Carpenter home—she lives near Forty-fourth, on Barnum. I got home about 9:30 and saw Herman's car in the driveway. He usually drives it into the garage, but I thought he'd probably intended to go out or something and then forgot. There were lights in the house, and I went in, expecting to see him in the living room.

"He wasn't there, of course, so I went back to the study and looked in. I saw him lying on the floor and those blood stains on the carpet. I ran over to his side, knelt down—"

"Did you touch him?"

She shook her head. "I started to, then I saw he wasn't breathing. I knew he was dead."

"Then you called me?"

She nodded. "I didn't know what to do. I went back into the living room. It was a shock, I suppose, and I had to collect my thoughts for a moment or two. But it wasn't long after I found him that I called you, Mike."

Murphy eyed me suspiciously. "Why'd you call him? Why didn't you call us?"

"It's just like Mike told Colonel Tanner," Hope said sweetly. "He's the crime reporter for the *Gazette*. I knew he'd know what to do."

Murphy looked unconvinced. But I was glad that Hope had picked up my cue from the telephone conversation with the Colonel.

FOUR

Murphy sat watching us from the other side of the rumpus room. Hope was uneasy about him and finally she asked, "Are we arrested, Mr. Murphy?"

"No, ma'am" he said.

"Then why can't we sit alone? Why are you watching us?"

Murphy shrugged. "Orders, ma'am."

I turned to Hope and said, "He doesn't want us to get together on our stories, in case we've got something to hide."

"But we have nothing to hide, have we, Mike?"

"No," I lied.

Murphy nodded politely, not believing a word of it. Everybody has something to hide.

Tyndall came downstairs a few minutes later and said the cops were overrunning the place upstairs. He asked what we knew about it. Hope told him the same story she'd told me: that she'd been upset when she found the body, and, not knowing what else to do, she'd called me.

Tyndall said he'd brought a photographer along and pictures were being taken upstairs. Then he disappeared.

We waited for a little longer and another cop came downstairs. "Lanson, you can go upstairs to the living room," he said. "Mrs. Osgood is to stay here."

On the way upstairs I met Guffy and two officers, one in plain-clothes, on their way down to talk to Hope.

I went upstairs to the living room with Murphy at my heels. A uniformed officer was running a vacuum sweeper over the gray carpeting in the living room. He motioned for Murphy to take me over by the picture window, where Tyndall and Jenkins, the photographer, were standing.

"Might as well sit down," said Murphy, lowering himself into a straight-backed chair.

"They found the gun," Tyndall said. "It was in a corner, at the end of the book case."

"What size?" I asked, thinking of the missing gun that killed Jeff Myler.

"Thirty-two," said Tyndall. "A Smith and Wesson target pistol."

"Probably Osgood's," I said. "He was a target man. Won some trophies at the gun club."

"Myler was killed with a thirty-two," said Tyndall. "I think I'll hint that it might be the same gun in my story."

"Ballistics will find out."

"Not till tomorrow. Think I'll get a by-line on this?"

"No," I said. "Because Colonel Tanner told me to handle the yarn."

"Huh?" I could see the disappointment in Tyndall's eyes and I felt sorry for him. The Colonel had taken the story right out of his hands.

"The Colonel said I was on the ground floor and he thought I could handle it easier," I said. "Don't feel bad. There'll be other stories and you can help me on this."

Tyndall stared at me with his red eyes. Then he turned and went to the telephone. The cop using the vacuum sweeper yelled for him to get off the places he hadn't cleaned, but Tyndall paid no heed.

While Tyndall called the office to check on what I'd told him, I watched the party on the lawn through the picture window. The cops were having themselves a ball.

Apparently they'd located the keys to both of the Osgood cars and had driven them into the garage. The driveway now was occupied by two squad cars, their searchlights playing on the grass in front of the house. Two uniformed cops with flashlights were walking over the lawn, probing the shadows and picking up scraps of paper like yard birds, apparently grabbing anything that might have looked like a clue.

I doubted that they'd find anything which would really throw a light on the case.

On the front walk, Sanders, Murphy's buddy, was keeping a small crowd of curious neighbors and passers-by at bay.

Tyndall returned from his phoning. "Okay. Taylor says you're the boss, but by God I'm not forgiving you on this. Or the Colonel either. I'll get even sometime. I'll horn in on one of your stories."

"I had nothing to do with it," I said. "I wouldn't horn in, except that it's what the Colonel ordered." It was a hell of a thing to do to a reporter.

Tyndall sat down on a divan. "How come Hope called you before she called the cops?" he asked. "Don't give me that malarky you gave the cops. What goes between you two? You still carrying the torch for each other?"

"None of your damn business," I said. Out of the corner of my eyes, I saw Murphy's eyebrows raise.

Tyndall grinned. He'd done that deliberately just to give me another headache from the cops. He was still mad about my getting assigned to the story.

"How'd you come out on that tip I gave you tonight?" I asked.

Tyndall sniffed loudly. "I got laughed out of the police station, almost."

"Laughed at?" This wasn't the reaction I'd expected from the cops. There was nothing to laugh at in an unsolved murder case.

"Yeah. Seems that the cops have a special idea about that bullet. They think some reporter sent it." He looked at me.

"Well, there are quite a few fellows at the *Gazette* and the *Globe* who worked there when Myler was boss," I said.

"The cops hinted that they could prove that the bullet came from the *Gazette* office," Tyndall said.

"How do they know?"

Tyndall shrugged. "You've already got your share of my sto-ries, pal. Read about it in the *Gazette* tomorrow."

"I've got a hunch this ties in with the Myler case," I said, thinking about the clipped phone book. Ozzie wasn't a reporter, of course, but cops call anybody who works for a newspaper a reporter.

Jenkins yawned and Tyndall turned to him. "How'd you come out next door, pal?"

"The old lady was sore, but I got a picture of her," the photo-grapher said.

I stared down at Tyndall. "What about next door? How does that fit in this case?"

"I thought the Colonel wanted you to handle this story be-cause you were so cockeyed smart," said Tyndall. "Next door is the residence of Mrs. Olive Myler, widow of Jeff Myler, former editor of the *Gazette* and the *Globe*."

"I'll be damned," I said. If I hadn't already been sure this linked in with the Myler case, this alone would have made me suspicious.

I sat down on the divan beside Tyndall. The cop finished his sweeping and disconnected the machine. He removed a paper sack full of sweepings from the vacuum cleaner bag; this he folded and carried out through the front door like it was gold dust from the Klondike.

"How about the other pictures?" I asked Jenkins.

"We got enough for a page," he said. "Several in the murder room. Extras, because the Colonel won't let us use one with a corpse in it."

One of the *Gazette's* sacred cows was corpse shots. This was overruled on occasion during safety drives when we showed vic-tims of fatal motor accidents strewn on the pavement. But in murder cases, corpses weren't generally permitted.

"Jenks took a shot of the medical examiner," said Tyndall. "After that, anything he did was okay."

Jenkins yawned. "Need one of the widow," he said. "Then I'll have to use your car to go back to the office. Okay?"

"Sure," said Tyndall. "I'll ride back with our star reporter." He nodded at me. He was still rankled about the assignment.

A detective came out of Osgood's study. He said to Murphy, "Tell Guffy we've cleaned up in there and we've gone back to the lab."

"What'd you find?" I asked the detective.

"Guffy'll tell you about it."

"What about the gun? Sure it's the one that killed Osgood?" I asked.

"Ask Guffy."

"You don't have to be so tight-lipped. Guffy's busy; give me a quick rundown on the case."

"Everything comes from Guffy," said the officer and he walked out the door. Murphy got up and went toward the stairway to the basement.

"Goddam storm troopers," said Jenkins.

Murphy returned and brought Hope with him. I got up as she came over to the divan.

"I'm going in town to stay," she said. "This house gives me the creeps and besides the officers say they'll be busy for quite awhile now."

"You're not—uh—arrested?"

She smiled. "Of course not. I'll be staying at the Creston Hotel. Call me tomorrow. Any time after noon."

"All right," I said.

"Guffy'll see you now, Lanson," Murphy said, gesturing toward the stairway to the rumpus room.

The uniformed cop had set up a card table and spread, a shorthand notebook on top of it. Guffy and the plain-clothes man were talking in one corner of the rumpus room.

When I appeared, Guffy pointed to a straight-backed chair in the center of the room. "Sit down," he said.

I sat and he stood facing me. His manner relaxed and for a moment he looked friendly. "I want a statement from you, Mike. Tell everything you know about the case, starting with the last time you saw Osgood alive."

I began with my visit to the Colonel's office after I left the police station in the afternoon. The only thing I omitted was Hope's unexpected call at my hotel. I knew he'd find this out, and I knew I'd be in trouble when he did, but I hoped that by that time he'd have a lead on the killer. If I told him now, he might concentrate on me and the real murderer would escape. That's what I told myself, and I almost believed it.

The uniformed cop took down my statement in shorthand and Guffy said it would be typed up and I could sign it later. He thanked me and said I could go.

"How about the lowdown, Guffy?" I said. "We've got to have a good story on this and I couldn't get anything out of the boys upstairs."

Guffy stared at the floor thoughtfully. "To tell the truth, Mike, we don't know much more than you know. According to the medical examiner, Osgood died about nine o'clock. He ate dinner downtown at the Longhorn Rib Room. We learned that from a detective who saw him there. He dropped in at the *Gazette* office, before eight o'clock. Apparently he came home here after that. We don't know when he got here. Mrs. Myler next door was watching a TV program and didn't notice when he came in, or if any other cars were here."

He paused and looked at me. "The one thing we don't understand is why Mrs. Osgood called you. She doesn't have a very good alibi, Mike, but we've got no reason to hold her. She was at a meeting at the Hotel Creston. A dinner meeting, but she got bored and went out into the bar about 7:00. She said she ducked in and out of the meeting after that, and even went out for awhile. Window shopping, she said. She went with Ruth Carpenter, a secretary at your office, and brought her home. She got here about 9:30."

I nodded. "That's about what she told me," I said. "About the gun?"

He said, "Belonged to Osgood. A thirty-two caliber S and W target. It was fired four times. Two of the bullets could have killed him. One went through the heart and the other pierced the main arteries leading away from the heart. There's no sign of the body having been searched. He wasn't robbed. Apparently nothing was taken from his study. Mrs. Osgood got some blood on her dress when she found the body and she showed it to the boys, who said that there was no use examining it, since it probably got on her dress the way she said it did.

"A chair in the study was overturned and we've been working on the theory there was a struggle. The murderer might or might not be bruised.

"The way we figure it, Osgood may have met somebody downtown. Or somebody might have come here. It probably was somebody Osgood knew and invited into his study. There was an argument, and the killer grabbed Osgood's gun and shot him."

"Do you suppose Ozzie kept his gun loaded?" For a timid little man, this seemed like a rash thing to do.

"Lots of people who don't have children keep loaded guns in the house."

"That's all?"

He nodded. "Mrs. Osgood doesn't know anyone who might have it in for her husband, but she didn't seem very grief stricken for a widow. She didn't get along very well with him, did she?"

"I guess you'll have to ask her about that, Clyde," I said. "I didn't know the Osgoods socially."

"I understand you used to know her before she was married."

"We had some times together," I said, "but that was three years ago. And if you think she killed him because she didn't like him, remember that divorces are easier to get than acquittals at a murder trial."

"But in this case there's a few million dollars difference between a divorce and widowhood," said Guffy. "She isn't in the clear, Mike. But we're not trying to pin it on her. We'll not move until we're sure. And I might say that you're not in the clear either. We want to know why she called you and not us."

"You'll just have to believe me," I said. "There's nothing between us. I ran around with her before she married Osgood— we were pretty good friends, but that's water under the dam. I don't know why she called me. I've hardly talked to her since she became Mrs. Osgood." Until tonight, I added to myself.

"What about this Carpenter woman? Wasn't she Osgood's secretary, the same job Mrs. Osgood had?"

"Yes. You think that Ozzie seduced all his secretaries?" I grinned when I said it.

"It has been done."

"She's a nice kid," I said. "Do you figure this ties in with Jeff Myler's murder, Clyde?"

He squinted at me. "You've got a fixation on the Myler case, Mike. We've got very little, except that both the victims were connected with the Gazette Publishing Company."

"Myler was killed by a thirty-two caliber bullet," I said. "So was Osgood. And did you notice Osgood's phone directory?"

"What about it?" he asked suspiciously.

"It's been clipped. The labels on the bullet package were clipped from Osgood's phone book."

Guffy turned and motioned to the plain-clothes man, who got up and went up the stairs. Guffy stood there frowning. "If the same man killed Osgood, it sort of lets out most of the young folks, like you and Mrs. Osgood. I don't think Myler was killed by a juvenile delinquent."

The detective hurried down the stairway carrying Osgood's phone directory. Guffy opened it on the card table. First to the C's. Then to the Ps. Then the M's. I didn't know about the M's. Now I saw *Myler* had been clipped. "The pillbox had Myler's name pasted on top of it," Guffy explained.

"I didn't see it."

"I know. We took it off to examine the paste."

"Oh."

"It was cornstarch paste. The kind you use in your mailing room, Mike. Not exactly the same, of course, because the consistency varies with each tubful you mix, but it was close enough. Besides, the wrapping paper was the same kind the *Gazette* uses."

"Came from our place, huh?"

"Yes. We've got a couple of other clues we're not mentioning. I suppose that I might as well level with you, Mike. This murder ties in with Jeff Myler's death with a very good knot."

FIVE

Tyndall had found a bottle of liquor upstairs and was feeling no pain when I finished with Guffy. Jenkins had long since departed in Tyndall's car and the squad cars were moved from the driveway, to allow Hope to leave.

Tyndall and I reached the office about twenty past twelve. The *Globe* staff had cleared the decks for the murder story. The night bulldog had carried a bulletin on the slaying, and that was all. The 2:30 edition, which went to outlying suburbs would have all about it.

Jenkins' pictures already had been processed and proofs of the zincs were being pasted up on the picture page layout. Luke Taylor and Colonel Tanner were in conference about the handling of the story and with them was gray-suited Dwight Deems, the day managing editor, who probably would succeed Ozzie as assistant editor. Luke Taylor, the night editor, was fluttering around but there was too much brass cluttering up the place for him to act very starchy.

He carried his picture-page dummy over to the Colonel, who gave it a glance and roared when he saw that one had Ozzie's corpse in it.

"But, Colonel," said Taylor, "in this case—"

"Consider Herman's feelings in the matter," said Tanner. "It was Herman's idea in the first place that these newspapers should never picture violent death, except when it taught a lesson. We want the *Globe* and the *Gazette* to be clean, family

47

newspapers, which no one would be afraid to leave in reach of growing children."

Taylor didn't know what to say, but Deems came to his rescue. Deems had a way of speaking his mind, possibly because he owned a few shares of stock in the company.

"Herman wasn't much of a newspaperman, Colonel," he said. "Good God, we've got to present reality, even the reality of death. It's not like putting something immoral on the picture page. Herman's corpse is news. If we can write about it, we can show it in a picture."

The Colonel turned to Taylor. "What's your opinion on this matter?"

"—uh—" Taylor cleared his throat, trying to decide whether to be truthful or diplomatic. "The picture is important, of course. But we must think of its effect on growing children."

"What effect?" asked Deems.

"Well, it might scare them," said Taylor.

Colonel Tanner pulled at his shaggy eyebrows. Deems had been positive in his views; Taylor had been groping for a good argument.

"I think," he said finally, "that this story may be important enough, after all, to alter our policy a little. But only one picture of Herman's corpse!"

"Yes, sir," said Taylor, and he trotted off with the dummy. The Colonel swung around to face me. "All right, Mike, tell me all you know."

I gave him the works, omitting the personal factors, which included Hope's visit and the fact that Guffy was suspicious of me. I mentioned the Myler angle and the Colonel snapped his fingers.

"That's the angle! Give it the full treatment. Play up the connection between the two—"

"I wouldn't do that, if I were you," said Deems quietly.

"You wouldn't? Why not?"

"All we've got to support Mike's hypothesis is a clipped telephone directory, and Guffy's assertion that our type of paste was used to mail the bullet to police headquarters—"

"Good God, Dwight! The gun that killed Herman probably was the same one that killed Jeff Myler."

"We don't know that it was," said Deems. "Why go out on a limb? Sure, let Mike mention the phone directory and the bullet, but let's not go overboard till we have someplace to swim."

"Did Guffy say anything that suggested what he might think?" the Colonel asked me.

"He was excited when I showed him the directory. He said there was a link with the Myler case."

"There!" The Colonel glowered triumphantly at Deems.

"I still think we should be objective," said Deems. "We shouldn't color the news with what we're thinking. Let the cops solve it."

This time the Colonel was only slightly swayed by Deems. "Write the facts, Mike, but don't underplay that Myler angle. Use it in your lead. We'll save the speculation for a later time."

"Yes, sir." I started to turn to go to my typewriter.

"Just a moment, Mike," said the Colonel. "Did the police find anything to indicate *why* Herman was murdered?"

I shook my head. "Guffy said somebody was mad, sir. There may have been a fight before the shooting."

"I'd say that any murderer was slightly mad. No hint of politics?"

"No"

"Myler was killed for political reasons," the Colonel said.

"That's speculation too, Colonel," said Deems. "Nobody knows why Myler was killed."

"Well," said Colonel Tanner, "what was a better reason for Myler being murdered? It took place just before a city election—a rather hot election, too, I recall. I remember everything very well." He smiled at Deems. "I was on the other side."

Deems nodded. "Yes," he said, "I was managing editor then, too. There was talk about a political motive, but no connection established. Myler had many personal enemies."

"Trouble is, Herman never got mixed up in politics," said Tanner.

"Osgood was active in many things," said Deems. "He was an Elk, a member of the Calais Country Club, and a member of the Editorial Association."

"That's not politics and it's hard to imagine anybody murdering him for anything those groups do," said the Colonel. "Myler was a member of the Creston Gun Club, too, wasn't he?"

"Yes," said Deems, "and so were you—for a short time."

The Colonel grunted and turned to me. "Write the story, Mike. We'll put the lead in twelve black, two columns for the first six graphs, then we'll cut to one, breaking inside and facing the picture page. Got time to do two thousand?"

I looked at the clock. It was 12:30. Deadline for the suburban edition was 2:00 a.m. "I can do three if you want it."

"Don't pad it, but run it to three if you can."

"Yes, sir." I went to my typewriter.

I managed to have nine pages of copy ready in an hour and fifteen minutes, which is pretty fair writing, even for rewrite men, who are always the swiftest on any newspaper.

Tyndall wrote some of my story, though, because he'd been around the cops while I was downstairs being guarded by Patrolman Murphy. I pasted Tyndall's backstopping in the middle of my story and gave it to Taylor a few minutes before two.

Taylor copyread my story, then gave it to the copy desk to split into short takes for the composing room. I sat around, smoking cigarettes and drawing overtime pay until Taylor noticed me.

"Get out of here," he said. "If Deems comes in and catches you loafing he'll raise hell."

"Yes, sir," I said. "I thought you might want another lead for the final."

"We can handle it if anything new comes in," he said. "Tyndall's down at headquarters now."

I got up and yawned. "What time shall I come down tomorrow?"

"The usual time, of course," said Taylor. "Hank will want a new angle for the bulldog. Tyndall says the autopsy report will be ready by nine o'clock."

The bulldog went to press at 10:30 and the deadline was 10:00.

"Okay," I said. I was feeling tired and very sleepy. If Taylor only knew how much it would mean for me to sleep till noon. Maybe he did, but he never let his sympathies interfere with his idea that reporters were born loafers and should be made to work at every opportunity.

It was ten minutes after two when I started for the elevators. In less than five hours it would be seven o'clock, time to get up. In six hours I'd have to be at work. But I'd lose an hour going home and going to bed and another hour getting up, shaving and breakfasting. Why not save that time?

On the fourth floor in the art room was a paste-up table, eight feet long and wide enough to be slept on. There were cushions in the chairs of the artists and retouchers which would make the table soft.

I rode up to the fourth floor. One light burned in the corridor.

It felt spooky and I glanced around uneasily, half tempted to go back downstairs and head for home. Then my eyes fell on the doorway at the end of the hallway. Ruth Carpenter's office. The door was ajar. I thought I heard a sound down there, too.

I didn't want to go, but I seemed to feel that I had to go down and close that door. I wondered who had a key to that office, or who had left it open. Then I remembered almost anybody could open any door in the building with the master key.

Tommy, the building superintendent, had a key to all the doors. A master key. His greatest fear was losing it. So he kept it hanging in an unlocked broom closet on the fourth floor. Either the brass didn't know about it or didn't care, but almost everyone else knew where Tommy's key was.

I reached the door and listened. I heard a rustling sound.

There was no light and I couldn't see through the crack of the partly opened door. I pushed it open a little farther.

A hand reached out of the darkness, grabbed my arm and swung me inside and around. For a brief instant I caught a glimpse of a shrouded shape and I heard a rustling, swishy sound.

Then something hit me heavily on the head and I saw a thousand stars. I didn't black out completely, because I was aware of someone stepping over me and I heard footsteps down the hall.

SIX

I must have been groggy for several minutes. Not out, but not in any mood to rise to my feet. I considered the idea of spending the rest of the night right there on the floor, but I guess my feet didn't get the message. Anyhow, before I knew what I'd done, I found myself standing, leaning against the door frame and swearing.

I put my hand to the back of my head and it came away sticky. In the light, I saw blood on my hand. Not much, but the burglar had hit me hard enough to break the skin of my scalp. I daubed it with a handkerchief and walked down to the john and soaked my head under a faucet. Then I rinsed out the hanky and held it on my head while I walked back to the office again.

The door to Ozzie's office was open a crack and I went in, turning on the light by the switch just inside the door. The room was neat and orderly. I tried the desk drawers and found them unlocked, but I couldn't tell if anything was missing.

There was a coat closet near the door and I looked in there, too. It had a few items in it, but nothing that looked like it would be worth a burglary. An umbrella, a portable typewriter in a case, an old suitcase, several empty coat hangers and a hat on a shelf. The hat looked like Ozzie had worn it only during heavy rains.

There was a bookcase near the desk and I looked it over, just for kicks. It had an almanac, a dictionary, several review copies of books, and a couple of jokers. One was entitled *Keeping Your-self Fit* and the other was *Master Judo Self-Taught*. The idea of Ozzie studying judo sort of seemed funny and I laughed.

Any reason for burglarizing this office must link with the murder, and the smartest thing I could do would be to find out who slugged me. But he was far away by now. I wasn't sure whether he used the elevator or the stairs, but I knew he wasn't on this floor any more. From the stairway it was easy to slip out the Sixth Street entrance without being seen. At this time of night there would be only a slight risk of being noticed stepping out of the elevator on the first floor.

I took the elevator down to the city room. I stuck my head in and saw Luke Taylor dozing at his desk and the other staffers working half-heartedly. Most of the desks were vacant.

Passing through the corridor, instead of going through the swinging doors in the city room, I went back to the composing room. Printers were busy getting the last pages ready for the autocaster. Some plates were already being sent by the tiny elevator to the pressroom in the basement.

Dwight Deems, in his gray suit, was standing near the make-up bank, his hands full of proofs, cutting stories where needed to make them fit into the right spaces.

A printer passed me from the rear. "You got blood on your head, reporter."

"I bumped it," I said.

That seemed explanation enough and he went on about his business.

I went into the john and lined up between mirrors on opposite sides of the room. A little blood was still oozing from a cut on my scalp, but it didn't look bad.

I got a Band-Aid from the first aid chest and put a patch on the cut. There was a small smear of blood on the collar of my shirt, but I was about due for a new shirt anyhow. The elevator took me back to the fourth floor. It was quiet, but the office door had been closed, probably by me although I couldn't remember doing it, and there was no sign of my encounter. I went the other way this time, back to the art department. I took off my shirt and draped it over a drawing board. I tried to remember if there were any women artists, but I couldn't think of any. If there were, I hoped they wouldn't be the first ones to come to work in the morning. I took off my pants and draped them over another board.

Then I took off my shoes and piled some seat cushions on the paste-up table. I was asleep almost the moment I lay down.

A couple of loud-mouth retouchers woke me up about 8:00 a.m. the next morning. They yelled that it was time for me to get to work and they needed the table.

I found my pants, shirt and shoes in a corner where they'd tossed them, and put on my clothes. The pants needed pressing and the shirt was a mess, but I figured my coat, which I'd draped over a chair, would hide most of the dirt and so on. If the office wanted me to look fresh, they ought to let me sleep a little.

I washed and combed my hair in the john and walked into the city room at ten minutes past eight.

Hank looked up and said, "Where do you think you're working? In a bank?"

I said, "Why yes. Isn't this the Federal Reserve?"

It didn't matter to him that I'd been up most of the night and that I'd been slugged, although he didn't know the latter part of it yet.

"You're not working in a bank. This is a newspaper office and you are ten minutes late."

"My alarm didn't go off," I said.

"Get a new one. This is going to be a busy day. Did you know you have red eyes?"

"Tyndall wears 'em, why can't I?" I wouldn't have been surprised if my eyes started to drip blood.

"To heck with Tyndall. Dwight Deems left a note and said that we'll need something new for the bulldog. The radio stations have been reading the morning paper over the air since 5:00 a.m. and they want something new to give to the people that can't read."

"I suppose you want about three thousand words?"

"Three hundred will do," said Hank. "Got an angle?"

"I'll dig up something. How much time have I got?"

Hank looked at the clock. It was still ten minutes past eight. "Nine-thirty at the latest," he said.

"Okay," I said. "How about a little help. Have Don Hilliard get the autopsy report on Ozzie, and check the lab on the gun."

"What are you going to do?" Hank asked suspiciously.

"I've got a new angle that'll take me an hour to check. And I'll need some time to write the story."

I could see from his expression that he didn't believe I had an angle, but he nodded. "Okay," he said, "but you'd better bring in something."

He got busy and I went to my desk. He hadn't noticed the Band-Aid on my head or the blood on my shirt, or maybe he figured reporters just naturally go around showing signs of battle. The only thing Hank cared about was whether you were drunk or sober.

I got my razor case out of my desk and went back to the printers' john, which has showers in it. I stripped off my clothes and let the water run over my skin. It felt good, except that I hate to dry myself with paper towels. Then I shaved.

Finally I got dressed again and took the elevator downstairs. I went out the side door and went up Sixth Street to Smitty's bar where I gulped down some hot coffee and a doughnut. Next I went to a haberdashery and picked out a new shirt. The store wrapped up my old one while I put on the clean shirt in a fitting room.

My next stop was a basement laundry, where I left my dirty shirt for washing. Then I headed back to the parking lot, got my car and drove to Charity Hospital, which is maintained by the city.

It was 8:45 when I reached the hospital. Instead of looking up an intern, I went down to the lab which is in charge of Doc Browne. Doc does a lot of testing for the police as well as pathological work for the hospital.

A technician, a blond woman well past thirty-five, was typing a report in the outside office. She looked up, recognized me from my previous visits, and asked what I wanted.

"Is Doc in? I'd like to see him," I said.

She pressed her lips together, looking very determined and belligerent. "Yes. But he's busy. He's running some tests this morning and doesn't want to be bothered. If it's about the Osgood autopsy, the police have the report."

"It's pretty important that I see Doc," I said. I knew he'd treat my head and maybe give me some quotes besides, if I rubbed him the right way. "This is a business call, you know." That meant he could send a bill.

This made all the difference in the world. She got up. She went into the lab, swishing her starched skirt. Something about that swish reminded me of the sound I heard just before I was slugged last night. Could it have been a woman in a starched skirt? Only nurses and people like that wore starched skirts.

She reappeared in a jiffy. "Go in," she said. "Doctor will see you for a few moments."

I entered the lab. Doc was an eagle-beaked old gent with thin hair that probably had been red when he was a lot younger. Now it was a dirty white. His face was pale, but he didn't look tired or worried like most doctors I'd met. He sat on a stool alongside a table filled with bottles, glass equipment, and stuff I didn't know anything about. He was putting a stopper in a bottle when I entered. "Hi, Mike," he said cheerfully. "I thought you'd be out catching Osgood's killer."

"Maybe I'll do that later," I said. I went up to him and turned my head around. "Take a look at this. Under the Band-Aid."

He reached up and pulled the Band-Aid off my head. The hair stuck to it, but he gave a jerk and my scalp didn't come off.

"Hmm," he said. "Somebody hit you with a beer bottle?"

"Nope," I said. "Might have been a bottle but there wasn't any beer in it. I got slugged."

"Did you report it to the police?" he asked casually.

"I will as soon as you tell me whether it's fatal or not."

"Tain't," said Doc. He pulled out a drawer and got some kind of mixture in a bottle. Then he took some sterilized cotton from a cabinet and poured some of the stuff on it. He daubed it on my scalp. It didn't even sting.

"You know I don't practice any more, Mike," he said. "But you oughtn't to run around with a cut like that. Might get infected."

"I'd have a dickens of a time finding a regular doctor at this hour," I said.

"They're all upstairs, seeing patients," he said. "It'd be like asking a plumber to fix a leaky faucet when he's putting in a new commode." He daubed some more. "I could put a stitch in it, but the scar won't show unless you get bald."

I told him how it happened. He grunted a couple of times and finished daubing.

"That one's easy to figure," said Doc. "The fellow that killed Osgood did it to get something. Osgood fooled him, and didn't have it. So the murderer broke into Osgood's office."

"How'd he know where to find the key?"

"Probably took it from Osgood after he murdered him," said Doc.

I didn't think so, but I could find out from the police if Osgood's keys were taken. But I couldn't figure what Ozzie could have had that the killer wanted, except the murder gun, the gun that had killed Jeff Myler ten years ago. And the murderer apparently didn't take that.

"Are the police holding Mrs. Osgood?" Doc asked. He was using some scissors to cut away the hair around the wound. I started to turn my head, but he pushed it back. "Sit still."

"Why should they hold her?" I asked.

"Usually when a man is killed the cops suspect the wife," he said.

"Half the town's saying the same thing you're saying, Doc," I said. "How about the connection with the Myler case?"

"I'd have to know more than I know to give an opinion on that."

"If they did connect, Hope would be eliminated because she was only a kid when Myler got bumped off."

"Not exactly a kid. She was fifteen. Some girls develop early."

"Would murder be a girlish prank?"

"I don't think the murders connect. Hope probably didn't have anything to do with the Myler case, but I'll bet she knows more about this one than she told the cops."

"You're bound to pin it on Hope, huh?"

"I'm not pinning anything on anybody. She's the best suspect we've got."

I had to admit that was right so far. "Is there any way to set the time of Osgood's death, other than between 8:30 and 9:00?"

"That's about as close as we can fix it."

"Can you tell me if Osgood was healthy?"

"He wasn't my patient. I don't know. He looked healthy."

"Was Myler?"

"How did he creep into this? I thought we were talking about Osgood."

"Were you Myler's doctor?"

"I was, and a doctor doesn't talk about his patients to total strangers."

"I'm no stranger."

"You were a stranger to Myler."

"Hell, Doc, the solution of two murders might depend on how healthy Myler was."

Doc thought for a moment. "I'll say this, Mike. Myler didn't have much left in the way of a future. He was pretty sick."

"What was wrong?"

Doc shook his head. "Only four people in the world knew that Myler wouldn't live another year," he said. "Four besides Myler. He knew it, of course. I was one of them. His wife was another. The third was a brain specialist, and Dwight Deems was the fourth."

I thought this over for a moment. "He had a brain tumor?"

"I didn't say that."

"Thanks, Doc."

"If you dare quote me, even in a faint whisper, I'll shoot leprosy germs in your hind end."

"I won't. Now what condition am I in? This is for quotes, so don't say anything you don't want printed."

"In medical terms, you've got a bump and a little cut," Doc said.

"Hell, that's the kind of terms I'd use. Talk like a doctor."

"I'd have to put you in the hospital under observation to give it a bigger name."

"Come on, Doc. My time's valuable."

"So's mine. Did it knock you out?"

"Not clear out; I knew what was going on, but I didn't give a damn."

"Been dizzy at all since it happened?"

"Not dizzy. My head ached for a little afterwards."

"That's understandable. I guess you ought to play safe. Don't take any violent exercise for a few days. Don't work too hard—as if you did. If you feel dizzy, lie down."

"Mind telling my boss all this, Doc?"

"Yes, I mind. Beat it."

"You haven't told me what's the matter with me. Have I got a mild concussion or what?"

"Well, if you want to make it sound worse than it is, you've had a very, very mild concussion. Also a slight laceration."

"Fine," I said. "Send your bill to the *Gazette.*"

"Don't worry, son," he said, "I'll send a bill. I'll charge mostly for my time and medical advice. I only put a little antiseptic and some adhesive tape on it."

SEVEN

Hank Newcomb was buried in copy when I came through the door of the city room, but he never misses a thing. He looked up and yelled like a bull moose, "What's the new lead?"

I stopped in my tracks and looked down at the bulldog jaw and flushed face of my city editor. Then I told him all that had happened to me in the wee small hours.

He swept up a phone. "Deems!" he yelled. Deems probably could have heard him through the frosted glass of his cubby across the room, but he answered the phone instead.

"Come over here! Mike had a brush with the murderer."

I went through my story a second time for the managing editors.

"Why didn't you tell us this before?" Deems asked quietly.

"Because I needed medical attention," I said. "If I'd told anyone about it this morning when I came to work—"

"At ten minutes past eight," Hank said.

"—I would have had to spend an hour writing the story and rehearsing the facts like I'm doing now."

"That where you've been? Seeing a doctor?"

"Yes," I said with a nod. "Doc Browne over at Charity said I have a mild concussion and it could get infected. He said for me not to work too hard."

Deems and Hank both snorted.

"Did you report it to the police?" Hank asked.

"Haven't had time," I said. "I will."

"Police officers are upstairs now, going through Herman's things," said Deems. "Don't make a special trip to see them. Just write your story and talk to them later. Maybe they'll be down before you finish."

Perhaps Deems was getting a little anxious about the time.

Hank looked up at him. "The full treatment?"

"Yes," said Deems. "First person, by-line, page one, with a picture." He turned and walked back to his frosted glass den.

There are certain things in life that are bigger and better than anything else. A by-line is big, so is your first story on page one. But nothing can compare with your first first-person story. An average reporter, who isn't a columnist, might have one in a lifetime.

"Get it done in twenty minutes." Hank's voice brought me down out of the clouds, "I'll have a rewrite man put a new lead on the main story about the murder."

"You bet," I said, and raced to my typewriter.

I finished the story in twenty-five minutes, although I could have done it in twenty, but there was no reason to spoil Hank Newcomb when there was still twenty minutes before the deadline for the bulldog. A photographer came down from the dark room to take my picture at my typewriter. He wanted me to wear my hat.

"Looks more like a real reporter," he said.

I didn't remember ever seeing a *Gazette,* or even a *Globe* reporter wear a hat while he was working. Only Walter Winchell does that and it could be because he's bald.

"No hat," said Hank. "You gotta show the adhesive tape on his head."

"What about my face?" I asked. "The patch is on the back."

"To hell with your ugly face," said Hank. "It's the adhesive tape we want to show."

So there was no hat, no face in the picture. Just Doc Browne's job of patching.

The cops hadn't come down stairs yet, and there was nothing left for me to do but to go up to Osgood's office and report what had happened to me before they read it in the paper. Cops are sensitive about things like that.

Ruth Carpenter was at her desk, looking a little sad. She told me that a Sergeant Russell was in charge and to go on in.

Sergeant Russell was a fat detective. I told my story and showed him the approximate spot where it happened, which was in Ruth's office. They found a little speck of blood on the floor and believed me. To them it was more convincing than the adhesive tape.

"You should have called up right after it happened," he beefed.

"Too groggy," I said. "Doc said I had a kind of concussion."

Sergeant Russell snorted. "It would take an ax to hurt a skull like yours." He paused. "What did he look like?"

"I couldn't see him," I said. "He was in the dark. But it could have been a woman."

"A woman?"

I told about the swishing noise, like skirts.

Somebody came into the room. It was Tommy, the building super, carrying a trench coat in one hand.

"What's that?" Sergeant Russell asked.

"Mistuh Osgood's coat," said Tommy. He started to hang it in Ozzie's closet.

"Hold it! Hold it! Where'd it come from?"

"One of the circulation men found it near the side door," said Tommy. He gave the coat to the sergeant, who went through the pockets. Then he looked at the label inside the collar and saw Osgood's name, written in India ink.

"Here's what the man that slugged you was wearing," said the sergeant.

"How do you know?"

"It figures," said the officer. "He was afraid he'd be recognized by his clothing, so he put this on when he heard you coming."

I thought of Dwight Deems' light gray suit. I reached out and shook the coat. I heard a faint swishy sound. "That's what I heard last night, all right."

Another cop who'd been going through the drawers of Ozzie's desk came over and looked at the coat. "What do you suppose anybody wanted here?" he asked. "I've been through everything. There's nothing that gives us a lead."

"The guy that wore this coat got what we want," said Russell. "He's the murderer."

"Through with me?" I asked.

Sergeant Russell eyed me with suspicion. "What's your hurry, Scoop?"

"This is company time," I said. "The *Gazette* expects a full day's work for a day's pay." I was quoting from employee regulations on page one of the *Gazette* stylebook, not that I believed the damned thing. The *Gazette* expected a week's work for a day's pay.

"Okay," said the sergeant. "You can go. We'll tell your boss if we want to talk to you again."

I didn't go back to the city room. I went out the back door and to the parking lot. It was only a matter of time before the cops would find out about Hope's visit to my room last night, and while I knew I didn't have much chance, I hoped I could turn up something that would keep them too busy to bother me.

Tyndall was in the lot, walking away from his car. "Look at the mess you got me in, eager beaver," he said. "You had to do my work for me last night, so Luke Taylor says, 'You gotta help out the *Gazette*.' So here I am. Just wait till a story breaks at 2:00 a.m. some night, and I have you called out of your nice warm bed."

"You're getting overtime," I said. "Why beef about it?"

"Nuts to overtime," said Tyndall. "But now that I'm here, what do you want me to do?"

I was about to tell him to see Hank, when I thought of something. "Why don't you check up on Ozzie's past life," I said. "See if you can find anything that links him with Myler, before Myler got killed."

"Sit in the morgue and read clips!" he groaned. "Don't you want me to go down to headquarters?"

"Hilliard's there," I said. "He can handle anything that comes up."

"Where you going?"

"Cops are clamming up as usual," I said. "I've got to see where they've been and what they're doing."

I got in my car and drove off. My first stop was on Clifton Road, at the house next door to Herman Osgood's place. The home of Mrs. Olive Myler, the widow of Jefferson Myler, deceased.

The front lawn was as neat and well-kept as Osgood's. Possibly they hired the same landscaper. The houses were much alike, but Ozzie's was newer.

Mrs. Myler, a short, busty woman with gray hair and gold-rimmed glasses, opened the door after I rang the bell. "Yes?"

"I'm Mike Lanson of the *Gazette,* Mrs. Myler," I said.

Her eyes fluttered beneath the glasses. "What do you want?"

"I want to talk to you," I said.

"I told the police everything I know about last night," she said.

"That's not the full reason I came here, Mrs. Myler," I said. "There's reason to believe that the murder of Herman Osgood is connected in some way with the death of your husband ten years ago. I wanted to talk to you about that."

She sighed deeply. "Do I have to go through all that again?"

"Don't you want to help the police catch the man who murdered your husband?"

For a couple of seconds she stood there. "Nothing the police can do will bring Jefferson back."

That was true, I suppose, but I had to talk to her. "Mrs. Myler, your husband was a newspaperman. You know that if this set of circumstances involved someone else, he'd insist on a reporter getting some kind of a statement."

Once more she sighed audibly. She stepped back, opening the door. "Come in," she said. "But I don't think I can help you."

She led the way into a large living room and directed me to the divan with a wave of her hand. She sat down across the room from me in an overstuffed chair.

"What do you want to know?" she asked.

"It might interest you to know, Mrs. Myler, that the last conversation I had with Mr. Osgood yesterday concerned your late husband's murder."

"Mr. Osgood talked to me many times about it," she said.

"Colonel Tanner believes that the bullet received by the police last week might open a new approach to its solution," I went on. "Mr. Osgood, for some reason, did not seem very anxious for me to follow it through."

"Perhaps, Mr. Lanson, he thought as I do, that too much time has elapsed and that reopening the case would only open old wounds."

"Mrs. Myler, did you read the *Globe* this morning?"

She nodded. "Yes, indeed."

"Then you must know there's substantial evidence that Mr. Osgood sent the bullet to the police."

"It could have been Mrs. Osgood, you know," she said. There was a trace of bitterness in her voice.

"I doubt if she could be involved in the murder of your husband, Mrs. Myler," I said. "Hope—Mrs. Osgood, I mean, was just a school girl when it occurred."

"A very precocious school girl, no doubt."

"You don't like her, do you?"

"Everyone knows what she is."

"What is she, Mrs. Myler?"

She wet her lips. "It's not necessary for me to answer that. I thought you wanted to know about my husband?"

"Yes, I do," I said. "Do you recall what happened the night Mr. Myler died?"

She nodded her head slowly. "I've been over that so often that I still remember every detail. I had been home all day. In the evening we had been invited over to the Osgood's. They were holding a house warming between 8:00 p.m. and midnight. Shortly before 8:00, while I was waiting for Jefferson to come home, the phone rang. Jefferson was calling and he said he'd been delayed, and for me to go on to the party and he'd meet me there later. I said that I would wait for him to return.

"I waited an hour. He didn't come home and he didn't call me again. I called his office, and the girl on the switchboard rang his extension, but Jefferson didn't answer. I assumed he was on his way home. The switchboard girl remembered my call afterwards and told the police about it. I think they suspected me a little at the time."

It was normal for the cops to check on the widow, of course. But as she spoke, I realized that Mrs. Myler's call did not necessarily have to come from her home. The switchboard girl would have no way of knowing from where Mrs. Myler had called.

"But Jefferson had not shown up at 9:30, and I knew that if he'd left the office about 9:00, he should be here. I began to get worried. Then I received a call from the police. My husband had met with 'an accident', they said. Officers were coming to talk to me about it.

"Almost immediately there was a knock on the door. Dwight Deems, who had been at Mr. Osgood's home, had received a call from the office. He came in and I broke down completely. When the police arrived, I was lying in my room on the bed. It was after ten o'clock before I was able to talk to them."

"Do you know of anyone who might have wanted to kill Mr. Myler."

"Absolutely no one," she said. "Of course, Jefferson had many enemies, but they were people who just did not like him. I don't believe that even his worst enemy would have wanted to kill him."

"Someone did, apparently," I said. "Did he show signs of being nervous, or apprehensive?"

"None whatever," she said.

I looked straight into her eyes and said, "Mrs. Myler, prior to his death your husband suffered from an incurable ailment. I have reason to believe it might have been a brain tumor. Yet you say he wasn't nervous or uneasy about it?"

Her face paled. Her eyes blinked rapidly and she gasped. "How—how did you know that? Did Dwight tell you?"

"Was it a brain tumor?"

She choked and put her hands over her face. "Please go, Mr. Lanson. I can't talk to you any more! I mustn't talk! I mustn't!"

EIGHT

Dr. Browne was in the office outside his laboratory when I reached Charity Hospital, about 11:15. Doc sat at the blond technician's desk, a copy of the *Gazette's* first edition spread out in front of him. He nodded toward it. "Made a hero of yourself, eh?"

"All in a day's work," I said, trying to be modest. "Did you see I mentioned you in the story? Gave you a plug."

"Don't need it; didn't even want it," he said. "Doctors don't advertise."

"That's a point, Doc, and maybe I could prove that they do, but I didn't come here to argue."

"That's nice. I don't feel like arguing. Why did you come? As if I didn't know."

"If you know, tell me."

"You think I'll tell you something you want to know. You want me to solve a murder for you. Take my advice, son, you'll live longer if you just sit back and let other folks be the ambitious type. Herman Osgood's dead because he was ambitious. Do you want to follow him to the grave?"

"What makes you think Ozzie was murdered because he was ambitious?"

"It's obvious, isn't it? If he'd been content to sit back and spend the money the gods dumped in his lap, nothing would have happened to him outside of breach of promise suits. But no. He had to earn a place in society like his grandad and his dad, so he got to be editor of a newspaper—"

"Assistant editor," I said.

"Maybe he wanted to be editor and Colonel Tanner bumped him off," said Doc. "But if that wasn't the case, he fooled around where he had no business to fool and got himself murdered."

"Could that housewarming Osgood had the night Jeff Myler was killed have anything to do with either murder, Doc?"

Doc studied for a moment. "I was at that party," he said. "Nothing suspicious happened. The only unusual thing was Dwight Deems getting a phone call about 9:30. His office called him to say that Jeff Myler had been murdered."

"Remember anyone else at the party, besides you and Deems?"

"Good Lord, you don't expect me to remember everybody, do you? There were about seventy-five people there. Osgood had set up a bar in the rumpus room. The heavy drinkers were down there. The more temperate folks were upstairs in the living room."

"But who was there?"

"Well, I do recall a Mrs. Smith and her daughter."

"Smith?" That could mean quite a few people. "Which Smith?"

"She was the caterer. Her daughter served drinks and passed canapes. They had a couple of high school girls doing that part of the job. Her daughter was named Hope."

"Hope Osgood?"

"Yes. Just a long-legged school girl then. Not even very pretty."

"I'll be damned," I said. "Could you swear she was at the party all evening?"

Doc scratched his head. "That was ten years ago. Good Lord, Mike, with half of the party in the rumpus room and half upstairs, you couldn't be sure of who was there and who wasn't. Besides, I did have a few drinks."

He had a point. "I've heard that politics was blamed for Myler's murder. Got any ideas on that?"

Doc nodded. "That I can answer. Myler was campaigning for some sort of reform party. He'd uncovered some graft. But the party that was in didn't have any trouble till Myler got killed; then they lost the election."

"Which side was Tanner on?"

"You trying to pin this murder on your boss?" Doc laughed.

"No. I just wondered how he stood—for or against Myler."

"He was for the crooked gang at City Hall," said Doc, "but I don't think he really cared much. Tanner, I understand, was getting out of the real estate business then. He'd taken the cream off the boom and rising construction costs were cutting into the gravy. But the City Hall gang was letting him get by with a few things, and Tanner naturally supported them. I'm sure though that Tanner didn't care enough to murder anybody."

"How did Osgood stand politically?"

"I don't think he stood for anything. He hadn't found a place for himself yet."

"Did Dwight Deems get along with Myler?"

"Deems? Oh yes. He was practically the only real friend Myler ever had, Myler was a funny fellow, Mike. He was a crusader. The only time you like crusaders is when they're knocking down your pet peeve. Sooner or later though, they'll take a poke at your pet hobby and you get mad at them. I shouldn't say this, because Myler was a patient of mine—I was in general practice then—but I didn't like him myself. The only time he ever got any praise out of me was when he started to wage war against some of the medical quacks in this town. Then he turned on the American Medical Association because we stood by each other in malpractice suits, and I got really teed off. But Deems was always on Myler's side."

"A yes-man, like Ozzie?"

"Not that boy! He'd tell the boss if he thought an idea was crazy, but nobody else had better call the boss crazy."

I nodded. This fitted pretty well with my opinion of Deems. As a newspaperman, he could run rings around Ozzie.

"What about this 'graft', Doc? You said Myler had found some in the city government?"

Doc thought a moment. "Are you digging up dirt to publish?"

"Doc," I said, "anything you tell me will be checked backwards and forwards and if it's printed, your name won't be mentioned. All I want is information—something to work on."

"Fine," Doc said. "There was a gambling hall on Tenth Street operated by a political character named Miggins. Myler sent a photographer with a concealed camera into the place and got some pictures of what went on. When the story was published, the politicians had a heck of a time explaining why the police didn't know about it. But they raised a big smoke screen by firing the cop on the beat. Suspending him, pending investigation. This was ammunition that Myler needed for his reform movement and he flayed the police force and the politicians. But after the election, the reformers that Myler supported turned right around and hired the cop back. Maybe you know him. He's a lieutenant now. Name's Guffy."

I whistled. I knew Guffy had been suspended at one time and that he hated newspapers. This explained it. "Think Guffy killed Myler?"

"Hell, Mike, I don't think something just because it sounds good. Laugh if you want to, but I'm a man of science. Everything I think ought to have some evidence attached to it. Unless something connects Guffy with the crime, I'm not going to suspect him."

"Doc, what are the symptoms of a brain tumor?"

"Whoa there, Mike. You're not asking me to reveal something about a patient?"

I shook my head. "Just curious, that's all."

He studied a moment. "The first symptoms are visual—poor vision, double vision and so on. Sometimes the patient can't see out of one eye or the other. Then they aren't able to coordinate their movements, or are paralysed—but the symptoms vary from day to day."

"Does a person's personality change?"

"Sometimes, but rarely enough almost to be an exception," Doc said. "When they occur, a person seems to lose his keenness of mind, or have memory lapses. Sometimes they have fits, resembling epilepsy."

"Did Myler suffer from anything like this?"

"I'm not in a position to reveal this, Mike." He paused and sighed. "You know you've got standards in your profession too that you don't break."

"Doc, I'm working on an angle in this case. I've got to know if Myler had a brain tumor."

"Find out from somebody else, Mike," Doc said softly. "I can say that Myler was a sick man. Whenever there's sickness, there's hope, but in Myler's case the hope was so slim that he could practically see the end."

"A brain tumor isn't always fatal, is it?"

"Of course not. But sometimes the tumor is in a spot that even the best surgeon can't reach without killing the patient."

"Probably lucky that Myler died when he did, even if it was a violent end."

Doc nodded gravely. "I don't know that I favor euthanasia, Mike, but sometimes suffering isn't worth living for. Even a man with guts can't see a percentage in living without hope."

"Wonder if Myler could have killed himself somehow?"

"That's a question nobody but Myler could answer."

This had covered almost all the ground. "You're a great guy. Doc," I said. "Anything you told me is as confidential as a communication to you from a patient."

"Gonna solve a couple of murders, eh, son?" There was a gleam in his eye.

"Maybe. No use trying to deny it, Doc. Osgood's and Myler's deaths are connected. I don't know how, but one must have resulted from the other. It's probably complicated, though."

"Not necessarily," Doc said. "Some things that look complicated are really very simple when you know all the facts."

I lit a cigarette. "Can I use your phone?" I asked.

"Help yourself."

I dialed the press room at Police Headquarters. Don Hilliard answered and I asked, "Got the ballistics report on the gun the cops found in Osgood's study."

"Yep," said Hilliard. "It was the one that killed Osgood."

"Did they try to match the bullet from that gun with the slugs from the Myler killing?"

There was a pause. Then Don asked, "Are you sitting down, Mike?"

"Yeah." I was perched on one corner of the lab technician's desk.

"Take a good grip on yourself," Hilliard said. "It ain't the gun that killed Myler."

"That *can't* be right."

"If it ain't right, we need a new crew of ballistics men down here at headquarters. They'll swear it ain't the same gun."

"Thanks, Don." I hung up the phone and turned to Doc. "We're right back where we started," I said.

"Where have we been, Mike?"

"I'm not exactly sure," I said, grinding out the cigarette in a tray on the desk, "but I thought the gun would be the one thing that would connect the two killings."

Doc laughed. "Why don't you stop trying to get two for one, and concentrate on catching the man that killed Osgood?"

"Maybe I will." It was beginning to look as if I'd have to.

At Police Headquarters a few minutes later, I checked the ballistics report myself. Besides clearing the weapon from being involved in Myler's death, the report stated that it had been positively identified as Osgood's own weapon through the serial number, which he had listed in his personal papers. He'd purchased the gun about twelve years ago to use for target shooting at the Creston Gun Club. The barrel was the original. The expert could tell if it had been changed.

The report blew up so many theories that might fit if Ozzie and Myler had been killed by the same weapon.

Hank Newcomb greeted me with a scowl as I came into the city room at 11:35. "I hope that putting out a newspaper isn't interfering with your day," he said.

"It's making the day interesting," I said.

"Where in the hell have you been since ten o'clock?"

I told him where I'd been, and that I'd found out a little background stuff, but nothing I could use in a story.

"We've got to have something new on the murder for the suburban edition," said Hank. "The fact that you were slugged doesn't really move the story along very far."

"That's what I've been trying to do," I said, softly and sweetly. "I'm working on a new angle."

That quieted him down a little, but he still acted as if he wasn't pleased with me. The trouble with Hank is that he's insecure. He's always afraid his reporters are spending their time in pool halls.

"Tyndall has really been working," he said, trying to make me feel ashamed. "He spent almost an hour in the morgue, checking on Osgood."

"I'll see if he found out anything I didn't know," I said.

The library, or morgue, is on the second floor. Mr. Johnson, the chief librarian, was a white-haired man who looked old enough to have helped Guttenberg print the Bible. He sat at a desk to the left of the door, behind a long line of books.

"What photos did Tyndall look at this morning?" I asked him.

Mr. Johnson checked a slip on a spindle on his desk. "He went through the Osgood file and cross-references, the Editorial Association, Elks lodge, Red Cross drives, Calais Country Club, Creston Gun Club, Dewey campaigns of 1944 and 1948, and—mmm, that's all."

"Did he find what he wanted?"

"I'm afraid you'll have to ask Mr. Tyndall about that, Mr. Lanson. He checked in everything except one picture. He said he'd bring that back later."

"What was the picture he held out?"

Again Johnson looked at a slip. "No. X-4B-112-39," he said. "It came from the Creston Gun Club folder."

"Do you know which picture it was—what it was about?"

"Heavens no. All I have is a number."

"Let me see the file."

The librarian went to a stack of folders on the desk occupied by one of his assistants. He went through them and came back with two. One was filled with photos, the other with clippings. I dumped the clippings out on the table. I saw they were all about the doings of the Creston Gun Club, apparently clipped from the sports section of the *Gazette* over a period of many years.

About half of them were headed: *Gun Club Elects Officers.* I went back to the early days of the organization and found that at first membership was limited solely to personnel of the city's banks. A headline proclaimed its purpose: *Bankers Improve Aim to Cope with Bandits.*

Later others were admitted and the attitude of the members became less bloodthirsty and more social. A story said that Jeff Myler, editor of the *Gazette* and the *Globe* was president one year. Myler was low man in the annual pistol match, but at least he didn't censor his own shortcomings, if being a bad shot was a shortcoming. Osgood was better than average. He placed second four times, and won the trophy once.

"Mr. Osgood must have been a pretty good shot," I said.

The librarian smiled. "Yes. I recall Mr. Myler's remark about him in connection with the club. He said, 'Herman Osgood has all the qualifications of a Western bad man, except the fortitude.' However, I don't think he really meant that Mr. Osgood would shoot anybody in the back. It was just one of Mr. Myler's little jokes."

"You knew Myler pretty well?"

"I worked under him many years. I was head copyreader on the *Globe* the night he died. As a matter of fact, it was I who discovered his body."

"You did?" I practically yelled the words, and the moth-eaten assistant librarians looked up in astonishment.

"Yes, indeed. Mr. Deems was out and he called in about 9:30, or a little before, trying to reach Mr. Myler. His phone didn't answer, and Mr. Deems asked the copy desk to send someone up to see why. I happened to be available, so I went."

"Can you describe what you saw?"

"I could never forget it," said Johnson. "Mr. Myler was on the floor. Apparently he'd been shot through the side of the head by the assassin as he sat at his desk. The body was in a great pool of blood."

"No sign of a struggle?"

"Nothing at all."

"And no clues?"

"Nothing."

"Funny somebody didn't hear the shot," I said.

"No. That wasn't strange," said Johnson. "The retouchers work at night until eight o'clock, unless there's some special reason to keep them later. There aren't many pictures at night, you know. After that the fourth floor is practically empty. There was no one around to hear the shot."

I examined the folder containing gun club pictures. Members were in group photos and single posed shots. I noted the guns and decided that nearly every member used a different kind. Colts, Smith and Wessons, Hi-Standard, even some foreign guns. Every model and probably every caliber, although I couldn't judge the sizes from the photos. Doc Browne was in a couple of photos and so was the instructor, Clyde Guffy, then a patrolman who had won the police sharpshooter match. I asked Johnson if he remembered how long ago this was taken.

"I don't recall," the librarian declared. "But it must have been sometime before Mr. Myler's death. Patrolman Guffy and Mr. Myler had a falling out some months before the tragedy. We have a file on Guffy—"

"I'll look at it later," I said. I figured I'd ask Guffy about it. "Sure you can't remember which photo Tyndall kept?"

Johnson shook his head. "We have so many . . ."

"Isn't there a negative, or a copy?"

"Sorry. Unless you'd want to go through the files. It was used either in the *Globe* or the *Gazette,* ten or twelve years ago."

It would take me the rest of the day to search through the files. I could find Tyndall quicker. "Thanks," I said.

I went back to the news room. In my typewriter was a sheet of copy paper on which a message was written with soft pencil in Tyndall's scrawl:

"Dear Chum(p): While you were playing Private Eye, I found something. See you in Smitty's Bar. Remember, the next first person by-line is mine. Love and kisses. Ward."

I got my hat and made a bee-line for Smitty's Bar, hollering to Hank that I was going out for lunch.

"Don't you ever work?" Hank asked as I went out the door.

NINE

There was a long bar on one side of an L-shaped room at Smitty's place. At the foot of the L were tables and a couple of booths where you could sit down if you were tired. Smitty served food as well as liquor, but only because the state law required food to be available in places where liquor was served.

Since I hadn't eaten a heavy breakfast, I ordered ham and beans and a mug of black coffee and carried it on a tray into the back part of the room, hoping to find Tyndall there. He hadn't been at the bar, but since he'd offered to meet me here, I assumed he'd show up before long.

From one of the booths, a soft voice called, "Mike."

Hope Osgood was sitting there sipping a highball.

I put my tray on the table and sat down in the booth across from her. "This is a hell of a place for a bereaved widow," I said.

"I hoped I'd see you here," she said.

"I was going to call you," I told her. "But you said not to call till after noon."

"It's almost noon," she said. "Besides, I wasn't going to be in my room at the Creston. Ruth Carpenter called me early this morning. She overheard officers talking. They've learned I was at your hotel last night."

That was no surprise. "They'll be looking for me too, then," I said.

"How's your head?" she asked. "I read your story this morning."

"I'd practically forgotten about my head," I said. "What did you tell Guffy last night?"

"Nothing," she said, smiling. "I said I came home from the meeting and found Herman and called you."

"You told him you'd been at the A.I.W.G. meeting all evening," I said. "Now he knows you lied."

"I'm going to see a lawyer, Mike," she said. "Of course that will make the police more sure than ever that I killed Herman, but they've got to prove I did, and since I didn't kill him, I'm sure they can't."

"Don't be so sure they can't build up a good case," I told her. "Where did you go after you left me last night?"

"Riding," she said. "I just drove around, thinking, trying to clear my head, wondering how much of a fool I'd made of myself."

"Why did you come to see me, Hope?"

"I told you," she said. "I just got to thinking about old times. I'd had a few drinks and it seemed like a good idea to go and see you. Lord, Mike, it sure was a blow to my ego. Don't I have any sex appeal any more?"

"Plenty," I said, "but I'm the kind of man that shies away from good-will offerings."

"Man, the pursuer," she said.

"I don't believe it was a good-will offering," I said. "Was that the *only* reason you came to see me?"

"Mike," she said, "the police are going to ask you that question. Don't you think you'd be better off not knowing the answer?" Her deep blue eyes burned into mine.

"I guess you're right. Do you think that your coming to see me had anything to do with Ozzie's death?"

She thought for a moment. "I think Herman would have been killed no matter what I did last night."

"What did you mean last night when you said you were going to be free?"

"I thought I made it clear. I intended to get a divorce."

"You had a lawyer?"

She nodded. "The same lawyer I'm going to see this afternoon. McCarthy."

"You had grounds?"

"I think so. I thought I had grounds to sue him on an adultery charge. I was wrong, but I think I had him frightened enough not to contest any action I brought."

"Adultery! Ozzie?"

"Why not? He was a male, wasn't he?"

Come to think of it, that was the way Hope got Ozzie in the first place. It wasn't fantastic that he'd do it again.

"Don't tell me . . . Ruth Carpenter?"

"I thought so, but I was wrong. She went to the Editorial Association meeting with him, but I gather she outsmarted him. Stayed with friends."

"But you had something else on him?"

Hope smiled. "This conversation is going in circles, Mike," she said. "Let's talk about something else."

"Hope," I said, "I've asked you before, but I've got to know for sure. Did you kill Ozzie?"

"I'll always give you the same answer to that, Mike. If I had grounds for divorce, why should I kill him?"

"Whether you had grounds for divorce or not, you might have killed him," I said. "You disliked him, probably hated him. Your marriage was on the rocks. An argument, four shots. It looks like whoever did shoot Herman was pretty down on him. Guffy says it was the work of somebody 'mad as hell' at Herman Osgood."

She lifted the empty glass, then set it down. "I need another drink, Mike. Bourbon and soda."

"To hell with a drink," I said. "Go see your lawyer. Get there fast. The cops won't let you get by with evasions. They'll want all the answers."

She hesitated. "Mike, we'll see each other again, after this is over, won't we?"

"If we're both not behind bars," I said.

She picked up her purse and rose. "Damn you," she said.

"Another thing," I said. "Don't lie to your lawyer."

She went out, her head high and her heels clicking. Some of the staffers saw her, looked at me, then bunched their heads together. They were reading a hell of a lot into the act.

I got up, leaving a dime for the bus boy, and then I saw Tyndall. He was sitting to one side of the booth, back where I couldn't have seen him without turning my head. He had a highball glass on the table in front of him and he was turning it slowly with his fingers. A grin was on his face.

"Cute kid, isn't she?" he said.

"Not bad," I said. "I got your note."

He got up, went to the bar and got another drink. I didn't follow him. This was a better place to talk. He came back, pulled a chair up to the end of the table and sat down.

"She didn't look like she was in mourning for Ozzie," he said. He took a sip from the glass. "She looked mad. What did you do, pal? Make a couple of million dollars mad at you?"

"Why don't you take a long walk off a short pier? Did you have something to show me, or didn't you?"

He took another drink. "Poor Ozzie. I'll bet he's spinning in his coffin, tearing his autopsy incisions asunder. Or do they sew 'em up? Before he's even laid away, his wife is out having a love spat with a lousy reporter."

"All right, Ward. You've had your fun. Now either get down to business or shut up."

He drained the glass. "Gotta get me another drink," he said, starting to rise.

I reached out, gave him a push back into the chair. "The drink can wait," I said. "The story's pretty hot right now."

"Lissen, pal. You can't push ole Ward Tyndall around," he slurred belligerently.

He started to get up again.

This time I pushed hard. Tyndall went backward and crashed into a table, overturning it. From the bar Smitty yelled at the top of his voice.

Somehow, Tyndall managed to stay on his feet. Now he came after me swinging both arms like a windmill. I waited and dove in with my fists. I felt his blows on my face and head and I punched with both hands.

Smitty's yells became louder; they were almost in my ear when I saw Tyndall lurch away, turn his back on me and dive out the back door. Someone seized one of my arms and another person grabbed the other and I found myself being held tightly by Smitty and his chef.

The next minute the cops came in the front door. Lieutenant Guffy was among them.

TEN

Guffy took me to Ozzie's office on the fourth floor. Ruth Carpenter was busy straightening out some files when we arrived.

"You haven't forgotten about our date tomorrow night?" I said.

"I didn't say I was going with you," she told me.

"You said Ozzie wanted you to work. Are you going to work at the morgue?"

She drew back. "That wasn't a very nice thing to say."

"I'm sorry. But if you don't let me spend the paycheck I've got coming today, I'll have a hell of a week end."

"All right," she said. "Try to stay out of trouble the rest of the day."

Gully heard it. "His idea of staying out of trouble is getting mixed up in a brawl at Smitty's bar," he said. "If you're smart, you'll leave him alone, Miss Carpenter."

"A girl has to have some fun," she said.

Guffy beckoned to me and took me over to Ozzie's desk where a cop sat with a notebook. Ruth went out to her office and we were alone.

"Nice girl," said Guffy. "Wish I were about ten years younger and still single."

"A swell kid," I said.

"Too swell for you," he said. "Mike, you've been a bad boy." He was no longer friendly and congenial. He was hard and gruff and his eyes looked like granite. "You've been telling me lies."

I was expecting this. "Well, Clyde, that's the way it goes. Sometimes you just can't depend on anybody. What have I been fibbing about?"

"Don't try to act smart with me, Mike," he said. "What about that guest you entertained in your room last evening?"

"What guest?" Make him work for it.

"The one the elevator boy told me about, who strangely enough answers a familiar description."

"Well, if you know all about it—"

"I want to hear about it from you."

"The visitor was a lady, and I am a gentleman."

"You're no gentleman and no lady would visit you in your hotel room."

"Supposing somebody did pay me a short visit last evening," I said. "What would it prove?"

"It proves that you haven't been on the level with, me," said Guffy. "Now I'm not sure of anything you told me last night."

"Everything else is true. Didn't you talk to the bartender at my hotel? Didn't he say I spent about half an hour in the bar?"

"Yes, he told me that. And we also know that Hope Osgood wasn't in your hotel room long enough for any monkey business, unless you're a hell of a fast worker. Now I'm giving you a break, Mike. Why did she come to see you?"

I shook my head. "Clyde, I honestly don't know. I keep telling myself it's because I'm irresistible, but if I am, no one else has ever noticed it."

"Didn't she say why she came?"

"She'd had a few drinks, of course, and she said something about the good old days. Could be she was feeling nostalgic."

"What does that mean?"

"Well, she was sentimental about old times. We used to run around together before she married Osgood."

Guffy raised his eyebrows. "Seems that I've heard that before. And she gave you the air because Osgood had a big bank account."

"Yes. And since she married him, I haven't had more than a few words with her. Just 'Hello, glad to see you,' and stuff like that. Not until last night, and then she came up and told me that she planned to get a divorce from Osgood."

"She wanted to pick up where you left off?" He was less bristly now.

I nodded. "She didn't make a point of saying that, but I gathered it was what she meant."

"Hmm."

"Can I ask a question, Clyde?"

"I'm questioning you. You're not questioning me."

"My question is going to determine just how much I talk to you . . ."

"You don't need to talk. We could lock you up right now—as a material witness if for no other reason. But you'd better talk if you know what's good for you."

"How much of an alibi does Colonel Tanner have?"

That seemed to stop him cold. He waved to the other cop to stop taking notes. "If Colonel Tanner killed his business partner," he asked, "would you run down the story?"

"Sure," I said.

Guffy's eyes were cold. "You'd double-cross your boss?"

"It's no double-cross," I said. "If my boss is a murderer, I'd just as soon pin it on him as you would. But I've got to have proof. Who are you loyal to, the mayor or the law? If the mayor committed a crime, would you arrest him?"

Guffy's face grew red. "Let me tell you something, paper boy. I got suspended from the force once because I was loyal to *my* boss. He was crooked as a corkscrew but I did what he told me to."

"You had to, or lose your job," I said.

"I wouldn't feel too secure in this job if I were you, Mike," he said. "Too many questions about Colonel Tanner might get you fired."

"Even if Colonel Tanner killed Osgood?"

"I'm sure he didn't," said Guffy.

"That may be," I said, "but on my list, he's number two suspect. For your information, a cop named Guffy is number three."

"Who's number one? You?"

I looked at him.

"Oh, I get it," said Guffy. "About your speed too. A girl comes up to your hotel room, and you suspect her for murder. Holy Toledo, Mike, I'm glad I'm just an acquaintance of yours. I'd hate to be your boss or your girl friend."

"You couldn't be either one. Anything else you want to ask me?"

"As a matter of fact, there are several things I want to know," said Guffy. "What were you and Tyndall fighting about?"

"I was trying to get him to stop drinking and go to work," I said.

"Could be you're telling the truth," he said. "What makes you suspicious of Colonel Tanner all of a sudden?"

"You told me I shouldn't talk about that."

"Trust me, Mike, I won't tattle."

"Has the Colonel got an alibi for last evening?"

"No. Neither have you. Nor I. Nor Hope Osgood. Nobody has an alibi."

"He was Osgood's business partner. That kind of thing leads to murder sometimes. And maybe the Colonel killed Jeff Myler and Ozzie found out about it."

Guffy shook his head. "Back to that again. Why would Tanner kill Myler?"

"They were on different sides of the political fence."

"So was I. I had a much better reason to kill Myler."

"Did you?"

"Don't be silly. If I did, I'd never tell a reporter."

"What about Mrs. Myler?"

"Well, Mike, what about her?"

"She was Jeff Myler's widow. Don't you always pick on widows first in a murder case?"

"As a matter of fact, Mike, we did question her. Not me. I wasn't on the force then, but I studied that case because, brother, they gave me one hell of a going over till I convinced them I didn't kill him. She was in the clear. Her alibi wasn't what you'd call solid, but I doubt if she had anything to do with it. The fact that the gun is still in existence ought to prove she didn't. She'd have tossed the gun in a lake or in a sewer. Maybe buried it in the back yard. She'd never put it someplace where it wouldn't rust."

"It wasn't rusted?"

"No signs of it on the bullet we got," said Guffy. "At least there was no rust in the barrel. We figure it's had a lot of good care over the years. Somebody thought it was valuable."

"A cop knows how to take care of a gun."

"So do lots of people," said Guffy. "Are you trying to pin it on me, Mike? I could do a lot better job on you."

"Guffy," I said, "let's stop kidding each other. You suspect me. I suspect you. Let's agree on that. But we're not getting anywhere right now. Why don't we call a truce and look at somebody else?"

"Like the Colonel?"

"He'll do."

Guffy stared at the desk. Finally he said, "Homicide is a funny business, Mike. Nearly everybody who kills somebody is new at the game. The few professional killers don't count because they're pretty rare. Now when a person goes into a business he doesn't know anything about, he's pretty apt to make mistakes, isn't he?"

I nodded.

"In Myler's death there weren't any mistakes. The person who killed Myler didn't leave a single scrap of evidence. He got away clean. Nobody saw him enter the building. Nobody heard the shot. Nobody saw him leave. He took away the gun, and he didn't leave a sign. It was different from any other murder I've ever tackled. It was timed right and executed flawlessly. Now you're trying to connect it with a bungling job—the kind that was done on Herman Osgood."

"Was it bungled?" I asked.

"It was the craziest murder I ever saw," said Guffy. "He left the gun behind—"

"Osgood's own gun," I said.

"That's the point," said Guffy. "The weapon and the four shots give us a very good insight in the murder. This murder wasn't planned. Myler's was. This wasn't a perfect crime, while Myler's was not only planned and carefully executed, but the murderer didn't give us a thing to work on except some very crazy theories, like you're working on now."

"You've got some evidence?" I asked.

"Enough to burn the man when we catch him," said Guffy.

"You've been holding out, Lieutenant."

"What have you been doing to me?" he asked.

I said nothing.

"Mike," he said. "I want the answer to one question. Why did Hope Osgood come to see you last night?"

"Clyde," I said, "if I knew I'd tell you. But I don't have the haziest idea."

"Then maybe you could give us an idea—just an opinion and nothing else. Do you think she killed Osgood?"

I shook my head. "I don't think so," I said. "But I don't know what goes on in her mind. The reason I don't think she killed Ozzie is because I know she was too young to have been involved in the Myler case. And I think the two connect, no matter what you say about the difference in planned and un- planned homicide."

"My job is to solve the murder of Herman Osgood," said Guffy. "Not Jeff Myler's."

"How do I stand in the case, Clyde? Am I suspect?"

"You are, but I haven't got enough on you to send you to the chair yet."

"Then I'm not arrested now, huh?"

"No. I only wanted the answer to one question. You can go."

I said good-bye and went into Ruth's office. I used her phone to call Hank downstairs and tell him I had to go home and change clothes; my new shirt was torn and I looked pretty messy. He'd already heard about my fight in Smitty's bar and Smitty was presenting his bill to the business office. Probably it would be taken out of Tyndall's salary and mine.

"When you get ready to do some work, would you mind let- ting me know, Mike?" he said sarcastically.

"Sweetheart," I said, "I've been working like a dog—no, like a crazy newspaperman."

He swore loudly and I hung up the phone because Ruth Carpenter was blushing furiously. Even over the phone, she could hear it.

While I was changing clothes in my hotel room, the phone rang and I answered it. Ward Tyndall was calling. "Hank said you were changing clothes, Mike," he said. "Believe me, I'm sorry. I had a couple of drinks too much."

"Forget it. My pants were wrinkled, anyhow," I said.

"Not sore, then?"

The guy rankled me, but I liked him in a go-to-hell way. "Water under the dam, chum," I said. "Sorry I punched you in the eye."

"It's a bruise I shall display with pride, since it came from the fabulous Mike Lanson who writes first-person byline stories in the morning paper. Anyhow, let's call a truce and work together."

"Okay," I said. "You sound reasonably sober now."

"I'm not," said Ward, "but I've got some dope. That's why I went to Smitty's, but you got mad."

"I'll be downtown in fifteen or twenty minutes," I said.

"No sense in your coming downtown," he said. "We've got to do some checking on University Hill. I'll come out to see you."

"Okay. Meet me in the Waltham Hotel bar in twenty minutes—"

"That's where I'm calling from, pal," he said. "Come downstairs and have a drink."

Ward had a little mouse under his left eye, which gave me a sense of accomplishment when I met him a few minutes later. He seemed ready for another drink, and I told him to have one on me and ordered one myself.

"What's the angle?" I asked, when I got the drink.

"This," he said. From his coat pocket he took a small envelope containing a photograph. It was from the *Gazette-Globe* morgue and had a caption written on the back: *Gun Club Wives Hold Match.* The typewritten cutlines gave the date and names of the women competing for the wives' trophy of the Creston Gun Club. Mrs. Althea Osgood was one. The only woman I recognized was Mrs. Jeff Myler.

"Take a good look at the pistol," said Tyndall.

I looked. It was a larger gun than most. "What about it?"

"Could it be a thirty-two caliber?"

"I can't tell from the picture."

"Did you ever see Osgood's gun?"

I shook my head.

"His was a thirty-two, and it looked so much like it, it could be a twin. Get a good look at the one Mrs. Osgood has."

I looked. Sure enough, the guns were almost identical.

"Trouble is," I said, "I think Smith and Wesson puts out that model in both twenty-two and thirty-two caliber."

"Well, let's ask Mrs. Myler," said Tyndall.

"What's it going to prove?"

"Maybe she did in Myler, and then shot Osgood because he knew she did."

"Let's go," I said, downing the rest of my drink.

Tyndall had already finished his, so we left.

ELEVEN

There were police cars all over the place, but we thought that they were intensifying the search for clues at the Osgood place. It never entered my mind that something else might have happened until we knocked on the door of Mrs. Myler's neat little house next door.

When the door opened Tyndall and I looked straight into the little granite eyes of Lieutenant Clyde Guffy. "You got here almost as soon as I did," he said. "Come on in, boys. Did Mrs. Myler call you?"

"Huh?"

Guffy didn't repeat his words, but he stepped aside and motioned for us to come in. On the floor in the living room was a body covered with a sheet.

Tyndall made a choking sound in his throat. "Mrs. Myler?"

"Mrs. Myler," said Guffy.

He glanced from Tyndall's face to mine. I suppose my expression was goofy.

"Would you mind telling me how you got here so quickly?" he asked. "I just put down the phone after calling headquarters when you knocked. You see I was next door, checking up a few details on the Osgood case when the maid came running over here. She arrives at work at 1:00 p.m., you know, and was a little late today. She came in the house and found the body."

"How?"

"You mean how did Mrs. Myler get killed?" he asked. "With a bullet, of course. I'd judge it was thirty-two caliber, but of course we'll have to check. Now will you tell me—"

"We didn't know a thing about it," said Tyndall. "We came out here to talk to her."

Guffy grinned. "Truth at last," he said. "But of course you're drunk, and don't know what you're saying. The only time a reporter is truthful is when he's liquored up."

"Clyde," I said, "can I use the phone?" Hank didn't think I was working, did he? I'd show him.

"Of course," said Guffy. "We've found no fingerprints on it. I've got a few things to do and you just make yourself at home till I'm ready to talk to you. Careful, don't step on the body."

I gave him a few cuss words and went to the phone.

I dialed the office and asked for the city desk. Hank answered the phone.

"This is Mike," I said.

"Well, *la-tee-dah!*" he said. "The country club kid himself. Enjoying your vacation?"

"Shut up," I said. "I got a big story."

"Sorry," said Hank. "We don't need any. What we want is something new on the Osgood murder to show our readers we don't go to sleep after the *Globe* goes to press."

"Are you going to listen?"

"No," said Hank. "Right now I'll settle for anything, even a report on the P.T.A. I'll switch you over to a rewrite and if it's not something new on the Osgood case, don't bother to come in except to get your severance pay. We've got a deadline hovering over our ears."

"But, Hank! It's hot—"

A click on the phone cut me off. Then the lazy voice of a rewrite man said, "Yeah?"

"It's me," I said. "Mike Lanson. Ready to go?"

"Okay, Mike," he said. "Let's have it slow."

"Here it comes," I said. I lowered my voice to a monotone, and dictated slowly. "The body of Mrs. Jefferson Myler, widow of the late editor of the *Gazette* and the *Globe* was discovered in her living room today. She had been shot—"

"Hold it!" yelled the rewrite. I heard his voice as he turned away from the phone and yelled across the room to Hank. "Hank! Hey! Mike's got another murder—Mrs. Myler!"

I hoped that when Hank heard it, he would have to leave the room and change his britches.

I gave the story then with Hank hanging on the extension. I had a few details to check and I told them I'd call back after I finished talking to Guffy.

"Mike," said Hank, after I'd finished. "I love you, boy!"

"To hell with you," I said and hung up.

I hovered around Guffy for a few minutes, asking questions. Whenever he got tired of hearing the questions, he answered me. I had a pretty good story and called Hank again. I was in plenty of time for the suburban edition.

By that time Guffy was ready to talk to us.

He asked about my conversation with Mrs. Myler in the morning, and didn't seem impressed. Then Tyndall showed him the picture of the Creston Gun Club wives. He grinned. "You're not telling me anything I don't know already," he said. "I was the club instructor at that time and I staged that match."

"This pic was taken just before Jeff Myler was murdered," I told Guffy. "She might have used that very gun."

"She didn't," he said. "That gun was Myler's all right. He used it several times and kept getting low scores with it, so he gave it to his wife. We checked it after Myler was killed. Not me, but the department did. The report said it was clear in the case."

"So you really suspected her?" I asked.

"Don't go drawing conclusions," said Guffy. "We check everything in a murder case. That's the way cases are solved—a lot of hard work. Not the way a silly reporter does it—by hitting a jackpot full of luck."

"Anybody else in the club have a gun like this?" Tyndall asked.

Guffy thought for a moment. "Tanner did, I think. I wouldn't be positive. But don't you try to send him to the chair, Ward. Mike's doing that. Both of you ought to get fired."

"The scientific approach, you know—follow every lead," Tyndall said. "I think you ought to check on Tanner's gun."

"We probably did," Guffy said, "Every scientific approach was tried in the Myler case, believe me. For your information Tanner is in the clear. We've also talked to him about Herman Osgood and we may talk to him again about Mrs. Myler. Tanner and Myler were at odds politically, but there were no hard feelings. They were good friends aside from their politics. I don't know how well acquainted he was with Mrs. Myler, but I don't believe he's involved here either—unless something turns up that links him with the other crimes."

"You think the same person committed all three crimes?" I asked.

Guffy had a strange look in his eyes. "I don't know if the same person is responsible for all three murders, but I am pretty sure that these last two murders would not have taken place if Myler had died a natural death."

I spoke quietly now. "Did you know that Myler had a brain tumor?" I didn't know for sure, but I thought it was probable.

"Yes," said Guffy, surprisingly.

"How did you know?" I asked. Doc Browne had said only three people knew besides himself—Mrs. Myler, Dwight Deems and a brain surgeon.

"There was an autopsy. The bullet was lodged in Myler's brain. The medical examiner found the tumor when he dug out the bullet."

Tyndall stared at me. "What's this? Myler had a brain tumor?"

I nodded. "I didn't think many people knew," I said. "But it seems that Hank Newcomb was right when he said there weren't any secrets in the world."

The phone rang and an officer called Guffy into the next room.

I heard him talking, and then he returned to the kitchen. "Headquarters," he said. "Hope Osgood has a lawyer." He waited for a moment but got no reaction from Tyndall or me. "He'll bring her in for questioning at nine o'clock tomorrow morning. Until then, she's taking the Fifth Amendment till she gets her story straight."

TWELVE

Tyndall was silent as we rode back to Police Headquarters. I parked my car in the parking area and went upstairs with him to the press room.

As soon as we entered the door, he flopped down into his chair and put his feet up on his desk. He lit a cigarette and concentrated for a while on blowing smoke rings at the ceiling. Finally he spoke.

"We're missing a bet on Colonel Tanner," he said.

"Guffy gave him a clean bill. The cops talked to him."

Tyndall shook his head. "You know as well as I do, Mike, that no matter how many ways a cop can catch a criminal, some of them get away. Call it luck if you want, but cops aren't always right."

"You think they're wrong on Tanner?"

"The Colonel has been around, and I don't think he'd let his inhibitions get in his way if he had to murder somebody—to save his own hide or to make a million bucks."

"Just how do you think we can find out?" I asked. "Should we go out to Tanner's house and say: 'Howdy, boss. I hope you won't fire us, but Tyndall and I think you murdered Herman Osgood. Maybe Jeff Myler and Mrs. Myler, too. Mind if we ask a few questions and take your gun down to ballistics for a quick check?'"

Tyndall laughed. "That'd go over like a lead balloon."

"How else can we learn things?" I said. "We can't sit on our fat cans and solve this thing."

"We can figure out just what we need to know," he said. "The Colonel's smart enough to commit a crime that would be hard to hook him up with. And I expect he'd kill if he had to. He was in the O.S.S. during the war. That outfit did a lot of things that aren't in the history books, and never will be."

"Killing was legal during the war."

"Some kinds of killing were. Not all kinds. And the Colonel never got caught when he went behind enemy lines. He's tasted blood; killing again wouldn't be as hard. Maybe Jeff Myler knew something about the Colonel . . . something that would ruin him."

Tyndall sounded convincing. Myler was a crusader. He went after his prey like a killer, but he used newspaper headlines for a weapon.

"Maybe the Colonel was gypping buyers on his new homes," I said.

"That, or maybe it was long before the war. The Colonel might have pulled a shady deal in the oil game. Wildcatting hasn't always been a lily-white enterprise, pal."

"It would be easy to check, if Tanner had pulled something," I said. "All we'd have to do is to call a newspaper where the Colonel operated. They'd know if he'd done anything that he shouldn't oughta."

"Where'd he operate?" Tyndall asked.

"Tulsa, I think. We could call the *Dispatch*. Surely somebody in Tulsa would know about oil operations before the war."

I lifted the phone and put in a call for the editor of the Tulsa *Dispatch*.

"The business office will raise hell about this call," Tyndall said. "We'll have to explain it."

"If it doesn't pan out, we'll say it's personal and pay for it ourselves."

Tyndall looked in the front part of the phone directory and found that it cost two dollars for a three-minute person-to-person call before 6:00 p.m. "A dollar apiece, pal. Don't talk too long."

The editor's name was Parkes and he had a pleasant voice. "Second call I've had today from Creston," he said. "What in the hell goes with you guys up there? Is Flash Tanner a murder suspect?"

"Flash Tanner?"

"Yeah. That's what we called him down here," said Parkes. "His first name was Gordon. Get it? Flash Gordon. Hah, hah."

"Heh, heh," I laughed politely. "We heard about the other call and wanted to find out who's checking on him." It seemed like a pretty good chance to cover our tracks and learn something in the process.

"The cops, of course," said Parkes. "A lieutenant named Guffy of Criminal Investigation. They're not trying to hang that killing on him, are they?"

"Don't know," I said. "There've been two killings since last night. You probably have the other story on your wire by now."

"That so? I haven't checked anything but the oil news today."

"What did you tell the cops about Tanner?"

Parkes laughed. "If that's what Flash is worried about, you tell him, I gave him a clean bill of health. I didn't have to lie a bit. I told those cops of yours that Flash Tanner was the squarest shootin' wildcatter that ever salted a duster."

I didn't know much about the oil business, but somewhere I read that salting a mine was faking mineral resources that the mine didn't have.

"That doesn't mean he did anything crooked, does it?"

"Hell no. I said Tanner was on the level and he was. Of course in those days, things were done that aren't legal any more, but they were legal then. Tanner may have cut some corners, but he always did the best he could. A great guy."

"He wasn't in jail any time was he?"

"In jail? No jail could hold Flash Tanner!" He chuckled. "Tanner was okay. When I needed a good story, I could always dig one out of Flash. If your cops think he killed anybody, they'd better go back to cop college. He wouldn't hurt a flea unless he had a good reason."

Murderers always think their motives are good.

"Thanks," I said. "Any time we can help you out, give us a call."

"Sure thing, pardner."

I hung up the phone and looked at Tyndall, who had finished his cigarette. "Well?" he asked.

"Down in the oil country, Flash Gordon Tanner is the patron saint of wildcatters," I said. "If Myler got anything on him in Tulsa, he didn't get it from a newspaperman."

"Ho hum," said Tyndall and his head went down on the typewriter. He didn't even revive when the phone rang a couple of minutes later.

The call was from the police laboratory.

"Lieutenant Guffy said to call you the minute we got something on the Myler case," said the cop on the other end of the wire.

I had to think for a couple of seconds. There were two Myler cases now. "You mean *Mrs.* Myler?"

"Oh, sure. The other one was ten years ago. But this has a tie-in."

"Yes?" I was straining my ears.

"The medical examiner said Mrs. Myler died between 11:00 a.m. and noon," the cop went on. There wasn't any tie-up here, and I waited for more. "We've also got a ballistics report. The bullet that struck Mrs. Myler came from the same gun that killed her husband ten years ago."

"How in the devil did you figure that out so quick?"

"Guffy had a hunch."

"Have they found the gun?"

"Not yet," said the cop.

"Anything else?"

"The lieutenant said to tell you the neighbors saw a man leave the house about 11:00 a.m. He was driving a red convertible."

"That was me," I said. "I told Guffy I was there."

"Yeah. I know. Guffy wants to talk to you about it. He said not to leave town."

Damn. I was up to my neck in this one, too. "I didn't have anything to do with the killing," I said.

"That's what they all say," the cop said, and he hung up.

I dialed the office and gave Hank the new lead for the home final. Hank treated me like I was the best reporter that a newspaper ever had. "I was just talking to Dwight Deems, Mike," he said. "He said you could go home an hour early today."

I was practically dead on my feet. "He's getting damn near human," I said.

"However," said Hank, and I knew there was a catch in it, "you were ten minutes late getting down to work this morning. So you'd better stay till ten after four."

"Okay," I said, without bitterness. I was used to this sort of thing.

"Check out with me before you leave." He hung up.

Tyndall was beginning to revive, but he wasn't very alert. He looked at me from his desk. "Let's don't talk about it," he said. "We keep going around in circles."

"I'm leaving an hour early," I said.

"Good." He put his head down on his arms on top of the desk.

I was just starting to go over my list of suspects again when Don Hilliard came into the room. He glanced at Tyndall, who was apparently asleep, then at me. "I just got the dope from the lab," he said. "Is it too late for the Home Final?"

"A cop called me," I said. "It's all in the paper by now."

He sat down and stretched. "I'm tired," he said. "I wasn't up all night like you, but I've been running my tailbone off."

"I'm knocking off at four," I said. "I'll drive you home."

He shook his head. "Hank said that you were leaving early and he wants me to stay till five."

"There won't be much to do."

"Think the cops will solve these killings?" Don asked.

"I'm tired thinking," I said.

I just sat in my chair, my mind dazed and confused.

I just sat. I tried not to think, but I did anyhow. I just couldn't stop. I got an idea, but it never seemed to make sense. I wondered if Myler could have killed himself. But if he did, who took the gun and why? Dwight Deems, maybe. But why again? Dwight got some stock in the *Gazette* after Myler died. Again why? Was it for something he did, or for something he didn't do? Like tell the cops all he knew about Myler's death.

The minutes ticked off. Don Hilliard drifted off. Said he was going to check something. I supposed it was that traffic accident he was working on. I didn't ask.

Finally the clock showed four. Ten more minutes. Then five minutes. Four. Three. Two. One. I picked up the phone and called Hank.

"Checking out," I said.

"Anything cooking?" he asked.

"No. Guffy's working on something. He's not around."

"Let me talk to Ward Tyndall."

I shook Tyndall and got him on the phone. He smelled like he'd been dipped in a brewery. Hank, of course, just wanted to make sure I was calling from Headquarters and not from a pool hall.

He gave Tyndall some nonsense and Tyndall yessed him. Finally he hung up.

Tyndall looked at me. "Get the hell out of here, he says." He went back to his desk and put his head on his arms again. I said good-bye, but he didn't even raise his head. I went out to the parking lot. Two men stood beside my car. Both of them were familiar to me, but I didn't know their names. They worked at the *Gazette,* downstairs in the mailing room.

"Howdy," I said.

The big one nodded and the short one said, "Hello, Mike. We've been waitin' for you."

He opened the door and climbed in behind the steering wheel.

I stared at him. "You've got the wrong car, haven't you, pal? Or are you going to chauffeur me home?"

"Get in, chum," said the big man.

He grabbed both arms and hoisted me into the car from the other side. He shoved me over into the middle next to Shorty and climbed in beside me.

"What's the big idea?" I asked.

"Shut up," said Shorty. "Give us your keys."

"To hell with you."

The big man held my arm and reached into my right pocket and pulled out the keys. He tossed them across my lap to Shorty.

"You got a nerve," I said. "This is right behind Police Head-quarters. If I yell, you fellows are going to have trouble."

"Keep him quiet, Bart," said Shorty, starting the motor and gunning it.

I opened my mouth to yell and Bart jabbed me in the ribs with his elbow. It knocked my wind out and I didn't yell.

THIRTEEN

Shorty turned the car into the two-lane drive toward the street. A police squad car was coming up the drive.

My ribs still hurt, but I tried to yell again and Bart's elbow landed again with a breath-squeezing jar. The only sound I made was a hoarse, "Whuush."

The cops didn't even turn their heads.

I was still gasping for air when the car went up Sixth Street to Bradley Trafficway. Then it turned south toward University Hill.

I had my wind back again. "You guys sure you got the right man? I haven't tried to muscle in on any mobs lately."

"Funny guy," said Bart.

"You're Mike Lanson, aren't you?" asked the little guy.

"Yes, but—"

"You're the right guy."

"Where are you taking me?"

"For a ride, Buster," said Bart.

"You're going to get in trouble over this."

"Look who's talkin'," said the little fellow. "You're the one that's in trouble."

"No hard feelin's," Bart said. "We ain't got nothin' against you personal. All we do is what we is told."

I decided it wouldn't do any good to argue with these men.

They drove slowly, but only because traffic was bad. It was nearly 4:15 and rush hour was underway. We stopped half a dozen times to let jams ahead of us iron themselves out.

At least half an hour later, we pulled up at the home of
the late Herman Osgood. Two cars in the driveway. The first
was Hope's red-and-white Edsel. The other was Dwight Deems'
Oldsmobile.

Shorty parked my car behind them. It was completely outclassed.

Bart got out and motioned for me to follow. "No funny business," he warned, "unless you want me to shine my knuckles on
your face."

I got out without trying to be funny. Bart held my arm till
Shorty joined him, and took the other arm. Then we walked,
chummy-like, up to the front door, which was opened by Hope
Osgood. A smile spread across her face.

"Hello, Mike," she said. "Sorry I had to get you out here like
this." Bart and Shorty released their grip on my arm.

I stood there, like a ruffled rooster, glaring at her. "What's
the big idea?"

Hope's smile grew broader. Without attempting to answer
me she spoke to my escorts. "You can wait in Mr. Deems' car.
He'll take you home in a few minutes."

Bart raised his hand to the tip of his hat, almost in a military
salute. "Yes'm. If you need us, just holler."

They turned and went to the car.

Hope spoke to me. "Come in, Mike. In answer to your question, I was afraid that if I invited you over, you'd suspect some
sort of an incident like the one we had last night."

I glanced at Bart and Shorty, who had paused to watch us
before getting into the car. It seemed best that I go in the house.
Hope stood aside as I stepped into the living room.

Dwight Deems sat in one of the modernistic chairs near the
fireplace.

I turned to Hope. "Party?"

"Just an informal reception," said Hope mirthfully. "Sit
down, Mike. We're going to play *Truth or Consequences.*"

I sat in a chair facing Deems, who seemed to be very upset.
His face was red. His lips twisted in a snarl and he ran his finger
under his collar as if it were choking him.

Hope brought another chair and sat between us. "I'd offer you a drink," she said. "But I'm afraid this reception isn't going to be entirely sociable. You may smoke, if you like."

There was no reason not to go along with a gag, and I lit a cigarette. Deems continued to look uncomfortable. Finally he spoke in a harsh voice.

"Blackmail," he said. "Blackmail! That's what it is. I could put you in jail for this, Mrs. Osgood."

"I'd think twice before I tried, Mr. Deems," she said. "And I think you've a much better chance of going to jail than I have."

"Were you kidnaped too?" I asked him.

He looked at me, then looked away as if he didn't intend to answer then turned his head back. "Not kidnaped," he said. "I was told to come here or—"

Hope laughed. "I need the answers to some questions, Mike," she said. "My lawyer said that the police are likely to arrest me for murder. A murder I didn't commit. Two or even three murders, perhaps, although I can't see how they can hang the Jeff Myler murder on me. Therefore, I thought it might be best for my own protection to get some information, before witnesses, that would prevent that awkward situation. You're the best person I know to be a witness, Mike."

"Mike," said Deems, "I can fire you on the spot, you know."

I looked him straight in the eye. I don't look bosses straight in the eye very often. Not defiantly, that is, and not when they're so mad their shirt collars feel tight. But I wasn't afraid of Dwight Deems. Probably because he was more afraid of something than I was.

"I don't think you'll fire me, Dwight," I said, trying to make it sound casual. "Under the Guild contract, you've got to prove just and sufficient cause."

"Damned union," he said. "Why do reporters have unions anyway? They only lower the dignity of your profession."

"Years ago, reporters tried to be dignified, Dwight," I said, "but it's hard to be dignified and hungry."

He snorted.

"Gentlemen," said Hope, "my reason for *inviting* you here was not to discuss the pros and cons of unions. Two people are dead because I kept a little secret for ten years. If I decide to keep my mouth shut, more people may die and I might be charged with murder."

She got up and walked across the room to a writing desk. She took a key from the pocket of her skirt, unlocked the desk and took a long manila envelope from a pigeonhole.

"I'm not going to let this document out of my hands," she said. "It's too much trouble typing it. I had a carbon, which I gave to Herman, but he made the mistake of leaving it in his desk. I think you got it last night, didn't you, Dwight? Just before you hit poor Mike over the head?"

I focused my eyes on the managing editor. "So it was you, huh?"

He avoided my gaze.

"I should have guessed it," I said. "You had on a light gray suit, which I'd have recognized in the reflected light in Ruth's office. That's why you slipped into Ozzie's trench coat before you slugged me. You talk about firing me? I could have you thrown in jail for assault."

"Why not sue him for damages, Mike? It's more profitable." Hope seemed to be enjoying this.

She pulled a long sheet of legal-sized paper from the envelope. "This is signed and notarized by Ruth Carpenter," Hope went on. "That's why I took her to the meeting last night. The carbon, of course, wasn't notarized, but it was simply something to let Herman know that he was in trouble if he didn't give me an uncontested divorce. Since Mr. Deems knows what is in the paper, I won't read it, but I'll simply brief you on it, Mike. Then we'll get to the bottom of things."

Deems turned sharply toward her. "Hope," he said, "I beg of you, don't tell this to a reporter. Olive is dead, so is Jeff Myler. What possible good can it be to bring these things to light?"

"This is the first I knew that Mrs. Myler was involved," said Hope. "The only reason for talking now is, as I've said before, to clear myself of possible murder charges."

She turned to me and continued. "Ten years ago, my mother made her living by catering parties. She was a widow and she was ambitious for me. She insisted that I finish high school and go to secretarial school. Fortunately, she didn't live to see me reach the goal she'd planned—marrying a rich boss. Otherwise she'd have been sorry. I'd have been much happier as the wife of a newspaper reporter.

"I worked for my mother at some parties and I was serving refreshments at Herman Osgood's housewarming ten years ago when Jeff Myler was killed in his office. About nine o'clock in the evening, Mr. Deems, who had arrived a little late, entered Herman's study. I was not nosy—in fact my mother had instructed me never to pry into anything or pay particular attention to what the guests were doing. But I chanced to pass the study and saw Mr. Deems inside, standing near Herman's gun case with a pistol in his hand. This unusual sight made me stop and watch. He was unaware of my presence because his back was toward me. I saw him remove a pistol from the gun case and replace it with the one in his hand. From where I stood they looked exactly alike. He put the gun he had taken into his pocket and turned and saw me.

"He was covered with confusion, and immediately he took my arm and pulled me into the room, closing the door. That door, incidentally, does not stay closed unless it is latched. Something I've learned since living here. Probably one of Colonel Tanner's slipshod bits of construction."

"This time the door was latched. Mr. Deems pulled a twenty-dollar bill from his billfold and put it in my hand. 'Forget what you saw tonight,' he said. 'Don't ever mention it to a soul—not even your mother. If you do, you'll get into very serious trouble.' Well, it was no trouble at all to take the money. I had an urge several times to speak out about it, since I read in the papers the next day that Jeff Myler, who was Mr. Deems' boss, was murdered. But I reasoned further. If I spoke out, I'd be accused of being sneaky and spying. My mother wouldn't get catering jobs, and if I caused Mr. Deems to be arrested for murder, his friends, whom I considered very upper-crust, would have it in for me. I didn't even know Mr. Myler, so why should I care whether he was murdered or not? I kept my mouth shut.

"Seven years later I married Herman Osgood. It was not what you'd call a successful marriage. My problem was to call it quits and come out of it financially ahead. One thing Herman hated above all others was scandal. I think he'd rather have died than be involved in one. The quickest way to get him to agree to a divorce and a large property settlement seemed to be to threaten him with a scandal. He married me to avoid a scandal, you know." She smiled as she said this.

She took a deep breath and resumed. "Of course I had no proof that the gun in Herman's study was the murder weapon. He might have discovered something unusual about it, and switched it, or perhaps Mr. Deems came back and changed guns again—"

"—tried," said Deems. "I tried but I never had the chance. I was never alone long enough."

"So I sent a bullet to the police," Hope went on. "I got it by taking the gun and firing it into a bucket of sand. Those two fugitives from a charm school, who brought you here, Mike, helped me wrap it. I pasted the clippings from the phone book on myself, when they weren't looking. I did it one afternoon in the mailing room."

"I'm glad you used union mailers," I said. I looked at Deems, who scowled.

"When the police announced they had identified the bullet as having been fired by the weapon that killed Jeff Myler, I was home and hosed, as the Australians say at the race track. I made the statement I have here, and got Ruth, who is the office notary, to witness it. Before that I gave a copy to Herman, telling him that I had the original in a very safe place. Actually it was in a safety deposit box I'd rented, which Herman didn't know about.

"I was to get Herman's answer last night, but he was dead when I returned home."

"Why did you come to see me, Hope?" I asked.

"Because, you big incorruptible newsman, you had the Colonel's ear. If the story was to be broken, you could do it without passing it first to Hank Newcomb, who would have consulted Dwight Deems, who would have halted it in its tracks."

I nodded. "Deems could have stopped it for a time," I said, "but even an editor can't stop a big story."

"Now, Dwight," said Hope. "We want the truth about Jeff Myler. Was he a suicide? And if so, why did you try to make it look like murder?"

The idea of suicide had been tossed around in my mind a few times along with the possibility of euthanasia, which under the law most certainly is murder in some degree. Homicide, anyhow.

"I see no reason why I should add anything to what you've said, Mrs. Osgood," said Deems. "There's no proof to anything you said. Herman Osgood did not have the murder weapon in his possession when he was killed, apparently, and except for your word he never had it."

"All right, Mike," said Hope. "Get the police on the phone."

I rose and started for the galley.

"Wait!" Deems' voice exploded in a croak.

I stopped and looked at Hope. "Go ahead, Mike. He just wants to waste time."

"Myler died as a result of an accident," he said quietly.

Hope shook her head, "No good, Dwight. People don't retouch accidents to look like murder."

Dwight Deems sighed. "There's really no reason now for my silence," he said. "Both Jeff and Olive are gone. Herman Osgood, too, but he was never really involved. Perhaps if I talk, the one person who is guilty of murder may be brought to justice."

I leaned forward. "Who?"

Deems shook his head. "I have only suspicions in that direction. Let's go back ten years." He rose from his chair and walked back and forth in front of the fireplace.

Finally he began. "Jeff Myler had a brain tumor, whether or not it was malignant, I don't know. Possibly it was. At any rate he had been subject to dizzy spells, double vision and other disorders for some months before his death. Dr. Browne diagnosed it as a tumor and his diagnosis was borne out by a consultant specialist who was called into the case at my request and Dr. Browne's suggestion.

"The tumor was in a spot where an operation would have only had a very small chance of success. Even if Jeff had survived, he probably would've been a hopeless paralytic the remainder of his life. If you had known Jeff, you would realize that to him this would have been worse than death. On the other hand, if nothing halted the growth of the tumor, he would grow worse and worse. His life would be a living death and he would be as helpless, as a paralytic. This, too, was unthinkable for Jeff.

"He discussed suicide, both with me and with Olive, his wife. We attempted to dissuade him. We never allowed him to be alone for any length of time. Even at work, I found excuses to call him at frequent intervals, or visit his office.

"Somehow he managed to keep his condition a secret from everyone except Olive and myself and the two doctors."

"Are you absolutely sure?" I asked.

"Yes," said Deems. "It was never mentioned."

"The police knew about it after the autopsy. Couldn't someone have learned during his lifetime." I was thinking of two people. Clyde Guffy, who at the time of Myler's death was under suspension from the police force, and Colonel Tanner, who was a political opponent.

"If you're thinking of Colonel Tanner," said Dwight, reading part of my thoughts, "get it out of your head. The Colonel had no reason to want Myler dead. Except for a difference in political opinion, they were friendly, even congenial. Myler had many friendly enemies like the Colonel."

"Okay," said Hope. "Let's not get sidetracked." She was a remarkable woman, one of the few who didn't let conversation meander in all directions.

"On that April night when Osgood had his housewarming, Jeff was at the office after dinner. Olive was to pick him up and drive him to the party, although I knew nothing of this plan.

"About eight o'clock in the evening I called Jeff from my office downstairs. It was one of those checks that I usually made, just to be on guard against anything he might attempt. He didn't answer the phone and I went up to his office immediately. I entered the office to find Myler dead and Olive sitting dazedly in a chair holding a pistol.

"Olive was not the hysterical sort, but she was in a state of shock. I found an envelope on the desk and I opened it. It was an editorial on euthanasia—"

"What?" Hope's face had a blank look.

"Mercy killing," said Deems, "Jeff contended that man should have the same rights as a dog—to be put out of his misery when he was hopelessly ill, or unfit to carry on."

He paced a few steps before going on. "Olive asked, 'Is that a suicide note? He tried to kill himself.' I told her it was an editorial endorsing euthanasia. She sobbed. 'He tried to kill himself. I came in the door just in time and I grabbed the gun. He struggled with me, but he had a seizure and I managed to get it out of his hand. At that moment the gun went off. I fired it, without realizing that I had done so.'"

Deems stopped his pacing. "We hear much in psychology nowadays about involuntary actions. About things that our subconscious mind makes us do, even against our ordinary natures. Olive Myler was in no sense a killer, yet she believed, like her husband, that death was in all respects preferable to what lay ahead for him. Her conscious self decreed that she must wrest the gun from Jeff, but her unconscious mind conceded that Jeff Myler at least had the rights that a sick dog has. She killed him. It was a mercy killing, yet it differed in no way legally from cold-blooded murder."

Again he stopped. I noted that Hope was watching him, cat-like, as if she did not quite believe what he was saying. Finally he continued. "I tried to persuade Olive that the situation could be set up to look like suicide. But she was unwilling. She did not wish to live and she wanted to surrender to the police. To me, this was unthinkable.

"Somehow I persuaded her to go home with me. I looked around the room, made sure no clues had been left behind, and took the gun—a Smith and Wesson Target pistol—with us.

"Both of you know how the elevators are situated at the *Gazette* building. They may be reached from Classified, from the Sixth Street entrance, or from the mailing room. During busy hours it is scarcely probable that anyone could get off on the first floor without being seen by someone. This was about eight o'clock in the evening, when the tempo of a morning newspaper begins to pick up.

"I knew that it was necessary that Olive be taken from the building secretly. She had managed to go upstairs without being seen. It was an accident, I'll grant, that no one saw her enter the building from Sixth Street. I could expect no such luck a second time. But the stairway can be used without much chance of being seen. Besides, the stairway ends right near the Sixth Street entrance.

"We walked down three flight of stairs and we slipped out without anyone seeing us. I drove her home in my car. She regularly drove Jeff because of his condition, but no one, you remember, knew of this condition, although it was daily growing worse and discovery of his seizures might be made any time. I felt, that the presence of Jeff's car on the parking lot might divert suspicion from Olive.

"On the way home, Mrs. Myler regained her composure. She realized now that there was no turning back. Whatever slim chance we might have had for a successful defense on the grounds of mercy killing had been lost when we fled from the building. The gun was still the big problem. Myler was a member of the Gun Club and the police would naturally want to see his weapons—just as routine investigation. If we cleaned the fatal weapon, it would be suspicious. If it were not cleaned, the police could certainly detect that it had been fired recently.

"Olive had recovered from her initial shock, as I've told you, and she recalled that Jeff had bought the gun because Herman Osgood had one like it. Herman had had great luck at the pistol matches and Jeff believed the weapon had something to do with it, although I doubt if it did. Anyhow, Olive knew Herman had an identical model.

"She suggested that I substitute Jeff's gun for Osgood's. The idea was logical. Only the serial numbers would identify the weapons and I hoped that the police would not check the numbers once they looked at Jeff's and determined that it had not been fired or recently cleaned. Osgood's would not be examined, I was certain. Osgood was giving a party and, as host, he'd have an unshakable alibi.

"I went to the party without letting on that I'd come from Olive's place or that I'd seen her that day. Mrs. Osgood has told how I substituted the gun and paid for her silence, which now is at an end."

"Ten years for twenty dollars is pretty cheap silence," she said.

"There was more involved than the money I paid you," Deems said. "At the party, I waited to hear from the office. I always left word where I'd be and I'd told Luke Taylor, who was night city editor, that I'd be at Herman's place. After 9:00, I grew impatient. Finally I couldn't wait and I called the office, asked to speak to Jeff Myler. Of course his phone didn't answer, but I had to be sure the discovery hadn't been made. Then I called Taylor, told him that I was worried about Jeff because he didn't answer the phone and asked him to investigate. Taylor sent Johnson, the head copyreader, up to Jeff's office and the body was found. Luke called the police, then called me at Herman's. I went at once to Olive's home, substituted Herman's gun for the missing weapon in Jeff's collection and burned the incriminating editorial on euthanasia in Olive's incinerator. I was with Olive when the police arrived.

"She broke down completely before police arrived, and since the police expected to find a hysterical and grief-stricken widow, she was not questioned very thoroughly until the next day. She did tell them that she'd been at home all day, and since no one came forward to break down her story, she was in the clear."

Deems stopped his pacing and sank down again in his chair.

"Since you burned the euthanasia editorial, you have no real evidence to support your story, Dwight," Hope said.

"Good God, Mrs. Osgood!" Deems exclaimed. "You don't think I killed Jeff Myler?"

"I understand you were given a block of stock in the *Gazette* corporation by Mrs. Myler," she said.

"But that was simply a token of gratitude," he said.

"Quite a token," was Hope's comment. She turned to me. "What do you think of this story, Mike?"

"It doesn't explain Ozzie's death, or the murder of Mrs. Myler," I said. "Those weren't mercy killings."

"That's what I think," she said. "What do you know about those deaths, Dwight?"

"Osgood showed me that document—the carbon of it," said Deems. "But I don't know why he was killed. Nor why someone killed Olive. I believe you committed those crimes, Mrs. Osgood. You're trying to pin them on me."

Hope sat very still. Her voice grew low and threatening. "I'm no murderer, Dwight. And if I had thought for a moment that you had killed anyone, I'd never risk being here alone with you this afternoon. No, Dwight. Herman must have known much of the story you just told. I don't know how he learned it, but perhaps he went to Mrs. Myler's home, after I'd threatened him. He told her about the affidavit even before I had the original notarized. He must have told her the story of my seeing you in the study when you switched the guns. She may have told him what you just finished relating. At any rate, she must have realized that Herman was in trouble through no fault of his and returned the gun that really belonged to him. The weapon that killed Jeff Myler was kept by her. Perhaps she planned to dispose of it. Perhaps she felt that it was no longer dangerous to have in the house. At any rate, it was used by the murderer to take her life."

"Who?" asked Deems. "If you thought I was innocent, you must have had reason to suspect someone else."

Hope Osgood smiled. "Colonel Tanner was taking a great deal of interest in the Myler case just before Herman was killed. Isn't it possible that Herman ran to him for advice and blurted out the whole thing?"

"But that's hardly a reason for murdering Herman," I said. I didn't like the way things were going. To me, Guffy was a much better candidate, although for the life of me I couldn't figure a motive for Osgood's murder, although he might have one for killing Myler.

"Why can't you drop the whole thing?" Deems asked.

"Because," said Hope, "I happen to be in the middle. The police probably will charge me with one murder, perhaps two after I'm questioned tomorrow. My alibi for the time when Herman was killed is nonexistent. And between eleven and noon today, I was downtown, on the streets, trying to avoid the police. I met Mike about noon, but Mrs. Myler was dead then. Mike, is there any way you can think of to determine if Colonel Tanner murdered Herman?"

"Not unless he has the gun," I said.

"Could we get into the house on some pretext and look for it?"

"That's not a job I have a particular taste for," I said.

"Why not? I'm willing to go with you."

"Whatever the result," I said, "the Colonel is going to see through it from the beginning. I don't think we can gain much by trying to outsmart him. He's smarter than I am, at least. Physically, he's had a great deal of experience in fighting and if it came to battling it out, the only thing in my favor is my youth."

Deems cleared his throat. "How are you on burglary, Mike?"

I looked at him sharply. "You ought to know that reporters sometimes have to do strange things. I've done my share of getting into places where I wasn't supposed to be."

"If Hope and I distract the Colonel," said Deems, "perhaps you might make a search for the gun."

For some reason, I wasn't half as eager to solve the murders now as I had been. I could think of all kinds of consequences for this kind of business, ranging from getting fired without severance pay to getting in jail on a housebreaking-charge.

"Would you do it for me, Mike?" Hope asked. "For old time's sake?"

I looked at her, without speaking.

"Would you do it for a fifty-dollar bonus?" asked Deems.

I turned my eyes in his direction. "What the hell," I said. "I've risked my life for less. You've got yourself a boy, Mr. Deems."

Hope looked at me with hatred in her eyes.

FOURTEEN

We had to explain to Bart and Shorty there had been a change in plans, and Dwight Deems advanced them taxi fare home.

Bart grinned at me, showing gold teeth. "No hard feelin's, eh, chum?" he asked.

My ribs still hurt from the punches he'd given me with his elbow during the ride out here, but I was willing to be as generous with him as I'd been with Dwight. "None at all," I said. "You fellows were just doing a job."

"Mrs. Osgood is a nice woman to work for," said Shorty. "Classy dame. Uptown stuff."

"Ever do any other work for her?" Deems asked suspiciously.

Bart looked at Shorty and grinned. "Nope," said Shorty, hastily.

I looked at Shorty. With Deems at my back, I wasn't afraid of physical violence. "That doesn't sound right to me, boys," I said. "We've just been having a truth session with Mrs. Osgood."

"What business is it of yours?" asked Shorty.

"None, if it doesn't involve Mr. Osgood," I said. "But Mrs. Osgood is up to her ears in trouble and we're trying to help her out."

Shorty shifted uneasily. "It wasn't nothing," he said. "She had us follow Ozzie around for a few days, to see if he spent his evenings legit."

"What do you mean, legit?"

"To see if he was chiselin'," said Bart. "He wasn't."

"Nice work if you can get it," I said. "Thanks, boys. And no hard feelings."

"You said it, chum," said Bart. They started off to hunt a taxi.

Colonel Tanner lived in an old-fashioned, rambling, three-story house dating back to the days when the size of a home was an indication of the owner's affluence. The place was an architectural atrocity.

The house was in the center of a wooded estate comprising at least three acres. At one time, Deems said, it had belonged to the Osgood family. But Herman had sold it to the Colonel when he moved into his more modern, and much smaller home on University Hill.

I don't know why the Colonel wanted such a big place, unless it was because he entertained a great deal and had many important visitors. All three of Colonel Tanner's wives had made pilgrimages to Reno before he moved into the place.

An iron fence surrounded the estate, and a brick and stone gateway was the only entry.

I scooted down to the bottom of the car as we turned into the blacktop drive that led to the front door of the house. Deems had already called Colonel Tanner on the phone, asking if he'd be in the position to receive Hope and himself on a matter of considerable importance. The Colonel said he'd be at home all evening. He was eating dinner at the moment, but wouldn't Hope and Dwight drop around in time for coffee and dessert? Indeed, Hope and Dwight would be glad to. I was only sorry that I wasn't an official member of the party; but I was getting a fifty-buck bonus, which would buy a lot of desserts and a lot of coffee if I felt underprivileged.

Leaving me in the car, Hope and Deems went to the front door. I heard a woman's voice, the Colonel's housekeeper; she was the wife of the Colonel's hired man, who sometimes doubled as butler.

I waited for several moments after I heard the door close; then I slipped out of the car, which had been parked in a surfaced area to the right of the house.

At the side was a little patio. French doors opened onto this from the house, and I noticed one of the doors was open a small crack. The September weather was warm and no doubt it had been left open for air.

I walked toward this door, careful to stay in the shadow of the house. I listened, heard nothing, and then pushed the door slowly inward. A moment later, I stepped into Colonel Tanner's study.

A large table occupied the center of the room, and an old-fashioned leather office chair was in front of it There was a reading lamp on the table, a few books and a stack of paper, which I immediately observed was a manuscript. I had time to glance at the title and noted to my amazement that it was a manuscript entitled *The Tiger's Middle Claw* by Reginald Van Duncan Rife. I'd read quite a number of Rife's mysteries. Now I learned to my amazement that it was the pseudonym of my boss. Good God! If he created murders in his mind, maybe he did research in his off moments.

There were two sectional book cases on the far wall. I had no time to investigate these, but a glass-fronted cabinet between them caught my eye. In it were several pistols, mounted for display. I recognized a German Luger, possibly a war trophy, an automatic pistol, probably an American made thirty-eight, and several smaller guns, including a couple of target-pistols.

I started toward it, when a voice broke the silence from the doorway to my right.

"I beg your pardon, sir. I was not aware that Colonel Tanner had other guests."

I turned and saw a man in a white coat, about forty-five years old, gray-haired and lean.

"I don't think the Colonel was aware of it himself," I said.

"Indeed?" said the man. "Then you must be a burglar."

"No," I said, thinking quickly, "I'm on his payroll, like you are. I work for the *Gazette.*"

The butler stared at me disbelievingly. "Perhaps I should announce you to the Colonel," he said. He pulled his hand from his pocket and with it came a nice leather-covered sap about six inches long.

"Yes," I said, "I think that might be a good idea." He stepped aside, and I preceded him into the dining room.

Deems almost choked, but Hope remained calm and unperturbed by my entry.

"Well, Mike!" said the Colonel. "You're just in time for pie and coffee."

"I found him snooping in your library, sir," said the houseboy.

The Colonel shrugged. "Well, I pay him for snooping. I suppose I shouldn't complain if he snoops on me. That will be all, Chester."

"Yes, sir," said Chester. He put the sap back in his pocket, turned and departed.

The Colonel sat at the head of a long table. Hope sat at his right and Deems at his left. Now, my host gestured to a seat beside Hope. "Sit down over there, Mike."

Deems had managed to keep from choking and now he said, "Colonel, I think we owe you an explanation."

The Colonel looked at him caustically. "No doubt you do, Dwight, but I'd rather hear it from Mike. Sometimes he's much more entertaining."

I sat down. A gray-haired, motherly woman brought in apple pie and coffee, just as if I'd been expected.

The Colonel passed me the cream, and I took a bite of pie; I hadn't eaten since noon and I was beginning to feel hungry.

"Between bites, Mike," said Colonel Tanner, "you might explain why we have the honor of your presence."

"It's this way, Sir," I said, "I was carrying out the assignment you gave me yesterday."

The Colonel smiled brightly. "Oh, yes! The Myler case. Any leads?"

"I've got the solution, sir, if you'd care to hear it."

"Mike!" said Deems.

"Let the man talk," said the Colonel, to Deems quietly. "I'm sure he's capable of it."

I gave the details as I'd heard them less than an hour before from Dwight Deems and Hope Osgood.

The Colonel listened intently. He didn't break in, until I finished. Then he nodded and said, "I suspected there was something very unusual about Jeff's death. It would seem, Dwight, that you're an accomplice after the fact. Is that what worries you?"

Deems spluttered and managed to say nothing. "It's not that I wish to suppress the truth, Colonel. I did what I did out of respect and esteem for my former employer and his faithful wife."

"I doubt if there is sufficient evidence to convict you," said the Colonel. "Any testimony Mike or Mrs. Osgood might give would be hearsay—except that intrigue with the gun, and even that's rather shaky, A fifteen-year-old girl might have imagined you were playing with guns in Osgood's study that night ten years ago. But the fact remains that the gun was not the one that killed Herman Osgood, and his murder seems more urgently in need of solving than any other right now. The murder of Mrs. Myler apparently is a byproduct. We can easily imagine there might be other murders."

"I'm speaking for myself, Colonel," I said, "but I'm sure that the others agree, that as long as we've laid our cards on the table, there's no reason for you not to do so."

"Then you suspect I had a part in a double murder?" he asked.

I shook my head diplomatically.

The Colonel drained his coffee cup, daubed his lips with his napkin and spoke directly at me. "I can add only one small detail to what you already know, Mike. I had nothing to do with the murders. What my suspicions were, or have come to be, is another matter, for I'm in the position here of being a bystander. It would appear, however, that we have all of the facts in the case, but no candidate for the electric chair."

"That's our problem exactly," said Deems. I don't know if it was an attempt to bring himself into Colonel Tanner's good graces, or possibly it was a sort of contagion resulting from exposure to Ozzie's job as yes-man and assistant editor. At any rate, Dwight Deems was eager to agree.

The Colonel spoke slowly, as if he was figuring things out as he talked.

"Last night someone visited Herman Osgood. Whoever it was had some sort of hazy idea that Herman Osgood knew who killed Jeff Myler. At any rate, he was convinced that Herman had in his possession a weapon which was involved in Myler's murder ten years ago."

"How do you know this, Colonel?" I asked, feeling that he had me in mind.

"Guesswork mostly," he said. "But I think the facts speak for themselves. Whoever killed Herman Osgood was guided by an incorrect hypothesis. You could have guessed it, Mike. Dwight here knew it. Hope suspected the truth very strongly. Mrs. Myler knew for a fact. And Clyde Guffy suspected that the Myler bullet was mailed anonymously by either Osgood or his wife."

"Dwight didn't tell me that," I said.

"Dwight had talked to one of our mailers," said the Colonel. "You weren't very smart, Hope, not to wrap that package yourself."

"Fingerprints, Colonel," she said softly.

"But the man or woman who visited Herman guessed the truth too late. We have no proof, but it's quite obvious that when the police received that bullet and began to reconsider the facts in the Myler case, Herman grew terrified. Hope had revealed what had happened, but he was afraid of Deems. He thought Deems was the murderer. I hope, Dwight, that he was wrong."

"I was an accomplice after the fact," said Deems. "But I had nothing to do with the murder."

"And you only have Mrs. Myler's word for it that it occurred as it did," said the Colonel. "Nevertheless, Herman dreaded being pulled into something that had scandalous, if not disastrous consequences. But he felt it his duty to confide in someone, and so Herman confided in Mrs. Myler. He felt that she was less dangerous than Dwight." The Colonel looked at gray-haired, mild-mannered Dwight Deems and smiled.

"Mrs. Myler probably told Herman that her husband died under circumstances that she could not reveal. Or she might have said her husband was a suicide, and she felt that it was far nobler to be thought a victim of assassination, or she might even have told him the truth. We'll probably never know how much Herman knew, but all he was thinking about was getting out of a bad situation. The upshot of it was that Herman received his own gun back and gave Mrs. Myler the actual death gun. This is the only way it could have happened, I think. Perhaps someone, can dream up a more far-fetched answer, but I'm sure this is the most logical."

"If anything about it is logical," said poor Deems.

"Herman displayed the weapon to his visitor last night. He suspected no foul play and he may have loaded the gun and asked him to fire a bullet from it and take it to the police for examination. Herman was sure he was in the clear now and he was anxious to prove it. Whatever happened after that, we can only guess, but I'm quite certain this is an extraordinary case and something most extraordinary must have happened."

I stared at the Colonel. At one point in the story, I had been acutely aware that he had been speaking directly at me, as if I were the murderer.

"Colonel," I said, "the way you talk, I wonder how you know so much."

He smiled at me. "I'm not sure I follow you, Mike."

"Are you sure you weren't at Herman Osgood's yesterday?" Sometimes I let my enthusiasm run away with me. But I'm a reporter, and even if it means getting fired, I have to dig up facts. And so here I was, practically accusing my boss of being a murderer.

"You ought to thank your stars, Mike, that I'm a tolerant man," the Colonel said. "And you should also be grateful that I appreciate how much guts you've got. I do appreciate it, Mike. The *Gazette* is a successful paper because its reporters and photographers have guts. I'm going to tell you something, Mike. No matter whether I killed Herman Osgood or not, my answer would be that I didn't. Sure, I'd lie to keep out of the electric chair."

He pressed a buzzer under his foot and the housekeeper came in from the kitchen. "We're through here, Mrs. Wilson," he said.

"We're going into my study. Please tell Chester we're not to be disturbed."

"Yes, sir," said Mrs. Wilson. She immediately began to clear away the dishes and the Colonel led us from the dining room, through a hallway to the study, where I'd been found by Chester.

The Colonel waited till we were all in the room. Then he crossed and closed the French doors and locked the study door.

He turned to us. "There are my guns," he said, waving his hand toward the glass-cabinet I hadn't been allowed to examine before. "Do you want to look at them, Mike."

"With your permission, Colonel," I said. I walked to the case. There was one gun that looked like a Smith and Wesson target pistol, and I pointed to it. "I didn't know you had one too, Colonel."

"Take it out, Mike," said the Colonel softly.

I heard Hope gasp. "Don't, Mike!"

Nevertheless, I opened the case and pulled the gun from its supports. I looked at it, then turned and smiled at the Colonel.

"Satisfied?" he asked.

"Yes, Colonel. It couldn't possibly have killed Myler, Osgood or Myler's widow."

"Why not?" Deems demanded.

"Because," I said, "it's a twenty-two caliber. Smith and Wesson makes the model in both sizes."

Hope breathed a sigh of relief. "Mike," she said, "why don't you let the police solve murders?"

"Maybe I want to prove something," I said.

"Mike is one of those adventuresome souls who would rather learn something than live safely," said the Colonel.

I hadn't been listening. Something about that gun suddenly set off a train of thought that led me to a conclusion like an express train running on an open track.

I knew who had killed Herman Osgood; I knew who had killed Olive Myler. I knew who had the gun and exactly where it was.

Colonel Tanner seemed to suspect something was going on in my feeble little brain. "You've got an idea, Mike?"

"I'm not sure," I said. "But I'd like a chance to prove something."

"You might be dead tomorrow if you try it, Mike," said Hope. I stared at her. Was it a threat, or was she worried about me?

"Okay," I said. "I'll wait till tomorrow and talk to somebody about it. Have you got enough dope to clear yourself with the police tomorrow, Hope?"

She glanced at Deems. "What will happen to you?" she asked.

Deems shrugged, but the Colonel answered for him. "Nothing. Myler's death was a suicide. He wanted to die. Let's forget that Olive Myler pulled the trigger. Nothing can be gained by telling the police she was a murderer. Let's say that she was opposed to suicide—she regarded it as an act of cowardice. She wanted the public to believe, whether it was true or not, that her husband was not a coward."

"I've lied enough already," said Hope. "One more won't make me much worse."

I turned to Deems. "My car is at Hope's house," I said. "Mind taking me back to get it?"

"Of course not, Mike," he said. "And I'm truly sorry about that bump on the head I gave you last night."

"You'll get a bill from Doc Browne," I said. "As for my personal feelings, the bonus covers that."

Deems looked sheepishly at Colonel Tanner. "I promised him a bonus," he said.

"I understand," he said. And he winked at me. That old boy never missed a trick. He knew exactly what the bonus was for.

FIFTEEN

My car was parked in front of Hope's house. I'd backed it out earlier in order to allow Deems to get his Oldsmobile out of the drive.

I waited till Deems drove off down the street; then I turned to Hope. "I suppose I've acted like a heel," I said. "I've had some pretty bad thoughts about you."

"I wouldn't be modest if I said I didn't deserve them," Hope said. "I'm what a great many people call a bad woman. I make no bones about being mercenary. I'm about as moral as a female dog in season and I've been married for money. But one thing I am not and never will be is a hypocrite."

"Well," I said, "as long as you're being honest, let's say that I'd like us to be friends again. And the fact that you're a rich widow isn't as important to me as the fact that I feel safer with you than I do with a lot of dames."

"That's because you don't think I'd marry you," she said. "But don't be too sure of that, big boy."

"I'll be cautious," I promised.

She looked serious for a moment. "Where are you going now?"

I shrugged. "Home, I suppose. I have some sleep to catch up on."

"Be sure you go home," she said. She put her arms around my neck and pulled her lips up even with mine. I've had many worse kisses from purer girls.

I departed in a somewhat tender mood. I didn't go home, but truth and Hope Osgood had always been complete strangers anyhow; and she knew I was lying when I said it. Who wants to go to a second-rate hotel when there's a murder to solve?

I drove out Bradley Trafficway to Police Headquarters and parked my car in the parking area. There were a few lights, but it was mostly dark and shadowy there. A good place for a hold-up. I sat in my car awhile, wondering if Clyde Guffy was on duty, or home catching up on his sleep like I should have been doing.

Finally I moved I got slowly out of my car. Somewhere in the shadows something was moving. I stood by my car watching. My eyes adjusted to the darkness and I recognized Ward Tyndall's car. Someone was moving around it, stealthily, like a thief. A thief operating in the parking lot at Police Headquarters. I moved around an empty squad car to get a clearer view.

Clyde Guffy was there, probing Ward Tyndall's car.

And then from another shadow, a hoarse voice said, "Is this what you're looking for, Clyde?"

The police lieutenant whirled and his hand went to the flap of his holster.

The hoarse voice warned again, "Hold it, Clyde. Look at what I've got in my hand."

A form emerged from the shadows. It was Ward Tyndall, and in his hand was a thirty-two caliber target pistol.

"That's exactly what I've been looking for, Ward," said Guffy. "I thought it was in your car."

"It was tucked in my belt under my coat," said Ward. "I thought I might have to use it again. I figured you were getting close and sooner or later you'd come up with the right answers. What gave me away, Clyde?"

"You were the only person outside the force that knew before Osgood was killed that the bullet came from him or his wife," said Guffy. "I figured somebody went out to see Osgood, got in an argument and lost his temper. That fitted you pretty well, Ward. You lost your temper today when you had that little fuss with Mike Lanson."

"I was late meeting Mike at Smitty's," said Ward. "I thought he'd wonder where I was, but he never asked. Of course, I wouldn't have told the truth, but I'd have loved to see the expression on his face if I'd said I was out killing a widder woman named Myler."

"There wasn't much to go on there, except that you turned up at the right time when my mind was full of suspicions."

"I wanted to discover the body," said Ward. "Look at how Mike cashed in on my work the night before. I thought I could at least get a by-line on the second murder."

"Why'd you do it, Ward?"

"I killed Mrs. Myler because I had to, just like I'm going to have to kill you, Clyde. But I lost my temper with Ozzie. It was a mistake. I thought I had it all wrapped up. I went out to his house, broke in by climbing through an unlocked window. I found the gun in the study, and I was looking at it when he barged in. I should have heard him, but I guess I was too interested in finding the gun to hear him.

"He was amused, not angry. And he said he knew that I'd come because I thought he had the Myler murder gun. Well, he said, why didn't I fire a bullet from it into the ground, or into a pail of sand, and take it down to the cops to be examined. He even loaded the gun for me.

"I knew I was licked and I said no thanks. I believed him. Then, he got uppity and began cussing me out. He said I was a low-lifer, a drunken newspaper bum. And that he was going to have me fired.

"I got mad and slapped him. Just an open-handed slap, nothing more. But that little squirt! Before I knew what had happened, I was sailing across the room, bouncing off a chair. He'd been studying judo in his spare time. Dammit, he was good."

I remembered now the physical culture books and the volume on Judo that I'd seen in Ozzie's office.

"I was mad because I'd been tossed around by a little pussy-footer like Ozzie. I grabbed the gun and told him to stand back. I was too mad to be reasonable. He'd already told me that I was going to be fired and I decided to tell him a few things.

But he was too damned sure of himself. He came right after me. I suppose that was Lesson Number Six—how to disarm an armed man. But it didn't work. I pulled the trigger—I pulled it four times and he went down like a feed sack."

"A very interesting confession," said Guffy. "It'll send you to the chair, Ward."

Ward tensed. "No, Clyde, I'm going to send you to hell. The reason I told you all this is because I wanted to tell somebody. But you won't live to tell it to anybody else. I'm going to kill you—

That's when I went after him. I don't pretend to be a hero. I didn't even think. I knew I had to do something and so I went charging in, crouching low, hoping he wouldn't hear me; if he did, I hoped I could get to him before he turned the gun in my direction.

I almost made it. I wasn't more than a step or two away when he turned, and even in the dim light I saw his eyes blaze recognition as he pulled the trigger.

The bullet spun me around. There was another shot, then two more. I heard shouts, yells and I saw uniforms all around me.

"Stop his bleeding somebody," I heard Guffy say. "He's a witness to Tyndall's confession."

"Tyndall doesn't need a witness," somebody replied.

Then my memories got confused and presently I felt tired. More tired than I'd felt since Dwight Deems slugged me early that morning. I needed sleep, because I'd had so little of it for such a long time.

A nurse was buzzing around and I saw Doc Browne standing at the foot of my bed. I was in a hospital.

"Howdy, Mike," Doc said.

I shook my head. "Hello," I was still a little cobwebby.

Doc turned to the nurse. "He's coming around. That sedative gave him all the sleep he needed."

My mind began to clear. "Doc," I said, "how about a steak? I'm damned near starved."

Doc shook his head. "The rallying powers of youth!" he said. "He wants to get up and go home. He doesn't know he's lost enough blood to float a battleship and he's got a smashed rib and a punctured lung."

I didn't know I was so bad off. Now that I'd been told, I began to feel sore. "Doc," I said, "I've got to get out tonight. I've got a date with a sweet kid."

"You'll never make it," said Doc.

"Well, give me some breakfast anyhow."

"Okay. I'll tell the nurse you can have a light snack—just steak and potatoes."

So I finally got to eat breakfast in bed. After I finished ham, eggs and home-fries, plus two cups of coffee with lots of cream, Doc came back and shot some stuff in me to ward off pneumonia.

"Guffy's been calling," Doc said. "He's changed his mind about one reporter, and lowered his estimate of another, which makes his opinion of the newspaper trade about par. But he wants to talk to you. If you don't feel up to it, I can stall him off. But if you want to talk to him, you can."

"I could talk if I was on my death bed, Doc," I said. "What happened to Tyndall?"

Doc lowered his eyes "He'll never worry about another story, Mike. He's in the morgue. He lingered long enough to fill in some details that he omitted when he talked before you and Guffy. It's all in the morning paper. I'll bring a copy."

Doc left. A nurse brought in a copy of the *Globe*. There was a big headline. *MURDERER SLAIN*. And it told about the shooting in back of Police Headquarters.

Tyndall was dead, and I was sorry. He was a worthless drunk, a newspaper bum, but I liked him in a crazy way, even though I knew he'd cut my throat on a story, just like I'd cut his.

He had told Guffy why. My tip-off the night Ozzie was killed had started a chain of events. He'd resolved to solve the Myler case and he'd checked up on the bullet that Hope had sent to the police. Like the cops, he figured that either Ozzie or Hope had sent it, and his choice was Ozzie.

Even a murder hadn't stopped him. He knew that Ozzie had the gun once. Ozzie hadn't been a good liar. So his next choice was Mrs. Myler. That picture he'd found in the Morgue had tipped him off to the fact that Jeff Myler had a gun exactly like Ozzie's.

He'd gone over to the Myler house, broken in and she caught him snooping. Finding some ammunition handy, he'd loaded the gun to fire a test shot. But the shot had been fired into Olive Myler.

Although I'd been responsible for Tyndall's tail spin, I didn't feel guilty. He had been the kind that would have wound up doing something like this anyhow. The only sad part was that two people had died as a result.

Guffy showed up in a few minutes. We talked for quite awhile. Guffy said he suspected Ward after he learned about the reporter's interest in the bullet. He'd suspected me for the same reason.

"Tyndall thought he was smarter than the cops," Guffy said. "I figured you had an urge, at least, to let the police do the solving."

"Not altogether," I said. "I wasn't backing away from solving the crime."

"Tyndall was envious of you," he went on. "You got all the glory. You had the big stories, the by-lines and all. He thought solving the Myler case was his one chance to be top man."

I nodded. "Tyndall didn't do much that any reporter wouldn't do, except murder. But he did that when he was crazy mad. And after he killed once, he didn't stop doing it again when Mrs. Myler caught him committing burglary—an act that might have exposed him as Osgood's killer."

"What made you suspect Tyndall?" Guffy asked.

"He practically admitted he killed Osgood," I said. "He knew what kind of gun killed Myler. That photo we showed you at the Myler place—"

Guffy laughed. "Oh yes. I overlooked that point."

"Sure. There were at least three thirty-two caliber pistols in that photograph, but his interest was in one—a duplicate of the gun that killed Osgood. He could only have known about it from Osgood. When he visited Osgood, he probably learned that there was another gun like it. And that's why he spent so much time in the morgue—trying to find out who had one exactly like it. He went right out to the Myler place then."

"Yes," said Guffy. "I remember what Tyndall told me as he lay there dying. 'What in the hell was I to do? She guessed that I'd killed Osgood. I told her that Ozzie had the wrong gun and I'd come for the right one. Then she said that it was a shame that I'd have to go to the electric chair but she would tell the police. If I'd killed Hope Osgood, she wouldn't have done a thing, she said.' She was a damned fool not to keep her mouth shut."

Tyndall was like the bank robber who shot the teller in self-defense.

I sighed. "I'm not such a hot reporter," I told Guffy. "I didn't trap the murderer. You did. I didn't figure out the solution till after you did. I didn't get the girl and I wind up in the hospital all taped up. And this story in the paper. Look at that!"

I pointed to the *Globe*. Don Hilliard's by-line was in twelve-point type.

"The lucky louse," I said.

"Hell, you can write a book about this murder, providing you change it around, making everybody fictitious and all—"

"Then it wouldn't be the same case."

"Who cares? Murder is murder. And think of the by-line you'd get on the front cover of a book!"

I listened, then said, "If I ever write a book, I don't think I'd use my name. It's not dignified. I'd use something that had class. Like the financial page. Bond. That's a good name. And to kid the reader along I'd use something crazy. Like that invisible rabbit named Harvey. Harvey Bond. Maybe I'd add a first initial for class. How does J. Harvey Bond sound?"

"Pretty good, but nobody would know you wrote it," he said.

"I don't want people to know I write fiction," I said. "I'm a newspaperman. If it gets around that I make up stuff, nobody would believe my stories. That could ruin a world-famous newspaperman."

Guffy stood up, laughing. "The only thing wrong there is that you're not world famous. And now, before I forget, there are a couple of dames outside that want to see you. You might not have gotten the girl, pal, but you sure have a nice-lookin' harem."

"Two?"

"Osgood's widow and a mighty cute babe named Ruth Carpenter. You want 'em one at a time, or can you handle 'em both at once?"

I thought for a moment. I was tired of making choices. "Send 'em both in, Guffy. Why should I try to decide which one I want to see first. I'm only twenty-five. Plenty of time to decide what sort of babe I like best."

"It might lead to murder," he said.

He grinned and left. I wondered if my hair was combed. But I didn't care much. Two girls means competition and they'd just have to take me as I was.

MURDER ISN'T FUNNY

FINAL DEADLINE FOR A COMIC STRIP ARTIST

MURDER ISN'T FUNNY

J. HARVEY BOND
Complete & Unabridged

Mike Lanson
No one believed him except the murderer.

Sherman S. Sydney
He got mixed up with the wrong people—those he
created on his drawing board.

Nora Donovan
She liked heroes, especially comic strip heroes.

Arthur Gervais
He was a ghost writer who almost became a ghost.

Max Vickery
Because he was a good artist, it was too bad
for him.

Phylana Kane
What did she know that made her dangerous?

ONE

I am not a punctual person, and I was fifteen minutes late when I walked into the *Gazette* city room on Saturday, May 9. City Editor Hank Newcomb looked at me with blood vessels swelling in his bull neck.

"Well, well. Good afternoon, Mike," he said with his usual effort at sarcasm. It was only eight-fifteen, of course, but for a reporter coming in late, any hour is afternoon to Hank.

"Sorry, Hank," I said with my usual restraint and good nature. "I had to stop at Smitty's for a little gossip."

Hank looked like a Prussian officer of Kaiser Wilhelm's day. I say this without authentication, since I was born more than a dozen years after 1918. But he had close-cropped hair, a mustache, and disdain for anybody he could outrank.

"I assume that gossip is a new name for breakfast?" he asked. "I hope you read the *Globe* during your midmorning snack?"

The *Globe* is called the morning edition of the *Gazette*. Both newspapers are published in the same building by the same company. They have different staffs, although it is not uncommon for a reporter for one sheet to be tumbled out of bed to assist the short-handed staff of the other in journalistic crises. My first thought was that Jimmy Brandt, my opposite number on the *Globe,* had pulled in a crime story I should have had for the late editions of yesterday's *Gazette.*

I had to read the paper. When you go to work for the Gazette Publishing Company, you receive a copy of *The Gazette-Globe*

Style Book containing the standard rules for spelling, punctuation and grammar which every editorial staffer is supposed to memorize. And it also contains certain regulations, one of which is that every man who writes words for these papers is expected to read them. You'd be surprised how many reporters don't read their own paper; but you wouldn't be surprised to learn that the best ones do. Being neither the best nor the worst reporter in the world, I sort of skim through my reading. If a story's hot, I read it.

"I read most of it," I said truthfully.

"The want ads, by any chance?" Hank asked, cagily.

"That's hitting below the belt, Hank," I said. "I don't read the want ads. And advertising isn't news."

"It pays your salary," he snapped. He arched his thick eyebrows and gave me a sinister look. "It happens, Mike, that there's a story in the lost-and-found column today. Let's see how long you take to find it."

He waved his hand and I hunted around for a spare copy of the *Globe,* having left the one I'd been reading in Smitty's Bar, where I'd had breakfast. Doughnuts and coffee, in case you think I drink hard stuff so early in the morning.

I found a *Globe* and opened it to the classified section. There was no mistaking the ad Hank was talking about:

> $25 REWARD and no questions asked if the six original drawings of the comic strip DREAM MAN are returned immediately. Strips were wrapped, addressed to Arnoth Features, Brent Building. Call Art Gervais, DAggett 5-4900.

I read the ad twice and picked up the telephone. I dialed the press room at police headquarters and got Don Hillard on the phone.

Don is quite a bit younger than I am, just out of college and full of journalism school indoctrination about the nobility of the Press. He has been my assistant for a little over a year, doing all the routine stuff and a lot of the leg work on the police beat.

He goes to work at seven a.m., an hour earlier than my starting time.

"This is Mikey," I said. "Anything going on?"

"Nothing hot. A couple of burglaries which didn't amount to anything. A filling station got held up for about a hundred bucks. But I've got a tip on something that might work out, if we can find a way to bust it.

"The feds had a guy in here last night. I don't know whether it's income tax or something bigger, but they talked to him a couple of hours, then turned him loose."

I snorted. That's the kind of a story you can't bust unless you get help from Washington. Federal officers just don't talk to reporters unless they're tired of their jobs. Most of them are nice about it, but firm. "How'd you find out about it?" I asked.

"Sergeant Russell mentioned it this morning," Don said. "He knew the guy the feds brought in. Russell thought this guy worked for us. Fellow named Jervis. He's an artist who helps the guy that draws *Dream Man*."

If I'd been a dog, my ears would have stood up. Maybe this want ad story was in my back yard after all.

"How do you spell Jervis?" I asked.

"I suppose it's J as in Jerusalem, E as in Earp, R as in rhubarb, V as in violets, I as in impatient, S as in Sam."

"It couldn't be with a G, could it? G as in golly, and ending in A as in ape, I as in Isadore, S as in Sam?"

"How should I know? This guy wasn't booked."

"What kind of federal officers nabbed him? Treasury? FBI?"

"FBI, I think. He's either a gangster or an income tax evader. Maybe a spy. When I started to ask questions, Russell got cagey, figuring maybe he'd been talking out of school." Don laughed. "Russell thought this guy was on our payroll, since the strip appears in the *Gazette*. He thought we knew all about the case. Asked me to give him the low-down."

"Know where this Gervais lives?"

"No, and Russell didn't know. He met Gervais—or Jervis—at the Society for Artists. You know Sergeant Russell is some kind of a painter. Does it as a hobby."

"Thanks, Don. Keep your ears open, and if you find out anything, let me know."

"Will do, sweetheart."

Just for luck I dialed DAggett 5-4900. A female voice answered, "Good morning, Beryl Road Hotel."

"Hello," I said, "is Mr. Gervais in?" I pronounced it like it was spelled Jervis, although I suppose it originally had been pronounced Jairvay when the family first came over from France.

The operator seemed to know whom I wanted, and said, "I'll connect you with room 717." There was a click, and silence. I waited for some moments, and finally the operator broke in, "Sorry, Mr. Gervais doesn't seem to be in. Is there a message?"

"Maybe you can help me," I said. "There's a classified ad in the *Globe* this morning, a lost-and-found ad which gave his name."

"If you found something that belongs to him, leave your name and phone number, and I can have him call you."

"Tell him to call Mike Lanson at the *Gazette* office," I said.

"All right, Mr. Lanson, I'll have Mr. Gervais call when he comes in."

Leaving the phone, I hunted up a copy of yesterday's *Gazette* and turned to the Whop and Wham page. I'd read the comic strip *Dream Man* before, but it wasn't one of my favorites. I won't say it is lousy, or even badly drawn, but it wasn't my type. I like humor in my comics.

The strip was signed Sherman S. Sydney, which wasn't Gervais any way you spelled it. Gervais was Sydney's assistant.

Dream Man is an adventure strip, which is a comic that is funny only by accident. The hero was a big, handsome devil whose name was Commando Green. He went into many breathless adventures, usually emerging without a scratch from the most perilous situations. He could do almost anything, and women swooned whenever they saw him. He had a different love interest in every adventure.

The current episode apparently involved the attempt of foreign spies to steal the plans for a moon rocket which a scientist named Ovahead—which I suppose meant egghead—was developing, although Green was telling him how to do it. There was a lady spy in the strip called Lulu Woohoo who had a good figure, big eyes, a cute face and hair which would have been silky blonde if the newspaper reproduction had been better.

I controlled my impulse to read more back issues of the *Gazette,* and phoned the newspaper morgue for dope on Sherman S. Sydney. Then I went to Hank Newcomb's desk. He looked up at me as though I offended his eyes. "Well, did you talk to Gervais?"

"I called his number but he wasn't in."

"Of course he's in. He wouldn't put the number in that ad and then not be there for replies."

"Shall we take this case to court?" I asked. Arguing with Hank was impossible because nobody was ever right but him.

"He'll call about five o'clock this afternoon if you wait for him. Find him."

I hesitated a moment trying to decide whether to tell him about the FBI angle. Then I decided that if I told Hank everything I knew, he'd know as much as I did. Besides, he'd expect me to get a story out of the FBI, which is next to impossible, as every reporter knows.

I asked Hank, "How come I'm assigned to this yarn? Not that I mind, giving my all for the dear old rag, but I thought I was the crime reporter, not a human interest hound."

"You're not supposed to think," Hank said. "I'll do your thinking for you. You just do as you're told, as long as it's gathering and writing news for this sheet. But just so you won't wear out your brain making wrong guesses, I'll tell you that Colonel Tanner asked me to put you on the story."

"Oh," I said. Colonel Gordon Curran Tanner is editor and publisher of both the *Gazette* and the *Globe.* The colonel title is a World War II leftover. He served secretly as a cloak and dagger man for the OSS, with a full bird on his shoulder straps. He had a lot of connections in Washington and he could have heard about the monkeyshines—whatever they were—that caused Gervais to confab with the FBI. Colonel Tanner might even have been consulted in the matter, and knew all the details, but couldn't break the yarn himself. But there was no law in the world that could touch him if one of his reporters got the info somewhere else.

Trouble was, I didn't know where to go to get it. Gervais had dropped out of reach. Maybe he was in a sputnik somewhere. Or maybe he was working out at Sherman Sydney's place.

That was an idea . . .

"Get the lard out of your skinny hind end and let's get on the ball," said Hank, in his usual cultured manner.

I moved. The newspaper librarian had dug up the dope on Sydney. Most of the morgue biography had come in the form of publicity releases from Arnoth Features, and was probably half lies.

Sherman S-for-Samuel Sydney was thirty-seven years old, a former magazine illustrator and gag cartoonist who had served during World War II as a Navy Department draftsman. After getting out of the Navy, he had freelanced awhile in New York where he met Nora Donovan, who helped create *Dream Man*. He married Miss Donovan, but after five years they separated. A divorce was pending, and probably had been granted, but the morgue material hadn't been brought up to date on this. Nor did the biography list his present writer. *Dream Man* appeared in about 150 newspapers in the United States and Canada and was exported to Latin America, Sweden, South Africa, Australia and to one client in Helsinki, Finland. A photo of Sydney, made five years ago, showed a clean-cut young man in his early thirties. He had a straight, pointed nose, and sharp features. He wore rimless glasses and had a mustache. His hair looked blond, but probably was a light red. His home address was "Greater Creston," which meant anywhere within twenty-five miles from where I sat.

The newspaper morgue had no material on Art Gervais, and there was no mention of assistants, save for his former wife. I returned the folder to the morgue and took the elevator up to the fourth floor, where the art department was located.

The artists occupied the end of the building opposite from Colonel Tanner's sanctuary. It was a well-lighted room, small, alongside the City Room, but it housed seven artists and re-touchers. Five of these, three artists, and two retouchers, were huddled over drawing boards sandwiched in between all sorts of weird equipment.

Separated from the common herd by a glass-and-steel partition were two additional boards for Max Vickery, the sports cartoonist, and Dick Aldwin, the editorial cartoonist, the cream of the paper's ink sloshers. I could see Max Vickery at work. He was about my age, big, broad-shouldered and gray-eyed. I often had been chummy with him in barrooms. He looked up and grinned as I entered.

"What's new, Mike?" he asked as I came in. "Or do reporters ever know anything new?"

"I just came up here to see how the other half of the world lives," I said. He knew I was kidding, of course. He was working on a picture of some ballplayer which was almost finished.

"Thought maybe you wanted to take a nap," he said. He was referring to the times I had slept on the paste-up table after working half the night. He could laugh, but it allowed me to get some shut-eye when otherwise I'd be driving to and from the office for an hour or so.

"According to Hank, I've slept half the morning," I said. "Maybe you could tell me a thing or two."

"Well, if I can help. I don't get around much though."

"Ever hear of an artist named Gervais?"

He looked up from his work. "You mean Jet Gervais?"

"Jet? Could be the same one, if his first name is Arthur."

"Uh-huh. Same guy." He dipped a brush into a small ink bottle and started blacking in the sweatshirt sleeves of the ballplayer he was picturing. "The Society for Artists calls him Jet because he's one of those slow-moving goofs who never seem to hurry."

"What does he do?"

"Draws the daily *Dream Man*. Most of it anyway. Sherm Sydney has two assistants and a writer, so all Sherm draws is the check."

"Ha, ha," I laughed, knowing that was what other artists said about any cartoonist who had an assistant. "You know Sydney, too?"

"A nodding acquaintance. He's a member of the Society."

"Where can I find Gervais on Saturday mornings?"

"How'd I know?" Max turned his drawing sideways and continued to put in more solid black. "What has Jet done that makes you so damn interested?"

"He lost a package of comic strips," I said. Max looked up and I told him about the classified ad.

Max put his brush aside and started crosshatching with a pen. "It figures. Jet's absent-minded as well as slow. He carries the weight of the world on his shoulders, that guy."

"Looks like we won't have any *Dream Man* strip next week."

Max looked up at me. "You kidding? Sherm works six or seven weeks ahead on the dailies. Sunday pages are drawn nearly three months ahead of release dates. Takes extra time for color separation and four plates. Feature men allow plenty of time for accidents, which are always happening. But there's a lot of work, even in making a four-column strip. More than folks imagine. And distribution takes time, too."

"Arnoth Syndicate's a local outfit, isn't it?"

Max nodded. Now he was showing his versatility by shading with a grease pencil. He was making the ballplayer stand out, though. I could tell it was Mickey Mantle. "A one-man outfit," he said. "He's got Sherm s strip, a couple of gag panels—both lousy—a bridge and a lovelorn column. Maybe a crossword puzzle. He's got some kids helping him for peanuts, and he cleans up. Heard he made sixty-five thousand clear on *Dream Man* last year. Sherm got the same amount; they split fifty-fifty."

"Does he make his own cuts and mats?" Mat is short for matrix, from which stereotypes are made by the newspaper.

"He farms the mechanical stuff. One outfit does the engraving and color separation, another mats and mails the stuff to Arnoth's clients. All Arnoth does is edit and sell. He's a lousy editor but a great salesman."

I wasn't getting anywhere toward my objective. "I've got to find Gervais. He's not at his hotel. Suppose he could be out at his boss's place?"

Max shrugged. "I don't know where he is. Could be at Sydney's. Why don't you give Sherm a ring? He lives somewhere around town, and his number's probably in the phone book."

"Guess I will."

A stockily built man came through the door and brushed past me toward the empty drawing board. It was Dick Aldwin, the editorial cartoonist, an older fellow, about fifty, neatly dressed in a dark blue suit, white shirt and bow tie.

He turned his head and recognized me. "Hello, Mike," he said. Then he nodded to his colleague. "Hi, Max. This reporter been bothering you?"

"If he were, I'd throw him out," said Max with a grin. He dipped another brush into white paint and started smoothing out the lines and corners. "He's looking for Jet Gervais. Seems like Jet lost some comic strips belonging to Sherm Sydney. There's an ad in the *Globe* about it."

"I wouldn't feel sad if all of Sherm Sydney's work was lost," said Aldwin, taking off his coat and putting it on a hanger. "He isn't even a good artist."

Max held his sports cartoon out at arm's length, upside down and inspected it. "Looks finished," he said, almost to himself. "Want to walk over to Engraving with me, Mike?"

"Sure," I said. We went back through the art room and into a hallway that separated the artists from the engravers. Max paused at the doorway to the photoengraving department and said, "Dick hates Sherm Sydney. His daughter Ella, who works for Sherm, has just gotten herself engaged to him."

"He ain't good enough for little Ella, huh?"

"Something like that. Mostly because Sherm's a divorced man—almost divorced, anyhow. I guess it isn't final yet; and that's all that's keeping Sherm and Ella from getting married. The old man doesn't like the idea of his darling daughter marrying a grass widower, especially since there's been some talk going around about Sherm and another gal—his secretary. But Ella's the kind of kid that always has her way, so I guess she'll do what she wants to do."

"They usually do."

"Yeah," said Max. "But I agree with Pops. Sherm's not a bad guy, and a better artist than Dick will admit. Still, he's not right for a girl at least fifteen years younger than he is. Even with the kind of money Sherm makes, it won't be a milk-and-honey marriage. Sherm's moody, and just a little neurotic about his work."

I left Max and walked to the elevator. Back in the City Room, Hank was yelling into the phone as usual. Something was cockeyed in a tax story the courthouse reporter had written. I searched in the city directory for Sherman S. Sydney, but he wasn't listed. Probably he lived in an outlying suburb. I looked in the phone book without any better result. Then I dialed Information. The gal told me Sydney had an unlisted phone number which she couldn't reveal.

I called Lieutenant Clyde Guffy of the police department. Guffy's in the Criminal Investigation division, which knows a lot about almost everybody. Guffy hates newspapers and newspapermen, but over the years he has learned to forgive me for being a reporter. Maybe he thinks I'm just misguided.

"Clyde, do you know where I can find a fellow named Arthur Gervais, also known as Jet Gervais?"

"Never heard of him."

"Sez you. Where does Sherman S. Sydney live?"

"Expect me to run down your stories for you, Mike?"

"I'm just asking for information, you damned cop."

"Listen, you newspaper rat, if it wasn't for the cops in this town—"

"Knock it off," I told him. "Just remember you depend on us, just like we depend on you."

Guffy snorted, "Mike, I'd help you if I could. But I can't. Understand?"

"Mmm. So it's hot, eh?"

"I don't even know what you're talking about." That's the way Guffy was. When he wanted to keep his mouth shut, even a cobalt bomb wouldn't jar it open. I knew Guffy could enlighten me about a lot of things, but the FBI had told him that silence, if not golden, was pretty damned important.

After finishing with Guffy, I called Arnoth Features to learn that Darryl Arnoth wasn't in, and his secretary told me she wasn't permitted to reveal the addresses or telephone numbers of their cartoonists. I tried to call Arnoth at his home, but nobody answered.

Finally I rang up the Society for Artists and scored. The houseman said that Sherman S. Sydney lived in Highland Heights. No, he didn't know his phone number.

I picked up the phone again and called Ruth Carpenter, Colonel Tanner's secretary. I tried to date her up for this evening, but she was busy. Then I asked her, "Do you know why the colonel's so hot on this Gervais story—the fellow who lost the comic strips?"

"The colonel hasn't come down yet, Mike," she said. "He didn't mention anything about it yesterday."

"Oh, well," I said, acting as if it were just a casual story, "I just wondered. If you hear anything, let me know."

"Sure thing, Mike," she said. "Sorry I can't be with you tonight."

"So'm I, sweetheart," I said. And I really was.

I got my hat and made for the door. Hank stopped me on the way out, and I told him that Sydney had an unlisted phone, that the story was beginning to sound hot, and that it might be a good idea to spot-cover it by driving out to see him.

Hank nodded. "Always use your head. Someday you may be a city editor yourself. Remember my teachings and drum it into your reporters."

I exhibited remarkable self-restraint. I didn't say a word till I got out of earshot. Then I whispered, "Heaven forbid."

TWO

My car was in the employee parking lot back of the *Gazette*
building. There's always a place for my car there because special
spots are reserved for the brass, reporters, photographers and
circulation trucks. Everyone else has to scramble for what's left.

I'd wasted thirty minutes getting nothing on a story that I
should have nailed down with a couple of phone calls, so maybe
I exceeded the speed limit a little taking Highway 182 across the
Wamego river. It's a freeway, and the cops aren't too strict about
speeding as long as you drive carefully.

Highland Heights is only twelve miles from the center of
town, and I should have made it in fifteen or twenty minutes,
but it started to rain. The top was up on my red Ford convertible, so I didn't get wet; but it was a heavy rain and I had to
slow down to a crawl. There wasn't much traffic, but I couldn't
see more than a few feet ahead. I felt like I was the only person
in the world.

It was about nine-twenty when I finally pulled up at a filling station at the outskirts of Highland Heights. It had stopped
raining by then, and a sleepy looking attendant came out with,
a raincoat over his shoulders. I asked him where Sherman S.
Sydney lived and he looked blank. Highland Heights was only
a little place, where everybody probably knew everyone else,
and what they did for a living. So I added, "The cartoonist who
draws *Dream Man.*"

"Mr. Sherman don't live in Highland Heights."

I figured I'd wasted another half-hour, probably longer. "Well, where does he live?"

The sleepy attendant pointed to a ridge to the east. "He lives atop that hill there," he said. "House is right on top. Blacktop driveway turns off the road."

"How do I get over there?"

"Turn around and go back to the first crossroad. About an eighth of a mile. Take the crossroad."

"Thanks." I swung my car around and drove north. I turned as directed, drove about a mile east up the hill and found the house right where the sleepy attendant said it would be, which is surprising considering that misinformation is so plentiful that you can get it almost anywhere.

There was a blacktop drive, wide enough for two cars to pass. The house was built on a slope, which made the basement the ground floor in the rear. There was a front door, facing south, and beyond it the driveway forked, one going to a garage large enough for two cars, with an apartment upstairs, and the other to a turn-around which circled what was supposed to be a flower bed, but which was mostly weeds. I took the turn-around so my car would be headed out, then parked opposite the front door.

I got out of the car, walked to the door and started to knock. A piece of paper was fastened to the aluminum screen with a piece of transparent adhesive. On it was a note, printed with brush strokes:

Gone to liquor store. Be back about 9. Don't go away, honey.

I wasn't Sherman S. Sydney's honey, but I wasn't going away, especially since it was after nine. I opened the screen, pushed on the front door and walked in after I found the door was unlocked.

The room in which I stood was one of those all-purpose things, where a person entertains guests, eats meals and watches television. Off to my left was a kitchen, separated from the rest of the room by a partition, and beyond that was a doorway leading to bedrooms, johns and probably the basement stairway.

A voice came from the kitchen. "Is that you, Sherm?"

It was a female voice, and I fixed my eyes on the kitchen door just as a head of platinum blond hair stuck itself through. This was followed by a face which was a dead image of Lulu Woohoo in the *Dream Man* comic strip. More color and more detail, of course, but this was Lulu. You couldn't mistake her.

Apparently this gal had expected Sherman Sydney, and had come through the door without the slightest fear that it might be somebody else. The body that came through didn't have much on. Just a man's white shirt, which hung halfway down to her knees.

Everything was there in the right places, but she was small. She wasn't a knockout, but she looked like she'd give a lot of mileage. Her features were plain, but far from disagreeable.

For a moment she stood there at a complete loss. For a moment I looked. Then she gave a little yip and jumped back out of sight into the kitchen.

"I beg your pardon, ma'am," which was very witty indeed.

The head stuck itself from the kitchen door again. Only the head and one hand clutching at the collar of the shirt. "Who are you?"

"I'm Mike Lanson of the Creston *Gazette,*" I said. "I want to talk to Mr. Sydney."

"He's not here. What do you want? I'm his secretary."

What secretaries were wearing nowadays certainly gave me a turn. "I understand some of his comic strips are missing."

"If you didn't get your mats, call Arnoth Features," she said. "Mr. Sydney doesn't have anything to do with distributing mats to his clients."

"It's not mats, it's drawings," I said.

"Originals?"

"Yes, I guess that's what you call 'em," I told her. "There was an ad inserted by Mr. Gervais in the *Globe* this morning. He said six strips were lost yesterday."

"Originals? *Lost?* Oh, my goodness! Did Jet lose those strips he was supposed to mail yesterday?"

"The ad said he lost six drawings, but not which ones."

She had forgotten her costume again and she came out of the kitchen door. "Sherm will be just sick over that," she said. "Three days' work all shot."

As she spoke, I glanced at the clock on the wall. It was nine-thirty. "How soon will Mr. Sydney be home?"

"I don't know. I don't even know where he's gone."

"There's a note on the door that said he'd gone to the liquor store and that he'd be back about nine. It's nine-thirty now."

"A note?" She looked puzzled. "Oh, that! I guess I didn't see the note, I mean. It was raining when I got here and I ran around to the kitchen door, so I wouldn't track up the place with my wet feet." She suddenly remembered her costume and jumped back out of my sight.

"I guess the note was intended for you," I told her. "It said, 'Don't go away, honey.'"

Again the head emerged from the doorway. "The note was for the Cream Puff," she said.

"Cream Puff?"

"Sherm's fiancée. I shouldn't have called her that. Ella Aldwin's her name. A very sweet girl. Her father works for the *Gazette*."

"That'd be Dick Aldwin's daughter," I said. "What's your name, ma'am?"

She must have decided I wasn't Jack the Ripper, so she came out of the kitchen again. "I'm Phylana Kane," she said. "Sorry I have to meet you in this outlandish costume. You don't know what it does to a girl to get caught with her pants off." She walked over to the doorway to the back part of the house. "Just a sec till I make myself decent."

She disappeared for a few moments, then emerged wearing a bathrobe which was too long and too big and didn't improve her looks in the slightest. It was a man's bathrobe, probably one belonging to her boss.

"You see," she explained, "I got caught in the rain. My house is down at the bottom of the hill." She pointed toward the front door which was south. "I usually walk out my back gate and up the hill—it's only a little way. But I got caught in the rain today and I got soaking wet. So I put my clothes in the drier downstairs as soon as I got here and put on one of Sherm's shirts. If Sherm came in, he wouldn't mind. He's painted so many nudes in his lifetime, there's no longer any mystery about the female form."

"Being an artist must be a great calling," I said.

She made a little face at me. "It takes a certain temperament."

A car came up the drive, stopped and a door slammed. "That must be Mr. Sydney," I said. I turned as the front door opened. Through it came the most beautiful woman I've ever seen. Phylana Kane was pretty and attractive, but the newcomer had the type of beauty that's referred to as glamour. Naturally, the glamour was distributed all over. She was statuesque, tall, with ample proportions. Her clothing was light and fresh, a cotton print, but she'd have looked good in anything. Her eyes were a greenish blue, and she looked intelligent. Her hair was a deep auburn. Her cheekbones were high, her mouth a trifle large, but alluring. To look at her was exhilarating.

She stopped and stared at Phylana's costume. "I hope," she said in a deep contralto, "that I'm not interrupting anything intimate?"

Phylana's eyes flashed. As I turned, I sensed that she felt at a disadvantage in the presence of this beauty. "That's not a necessary remark, Nora."

"Miss Kane . . . er . . . uh . . . got caught in the rain," I said.

"Nora," said Phylana, "may I present Mr. Lanson? Mike Lanson, this is Nora Donovan, Mr. Sydney's writer. Mr. Lanson is also a writer, a reporter from the *Gazette*, a client paper." Phylana emphasized the word client. I felt important.

I bowed and took the hand Nora Donovan extended. "Always glad to meet a customer for our brain child," she said. Her ungloved hand was soft and smooth.

She sat down in an overstuffed chair. "My!" she exclaimed. "Did you ever see it rain like that? I came out in a taxi and we positively crawled all the way—couldn't see ten feet ahead. Where's Sherm?"

"Mr. Lanson said there was a note on the door," said Phylana. "What did it say, Mike?"

"That he'd gone to the liquor store and he'd be back about nine."

"Way past nine now." She turned to me. "I'm Sherm's ex-wife, you might as well know, and I can say after living with that man, that you can't depend on him. He has no sense of time at all."

"Oh, yes," I said. "You helped Sydney get *Dream Man* started."

"Yes. I've always been his writer. Still am, in fact, though Sherm's a jackass."

"Sherm's a very nice man," said Phylana. "A gentleman."

Nora Donovan laughed. "Of course, dearie. You've been in love with him all these years. Too bad Sherm never realized it."

Phylana's eyes snapped. She turned and went back to the doorway. "I think my clothes are dry now," she said. "I'll get into something more presentable."

Nora Donovan took off a little hat that was hardly a hat at all and put it away in a closet. Then she walked back toward the kitchen door. "Wonder if there's anything in the house to drink," she said. "I don't suppose there is, or Sherm never would have deserted his precious work to go to the liquor store."

She disappeared through the door. I heard the rustle of paper and she reappeared carrying a brown package. "He must have come back," she said, tearing off the paper and exposing a bottle of Old Charter. "Wonder if he could be in the studio?"

I looked blank. "Downstairs?"

"Heavens no," said Nora Donovan. "He's turned the garage apartment into a studio. I hated it, but he said it keeps his work separated from his home."

"Well," I said. "In that case, I'll just—"

"Surely you can have a drink first?"

I shook my head. "Too early. Besides, I'm working."

Nora Donovan laughed. "Don't tell me you reporters don't take a snort now and then when you're on the job."

She studied me a moment, still holding the bottle. She moved into the kitchen. "How'll you have it? On the rocks, water or ginger ale."

"Tap water, please."

"You must come from Tennessee. That's the way people down there drink moonshine—when they don't drink it straight. Ever taste moonshine?"

"No."

"Great stuff. Only this is better." She came out of the kitchen carrying two highball glasses, one of which she gave to me.

Phylana came back when we were halfway through the drink. She was wearing tan slacks and a brown midriff blouse which exposed a cute little expanse of belly. She had on Capezio shoes. Fully dressed, she looked even more like the counterpart of the lady spy in the *Dream Man* comic strip I'd read this morning.

"Aren't you the model for Lulu Woohoo?" I asked.

She wrinkled her nose. "Yes, Sherm often uses me as a model."

"He uses anybody," said Nora, a little unkindly I thought. "He's used me again and again. Very soon he'll introduce a new girl named Glenda. The Cream Puff modeled for her."

"That's Miss Aldwin," I said, remembering that Phyl had used the name.

"Yes, the poor girl!" Nora sighed, then turned to Phylana. "I found a bottle of panther sweat in the kitchen, dearie. That means he must have come back from the liquor store. Did it ever occur to you that he might be in the studio?"

"Gee! I wonder if he is," said Phylana. "I was so bothered about my wet clothes, I never thought to look." She went to the kitchen and glanced out of the kitchen window, which I could see from where I sat. She returned. "The light's on in the studio."

I killed my drink. "I'll go and look."

"I'll go with you," said Phylana. "Coming, Nora?"

"I'll finish my drink first," said Nora.

Phylana led me through the kitchen, all steel and very modern. Another screen door opened onto a sort of patio in front of the garage, which we entered through a side door. Just inside the doorway was a narrow stairway, which we climbed. At the top was a small vestibule and doorway. Phylana opened the door as I came up the stairs behind her.

"Sherm. . . ."

Her call ended with a gasp. She took another step into the room, stopped, then turned around and looked at me with a twisted expression on her face.

I looked through the doorway.

He was on the floor beside a drawing board and a cushioned steel chair. His face was turned upward and I could see a dark hole in the center of his forehead. Blood had run from that hole down over his eye and the side of his face and stood in a murky puddle around his head.

There was no doubt that Sherman S. Sydney, creator of the comic strip *Dream Man,* was dead.

THREE

Phylana Kane's left hand gripped my right arm as I stepped forward. She made a choking sound, then turned and buried her head against my shoulder.

I pulled her back into the vestibule. There I held her for a moment while she sobbed. "It's—it's horrible!"

"Let's go to the house," I said quietly. I remembered now what Nora Donovan had said about Phylana having been in love with Sherman Sydney.

"Yes," she whispered. "Take me to the house."

The steps were narrow, almost too narrow for us to walk down side-by-side, so I went ahead, holding onto her hand. At the bottom she halted and wiped the tears from her eyes with a small handkerchief.

"He had no reason to kill himself on account of the Cream Puff," she said.

"I didn't see a weapon," I said. "Unless he was lying on it. It didn't look like suicide to me."

Her fingers dug into my arm again. "You mean—you mean he was murdered?"

"Probably," I said. "We'll have to call the sheriff anyhow."

Her grip relaxed as I opened the door and took her to the house.

I opened the screen door to the kitchen and helped her inside. She stifled a sob, and then her eyes fastened on Nora, who was pouring another shot into her highball glass.

161

Nora saw the tears. "What's wrong, Phyl?"

The words came wrenched from Phylana's throat. "Sherm's dead."

Nora set the bottle down and looked blankly at me.

I nodded. "Shot through the head," I said.

Nora leaned back against the sink. "Good God!" She reached out, picked up the glass she had poured and raised it to her lips and drank. Then she looked at Phyl, who was sobbing into a paper napkin she had picked up off a shelf. Nora took the bottle, found a glass in a cabinet and poured a drink which she held out for Phylana. The girl shook her blonde head. "Drink it," said Nora. "You need it." As Phyl slowly reached out and took the glass, Nora turned toward me. "It *would* happen with a reporter in the house."

"Sooner or later a reporter would have been here," I said. I found the phone. I noted the unlisted number RIdge 7-3355, and I was glad that the phone company hadn't been permitted to give it to me. It had saved me time in the long haul.

I dialed the sheriff's office. Sheriff Lindley was in and I spoke to him personally. I'd known Lindley from the time he'd been a deputy about the time I became police reporter more than six years ago.

Lindley asked for directions for reaching the Sydney place and then said, "I'll notify the coroner and we'll be there in a few minutes. I suppose you've got enough sense to leave things alone. Anybody with you?"

"His secretary and his writer," I said. "Both women."

"Well, keep them out of mischief," the sheriff said. "Remember you're a deputy sheriff, and I'm ordering you to take charge till I get there."

"Okay, sheriff," I said.

Sheriff Lindley, as other sheriffs had done in the past, issued Special Deputy Commissions to all police reporters. These were little green cards signed by the sheriff and registered by the county clerk. They empowered me, theoretically, to act as a sheriff, and even to carry a gun, although I never did. In actual practice they were courtesy cards similar to the identity cards issued by the Creston police and the State Police which let reporters go places where the general public is excluded in times of emergency. This was the first time I'd ever used my special deputy commission, although I'd used police identity cards frequently.

By the time I'd finished calling, Phylana had finished her drink and Nora was escorting her to one of the bedrooms.

I dialed the office and got Hank Newcomb on the line.

"This is Mike," I said. "This is really a police case, Hank."

"Oh yeah?"

"Yeah. Murder. Looks like it anyhow, but the sheriff hasn't gotten here yet. Mysterious circumstances will cover it for the bulldog."

"Who for God's sake? Gervais?"

"Sherman S. Sydney," I said.

Hank sucked in his breath. "All right, Mike. Hold it a minute. We'll use a bulletin and maybe a couple of paragraphs for the bulldog—not much time for any more. And you call as soon as you get the other details."

"Right," I said. I heard a click and a voice on the line said: "Rewrite."

"Mike Lanson," I said. "Here goes. Ready?"

I gave him the facts. He could pad out the story with dope from the morgue. As soon as I'd finished, Hank—who had been listening on an extension—came back on the line. "I'll send Jenkins out for pix, Mike. How does Gervais tie into this?"

"Don't know," I said. "I haven't found him yet."

"Okay. We'll try to find him. If you need any help, call us."

"Will do." I hung up, turned and saw Nora Donovan watching me from the doorway.

"When did it happen, do you suppose?" she asked.

I shook my head. "I don't know. Not too long ago, I'd say. But the blood hadn't dried. . . ."

"Please!" she said.

"Sorry, but you asked."

"And I'm *sorry* I asked. What does a person say at a time like this? I'd like to bawl like Phyl but I can't."

"You were married to him."

"Yes, but it didn't take. All we ever had in common was a comic strip. He wasn't married to me; he was married to a drawing board."

"A pretty nice living, from what I hear," I said. I could see that it was from the house, too.

"Sherm never saved a cent," she said. "Everything he ever made went the same year he made it. I got the small end of a 65-35 split. I could retire tomorrow, only I don't want to." She sighed. "Maybe I'll have to now."

"You can always write, can't you?"

"Sure. But not the kind of stories that make this kind of money. I was living hand-to-mouth when I met Sherm in New York. He was worse off than I was, trying to sell gags to magazines. We got together and did a little better. I wrote the gags, he drew the pictures. One day I came up with the idea for a comic strip. We peddled it to all the big syndicates and almost gave up until we met Arnoth at an editorial convention. He had a couple of features and was looking around for something else. He's a one-man syndicate, you know. He decided it would sell, and it did. We got forty papers right at the start. There are 150 now."

A car was coming up the driveway. It was too early for the sheriff and I went to the window, with Nora at my heels. She stared at the blue-and-white Chevrolet Bel-Air that was making the turn in front of the house.

"My God!" she said. "The Cream Puff."

I recognized her now. Dick Aldwin's daughter Ella had been down to the office several times since I became a reporter, but she hadn't been very friendly. I'd met her, but that was about all.

The Cream Puff appellation wasn't hard to understand. She looked soft and pretty, but not very stable. She knew she was pretty and expected admiration, even passes, but not from the hired help at the *Gazette*. In short, she was a spoiled brat.

I went to the front door as she got out of the car. She glanced at the house, then toward the garage. Probably she saw the light burning because Phylana and I hadn't waited there long enough to turn it off. She started toward the garage as I came out the door after her.

She heard the screen slam, stopped and whirled. When she saw me there was puzzlement in her glance, as if she were uncertain whether she knew me or not. The three or four meetings at the *Gazette* office apparently hadn't impressed her.

She was dark-haired, and round-faced. She had an Italian haircut and orange lipstick. Her mouth was pouty and her eyes insolent. Her figure wasn't bad, but it didn't hold a candle to Nora's or Phylana's. Yet I had to hand it to Sherman Sydney for getting himself surrounded by beautiful babes. The woman he had married, the woman he could have married, and the woman he wanted to marry were all knockouts.

"Hello?" she said, with a rising inflection.

"I'm Mike Lanson of the *Gazette*," I said.

Then she said, "Oh, yes! I remember you. I'm Ella Aldwin. Where's Sherm? In the studio?"

I hesitated. She started to smile, and then some expression in my face must have stopped her.

"There's been an accident," I said.

"Not to Sherm? What happened?"

"Miss Aldwin," I said, "uh . . . Mr. Sydney is dead." I decided you had to come out with these things. There was no way to soften the blow.

She looked past me toward Nora, who had come out of the house and who was advancing toward her. "Dead?" she asked, as if she expected Sherman Sydney to live forever.

"Now take it easy, Ella," said Nora. "Nothing can be done about it."

"A heart attack?" she asked.

"A bullet," I said. "He was murdered."

"Oh. . . ."

Her voice trailed off and I waited for the hysterics that didn't come. Nora Donovan hadn't shown a great deal of grief when she heard the news. She'd reacted as though shocked, but I believed her when she said all of the romance was dead between Sherman Sydney and her.

Phylana had been shocked too, and there was grief besides.

Now Ella reacted quite differently from either one of the others. She turned, looked up at the garage window with the little glow of light from the fluorescent lamp showing through. "Who's up there now?" she asked.

"No one," I said. "We're waiting for the sheriff."

"I must see Sherm," she said.

"He's dead, Ella. Don't you understand?" Nora said softly.

Ella started toward the garage.

"Don't go up there!" I said, and I started after her. I caught up with her at the door. She started to open it; I grasped her arm. She wrenched her arm free and darted through the door.

The move was so quick that it caught me off-balance. I made a wild reach for her again but missed. Then she was goner. She slammed the door in my face and by the time I got it open, she was halfway up the stairs.

There was nothing to do but follow her. I was right behind her as she entered the studio. She didn't hesitate at the sight of the body; she moved across the room to the drawing board.

Beside it was a small table, covered with brushes, pens, erasers, triangles, rulers and all the items an artist must work with. She went right and left.

The fluorescent light shining in her face gave it a greenish tinge. There may have been sorrow, there may have been shock in that expression, but as I looked at her there I thought of Dracula's girl friend, whatever her name was. I don't know how to handle women, because they do things you don't expect them to do. Sheriff Lindley had ordered me to take charge till he got there and technically, at least, I was an officer sworn to uphold all the laws of the land, half of which I didn't even know.

"Please, Miss Aldwin," I pleaded inanely, "You mustn't disturb anything."

I might as well have yelled at the man in the moon.

I started across the room after her, not sure just what I was going to do. Just as I reached her, she found whatever it was she was looking for—something bright and glistening—a ring.

She put it on her finger. It was a diamond ring—an engagement ring.

I grasped her arm and pulled her back toward the door.

"That was a crazy thing to do," I said.

Once more she tried to jerk away, but this time I held on.

"Please, Mr. Lanson. Let go of my arm."

"I will if you behave."

I was holding her right arm and she held up her left hand so that I could see the ring. "It's *my* engagement ring," she said. "I left it here last night."

"You mean you gave the ring back? Broke off the engagement?"

"Surely you understand, Mr. Lanson? It was only a little spat. We quarreled over something that was utterly trivial."

"Like what?"

"I don't know if it's any of your business," she said. "But you must realize how it would look if that ring was found here . . . after Sherm was. . . . was . . . was . . . *murdered!*" She finally got the word out.

"All I know, Miss Aldwin, was that Sheriff Lindley gave me orders not to let anything be disturbed. I'll have to tell him about the ring."

"But he might believe I did this horrible thing."

"I'm sure he won't believe anything until he's made a thorough investigation. The fact that your ring was here doesn't prove you . . . uh . . . were responsible for what happened. You shouldn't have messed things up. You might have disturbed an important clue."

"I know what he'd believe." Her tone was arrogant. Here was a young woman whose fiancé had been murdered. He lay within a few feet of her in a dried puddle of his life's blood; yet she was angry because I hadn't let her come up here and carry away the engagement ring she'd left, or carelessly thrown, on the table beside that drawing board.

"He's going to hear about it," I said.

"You won't tell him—you *won't*."

"I must," I said.

"You're not an officer."

"Unfortunately, I've got a deputy sheriff's commission." I was beginning to be sorry I had it.

"You've got to keep me out of trouble."

"The sheriff won't try to pin a murder on you just because you left the ring here," I said.

"Yes, he will," she said. "He'll learn that I quarreled with Sherm. Even yesterday afternoon, when Phyl was here. She doesn't like me, she wanted Sherm herself."

"I'd be careful what I said, too," I told her.

"Just you be careful. Keep your mouth shut about that ring." She sounded like she could order me around, and I didn't like it. "The minute the sheriff learns about the quarrel, he'll put me in jail. There'll be a scandal. Even if I'm acquitted my life will be ruined."

"You haven't been arrested yet and your life isn't ruined," I said. "Be sensible. Even if I did clam up about your being here now, Nora Donovan saw you come in the garage. Phylana Kane's in the house too. She probably knows you're here."

"I can handle them."

"But you can't handle me," I told her. "Come on, let's go downstairs." I tugged on her arm, but she braced herself against the door frame and wouldn't budge.

"Not until we get to an understanding," she said.

I tugged again. I even jerked on her arm. But she was set and I knew that no petty jerking would pry her loose.

"Stop it," she said. "Listen, Mike, maybe you don't know that my father is very influential at the *Gazette* office. Colonel Tanner's his friend. He could get your job, you know."

That made me angry. Even if I hadn't felt I had the greatest job in the world, come hell and Hank Newcomb, I would have been angry at a threat like this. She wouldn't have made me any angrier if she'd tried to knife me in the back. I'd had enough of this fooling around and treating her like a lady. Instead of pulling, I gave her a little push, throwing her off-balance and away from the door. I went in low, flopped her over my shoulder headfirst like a sack of flour. She screamed and kicked and hit, but I held her tight.

I carried her down the stairs, out the side door, and then dumped her on the patio beside the garage. I meant to put her down feetfirst, but she was kicking and hitting at me and I couldn't manage things very well. I set her down hard, and as I released my hold on her, she swung her left hand and that blasted diamond ring caught my cheek, scratching a groove across it. Naturally I dodged, and in dodging I gave her a push. She staggered back, fell, and ripped her pretty black and white skirt.

She sat there screaming and bawling. "You'll pay for this."

"Miss Aldwin," I said, "I don't give a damn if your old man is Big Shot Number One of the whole wide world. Nobody can threaten to have my job and not make me fighting mad. And furthermore, I'm going to report everything that happened to Sheriff Lindley. Now go tell your old man."

"I will!"

She scrambled to her feet, ran to her car and started the motor. I probably should have tried to stop her, but I didn't. I didn't want her around.

As her car roared around the turn-around, and headed back out, I heard gentle applause. I turned and saw Nora clapping her hands.

"You should have blacked her eye, too, Mike," she said.

Phylana Kane came out of the kitchen door. "I enjoyed every minute of it," she said. "Your face is bleeding, Mike. Let me put something on it."

I raised my hand to my cheek. As I looked at my fingers, I saw blood on the tips where they had touched the scratch made by Ella's ring. "It's all right," I said.

We went out into the all-purpose room just as Nora came in the front door. "Sheriff's coming," she said. "Got your alibi ready, Phyl?"

"What about yours?"

"Lord, I don't even know what time . . . uh . . . it took place," said Nora. "But I may have an alibi. You don't know who I spent the night with."

A sudden thought struck me.

And then I heard the brakes squeak on the sheriff's car outside.

FOUR

Sheriff August Lindley can't be described without using the word enormous, which is a good word so we'll use it. I'm no good at guessing height, weight and age, but I'd wager a respectable amount he was over six-five, over 275, and over forty. He was slow-moving, as becomes a man of such proportions, but not especially awkward even if the stoop to his shoulders made him appear ungainly.

He piled out of his big Buick two-door with two deputies. The deputies went around and opened the trunk and took out a camera and a case containing fingerprint equipment, The sheriff came over to where I was standing with Phylana and Nora.

"Hi, Mike," he said. "What did you do to your face?"

"I'll tell you about it in a minute, sheriff," I said. "First I'd like you to meet Mr. Sydney's writer, Miss Nora Donovan."

The sheriff took off his hat and nodded. "Pleased to meet-cha."

"And his secretary, Miss Phylana Kane."

"Pleased to meetcha." Again he nodded, then turned to me. "Well?"

I gestured toward the garage. "In the studio, over the garage."

The sheriff gave the upstairs windows a speculative glance. "Reckon that part will keep for a few minutes. We'll wait for the coroner." He turned toward his two deputies. "Stick around out here. Let me know as soon as Doc Stone gets here."

"Okay, sheriff," said the taller of the two deputies.

"Won't you come inside and wait, Sheriff?" Nora asked pleasantly. "Maybe Phylana and I could tell you what we know and leave. This is not the most pleasant place to be right now for either one of us."

The sheriff looked at her like he'd like to eat her. "Yes, 'twon't hurt to hear your stories now."

I followed him into the living room. Sheriff Lindley sat down on the divan and spread out. The rest of us found chairs."

"Any ideas when this thing happened?" the sheriff asked. He glanced from Nora to Phylana and back to Nora. Neither woman spoke.

"Who saw him alive last?" he asked.

"It must have been you, Phyl," said Nora. "You were still here when I left yesterday afternoon."

"What time was that?" Sheriff Lindley wanted to know.

"Must have been about three, wasn't it, Nora?" asked Phyl.

Nora nodded. "Yes. About that time. Sherm and I thrashed out the kinks in our story after lunch. I said I was going to town, and started to call a taxi. Sherm said that Jet was almost through with the strips he was finishing, and that he'd leave within an hour—that was about two o'clock, I think. Jet would drop me off at the hotel on the way to the post office."

"You waited a full hour?"

"Not that long. Jet was through in a few minutes, but Sherm offered us a highball, so all of us—Phyl, Ella Aldwin, Jet and I—went with him over to the house. We had our highballs, and Jet and I rode into town."

"This Jet. Who's he?"

"Art Gervais, Mr. Sydney's assistant."

"Where's he today?"

"How should I know?" said Nora.

"He only works five days a week," Phyl explained. "He's never here on Saturday."

"Rest of you work Saturdays?"

"Sherm usually attends to his correspondence on Saturday morning," Phylana said. "I come in for a few hours. Nora, of course, isn't here most of the time. She lives in Florida and is only here for a story conference. Miss Aldwin seldom comes down on Saturday—on business, I mean. She's Sherm's fiancée, you know, and sometimes they go out together in the afternoon to play golf or something."

The sheriff looked at Nora. "You're a writer, huh? I didn't know comic strips had writers. What do you do? Make up them words in the pictures after the artist draws 'em?"

Nora smiled patiently. "I plan the action—the stories—and write out the scenes for the artist to draw. Yes, I write the dialogue too."

"How come your name ain't on the comic strip, Miss Donovan?"

"Because I'm not the artist. Sometimes the writer gets credit, but nearly always he's secondary to the artist. Sherm had the right to change my script, and he did, quite often, much to my disapproval."

"You didn't like that?"

"Of course not, but don't get the idea that it made me mad enough to shoot him. After all, Sherm and I had the same idea—make the strip better in every way we could."

The sheriff shrugged. "All this is Greek to me, Miss Donovan. I guess I'd better find out about what you know and where you were. That's stuff I can understand. I'll get a complete statement from you later. Right now I'm not even sure this is murder; I'm just taking Mike's word for it till the coroner gets here. Supposing you give me a rundown on what you did after you left here yesterday, up to the time the body was found?"

"Certainly, sheriff. I'd like to clear myself of suspicion."

"Nobody's a suspect yet. I'm just looking for information."

"Well Jet and I left about three o'clock," she began. "He drove me to my hotel, the Hotel Creston. My room's 1219. I told him I'd buy him a drink for hauling me to town. We went into the cocktail room and had two or three drinks. If you want to check, there weren't many people there and the young woman who waited on us might remember us. Jet left me about four to mail the strips."

"Those strips were lost, sheriff," I said.

The sheriff looked at me and raised his eyebrows. "Does that have anything to do with Sydney getting killed?"

"I don't know," I said, "but I thought you ought to keep it in mind."

"I'm certainly glad you told me how to run my office," said the sheriff. "Go ahead, Miss Donovan."

"Well, there's not much more. I went to my room, changed my clothes, met Mr. Gervais about seven o'clock, had dinner with him and, after he left, which was about eight-thirty, I went upstairs to read until bedtime."

"And this morning?"

"Good heavens, sheriff," said Nora. "I got up—I haven't any idea what time. Must have been early though because I went to bed early last night. I went out for breakfast, came back to the hotel and sat in the lobby till about nine, then came out here. Must have been about nine-thirty when I got here, wasn't it, Phyl?"

"About that," said Phyl. "Mike and I were talking."

"Hmm." The sheriff turned to Phylana. "What's your story?"

"About the clothes?"

"No. I don't think Mike is lying. I mean what happened here after Miss Donovan left yesterday?"

"Since Miss Donovan was so nice as to mention how I was dressed when she arrived, I'd like to go back farther than that, if I may, sheriff," said Phyl, bitingly, as she glanced at Nora Donovan.

"Please do, dearie," said Nora.

"Miss Donovan came here Thursday. Since that time, up to the time she left yesterday afternoon, she and Sherm bickered continually. It was all any of us could do to keep on working with that continual arguing going on."

"Sheriff," said Nora, "Sherm and I have argued about the *Dream Man* story since we launched the strip about six or seven years ago. We were both trying to get a good story out of it. Is it a motive for murder when your partner wants to make your product better?"

"You're his partner?" the sheriff asked.

"Also his ex-wife," said Phylana quickly.

Nora winced and gave her a sharp glance. "She does like to stab me in the back, doesn't she? Yes. I was married to Sherm for five years—since soon after the strip was sold. We agreed to a divorce about a year ago, and the divorce would have become final in three more weeks. But even while the divorce was pending, I kept on writing the script for *Dream Man* and sending it to him by mail. Any emotional relationship between Sherm and me was ended within a few months after we were married."

"Let's stick to cases, please," said the sheriff. "Miss Kane, let's hear what happened after Miss Donovan left yesterday."

"It was very peaceful for one thing," said Phylana, bitingly. "I wrote several letters to novelty firms that are using *Dream Man* ideas on paper plates, napkins, valentines and greeting cards, coloring books, and so on. I left about five o'clock."

"Was Mr. Sydney alone when you left?"

"No. Ella Aldwin was here. She's Mr. Sydney's fiancée. She's also the young woman who scratched Mr. Lanson's face a few minutes ago."

The sheriff looked at me and I turned my cheek so he could see it. "I wondered how that happened," he said. "Tell me about it."

I told him and he said, "I hope she didn't wreck any evidence. What time did you get here this morning, Miss Kane?"

"I don't know the time exactly," she said. "It started to rain when I was about halfway between my house and here. My home's at the bottom of the hill, to the south. It's about a quarter of a mile walk on a path through the woods."

"I guess that'd be about eight forty-five," the sheriff said. He took out a notebook and made a few notes. "I'll want to get a signed statement from both of you ladies, so you sort of go back over your stories and try to remember anything you left out. Where can I find this fellow you call Jet, Miss Kane?"

"Mr. Gervais stays at the Beryl Road Hotel," said Phylana. "Miss Aldwin doesn't live with her father, Dick Aldwin, in case you should want to get in touch with her. She has an apartment in Creston, near her father's home. The address is in the phone book."

A car was coming up the drive. 'That's the coroner," said the sheriff. "Are you going with me, Mike? I wouldn't blame you if you stayed here with all these pretty young women."

"Always the politician, aren't you, sheriff?" I said with a smirk as I followed him through the kitchen.

FIVE

The sheriff and the coroner and the two deputies went over the room inch by inch. They found hundreds of fingerprints, but none in the right places. Sheriff Lindley figured that the murderer, if he were an outsider, wouldn't bother to leave fingerprints on drawing materials, and, if he were an insider, his prints were all over the place anyhow.

The sheriff was positive that robbery wasn't the motive because Sydney had more than two hundred dollars in his billfold.

The pertinent facts that were gleaned after about two hours of work were that Sherman S. Sydney had died of a bullet—probably a .32 which would be extracted at the autopsy—through the forehead, fired at close range. From the position of the body, he judged that Sydney had been standing when shot. The buffet had coursed upward, but it didn't mean that the assailant was shorter. Almost anybody would have to point the gun up a little to shoot a man in the forehead. Sydney, while not tall, wasn't a shorty either.

Doc Stone said there'd be an inquest at two o'clock Monday afternoon.

One item was found that probably was a clue although it didn't look like much. It was a piece of gummed mailing paper on the floor near the paste-up table. It had been used, apparently from a package of some sort, but there was no used wrapping paper in any of the wastebaskets in the room. I wondered if it could have come off the package of comic strip drawings which had been wrapped for mailing in this very room the afternoon before the murder, and which had since disappeared.

"I can't see how a comic strip could figure in a murder," the sheriff told me. "What is there about a drawing that would make one human being kill another?"

"I don't know, sheriff," I said, "but you and I aren't in the comic strip business. We don't know all the angles."

"I know it takes a mighty strong reason for a man to kill another man," he said.

"The comic strip business is pretty big, sheriff," I said. "There's a lot of money in it for the artists. And where you find money, you find murder."

The sheriff shook his head. He still couldn't see a comic strip as a murder motive.

Probably the most important fact that we learned was that Sherman Sydney had died about six o'clock in the morning. This, quoting Sheriff Lindley, "was a hell of a time for murder." It also meant somebody got up early or possibly stayed out all night.

But close inspection of the body revealed that Sydney had not shaved and he had on a clean T-shirt, which probably would have been soiled if he'd worn it all night long.

I did make one little contribution to the investigation, although I'm not proud of it and I should have kept my mouth shut instead of trying to besmirch a young lady's reputation—probably an innocent lady at that.

"Sheriff," I said, "Miss Aldwin said she returned her engagement ring to Sydney last night."

"Yeah? Got a hunch about it?"

"Night means after dark to most people. Miss Kane left at five o'clock, the usual quitting time. That's daylight. Do you suppose Miss Aldwin stayed till after dark?"

"Might have had dinner with him," said the sheriff. "Maybe they went out together afterwards."

"Maybe she stayed all night," I said.

The sheriff squinted one eye. "Tain't likely. Most folks try to keep their engagements respectable."

"But such things *have* happened."

"Till somebody proves it otherwise, I'd prefer to think Miss Aldwin slept alone in her own little bed," he said. "Maybe she got up early and came over and shot him, but murder is different. And that's speculation, boy. As far as I'm concerned, there ain't a real live suspect on the list yet."

"But you have got a list?"

"Yep. And I'm going to start right now talkin' to people. Maybe by sundown, I'll have something to work on."

We went down the stairs, with the deputies. The sheriff locked the garage door with a key he got from Phylana. He said that if he learned nothing after interviewing everybody he intended to interview, he might have some men from the Creston police lab come out and go over the studio again. The county would foot the bill and, being experts, the cops might find something he missed.

We found Nora Donovan sitting in the house with a highball glass in her hand. A cigarette was burning in the smoking stand at her right.

"Phyl's gone home," she said. "She said to tell you to be sure the house is locked when you leave. She has another key in case you want to get in anytime."

"Okay," said the sheriff. "Where's the laundry room, Miss Donovan?"

"Laundry? Mmm. Sure! You want to see if Phyl washed her clothes as well as dried them. Think there was blood on them, sheriff?"

"I'm not sayin' what I think," the sheriff said.

"Stairway to the basement is just beyond that door over there," Nora said, pointing. She turned to me. "Can I ride back with you, Mike?"

"Sure," I said. "I'll have to call the office first."

"Phone's in the kitchen."

It was ten minutes-to-twelve when I dialed the office and asked the operator for the City Desk. Hank answered with his usual shout.

"Mike Lanson calling," I said.

"All right, Mike, what have you got?" There was a sour note in Hank's voice. Usually he was sarcastic, and I missed it.

I told him about the coroner's findings, which would be subject to confirmation at the post-mortem. I also gave him a brief account of what was known of the movements of Sydney's staff after three o'clock yesterday afternoon, also subject to confirmation by later interviews.

"You've been a long time finding out nothing," said Hank. "Is everything cleaned up out there?"

"Just about," I said. "The sheriff will leave in a few minutes. Jenkins already has gone back. I might as well come in."

"No sign of the missing comic strips?"

"No."

"Funny thing, Mike, we got hold of Gervais."

"Huh? Where was he?"

"At his hotel where he should have been," said Hank. "Are you sure you tried to reach him?"

"Of course. He's staying at the Beryl Road Hotel, isn't he?"

"Yes," said Hank. "You shouldn't have let the desk give you the run-around. You should have gone over to the hotel."

"Has he gotten the strips back yet?"

"He said they never were lost," said Hank. "Gervais told me that apparently he left them at Sydney's place. Maybe he had had enough drinks that he walked off leaving them. Last night he rang up his boss to make a clean breast of it all, and Sherm told him that he had the strips at his home—or in his studio."

I was doing a helluva lot of thinking, and it didn't all add up to right answers.

"You haven't done very well on this assignment, Mike," Hank continued. "Come into the office as soon as you can. I have something to talk to you about." I didn't like the sound in his voice. He made even less sense than the murder.

"Okay," I said. "I'll come in." I hung up the phone.

Sheriff Lindley came into the kitchen. "You ready to pull out?"

"Yes," I said. "What'd you learn in the laundry room?"

"Only that the automatic washer hasn't been used today and the drier has," he said laconically.

"You didn't find those missing comic strips in the studio, did you?" I asked.

"There were a lot of strips there—mostly old judging from the dates stamped on the back."

Nora appeared in the doorway. "The missing strips were wrapped in brown paper and addressed to Arnoth Features," she said.

The sheriff took the little scrap of gummed tape from his pocket. "They done up with this stuff?"

"Why, yes," said Nora. "Did you find that around here?"

"It was on the floor of the studio. No tellin' where it come from though. Might have been kickin' around from any package."

"The missing strips were dated 6-29 to 7-4," Nora said. "The dates were in the lower right-hand corner of the last frame of each strip. Sometimes in other places, but usually in the last frame."

"The dates I saw were rubberstamped on the back."

"Those are the dates the originals are received by the engraver," Nora explained.

"June 29th to July Fourth," I said. I counted on my fingers.

"Eight weeks ahead," Sheriff Lindley said. "You work that far ahead all the time?"

"Not always," said Nora. "But we can't work closer to the release date than five weeks without running into extra mailing expense. Sherm has to pay extra expenses like overtime for the mailers, special delivery fees and all that. On the Sunday Page we work about eleven weeks ahead, as a rule. That's because color separation takes longer than regular etching."

Sheriff Lindley shook his head. "Like I said, it's all Greek to me. You folks ready to go?"

"I'm ready," said Nora.

"So'm I."

We trooped out of the house while the sheriff closed all the doors and made sure they were locked.

I got into my car, after helping Nora into the front seat. "See you in town, sheriff," I said. "Later."

"Not if I see you first," Sheriff Lindley called back from his car.

The pavement was dry, but there were still puddles of water by the side of the road.

"The office got in touch with Gervais," I told Nora. "He said the strips never were lost. He went off and forgot them here at the house."

She turned her head quickly toward me. "He said *that?*"

"According to my city editor, that's what he told the reporter who talked to him."

Nora Donovan frowned, and a very pretty frown it was, although I was driving and couldn't look at it very long.

"What's the matter? Doesn't it sound right to you?"

She paused before she answered. "I don't know what to think, Mike. I mean, well, Jet was so upset about the strips last night. After he went back to his car to mail them he called me. He was positive someone took the strips from his car in the parking lot. He said then that he was sure he had them in the car when he left Sherm's place."

"But he'd had several drinks when he said it," I reminded her.

"Several, but not *too* many."

"Remember *how* many?"

"Well, we had a highball at Sherm's. Then we had three at the hotel. I bought him one for bringing me to town, he bought me one for buying him one, and I bought another round just to make it even. Four drinks."

"In the space of an hour and a few minutes," I said. "He was feeling no pain."

"Is that why you asked Sheriff Lindley if he found any originals in the studio?"

"Yes," I said, with a nod. "The murderer must have taken them away with him. Looks to me as if the strips really were the motive for murder. Remember what they were?"

"There was certainly nothing in any of them that would lead to murder," she said. "I wrote the script, and I even saw the drawings after they were finished. You been following the strip?"

"No, to be honest."

"Well, these strips are the tail end of a yarn that is beginning now in the paper. Commando Green is helping a scientist construct a moon rocket. There are spies—"

"Lulu Woohoo," I said.

"Yes, Phylana modeled for that one. She often models, and Sherm changes her features enough so that the reader never catches on."

"Models for comic strips!"

"Nothing unusual in that. Lots of comic artists use models. The usual procedure is, though, to build up a good photo collection. Sherm is one of those artists who can't draw a straight line without a model. I spend half my time running down pictures to use for backgrounds, and action scenes that Sherm can incorporate into the strip. Most of my job is research."

"Let's hear the rest of the story about *Dream Man.*"

"Well Commando Green, that's Dream Man, manages to keep the lady spy from getting the rocket plans, and in desperation she and her henchmen kidnap Glenda Ovahead, the scientist's daughter. Dream Man rescues her and of course the love interest creeps in."

She was getting off the track. "Why did you say you came here from Florida?"

"Sherm was lousing up my stories. Or maybe Phylana was. She thinks she can write. I had to put him straight."

"Was that why you argued with him?"

"Yes, and for your information, the best I could do was compromise. Sherm always had the last word, because he had a contract with Arnoth. I had an agreement with Sherm, so he was my boss."

"I understand Sherm got a fifty-fifty split for drawing the strip."

"Yes," said Nora. "That's the usual arrangement with the originator of a strip. But there are as many different contracts as there are artists. Sometimes the expenses are deducted first, sometimes it's fifty-fifty on the gross. A few big names get 60-40 with the syndicate. Sherm paid his assistants and gave me my cut out of his share. I don't know what he paid Gervais, Ella and Phyl, but I got thirty-five percent of Sherm's sixty-five percent. But I didn't get anything from the gadgets—comic books, toys and so forth."

"Did that amount to much?"

"Two or three thousand a year, maybe. I'm just guessing."

I figured that Nora must have received about twenty thousand. If the combined salaries of the others was about fifteen thousand, Sherm Sydney received about thirty thousand from *Dream Man*.

"What happens to you now that *Dream Man's* dead?"

She stared at the road ahead. "I don't know. Gervais told me once that he'd find something for me if anything ever happened to Sherm. But I have no real contract, not one like Jet has. And now the strip belongs entirely to Arnoth. Very few comic artists own their strips, you know, even though it's their idea. Arnoth'll probably get someone else to draw it. Probably I'll keep writing."

"Will Jet be the new artist?"

She nodded. "Probably. He can imitate Sherm's style so well that only a few people can tell the difference. Besides, Jet has drawn almost all of the dailies for several years. Sherm only drew certain spots he wanted to do, or which he thought Jet couldn't do the way he wanted them done."

"How many strips of that last batch did Sherm work on?"

She thought for a moment. "None that I know of. He could have done a little touching up here and there, though."

"What happened in those strips?"

"I told you it was the windup of the story that's just starting in the papers now," Nora said. "We were going to wash it up next week. You see we always end a story in the middle of the week. Papers buy a strip a week at a time and if we end a story when a week ends, there's a chance that some of the papers that aren't so hot on it might find the temptation too great and stop the strip. But if we end a story on Wednesday or Thursday, the paper either has to throw away something it has paid for or go on as a client."

"What's to stop them from quitting any time?"

"Reader reaction. No matter how lousy a strip is, it usually has a few fans. Some advertising outfit made a survey of what was read in newspapers a few years back and all of the comics, even the worst ones, had better ratings than a lot of regular news features."

"And just what did the strip show?" I said, guiding her back to the subject.

"We really had trouble on this one," Nora said. "Sherm wanted one ending and I wanted another. But we finally compromised. Sherm was feeling a little soft because of his romance with the Cream Puff and he wanted Commando Green to fall in love with Glenda. But it just wouldn't do. He has to jilt Glenda and go on with another adventure. He has a new sweetheart in almost every story."

"Don't the readers think he's a heel?"

"Not especially because we make the women the aggressors," she said. "In the last part of the story, he'll leave Glenda with a broken heart, but she'll realize it was hopeless from the start."

"So the strips that were missing led up to the breaking off of Commando Green's current love life?"

"That's it, exactly," said Nora.

Nothing that she had said seemed to be a motive for murder. Yet I was convinced that Sydney had been killed because of something he had drawn. Or something he intended to draw. Love can cause murder, of course, but the love involved here had nothing to do with any real person. It was all fiction.

How would the murder affect Sydney's associates? Nora had much to lose. She collected thirty-five percent of sixty-five thousand dollars a year—more than twenty thousand dollars. That would be a good argument for her innocence. She'd never kill the artist who drew the golden pictures.

Phylana Kane? What could she gain by murder? She was a little sweet on Sydney, I guessed, but murder wasn't the answer. A woman scorned maybe? That could fit. I'd have to think about it. Gervais might have a motive if he inherited the strip. But he would know, when he killed, he'd be suspected. How did the FBI fit into this thing?

"Did you hear from Gervais after he left you last night?" I asked Nora Donovan.

"No."

"You don't know where he went or what happened to him after eight-thirty?"

"No. Except that he must have talked to Sherm if he told your reporter that the strips weren't lost. He was still worried about them when he left me."

"Did you know Jet was picked up last night after he left you and questioned by the FBI?"

"The FBI? Good heavens, no! What would they want to talk to him about?"

"That's what I'd like to know."

She was thoughtful for a few moments. "I wonder if it could be the moon rocket?"

"What moon? Oh, you mean the rocket in the comic strip?"

"Yes. I sketched a rocket that was being tested at Cape Canaveral. You know I live in Florida."

"Yes. I know. But if you had permission to see the rocket and to sketch it—"

"I didn't have either one. I was a couple of miles away—maybe farther—but I had good binoculars."

That could be it, of course. "They didn't talk to you?"

She shook her head. We were approaching the downtown exit on the freeway. She was silent until I turned on Seventh Street. Then she said, "You solved a murder once, didn't you, Mike?"

"After a fashion," I said.

"Phyl told me you did. Why don't you rest on your laurels and let the sheriff solve this one?"

"Trying to warn me?"

"It would be too bad if you got hurt," she said. "Whoever killed Sherm had a good reason, and the killer intends to get away with it—even if he has to kill again."

"Nearly everyone who murders thinks his crime is excusable or justified," I told her.

"In this case you're up against a peculiarly determined group
of perfectionists, Mike. They plan carefully, fight hard, play for
high stakes, and they know how to erase or white-out errors."

"Sounds like you think an artist did it."

"Nearly everyone connected with Sherm was in the art business," she said. "And you seem to think those missing comic
strips have something to do with the case."

"But nothing to prove they do so far," I said. "Besides, I'm
also determined. I fight hard, too; and I know how to recognize
erasures and fixes."

"But the stake you're playing for isn't high. Get smart."

We drew up in front of the hotel and as the doorman opened
the door, she asked, "Can I buy you a drink?"

"I'll take a raincheck," I said. "My boss wants to talk to me."

I left her and drove to the *Gazette*. I parked my car in the
spot reserved for reporters and photographers, and as I got out,
my right foot struck something protruding from under the seat.
I reached down and pulled out a long flat package.

It was two-and-a-half feet long and six or eight inches wide.
On it was a brush-printed address, "Arnoth Features, Brent
Building, Creston," and a return with Sherm Sydney's name on
it. There were eight uncanceled three-cent stamps in the upper
right-hand corner.

I knew at once that the package contained the missing comic
strips.

SIX

Most of the stories of success that I've read, leave out the most important element necessary for getting to the top of the heap. I don't mean genius, I don't mean skill or brains or daring, and I don't mean luck, although those things are part of the recipe for success. The most important thing is timing. Things have to be done at the right time, not too soon, never late, but exactly when things are right. If I'd torn open that package, disregarding that it carried postage and wasn't mine to open, the murder could have been solved in a few hours. But it wasn't my day to do things right. I decided to wait awhile before I opened it.

I went to the back door, through the mailing room, to the elevators and rode up to the City Room on the third floor. Mose Kapso, the assistant city editor, was in Hank's chair. He looked up at me glumly when I asked where Hank was.

"Over at Smitty's eating lunch," he said. "Stick around, Mike, he wants to talk to you."

I didn't like the tone of his voice. I went over to my desk and put down the strips and wondered if I should open them. Technically, I suppose, I didn't have the right as long as those eight three-cent stamps were on the package. Those stamps gave Uncle Sam some authority. But technicalities had never really bothered me, and I was working on a murder case. If those were the missing comic strips, I figured they were a very important key to the whole business.

"Mike!"

I had dillydallied too long. Hank, was calling me from his desk. He had returned from lunch.

I walked over to Hank's desk. He was standing beside it and Mose was still sitting down. He beckoned to me. "Come on," he said. "I want to talk to you."

Mose had told me that much. I followed Hank over to a little private office that Night Editor Taylor uses on his shift. We went in and Hank closed the door. This was going to be a private conversation.

"Rewrite has handled your, story, Mike," he said. "It's not a bad yarn, although you didn't give us much detail—"

"There's a lot more coming, Hank," I said "I've got a hunch it's going to—"

"Mike," Hank interrupted, "just what in the hell did you do to Ella Aldwin? Did you try to rape her?"

The question took me by complete surprise. I just stood there with my mouth open, not saying a word.

"Dick Aldwin has been up talking to Colonel Tanner," Hank went on. "From what he said you were pretty rough."

I found my voice, "I was doing what I was supposed to do, Hank," I said. "I told her to stay out of the studio. Nothing was to be disturbed till the sheriff arrived. She disregarded me, went up the stairs—the studio is over Sydney's garage, you know—then she started messing around with his things. She was looking for her engagement ring, which she'd returned to Sydney the night before."

"And you barged in, knocked her down, practically dragged her down the stairs and threw her on the pavement, tearing her dress, skinning her arm and treating her in a way that no gentleman treats a woman."

"No, Hank," I said. "I went in, took her by the arm and tried to take her out of the room. She refused to go. She threatened me. She said that if the sheriff found the ring she'd be suspected of murder—"

"Maybe she was a little mixed-up, Mike," said Hank. "You've got to remember that the dead man was her fiancé. She was in love with him. She was grief-stricken, in a state of shock, and not responsible. You had no right to be brutal."

"Brutal!" I pointed to the bandaid on my right cheek. "She tried to slug me. She said she was going to have me fired. What was I to do? The sheriff had given me orders."

"You're not working for the sheriff. You're working for us. You should have told the sheriff to go to hell."

"I have a deputy sheriff's commission."

"A damned courtesy card. It doesn't mean a thing. The sheriff passes them out to all his friends. It's about the same as a Junior G-Man card that you get with box tops."

"It was still my duty as a citizen to see that no evidence was destroyed. The only way I could get Ella Aldwin downstairs was to carry her; so I did. She fought and struggled and I lost my balance when I started to set her down outside the garage. She slipped and fell and tore her dress. I didn't know she skinned her arm, and I'm sorry."

"Is that your story?" Hank glared at me.

I looked at him. "What more do you want? I haven't done anything that I wasn't supposed to do."

"Haven't done anything?" Hank screamed. "Why you goddamn lunkhead!" He went to the door. "Wait here." He disappeared, and I waited.

The way Hank told it wasn't far from the truth. Maybe I had been a little rough on the girl, but somebody should have been rough with her long ago. Hank made it sound like I'd been deliberately brutal and vicious, and I hadn't been. Five minutes passed, then the door opened and Hank came in.

"Your paycheck and severance pay will be ready Monday, Mike," Hank said. "I've talked to the colonel and he's contacted the Newspaper Guild. He told the Guild that your conduct is unworthy of a newspaperman. You're fired."

"What are you telling me, Hank? That a spoiled brat like Ella Aldwin can get a reporter canned any time she wants?"

"Any time a reporter manhandles a woman without a good reason, he deserves to be fired," said Hank. "And don't kid yourself, Hank. Journalism schools all over the country are turning out good newspapermen every year. We'll never miss you."

"Okay," I said. "So I'm fired. Will you do me a favor, Hank?"

"I might, Mike. What is it?"

"Step out in the alley with me for about ten minutes!"

Hank snorted, opened the door and walked out. Maybe I'd overdone it, but I was mad. I wanted to slug somebody. Hank had had it coming for quite a long time. But again my timing was wrong.

I went over to my desk and opened the drawers. There wasn't much personal junk there that I wanted. An old razor that I used sometimes before night assignments, a couple of snapshots of friends, including Ruth Carpenter, the best-looking secretary in the place. I stuffed these into my coat pocket.

Then I remembered the comic strips. They weren't on my desk.

I turned to the reporter at the next desk. "Has anybody been here since I came in?"

"Sure," he said. "There was a regular convention. Even the colonel was there a few minutes."

"Who else?"

"Dick Aldwin, Max Vickery, Hank Newcomb and the straw boss." The straw boss was Dwight Deems, managing editor and Colonel Tanner's assistant.

"Which one of them took that long narrow package off my desk?"

Johnson, the reporter, shook his head. "I didn't see any package on your desk."

I went over to Hank's desk. Hank was sitting there angry and red-faced. He looked up at me.

"I told you to get out. There's nothing more for you to do around here."

"What became of that package on my desk, Hank?" I demanded.

"What package? I didn't see any package?"

"Okay," I said. "Somebody took it and when I find it, somebody's going to find himself in a hell of a lot of trouble. And I don't care if it's Colonel Tanner."

I put on my hat and left the building.

SEVEN

There were hard economic facts to consider. As Hank had said, schools could turn out passable reporters who, with a little experience, would eventually become good reporters.

What could I do? Where could I even get a job now when I needed one? And I'd have to have one soon. My severance pay, running a week's salary for every four months I'd worked for the *Gazette* meant nineteen week's pay. I had to have a job in about four months. And I had to be a reporter—nothing else.

Suddenly I wondered if I didn't have a special talent. Once I'd solved a crime—a murder. Of course the cops solved it, too, but I'd done what every crime reporter wants to do and few of them actually have done. If I could solve another murder, I'd prove I had a special talent. I'd be valuable newspaper property, and maybe I could work for a syndicate.

In a phone booth I got a directory and looked up the number for Arnoth Features. The girl who answered my call said Arnoth was in, and after I gave my name, she put him on the line. He agreed to spare a few minutes, if I'd come right over.

The Brent building was on Tenth Street, an easy walk, and since I wasn't on a gasoline expense account, I walked. The offices were in a suite on the ninth floor. While I'd heard it called a one-man syndicate, there were several employees. Some girls were filing and typing. One of them took me into an office room at the rear.

Mr. Arnoth, a heavy-set, dark-featured man with rimless glasses, put aside a bulldog edition of the *Gazette* which he had been reading as I came through the door.

"Mr. Lanson?" he extended his hand as he half-rose from his chair. I took the hand. It was soft and moist. The girl left, closing the door behind her, as I said I was Mr. Lanson and I was glad he could spare me some time.

Arnoth offered me a cigar and a chair. I took the chair. I don't smoke cigars. "You're the crime reporter for the *Gazette,* are you not?" he asked, and without waiting for me to answer he added: "Horrible thing that happened to Sherm."

"Yes," I said. "I covered the story."

"Ah! I suppose you want some background material?"

"No," I said. "I've just been fired."

He raised his eyebrows and took the cigar, which he had just lighted from his mouth. He stared at me for a moment, then said, "When I was a newspaperman, getting fired didn't mean a thing. In some cases it was a recommendation. It all depended on who fired you, and why."

I told him about my run-in with Ella Aldwin.

"Bad business," he said. "Tanner ought to listen to you, but I guess he can't afford to lose a man like Aldwin. Do you expect me to do something about it?"

"Would you?"

"No," he said. "Tanner's a client. I don't try to tell clients how to run their business."

"I figured if I solved this murder, he'd hire me back. It would make me something special as a reporter."

"Leave it alone. That's the cops' business." He spoke a little too quickly.

"Why? Afraid I might dig up some dirt that would hurt your syndicate?"

Again the eyebrows went up and down. He laughed. "Partly, since you're recalling things by their right names. Mostly, because it's a waste of time. You hear about reporters solving murders, but it doesn't happen too often."

"I solved one murder, Mr. Arnoth. I think I can do it again."

He leaned forward. I noticed he was a little on the beefy side. "Yes, I remember that case. You know, if you solved this one it might be good for a special story. Yes, I'd use one and it would pay two or three times what you get for a week's work on a newspaper."

"You can help."

"I can? How?"

"I've got a sort of theory that Sherman Sydney's murder is tied up with the *Dream Man* comic strip."

"Why?"

I had a number of good reasons, but as I said before, this wasn't my day. I gave the reason that was the worst.

"Did you know that Sydney's assistant, Art Gervais, was questioned last night by the FBI?"

He took the cigar out of his mouth and laughed. "So that's what's eating you! I'm afraid you're on the wrong track, son."

"What makes you think so?"

"Because Gervais told me all about it. It seems that some of the pictures of rockets in the strip were too much like some new models the government is trying out down at Cape Canaveral. The security setup thought they had a leak somewhere and decided to work on Gervais to find out where Sydney got his material. As soon as they learned about Sydney's writer, Miss Donovan, and how she lived a few miles from the rocket center, it all became clear to them. They sent word to Sydney to be more careful. Of course the designs, don't mean a thing—one rocket is usually the same shape as all the others. It's the fuel, and so on, that's important, and Sydney didn't know anything about that."

"Did the FBI talk to you?"

"Yes. They called Colonel Tanner too. Wanted a line on Sydney and who worked for him. Tanner knew about Gervais and they decided he'd be their man."

That was why Colonel Tanner put me to work on the story of the missing comic strips, I decided.

"How'd you know all this?"

"Gervais called me about eleven o'clock last night, after the G-men got through with him. I told him to come over to my place and tell me about it. He gave me the whole story. He told me about the missing strips, and I figured he might have been confused yesterday and left the strips at Sydney's place. So we called Sherm, and sure enough, Sherm said he had the strips."

"Gervais forgot them?"

"I suppose so. Sherm said he wanted to make a change in one of them and he'd bring them in today himself. You didn't run across them at Sydney's place, did you?"

I nodded. "I ran across them, but not at Sydney's place. I don't know how they got there, but somebody put them under the seat of my car."

"What?"

"I said somebody put them under my car seat. I don't even know when. It must have been at Sydney's place after I got there this morning—*if* Sydney had them this morning."

Arnoth knocked the ashes from his cigar into a huge glass ash tray on his desk. "Are you trying to suggest that Sydney's murderer was lurking around the garage this morning about the time you discovered the body?"

"Whether it was Sydney's murderer or not is a question to be solved," I said. "But somebody wanted the strips where Sheriff Lindley wouldn't find them. At least that seems like the only logical solution."

"Where are the strips now?"

"I took them into the *Gazette* office with me. While I was getting fired, somebody swiped them."

"Whoa there! You think somebody at the *Gazette* is implicated?"

"Could be that somebody at the *Gazette* is implicated. Mr. Arnoth," I said. "Dick Aldwin wasn't making a secret of the fact that he regarded Sherman Sydney as a poor type of son-in-law."

Again Arnoth was silent for a moment. Finally he said: "But his daughter's engagement didn't have anything to do with Sherm's strip. I realize that Glenda Ovahead, the girl in the strip, has a resemblance to Ella Aldwin, but Sherm used lots of girls for models, and he certainly didn't use Ella without her permission."

"Maybe Dick Aldwin objected to his daughter being in a strip?"

"That's not a very strong motive for murder."

"People have been murdered for less—"

The phone cut me off. Arnoth answered. He listened and said, "Send him in." He hung up the phone and looked at me. "Art Gervais is here. Maybe you'd like to talk to him."

Gervais, who came through the door, was about my age. His eyes had a defeated look, as if he felt that the world was too big and too complex for him to cope with. He was slender, rather slight in build, and he had black hair and a little black mustache on his upper lip. Arnoth introduced me and Gervais pulled up a chair in front of the desk.

"Are you going to be Sydney's successor?" I asked.

A strained look came into Gervais's eyes and Arnoth answered, "Any announcement on that would be premature right now, Mr. Lanson. We'd prefer not to comment on that."

"I'm not a reporter at the moment," I said.

Arnoth turned to Gervais. "Mr. Lanson thinks that he can solve Sherm's murder. He wants to try, and maybe we can use an exclusive story. Know anything that might put him on the right track?"

Gervais shook his head. "Sherm was a funny guy," he said. "Not the kind of a man you could get close to."

Maybe Gervais hadn't gotten close to Sydney, but I could name three women who did. "I don't know exactly what I'm looking for," I told Gervais. "But I think the clue is something in the comic strip that was for release on July 4."

"That? Why it was a nothing strip," he said.

"A nothing strip?"

Arnoth explained. "The story just marked time. A lot of papers don't publish on July 4 and in order not to foul them up, we don't advance the plot on a holiday."

"Do you remember what was in the picture?" Nora had been rather indefinite when I talked to her about the missing week of strips.

"Well, the first frame caught up with the story from the preceding day," Gervais said. "It was a rehash of Commando Green's announcement that he was going to the South Pole. Glenda, the love interest, was taking it rather badly. She's been trying to hook him, you know. Green, in the second frame, repeats what he's often said before, that he can't live without adventure—that he'll never settle down. In the third frame, Glenda realizes she's lost him. The last frame is a close-up of her deep in this realization, with a tear on her cheek."

"Sounds pretty dull, doesn't it?" said Arnoth. "If we did that every day there'd be no readers."

"That's what Sherm thought. He told me he wanted to change the last frame to zip it up a little, but Nora told him to stick to copy." Gervais laughed. "They argued all yesterday morning about it."

"Argued all morning over something half the clients won't print," chortled Arnoth. "That's one of the things I liked about Sherm. Everything he did was important to him."

I studied it over and I couldn't see anything yet that looked like a murder motive. "Supposing you tell me exactly what happened after three o'clock yesterday, Mr. Gervais?"

Gervais leaned back in his chair. "I've already told the sheriff."

"I'd like to know too," said Arnoth.

Gervais shrugged. "All right. Miss Donovan had asked to ride into town with me. I finished up a little before two-thirty, and Sherm suggested we have some cocktails. I put the strips in the car—no, I guess I didn't because I couldn't have . . . but I did! I *remember* putting them in the car!"

"You're sure?" I said, leaning forward.

"But when I went to look for them after I had cocktails with Miss Donovan at her hotels they weren't there."

"Where did you put the strips?"

"In the back seat."

"Did Sydney have a chance to get them out of the car while you were having a highball in the house?" I asked.

Gervais thought a minute. "Why, yes, I suppose he did. We were talking and moving around a lot. He could have slipped out of the kitchen while he was mixing the drinks. I had my car in back of the house, not far from the kitchen door. But why would he have done such a thing and not told me?"

"Maybe he didn't want you to know," I said.

"But why? He was my boss. I had no right to object if he wanted to go over my work."

"I don't know why," I said. "You had dinner with Miss Donovan last night. Is there anything between you two?"

"What do you mean by that?" Gervais spoke in a tone that sounded a little miffed.

"I wondered if it was just a casual dinner, or are you . . . uh . . . courting her?"

Gervais laughed. "Miss Donovan is a couple of years older than I am. We're good friends and work together. However, I don't mind telling you that she's a very beautiful and attractive woman. On the other hand, you must realize that she's almost in the position of being one of my employers. She and Sherm were the bosses of *Dream Man*. I tried to keep my relations with her on a strictly employer-employee basis."

"That ought to answer your question," said Arnoth.

"It does," I said, "How did the FBI find you last night?"

"I left word at my hotel that I would be at the Creston. I hoped somebody would get an early edition of the *Globe* and report finding the strips. The FBI found out where I was and met me when I left."

"You left before the first edition was printed," I said. "Afterwards, you called Mr. Arnoth? And he called Sherman Sydney and found out where the strips were?"

"Yes. And I don't think Sherm took them out of my car. If he had, he would have mentioned it to Mr. Arnoth."

"He didn't," said Arnoth. "But that doesn't prove that he didn't take them himself."

"Who else could have?" I said.

"Phylana might have? She was gone from the room after Sherm served the highballs."

Phylana hadn't mentioned getting the strips, neither had Nora, "How about Ella Aldwin?"

"Why would she do such a thing? She has very little to do with the drawing."

"Where did you spend the night, Mr. Gervais?" I asked suddenly.

Gervais smirked at me. He was beginning not to like my questions. "I don't know why I have to clear myself of a murder charge to you, Lanson. You're not a policeman. But to put your mind at rest, Mr. Arnoth and I stayed up so late talking over the FBI angle and the missing comic strips that he suggested I spend the night in his spare room. Is that a good enough alibi?"

"Not quite," I said. I turned to Arnoth. "He had breakfast with you this morning?"

"No. He was gone when I got up. I'm a late sleeper on Saturdays, especially when I'm up late the night before. I might have slept till ten, only some damned fool rang my phone about eight-thirty and woke me up. When I got up and answered the phone, the party was gone."

That was my call when I was trying to locate Gervais. Like I said, this was my day for bad timing.

"What time did you leave?" I asked Gervais.

He shrugged. "I didn't notice. I got up and slipped out quietly. It was about seven o'clock when I had breakfast at a café downtown."

He didn't have an alibi, I decided. Arnoth probably had one, although I couldn't be sure.

"Is that all, Mr. Lanson?" Arnoth asked quietly. "If it is, Mr. Gervais and I would like to talk business this morning."

"That's all," I said. "Sorry I took up so much of your time."

"The pleasure is ours," said Gervais. He didn't look pleased. He seemed very glad that I was going.

EIGHT

Home is where I keep my clean shirts. I went to Smitty's first because his ham and beans are cheap. After washing the food down with a mug of muddy coffee, I went to the place where my clean shirts hang out, which was the Waltham Hotel.

My room is on the fourth floor. I took off my coat, hung it in the closet, then I dialed Tate Harrison, a copyreader for the *Globe* who doesn't go to work till five p.m.

Tate told me he'd heard about my getting fired. Tate is the chairman of our Guild grievance committee. "Hank may have told you you were fired, Mike, and maybe he can make it stick," Tate said, "but we're going to listen to your side of the story."

"You've made me feel better," I said.

As soon as I hung up the phone, the desk rang to say another party had called during my talk with Tate. The party had left a number, RIdge 7-2027 but hadn't given her name. Yes, it had been a woman. I thanked the clerk and remembered that Ridge was a Highland Heights exchange.

I dialed the number. A voice, soft and low, answered. "Yes?"

"This is Mike Lanson," I said.

"Oh, Mike. This is Phyl . . . Phylana Kane?" It was a question.

"Yes, Miss Kane."

"Phyl to my friends, Mike. I called your office, and the man who answered said you weren't working, that I could find you here. Are you ill? Or do you always go home early in the day?"

No use beating around the bush. "I've been fired."

"Fired?" There was a horrified tone in her low voice.

"Miss Aldwin's father talked to my boss and he got the wrong impression about what I tried to do today."

"Well, you just tell your boss to call me. I'll tell him what happened. I'll even call your boss myself. Do you want me to?"

"No need, yet. Maybe later," I said.

"Well, I'm not going to let Ella Aldwin throw her weight around," she said. "Remember, just one word from you and I'll give Colonel Tanner an earful."

"That's certainly nice of you, Miss Kane. How do you feel now?" She hadn't been feeling so pert, the last time I saw her.

"Much better, Mike. It's been a terrible shock, but . . . well, there's nothing I can do about it."

"You're wrong, Phyl. There's something you *can* do."

"I can? What can I do?"

"Maybe you can help bring the murderer to justice."

There was a hesitancy in her voice when she spoke again. "Mike, that wouldn't bring Sherm back. What's done is done and—"

"I've got a feeling you didn't tell everything you knew today."

"I did!" She protested too much, as a guy named Shakespeare once said.

"Okay," I said, "but if you remember anything you forgot to tell, call me up."

"I will. Mike, the reason I called you is that I wanted to ask you a favor."

I wanted to remind her that I was also asking for a tiny little favor, and then I considered the inequality of it all. What she hadn't told the sheriff might have been the fact that she killed Sherm Sydney. She probably wouldn't ask me to confess any crime. "Okay, ask it," I said.

"Mike, under the front seat of your car is a package. I want you to mail it for me."

"You mean that package of comic strips? The ones Jet Gervais lost last night?" I asked.

"Oh!" She paused, then asked: "You found them, then?"

"Yes, I found them."

"Then mail them for me. It's very important."

"Miss Kane—Phyl, I mean—I understood you to say this afternoon that you didn't know anything about those strips."

"When I told Sheriff Lindley that, I didn't," she said. "It was afterwards, while you and the sheriff were in the studio, that I went into Sherm's bedroom and found them on his dresser. He probably intended to drive into Highland Heights and mail them today."

"Didn't you know he had them all the time?"

"Of course not. It's perfectly clear what happened. While he was mixing drinks yesterday afternoon, he figured out a change he wanted to make. He slipped out the kitchen door, got them out of Jet's car and none of us noticed it."

"Why didn't he mention it to Gervais?"

"I don't know why. Maybe he didn't think of it."

It didn't seem like a good reason. "Phyl," I said, "I'd like to talk to you—in person, that is. Can I drive out now for a little chat?"

She hesitated. "You'll ask me a lot of other questions, won't you, Mike?"

"Probably, but you don't have to answer."

She sighed. "I suppose the sheriff has already learned I lied to him about one thing anyhow. I've got to talk. Maybe you can tell me what to do."

"I can advise you to see a lawyer," I said.

"But . . . but . . . Mike! You don't think *I* killed Sherm?"

"Like the sheriff said, 'I don't know enough yet to consider anybody a suspect.'" I was beginning to feel that the guilty party was among a very tight group of people.

She thought for a moment. "Why don't you come out for dinner, Mike. It's horrible to be here alone, thinking about Sherm. I think I'd like to have your company."

"Sure. What time?"

"Would six-thirty or seven be too late?"

"Just fine," I said.

"About those strips, will you mail them. I'll explain tonight."

"Sorry, Phyl," I said. "Somebody swiped them from me at the office today."

"Swiped? Somebody stole them?"

"Yes."

"Who? Who could have done such a thing? Was Nora in the office with you?"

"No. It must have been someone that works on the *Gazette.*"

Afterwards, I took a little nap. I never seem to get enough sleep and a mid-afternoon nap is something of a novelty for me. Around five o'clock I arose, bathed, shaved and dressed. In my dresser drawer I had a tiny .32 caliber automatic that I bought some years ago. I stuck that in my coat pocket, not that I was afraid, but I was dealing with a killer, and the killer might be a woman. I wasn't going into the spider's parlor without being ready. Besides, my deputy sheriff's commission entitled me to carry a gun.

Phyl opened the door wearing a white peasant blouse and a blue and white print skirt. She had on flat heels, which made her pretty short alongside me.

"Come in, Mike," she said with a smile.

"There's whiskey, ginger ale and soda up there." She pointed to the top shelf of a cabinet. "You mix the drinks and I'll put on the steaks."

"Steaks! You wonderful woman."

"I have to bribe you," she said. "How do you like your steaks?"

"Medium rare. How do you like your drink?"

"With ginger ale."

I got the makings, down off the shelf and some ice cubes from the refrigerator. I found two tall glasses and measured out the principal ingredient. Then I filled her glass with ginger ale and mine with branch water. I was standing near the back door and I thought I heard someone outside.

I looked at Phyl, expecting her to open the door. "Didn't you hear someone?" I asked.

"Where?"

"At the back door." I took a step and threw the door open.

The twilight showed a large, grassy lawn, enclosed on three sides by a lattice work covered with vines. The fourth side was enclosed by the house and garage with a little open space between. At the back of the lot was a little white gate, probably the one used by Phyl when she went to work on top of the hill. Along this path, moving up the hill through the trees, I thought I saw movement.

But there was no one in the yard.

Phyl's hand rested on my arm. "Who is it?" she asked.

"I thought I saw someone up there." I pointed to the path.

The grip tightened, then relaxed and I heard a soft, nervous laugh from her lips. She stooped and picked up a bottle of milk from the doorstep.

"The milkman," she said. "This is my breakfast for tomorrow."

I felt like a nervous grandma and followed her back in the kitchen. She put the milk in the ice box. Far away I heard a car start explosively. "Doesn't sound like a milk truck," I said.

"No. That's up on the road that runs past Sherm's place. The milkman comes down the street in front of the house."

"I didn't hear a car in front of the house."

"The milk's here, isn't it?" she asked.

There seemed to be no argument about that.

The steaks were on the grill and we sipped our drinks. "Why don't you let the sheriff solve this case, Mike?"

That was the third time I'd heard this question asked. I was getting a little tired of it.

"Are you trying to tell me to lay off?"

"Yes. The person who killed Sherm won't stop at a second murder,"

"The way to stop him is to get him in jail. You got any ideas who did it?"

"Yes," she said. "The same person that got you fired today."

"Ella Aldwin?"

She bent over and opened the oven grill. "The steaks are done, Mike. Let's eat first and talk later."

The steaks were just right. She also had French fries and a salad, which is about all you can say for a salad. For dessert Phyl served me a full quarter of one of those frozen pies you get at a supermarket and put in the oven at home. Her coffee wasn't bad either. We finished up everything and lit cigarettes.

"It seems a shame to spoil this lovely evening by talking about that awful thing that happened today," she said.

"You feel like talking about it?" I asked.

She sighed. "I thought a great deal of Sherm, Mike," she said. "I've worked for him about four years—more than four years, I guess. He's the best boss I ever had."

"You had no reason to kill him then," I said. "Why do you think you might be suspected by Sheriff Lindley?"

"I don't have an alibi. I live within easy walking distance of Sherm's home; I just go out my back gate and up the hill. And, after all, I'm a jilted sweetheart."

"A jilted sweetheart?" I looked at her closely.

She nodded. "That's what I lied about to Sheriff Lindley, Mike. I told him there was nothing between us. Nora is sure to tell the sheriff about us—Sherm and I."

"I don't think so, not unless she thinks you killed Sherm."

"Shall I tell you about it?"

"Not unless you want to."

"Are you going to—to—put it in the paper?"

"Not unless it has a bearing on the case," I said.

"I have a lot to tell. I have to get it off my chest," she said. "The minute I started working for Sherm, I knew that he and Nora weren't suited for each other. They weren't like other married couples, I'd known. They didn't act . . . well, chummy together. The only thing I ever heard them talk about was the strip. And it wasn't because I was with them only during business hours. I used to go places with them, and I was a guest in their home very often. I even took trips with them. Sherm was much nicer to me than he was to Nora."

"What about Nora? Didn't she resent this?"

"No. She didn't love him. She used to kid me about being grounds for divorce if she wanted one. Then she'd say that as long as Sherm kept her in fur coats, she'd stick with him. Later, she said, I could have him."

"Sort of cold-blooded, eh?"

"Yes, until Sherm hired Gervais. That was about a year after I went to work. Jet had his eyes on Nora. He thought I was making a play for Sherm—he listened to Nora too much. And he said one day it might be profitable for both of us if they got a divorce. I refused to listen to this kind of talk."

"But you liked to hear it?"

"No!" She still protested too much. "I've been raised to believe in marriage, Mike. Besides, I knew that if they ever really separated, *Dream Man* would flop. Nora was the one who made it go. Sherm couldn't work out a good story. Sure, he tinkered with her plots, but she gave him something he could tinker with, and he never got far off the storyline.

"But Sherm liked me and I liked him. There was something about him that attracted me terribly. Nora always made fun of Sherm by saying he was as sexless as Commando Green. She didn't know!

"One day Nora and Gervais came in together and found me in Sherm's arms. That was all she needed for a divorce. She made Sherm agree to keep her on as a writer at a thirty-five percent split from what he made from the strip in order to avoid a scandal. Sherm was afraid a scandal would lose papers.

"The divorce becomes final in about three more weeks. But I lost Sherm. Maybe she got Jet. I don't know about that."

"And Ella almost had Sherm?"

Her eyes snapped. "The Cream Puff deliberately took him away from me. Oh, I had a motive to kill Sherm, all right—Ella too. If I had been the type, I would have. But of course I didn't."

She'd lied to the sheriff and there was less reason to lie to him than to me. Everybody lies to reporters. "You knew Sherm had those comic strips, didn't you?"

"No. I really didn't, Mike. I knew he was busy last night, but I thought he was working on his Sunday page."

"Were you here last night?"

She hung her head. "That's another thing I lied to the sheriff about." Her cigarette, which she'd put in the ash tray was still burning, and she put it out before answering. "Ella was there too. Yes, Mike, I was there. After I went home last night, Sherm called me on the phone. He said he and Ella had quarreled. He told me he'd been a fool to let her lead him around by the nose. That's the exact words he used, Mike. He said; 'lead me around by the nose.' He said why didn't I come over and fix one of those meals like I used to. I told him the only thing I could fix at that late hour was spaghetti, or something easy. He said that would be fine.

"I went right over. I don't know what time it was, but not much after five-thirty—maybe six. We had dinner and Sherm said he had some work to do. He went into the studio. I washed the dishes. I thought that when he finished we'd have a drink or two together, but I looked around and found he'd used all the liquor in the afternoon, so I went to the liquor store."

I whistled. "Then *you* wrote that note I saw on the door this morning?"

"Yes. I didn't dare tell for fear that I'd be suspected. You mentioned the note, and I decided it was none of your business, so I didn't explain. And of course I wouldn't let on to Nora. Then we found the body. After that I kept my mouth shut. I took the note down while you and the sheriff were in the studio."

"He never attached much importance to it. He thought the note was for Ella."

"He probably knows otherwise now," she said. "I suppose he's talked to Ella and she said she didn't write it. The 'honey' was my signature."

"Go on. After you went to the liquor store. . . ."

"Well, I came back. It was about nine. Ella was in the studio. Her car was in the drive and I heard her voice. They were quarreling. I heard her say, 'Father knows about you and Phylana.' I was angry because I thought she was trying to make him fire me, get rid of me. I almost went up there to have it out with her, but I knew it wouldn't do any good." She stopped. I knew better than ask her why. She went on, just as if I'd asked her, "You see, Mike, Sherm was an awfully funny man. He'd drawn *Dream Man* for so many years, he identified the strip with himself. Even though he didn't write it, Commando Green was himself. He lived like Commando Green, he wanted to be surrounded by pretty girls. A new girl in every story. Ella was the new heroine. I was the villain now. Until our status changed, I couldn't do anything with Sherm."

"You didn't go back again after you came home?"

"Are you still convinced I killed him, Mike? I've told you I didn't. As a matter of fact, I'd had a previous engagement that evening. A friend was going to call. But I stood him up. After I went home, I waited, hoping my friend would show up. But he didn't."

"Did you look at the strip that Sherm redrew?" I asked.

She shook her head. "No. I saw the ones that Nora planned for the week. They argued about the July 4 strip. I suppose that's the one Sherm changed."

"What was it?"

Phylana shrugged. "It was a holiday strip. Nothing happened. Commando Green was jilting Glenda. Of course, it wasn't a jilt, exactly. Commando Green never really jilts girls, he just says what Sherm says to his woman, that they aren't good for each other. And Sherm is quoting Nora's script. Sometimes I think Nora wrote Sherm, as well as *Dream Man*."

"Have you made up with your boy friend?"

"I haven't heard from him. He really didn't matter. He wants to be a comic strip artist and thought I could persuade Sherm to help him."

"You weren't in love with him?"

She reached out and patted my hand. "With Max? Of course not. I—" She broke off as she suddenly realized she'd spoken a name.

"Max? Not Max Vickery?"

"Mike! Don't get him involved in this. Max was in love with Ella Aldwin too. That's how we got acquainted. I let him cry on my shoulder and I cried on his. But he couldn't have murdered Sherm."

"That's the trouble. Everybody seems to have a motive, but everyone else says, 'no—they couldn't have done it.'"

She withdrew her hand. "You think I killed Sherm?"

"Right now, I don't know what to think. Your story might be true and it might not. I don't know why you didn't tell it to the sheriff straight, as you've told it to me. He'd have questioned you, but he probably would have believed you in the end. Now, because you lied, he'll think you're concealing something. The fact that you're guilty, maybe."

"I wanted you to help me make him believe me, Mike," she said. Her eyes were pleading. "He'll find out I lied."

I got to my feet. "One thing I can't do," I said, "is persuade the sheriff to believe anything."

She got up from the davenport. "You're going?"

"Yes." I went to the closet where I'd left my hat. This babe was a mental case, and I wanted to get out of here.

As I got my hat, she got between me and the door. Her arms stretched out and clasped themselves around my neck.

"Don't go," she whispered. "Please stay!"

I knew then that she was crazy. She was trying to get her hooks in me like she once had had them in Sherm and in Max Vickery and heaven knows how many others.

But I couldn't avoid those full red lips. Then I had myself under control. Like the little Sir Galahad I was, I pushed her away just as the front door opened and Max Vickery came in.

He saw me pushing her. "Hello, Mike," he said. "Still pushing women around, I see."

NINE

Max Vickery was shorter than I, but a lot heavier; so I wasn't thinking of entering any athletic contest with him at the moment. I checked my impulse to sock him, which I should have heeded.

Phyl must have sensed that I was angry. She swung around and faced him. "Mike wasn't pushing me around, Max. I invited him here. I didn't invite *you.*"

Max smirked, almost leered. "Okay, if that's the way you say it is. You don't seem to be grieving over Sherm."

"How can you say such a thing!"

For a moment, Max looked as if he were sorry. He even said so. "I'm sorry, Phyl. I came here on business. I need your help—"

"After what you just said, Max, you can't expect anything from me."

"But, Phyl—"

"Move along, buddy. You heard what she said," I told him.

He scowled at me. "For two cents, I'd put a dent in that long nose of yours," he said. "Beat it. You're nothing but a fired snoop."

"Don't be so sure I'm fired," I said. "Even if you were part of the mob that tried to lynch me."

"How can you stand this crud, Phyl? He'd hang a murder rap on you, if he had half a chance. Just to get his by-line over the story."

"Please go, both of you," Phyl said. "I don't want to see anybody any more tonight. I don't want any more bickering. I've had all I can stand for one day. Go, Mike."

I got my hat and put it on. Max still blocked the door. "You heard the lady, Max," I said.

He turned sullenly and went through the door. I walked behind him to the tree lawn where I stopped. His car was parked behind mine. Probably he saw it when he drove up, and that's why he barged in without knocking. He turned suddenly.

"Mike!"

I stopped. "Yeah?"

"Take off your coat," he said.

"Are you crazy?" I had better reasons for wanting to punch him in the nose than he had for wanting to punch me, but I knew that any way the battle went, I'd get a few bruises and it just wasn't worth the bother.

"I'm going to knock the hell out of you," he said.

Well, there was no way to get out of it now without looking yellow. I had a longer reach than he and I was taller. I might not come out so badly after all.

I started to peel off my coat, but while both arms were in the sleeves and my belly unprotected, he let go with his coat on. He drove a pistonlike punch right into my guts.

I grunted and doubled up and his other fist crashed into my chin, knocking my teeth together. The world seemed to shake under my feet and I went down. I coughed when his foot kicked me in the ribs.

He waited while I struggled to my feet, trying to get my arms untangled from that damned coat.

He wasn't having any fight from me. Before I could get my arms loose he swung. This time I got my shoulder in the road and blocked it. Then I pulled and my coat ripped up the back. But it was too late. His fists landed again. First in my belly, then on my chin. I went down a second time and didn't try to get up. He kicked and kicked and kicked.

I heard somebody yelling, "Call the cops!"

Then I heard Phyl screaming. His car started and went away and I felt Phyl Kane's soothing hands on my face. She tried to pull me to my feet, but I didn't want to get up.

"Mike! Get up!" she pleaded, almost hysterically. "Let me help you into the house."

"Don't bother," I coughed. "I'm perfectly comfortable here."

As she was trying to lift me and nearly killing me in the process, I heard a siren. It grew louder and louder, then stopped. I looked up and saw two cops in uniform standing over me.

"Drunk?" one asked.

"They were brawling!" a woman yelled from the next house. Mrs. Blackett, no doubt.

The cops lifted me. My sides hurt where Max had kicked me, and my legs were like rubber. Somehow they got me in the car. One of them went back to get my hat and the two halves of my coat. He whistled when he found my gun. "Heeled!" he said.

We got in the car—both cops in front, and me in the back. One leaned over and frisked me. "What you doing with a gun, buddy?"

"It's a .32. Same kind that killed Mr. Sherman," the other said.

"Why don't you charge me with murder?" I said.

"We might do just that."

"For your information, I'm a deputy sheriff. I'm also a newspaper reporter. Name is Mike Lanson."

"Oh," said the first cop. "In that case, Sheriff Lindley's looking for you. You're just the deputy he wants."

The car started up, and in a couple of minutes they unloaded me at the two-story brick building that is a combined police station and pokey. I was taken upstairs and put on a foul-smelling cot in a dinky cell. My ribs hurt like hell, and I had a sore chin and sore belly where Max's fists had landed.

A doctor came in. He punched my sore ribs and I yelled. "Cracked rib," he said. "Take his shirt off."

An officer peeled my shirt, which was dirty and grass stained and then they got my undershirt off. It nearly killed me when I raised my arms.

Doc took some adhesive tape out of his satchel and began to tape my ribs so tight I could hardly breathe.

The cop who had found the gun was in front of me. I asked him, "What charge you holding me on?"

"You disturbed the whole north end of town. You were packin' a gun. And you ask what charge?"

"I got a deputy sheriff's commission. I can carry a gun."

"One of those green cards? They don't mean a thing. The sheriff gives one to every ward heeler in the county."

"I can make bond. How much?" Twenty-five dollars or so, I hoped.

"You just take it easy for awhile. The sheriff's on his way out here."

For a second I felt better; then I didn't like the way he said that. I thought the sheriff was a friend of mine, but the way this cop sounded something pretty bad was in store for me.

Doc finished winding me up in adhesive tape and I put my dirty shirt back on. The cop showed me the two halves of my coat and I decided it wasn't worth messing around with. The night was warm anyhow. "Throw it away," I said.

The cell door closed and I was left alone for awhile. Then Sheriff Lindley and the deputy named Archie came into the jail. The sheriff looked at me. "Hello, boy. You got yourself in a mess of trouble."

"For instance?"

"I got an assault and battery warrant for you, sworn out on complaint of one Richard Aldwin of Creston." He drew the warrant from his pocket. "It charges you brutally assaulted his daughter without cause."

"What the hell, sheriff?" I said. "I told you about that. You know I was acting on your orders and that she'd already fouled up the evidence in a murder case."

Sheriff Lindley shrugged. "You went beyond my orders, Mike. I didn't tell you to beat up women. Besides, he swore out the warrant and I'm only doin' my duty servin' it."

"Yeah. You're afraid that if you don't toss me in jail, Dick Aldwin will draw a cartoon that'll ruin your chances for re-election."

"Better be careful what you say, Mike. It's a long drive back to town and you ought to keep friendly with me." He straightened out the stoop in his shoulders to let me see how big he was. "Too bad you got fired today."

A turnkey came and unlocked my cell and I stepped out. The sheriff snapped handcuffs on my wrists. "That isn't necessary, sheriff. I'm not a desperate criminal."

"That's what they all say," he said.

It takes things like this to prove how unimportant you are the minute people know you aren't a newspaper reporter who can write up what they do to you. The sheriff took me by the arm and guided me out to his car, the same black Buick he'd driven up to Sherman Sydney's place that morning.

They put me in the back seat and the sheriff and his deputy rode in front. I was still sore, but I could think now and so I asked, "Who's going to take care of my car?"

"The Highland Heights cops have it. They've got the keys. You can take the Greyhound bus out when you get out of jail—if you make bail."

The car hit Highway 182 and headed toward Creston.

"Max Vickery is mixed up in the Sydney murder, sheriff," I said. "He was lovey-dovey with Sydney's secretary and in love with Dick Aldwin's daughter—Sydney's fiancée."

"You leave the lawin' to me, sonny boy, and I'll leave the newspaper reportin' to you. Right now you'd best think about your own troubles. You can get six months in jail for what you did today, and judges don't look kindly on slappin' a woman around, especially a pretty one."

"If I were still a reporter, you'd never arrest me," I said. "You'd worry about how I could louse up your re-election. But because Aldwin still works for a newspaper, he can throw his weight around."

"Shut up," said the sheriff sharply.

The car reached the Creston city limits and was heading through town before he spoke again. "You want a lawyer?" the sheriff asked. "You'd better get one. He might get you off with thirty days."

"I won't even spend the night in jail," I said.

"Not without bail you won't get out of jail. You'd better call a bondsman to get you out tonight and see a lawyer tomorrow. I can give you the name of somebody who'd put up bail for you."

"How much of a kickback do you get for recommending him?"

"You'd better be careful, what you say, Mike. I'm warning you; I got patience but you're pushin' it real hard. Anyway, who slugged you around?"

"Max Vickery. And I'll take care of it my own way."

The car turned off the freeway and pulled up in front of the county jail. I was sore and it was painful for me to climb out. My hands were handcuffed and I couldn't use them to help very much. I was led into the sheriff's office where a sleazy looking turnkey took my name. The sheriff took off the handcuffs while Archie searched my pockets.

The sheriff took the .32 automatic from his pocket. "This belongs to him too," he said. "Put it with his stuff. By the way, Mike, give me that green card I gave you."

"With pleasure," I said, "it's in my billfold."

The sheriff took it out. Then he said to the turnkey. "Let him make a phone call if he wants."

"Phone's over there," said the turnkey, pointing to a booth.

"Here's some money." He took a dime from the money Archie had taken from my pockets and handed it to me.

I went into the booth and looked up Dick Aldwin's phone number and dialed it.

"Hello," his voice came over the wire.

"This is Mike Lanson."

"You—" whatever he called me ended in a splutter.

"I'm in jail, Mr. Aldwin," I said pleasantly, "thanks to you."

"That's right where you belong," he said, "and you can stay there till you rot."

"I'm not staying without compensation, Mr. Aldwin," I said. "The longer I stay, the more it's going to cost you for false arrest."

There was a moment of silence. Then, "What are you talking about. My daughter told me the whole story. . . ."

"If she told you it was an unprovoked attack and malicious, you've got the wrong facts, Mr. Aldwin," I said. "I was acting under Sheriff Lindley's orders."

"You had no orders for what you did. Sheriff Lindley told me so himself."

"Sheriff Lindley is concerned with his re-election," I said, "and after he sees the light, he might not testify exactly as you expect him to. Did you know I had two witnesses for what happened today?"

"Two—" He stopped, and there was silence again for a moment. I waited patiently. "You're bluffing."

"I'm not bluffing, Mr. Aldwin. And a lot of lawyers will be glad to bring a nice big fat lawsuit against you if I spend tonight in jail. If I were you, I'd do something about it."

I hung up the telephone and went out of the booth.

"You get a bondsman?" the sheriff asked.

"In a manner of speaking," I said. "He'll be here shortly."

The turnkey asked the sheriff, "Shall I lock him up?"

The sheriff looked at me. He suspected something. "Who'd you call?"

"Dick Aldwin," I said.

The sheriff turned to the turnkey. "Keep him out here for a few minutes. Maybe Mr. Aldwin will call back."

He did in exactly five minutes. The sheriff took the call on another phone in his office and then he came out and looked at me. "Mr. Aldwin said he wasn't going to press charges."

"You can't release me, sheriff," I said. "It takes the court or the county prosecutor to do that."

"I know. That's what I told him. He's coming down here with a lawyer to talk to you."

In about thirty minutes, at ten minutes past eleven, Dick Aldwin, Ella Aldwin and a lawyer Hamed Sparks appeared at the county jail.

The lawyer did the talking. "We have no desire to embarrass you or to retaliate for this attack on Miss Aldwin today," he said. "Mr. Aldwin tells me that if you apologize to Miss Aldwin before witnesses, that he'll agree to a dismissal of the charges against you."

"Sorry," I said, "but I didn't do anything to apologize for. If apologies are due, I'm the one that ought to get them. Miss Aldwin scratched my face." I pointed to the bandaid on my cheek.

"He skinned my knee and tore my dress!" said Ella. The lawyer raised his hand. "I told you, Miss Aldwin, that I was to do the talking." He turned to me. "But as Miss Aldwin says, the damage to her person was considerably greater than that suffered by yourself."

"I don't feel like talking about it," I said. "Sheriff Lindley gave me orders to see that nothing was disturbed in Mr. Sydney's studio when I reported the murder yesterday. Even if he hadn't given the orders, it was my duty as a private citizen to protect the evidence in a murder case and to see that no one interfered with the operation of law enforcement officers. Miss Aldwin paid no heed to my demand that she stay out of the murder room. Instead, she went willfully into the place, disturbed a number of things and took away a diamond ring that might throw considerable light on the slaying. When I demanded then that she leave immediately, she refused. She even braced her foot against the door frame, and I had to pick her up and carry her down the stairs. Outside the garage—and I have two witnesses to bear me out on this—I attempted to put her on the ground gently, without harming her. But she was kicking and screaming and hitting me and I lost my balance. I sort of dropped her. If she was injured, it was her own fault."

Aldwin looked sharply at his daughter. It was apparent that her story didn't quite jibe with mine.

"Miss Aldwin tells us differently," said the lawyer.

"Has she got witnesses?"

The lawyer cleared his throat. He motioned to Aldwin and took him aside. The two men talked in low tones.

Finally the lawyer came back to me. "Mr. Aldwin is a busy man, and as I said, he has no desire to punish you. Perhaps you did act in good faith, but you exceeded the proper limits—"

"I exceeded nothing, and I'm going to sue the hell out of him."

The lawyer glanced quickly at Aldwin, who was looking very sick. Ella Aldwin was strangely subdued.

"We will pay you a reasonable amount because of the misunderstanding and that tiny scratch, and have you released immediately if you sign a release—"

"You don't get off that easy," I said.

The lawyer stiffened. "You won't get much in court."

"I don't want much," I said. "I want some answers."

The lawyer exhaled. He turned to the sheriff. "Can we use your office . . . er . . . privately?"

"Sure," said the sheriff. "Like I told you, Mr. Aldwin, Mike's a good boy. Just a little impetuous, that's all."

We filed into the sheriff's office.

Ella remained outside.

I sat down, Aldwin sat down and the lawyer remained standing. "You don't look very well, Mike," said Aldwin. "The sheriff said you had a fight with Max Vickery."

"I've still got things to settle with him," I said, and I looked up at the lawyer. "And don't say that's a threat."

"It depends on what happens, Mr. Lanson. Now let's get down to cases. What is it you want?"

"First off," I said, "I want the charges against me dropped."

"I've already talked to the county attorney," said Sparks. "He's getting an order for your release and it'll be here in a few minutes."

"Next, I want a signed statement from Aldwin and from his daughter regarding their movements from five o'clock yesterday afternoon until ten o'clock this morning—or yesterday morning. I guess it's about midnight now."

The lawyer glanced at Aldwin. "You don't have to do that unless you want to, Dick."

"If he doesn't I'll bring suit. Even though charges are dropped, I've been placed under arrest. I've suffered embarrassment and loss of dignity by being brought to the jail in handcuffs. That's the basis of a pretty good suit, Mr. Sparks."

Dick Aldwin's head dropped. I went on:

"And the next thing I want Aldwin to do is to retract any statements he made against me to Colonel Tanner which caused me to be suspended from my job. In other words, if Aldwin doesn't get my job back, he's going to be sued from the ground up for getting me fired."

"I'll do that," Aldwin said. "And I'll sign the statement. But any decision Ella makes is her own. If she doesn't want to tell where she was or what she did last night, you can sue till hell freezes over."

"Call her in," I said.

The lawyer called Ella. She came in silently, her face a trifle pale. The lawyer said, "Mr. Lanson wants you to sign a statement of your movements and activities between five o'clock yesterday afternoon and ten o'clock this morning."

"That includes our little hassle, Miss Aldwin," I said.

She glanced angrily at me. "Will it help dad?"

"If he goes along with me on the rest of our bargain," I said.

She looked at Dick Aldwin and he said, "He hasn't asked too much," he said weakly.

"All right. I will," she said. "Will you write it down, Mike? I'm not very good on a typewriter."

There was a machine in the corner. At the lawyer's request I made a carbon for his files and she dictated. Her statement was:

"On the afternoon of May 8, Sherman Sydney and I went into the studio after the others had left. We had been quarreling because I'd noticed that he'd been paying a great deal of attention to Phylana Kane lately. He said that Phyl was an old friend and that, naturally, he wanted to be nice to her. He said that he had taken the comic strips that Jet—that's Arthur Gervais, Sherm's assistant—had planned to mail from Jet's car and was going to redraw the last frame of the July 4 strip.

"I asked Sherm why, and he said it was a matter of giving the readers something they'd asked for. Besides, he said, the strip had no punch and the story had dragged all week. He wanted to put some snap into it.

"I sat in the studio while he got 1-ply paper and began penciling in the new drawing. I didn't notice what he drew because I was angry with him. Besides, I have nothing to say about what goes into the strip. That is Sherm's worry. And Miss Donovan's, although Sherm has the last say. I told him finally that I didn't want to sit around twiddling my thumbs, that I was going home. He didn't seem to care.

"I went to my apartment and fixed dinner. Afterwards, I began to feel sorry about quarreling with Sherm. I changed my clothes and got into my car and went to the studio. That was about nine o'clock. Sherm was in his studio. He'd finished the new drawing and was just pasting it in place on the strip.

"Sherm didn't even seem glad to see me. He told me Phylana had been over for dinner, and I told him that after we were married, he would have to fire Phyl. Sherm got angry, and one thing led to another, and finally I took my ring off my hand and threw it down on the table beside his drawing board. I told him I was quitting my job, too, and that I never wanted to see him again. Then I left and went to my apartment at 210 Margaret Street. I went to bed about eleven o'clock.

"I woke up about eight-thirty this morning—that's Saturday, May 9—and felt that perhaps I'd been unreasonable. I was sorry I'd been jealous of Phylana, and I decided to go back to the studio and make up with Sherm.

"At the studio, I met Mike Lanson and he told me that Sherm had been shot. I remembered that my ring was still in the studio, and I had some idea that if the officers found it there they'd think I'd killed Sherm. At the moment that seemed to matter more to me than Sherm's death. I started off to get it. I heard Mike call but I paid no attention. I entered the studio and saw poor Sherm lying on the floor with a bloody wound in his forehead. Mr. Lanson had just asked me if Sherm was dressed the same way he'd been dressed the night before. He was not. He was wearing slacks and a T-shirt this morning. He had on light gray trousers and a white shirt and a necktie the night before.

"The thing uppermost in my mind was the ring. I found the ring right where I left it the night before. Sherm had not even picked it up, and I realized he had not loved me. Perhaps I had not loved him. My father was right—the idea of marrying a celebrity had blinded me to the fact that love is important in marriage. But I admired Sherm. He was always considerate and good.

"Mike Lanson, who had followed me into the studio, insisted that I leave. I refused to go and threatened him, telling him that my father could get him fired. I was very hateful and foolish. Mike carried me down the stairs, but when he tried to put me down, he must have slipped. I believed at the time he had pushed me. I fell, tearing my dress and bruising my arm. I was angry and went home. I called my father by telephone and told him what I thought had happened. My father said he would attend to Mike Lanson and see that he got what was coming to him."

Sparks objected several times as Ella told her story, but Ella insisted on telling it straight

Next Dick Aldwin gave his statement

"At five o'clock yesterday afternoon I went home and called my daughter on the phone. She was not at her apartment and I realized that she was still at the home of her employer, Sherman S. Sydney. I had never approved of my daughter's engagement to Sydney because he was a divorced man. In fact, his divorce was not even final, and his former wife was still associated with him. Although the former Mrs. Sydney was associated with her husband in a business capacity, I suspected that the present relationship was not altogether in a business way.

"I called Mr. Sydney's secretary, Miss Phylana Kane, who confirmed my suspicion that my daughter was at the studio. Miss Kane said that Miss Donovan, the former Mrs. Sydney, was staying at the Hotel Creston. I telephoned her. I told her that I didn't approve of my daughter's engagement to Mr. Sydney, and I asked if there was anything she could do to make Ella break off the affair. Miss Donovan told me, and I remember her exact words, 'Mr. Aldwin, what my ex-husband does, except draw that creepy comic strip, is none of my business. If your daughter wants to marry a man who is handcuffed to a drawing board, it's her affair and I'll not get mixed up in it.'

"I tried later in the evening to reach my daughter by telephone and was not successful. I spent the rest of the evening at home, reading and watching television. I went to bed about midnight. Got up about seven in the morning and went to work. I reached the office about eight-thirty—I don't know the exact time. Mr. Lanson was in my office talking to Max Vickery, the *Gazette* sports cartoonist. I think I spoke to him, but my mind was on Ella and I don't remember what I said. Mr. Lanson and Mr. Vickery left. Mr. Vickery returned in a few minutes. I worked steadily until about ten o'clock when I received a phone call from my daughter. She said that Mr. Lanson had attacked her without provocation at the Sydney place. Mr. Sydney had been killed, she said—shot through the head—and she had been overcome with shock and grief. Mr. Lanson had brutally ordered her off the premises, and when she refused to go, he hit her, knocked her down and tore her dress. I think that my daughter was overwrought and that her version of the affair was due to her shocked condition."

I smiled at the last statement, but let it stand.

"Is that all you want?" Sparks asked.

"Yes."

"The release order has arrived and you can go," the lawyer said.

"I apologize, Mike," said Ella Aldwin. "I behaved terribly."

"In my work, that kind of behavior is par for the course," I said.

"I'll talk to Tanner tomorrow, Mike," said Aldwin. "And I apologize too, for all the embarrassment and inconvenience I've caused you."

"The Christian thing to do would be to forgive and forget," I said. "As soon as I get my job back, I'll do that."

TEN

Sheriff Lindley gave me back my pocket change and watch and my little green card and said, "I'm sending your gun to police ballistics tomorrow, Mike. I'll return it as soon as it has been checked."

I gave him my Sunday sneer. "Think I killed Sherman Sydney?"

He shrugged. "Somebody did the job, and until we find the right party, we're checking every .32 caliber gun we find."

"Humph."

He knew I didn't like it. "I hope you look at this in the right way. I'm only doin' my duty."

A reporter has to take a lot from many people, but this was almost too much. Still I swallowed my pride and said, "It could happen to any politician, sheriff."

He looked a little mad himself.

I took a taxi back to the Waltham hotel, since my car was still in Highland Heights. I hung a *Do Not Disturb* sign on my door knob and turned in. My cracked rib hurt so badly that it was hard to get comfortable and I slept only off and on. Finally, about dawn, I got down to real slumber, dreaming that Phylana Kane's arms were around me, squeezing the breath out of me. I finally woke up, discovered it was only nine o'clock. But my ribs hurt so bad I got up anyhow.

I had an extra suit of clothes. I put it on, plus clean shirt and underwear, and had coffee and a roll for breakfast in the hotel coffee shop. Then I called Tate Harrison and reported that everything probably would work out without the Guild getting into a stew about it. I explained that statements from Dick Aldwin and daughter would clear me, and that I'd probably talk to Colonel Tanner later in the day.

"How in the devil did you do it, Mike?" Tate wanted to know.

"'Twasn't easy," I said.

"I envy you reporters," he said. "You've got a knack for falling in a cesspool and climbing out sweet as springtime. Copyreaders are stodgy bastards."

"You get paid more," I said.

We said good-bye and hung up.

I had a lot of things to do. I called the sheriff's office and learned they'd already run ballistics test on my .32 and given it a clean bill. The cops said the medical examiner put the time of death at between six and seven a.m., which was what Doc Stone had said.

Afterwards I looked up Max Vickery's address. He lived in a flat in the University Hill section. It was still early so I took a cab to the Greyhound station. I checked an impulse to talk to the dispatcher about early morning riders yesterday. I bought a ticket on the ten a.m. bus that ran to Highland Heights. I needed my car.

The bus stopped at a restaurant in Highland Heights, and I walked over to the police station.

The desk sergeant wasn't the same one that was on duty the night before, of course, and I had to go through a lot of red tape identifying myself and showing the receipt for my car keys that they'd given the sheriff the night before. While I was going through this business, a big husky patrolman came in and looked me over.

"I thought the sheriff had a warrant for you," he said. "Did you make bond?"

"It was all a mistake," I said.

"He's clear, Henderson," said the sergeant. "I checked with the sheriff's office." The sergeant turned to me. "Hope you don't blame our boys for hauling you in last night," he said. "We were acting in good faith."

"No hard feelings," I said. "All I want is my car."

He gave me my keys and told me it was out behind the station. Henderson eyed me suspiciously and even followed me to the car. There's nothing I hate like an officious cop, and I could see that he was top grade in his class.

On the way out of town I drove past Phyl's house. The blinds were drawn, so I didn't stop. I got on Highway 182 and headed back toward town.

It's funny how a night's sleep will give you the answers to a lot of things. As I drove I got to wondering who had stolen those comic strips from my desk the day before and all of a sudden I knew what had happened to them. The answer was so funny and so simple that I darn near went off the road laughing.

I stopped at a filling station. I looked up the name Somerset in the directory and discovered there were five families by that name. I'd called three before I learned that Hugo Somerset was the father of Joe Somerset, *Gazette* copyboy.

"Joe?" said Mr. Somerset "He's just getting ready for church. Is it important?"

"Pretty important, Mr. Somerset. This is Mike Lanson, one of the reporters for the *Gazette*. I think he can help me on a big story."

"Just a minute," said Somerset and I heard him call Joe to the phone.

"Hello, Mike," said Joe. "I thought you got fired yesterday. You working again?"

"It was all a mistake, Joe," I said. "Listen, about noon yesterday, did you pick up a long rectangular package off my desk in the City Room."

"Sure, Mike. An oblong package with a lot of three-cent stamps on it?"

"That's the one. What did you do with it?"

"Mailed it, of course. It was all ready for mailing so I took it down to the mailing room. Did I do anything wrong?"

"Nothing that a bottle of aspirins wouldn't cure," I said.

"Huh?"

"Never mind, Joe. You did the right thing. I just wondered what happened to it."

"Gee, I'm glad, Mike. I guess I'll be seein' you Monday, huh?"

"I hope so," I said. I hung up the phone.

I looked up Arnoth's number and called him. A voice answered, "Hello?"

My timing, which was so bad yesterday, was right today. I was finding people home. "Mr. Arnoth?"

"Speaking. Who is it please?"

"This is Mike Lanson. Remember me?"

"I certainly do, Mike. Ready to talk business on that proposition we talked about yesterday?"

"Well, I'm thinking it over, Mr. Arnoth, but something important has come up." I told him about the comic strips.

"Hmm," said Arnoth, "there's not much I can do about it now. We don't usually get the mail until Monday, and—"

"Don't you have your mail delivered to a box so you can pick it up anytime?"

"Why, yes, but it may not be in the box. The post office sorts mail just when it feels like it nowadays. You can't hurry 'em up for love or money."

"It just so happens, Mr. Arnoth, that that set of strips may be the key to Mr. Sydney's murder."

"Mmm. You trying to solve it by yourself?"

"Not especially. I'll bring the sheriff down with me if you'll open the box this morning."

He hesitated. "Listen, Lanson, if we could get an exclusive on this it would be money in the bank for both of us."

"How do you mean?"

"I mean I know at least twenty-five papers that would pay a good price for a story on how you solved the murder of Sherman S. Sydney. Maybe fifty papers. You got any idea how much that would be?"

"A lot, huh?"

"We'd charge from five to twenty-five dollars each. And maybe we could stretch it out into a series of five or six articles."

My head was swimming. "Okay, Mr. Arnoth. It's a deal. But first I've got to see those strips."

"We aren't likely to get into trouble if we open the package without the sheriff around, would we?"

"Hell no, Mr. Arnoth. We don't even know what's in the package. How do we know it's the key to a murder?"

"Okay, boy. We'll split fifty-fifty—that's the regular syndicate deal."

"Sure, Mr. Arnoth. I'll agree to that. How soon'll you be at the post office?"

"Thirty minutes," he said.

I hung up the phone.

I bought a tank of gas on the basis of the money I was going to make on my first syndicated series and then I drove to the post office. I got there ahead of Mr. Arnoth, but he drove up in his Cadillac after I'd waited about five minutes.

He waved and beckoned to me. I went over to his car. He opened the door and spread some papers on the car seat in front of me.

"Just in case there's a misunderstanding," he said, "I want you to sign this agreement now."

There were two copies exactly alike, which said that I was liable for all damage suits resulting from the articles and that I was to receive fifty percent of the money the client newspapers paid for them. I signed both copies and Mr. Arnoth signed them. A man was mailing some letters in the mailbox in front of the post office and Mr. Arnoth called him over to witness our signatures. His name was Krumpacker.

"Okay," said Arnoth, when Krumpacker signed his name. "Let's got to work."

We went into the post office and Mr. Arnoth went to an oversized box and opened it with a key.

ELEVEN

The big package with Sherman Sydney's return address on it was at the bottom of the box, showing that the mail clerks had done quite a bit of sorting since the strips got to the general post office.

Arnoth carried it over to a counter and opened it right there while I hung over his shoulder. He shuffled the strips with almost deliberate slowness until he came to the one dated 7-4.

It looked innocuous to the point of being uninteresting for three frames, but the last one was a whinger. I could see no difference in the drawing between the first three frames and the last, although Ella Aldwin had told me that Gervais had drawn the first three, and the last, which was changed, had been drawn by Sydney. The characters looked the same, except in different poses.

The last frame was a new picture, apparently pasted over the old. It showed Glenda, the black-haired love interest who resembled Ella Aldwin, swinging a roundhouse slap which had landed with a big star-shaped splatter on Commando Green's cheek. There were no balloons, but there was a large blackfaced *WHOP !!!* followed by three exclamation points.

Arnoth looked at me a little disappointed. "Is this what you're looking for, Lanson?"

I was mystified myself. I expected more. The slap and the *whop* were pretty, but as for solving a murder, the strip might as well whop dead, to make a bad pun.

"It might," I said, "if I could see the picture underneath."
Gervais had described it to me, but there's nothing like seeing.

"That's easy," he said. He took his fingers and peeled the
overlaid picture right off the strip. "Rubber cement," he explained. "It comes off easy and holds fast. A comic strip artist
would be lost without it."

The picture underneath showed a different type of reaction.
Glenda was shown in a closeup. Her head was bowed, her eyes
were sad and a single highlighted tear rolled down her cheek.
There were no balloons. None were needed to show that Glenda
was broken-hearted.

"Well?" Arnoth looked at me.

"I don't know what to make of it, Mr. Arnoth," I said.

"You'd better make something of it, Lanson. It may mean at
least two hundred dollars in your pocket, maybe a thousand if
we can run a series of five or six articles."

I studied it hard. For that money I'd study a *No Smoking*
sign real hard. The girl looked like Ella Aldwin, but I'd been
told an artist doesn't identify a model with anything. She meant
no more than his brush or whatever he was working with at
the time. Ella Aldwin might be Sherm's light of love outside of
working hours, but when she posed for pictures she was just a
tool of his trade.

Commando Green looked like nobody in particular. Maybe
when the strip was started there had been an original model, but
it was a good bet that he no longer resembled even the original.
This probably was the only thing in the entire strip that Sherm
drew without a model or guide. Did the slap mean something?
Or was the thing I was looking for in the other picture, the one
Sherm Sydney decided the public should not see?

I couldn't see where one picture meant any more than the
other. I liked the second drawing—the one Sherm did—better
because it was action. Glenda wasn't taking her jilting lying
down, or should I have said that?

But either reaction was believable. It depended entirely on
Glenda's character and I hadn't followed the strip long enough
to be a judge.

"Do you know what's going to happen in the strips before you see them?" I asked Arnoth.

He shook his head. "No, not exactly," he said. "Sherm usually sent me an outline of Miss Donovan's stories before he used them. Once in a great while, I made a suggestion or told him to omit something that I didn't think would go over well with the clients. Usually I just told him to go ahead. But almost every story underwent revision as it was developed on the drawing board."

"Did Miss Donovan plan the pictures?"

"Yes indeed. A comic strip has a shooting script just as complete in detail as a movie shooting script. Not only did Miss Donovan describe every scene, the expressions of the characters and their positions, very often she also ran down drawings and photos which Sherm could use for backgrounds. Especially if the adventure were in some strange foreign place. She has a complete file of *National Geographics* and hundreds of travel books, but Nora always was finding other pictures in magazines and newspapers."

"Quite a job of research."

Well, there it was. A woman slaps a man, the hero, and what happens? The man who drew the picture gets murdered. It didn't make sense. Not even when you considered the tangled love life of Sherman Sydney who brought the woman he married, the woman he wanted to marry and the woman he could have married all under one roof.

I shook my head. The more I looked at the picture the more I realized that murder could hardly have come from Sherman Sydney's love life. Had that been explosive, he'd have been murdered long ago. It must lie in the comic strip. If sex was involved, it was incidental. There was something else. There had to be a clue underlying this picture. It was something deep, something I didn't understand.

"You don't seem to be getting anywhere," said Arnoth.

"The answer is something that's back of the picture," I said. "It's something that underlies the whole strip, but I just can't grasp it."

"You've *got* to grasp it," groaned Arnoth. "That money should mean something to you."

It meant a hell of a lot more to me than to Arnoth.

"It's there," I said. "It's gotta be there. Give me time to think about it—alone."

"You think it proves who killed Sherman Sydney?" he asked.

"It might." I wondered if it would be enough proof to convince twelve jurymen. It might convince twelve psychiatrists, providing they weren't all from different schools.

Arnoth sighed and began rewrapping the strips, taking care to put the loose picture on top of the pile. "I think I'll use the one where she slaps him," he said. "I've always wanted to see somebody slap *Dream Man.*"

"I may have my job back tomorrow."

"Perhaps by tomorrow I'll be ready to announce the new artist for the strip."

"Gervais?"

Arnoth hesitated. "That isn't certain yet. Please do not mention Gervais in connection with the strip. You will be doing both me and Gervais a big favor."

"You mean Gervais may not get the job?"

"I cannot make a statement—yet. The contract hasn't been signed."

"But who else would it be?" I stared at him. "Just give me a lead, Mr. Arnoth, so I'll know where to reach him when you do make the announcement. In a case like this, I promise not to break the story until I hear from you."

Arnoth looked at me as if he wanted to be sure if he could trust me. "I think if you talk to Max Vickery you'll learn more details," he said. "But any announcement before the contract is signed is premature."

That nearly took the wind out of me. Max Vickery! The guy I wanted to punch in the nose.

"Thanks, Mr. Arnoth. I'll keep it under my hat."

We went out of the post office together. He got in his car with the strips tucked under his arm. I decided to go out and see Max. Maybe I could get the story and afterwards give him a punch that I owed him.

Max lived in a modest little walk-up, but I bet he paid through the nose for it. The University Hill section is a "good location" address and landlords charge high for the privilege of impressing people who probably don't care anyhow.

There were twelve mail boxes in the apartment house vestibule. Max Vickery's name was on the box for 2-D, which meant second floor.

Apartment 2-D was the second door on the right, the rear apartment on the second floor.

I pounded on the door, listening for sounds from within. There was no answering call, or opening of the door. I knocked a second time. Still no answer. I tried the knob and found the door unlocked. Naturally, I went in.

The apartment looked empty. It had a large living room. To the left was a bedroom and to the right was a modest kitchen. That was all, excepting a john and a clothes closet, which I couldn't see from where I stood. Probably off the bedroom. Max was a sucker to pay high rent for this dump. The whole thing wasn't much larger than my hotel room.

The shades were drawn and the room was dark and sinister. The quiet didn't sound right either. Nobody was home, I guessed, unless Max was sleeping in. Just for luck, I crossed over to the left and looked through the bedroom door.

One glance was enough.

Max was fully dressed, lying on the floor, and he was as dead as anybody ever gets. There was a hole in his head, near the right temple, and there was a puddle of blood around him.

I tiptoed back and found the phone. I dialed Lieutenant Guffy at his home. His Sunday was going to be spoiled.

"Stick around, Mike," he said, after I told him what I'd found. "I'll send the boys over." He paused. "And I'll be along myself." He sighed heavily.

"I thought you would," I said. He'd be the best man on this case.

"It's not that I like your confounded company, you newspaper rat," he said, "but every darned time you turn up a body, I know the case is going to be a stinker and I'll probably have to lose sleep over it anyhow."

"You ought to hire some smart cops then," I said.

He growled and slammed the receiver on the cradle. I waited only a little while before the cops got there. They pushed me into the kitchen, where I sat down at the table to wait for the inevitable Guffy.

I was sure Vickery's murder tied in with Sherm Sydney's killing somehow. Max had inherited death with his new job. Somebody didn't want certain things to happen and would kill to prevent it.

I figured Guffy would be asking a lot of questions after he heard of my trouble with Max, and I decided to tell him the whole story, not holding back a thing. He'd find it out anyhow. Guffy would suspect me because he was a cop and it was his business, but I knew he'd never really think I killed Max.

The coroner, Doc Stone, stuck his head in the kitchen and saw me. "You get around as much as I do, don't you, boy?"

"Nope," I said, "I only go where people get shot in the head. I'm a specialist."

I went to the door and watched him work over the corpse.

"Same size hole as the one we had yesterday," he said. "This one ain't been dead so long. Maybe an hour or two. Rigor mortis ain't complete. Couldn't be over two hours."

It was noon, which meant the killing took place between ten and eleven.

Finally Guffy came. He came into the kitchenette and I told him about the fight with Max. "You'll have to testify at the inquest, Mike. You might have a rough time with the sheriff, but if you can account for your movements this morning, I doubt if you'll have much to fear. I guess I'd better call the sheriff in on this. Looks like this case ties in with the killing he had yesterday."

"Give him my love," I said.

Guffy gave me a dirty look. "And just for the record, Mike, do you mind telling me why you came here?"

"To give him a punch in the nose mainly," I said, "but I had another reason. Arnoth had Max slated for Sherm Sydney's job."

"Huh? I thought Gervais was going to inherit that."

"So did I, but apparently Arnoth thought Max could do a better job. Now Gervais will probably be in."

"Not by a longshot. Gervais is going to jail for murder," said Guffy. "It's as plain as the nose on your crazy face. Gervais killed Sydney, expecting to inherit the strip. When Arnoth said no, he was going to hire Max Vickery, Gervais removed Max."

Damned if it didn't sound good. Except for one thing. I asked Guffy, "How does the hocus-pocus about the missing comic strips fit in?"

"Does it *have* to fit in? I'll admit it makes a good story for your crummy newspaper, but I'm solving a murder, not filling up the news columns," Guffy said.

Sheriff Lindley came over in a few minutes. He greeted me a little too warmly and said, "Aldwin thinks I was pretty smart not throwing you in jail. It could have cost him a lot of money if you'd sued him."

"I'll bet he'll vote for you, sheriff," I said.

"Huh? Oh, yes. Ha, ha. If Colonel Tanner doesn't give you your job back, just call me and I'll go over and talk to him. You may not realize it, Mike, but I'm a great friend of his."

"Yeah?" I decided what the hell was the use trying not to be sarcastic. The sheriff heard it and shut up. He and Guffy walked off into a corner of the living room, while Guffy told him most of the things I'd told him, plus what they had learned that they hadn't told me. Finally Guffy motioned for me to come over.

"Sheriff said he already tried to locate Gervais this morning and he wasn't home. Looks like he's our boy. I'll get an A.P.B. out on him, and we ought to have him by nightfall."

"Yeah? And what if he isn't your boy? What if somebody gets murdered while you go chasing Gervais?"

"Nuts to you," said Guffy. "Sheriff Lindley and I thought a little chat with Phylana Kane might turn up a few things. As soon as she learns that Max Vickery was killed, she may spill everything she knows. Want to go along?"

"Sure," I said.

"Phylana was trying to be Max's girl friend," Guffy explained. "At least that's what the boy Horace Greeley told me. Shall we use my car or yours?"

"We'll use mine," said the sheriff. "I get mileage."

As long as we were using the sheriff's car, I put mine in the parking lot of the apartment house and rode with them.

We didn't turn at the road running east to Sherm Sydney's place, but instead we continued south till we passed the filling station where I'd stopped after the rain yesterday morning. I saw the sleepy attendant outside fixing a tire. A little farther on was another road, running east I told Guffy to turn and the street took us right up to Phylana's cottage. We parked in the drive.

It still looked deserted, as it had the first time I went past the place early this morning.

"Maybe she's still in the hay," said Guffy.

We climbed out of the car and walked up to the front door. I rattled the brass knocker, but there was no sound from within. "Sound sleeper," said the sheriff.

I had an uneasy feeling, which was, by this time, natural. I'd already turned up two corpses in two days. "Let's go around to the back."

I started and they followed. "I've got a feeling something is wrong," I added.

"You're crazy," said the sheriff.

"Don't ever argue with him when he says something like that," said Guffy. "This boy has hunches."

I led the way around to the back. The back door was locked and I pounded on it "Let's break in," I said.

"Don't be silly," said the sheriff. "You know damn well we've got no right to do that without a warrant."

The door didn't fit very well. And through the cracks around it I smelled something.

"Gas!" I said. "Smell it?"

The sheriff sniffed. "By God, you're right."

I backed up and threw my weight against the door. Then I screamed with pain. In the excitement I'd forgotten about my cracked rib.

"Out of the way," said the sheriff. I limped aside, still aching. He swung his huge foot. The door splintered. Then he threw his shoulder against it. There was a sound of ripping wood and the door crashed inward.

A wave of gas-laden air struck us in the face. I followed the sheriff into the house and into the bedroom.

Guffy halted by the gas stove long enough to turn off all four burners and the oven.

In the bedroom there was more gas. At one time somebody had had a gas heater installed there. One of the old-fashioned kind which fits with a rubber hose. The heater was no longer used, but the petcock was still there and it had been turned on.

The sheriff halted.

Phylana Kane, fully dressed, lay on the bed. I couldn't tell whether she was breathing or not.

I picked up a small chair and heaved it through the window.

"That was a silly thing to do," said Sheriff Lindley.

He reached down with both hands, picked her up and then carried her out into the back yard as if she were a baby.

TWELVE

The ground sloped upward in back till it met the hill on which Sherman Sydney's house was located.

Sheriff Lindley found a nice grassy spot without wasting any time looking around, and he put Phylana down on it, with her head toward the house. He turned to me and said, "Get blankets!"

I ran back into the house. Guffy had opened the kitchen window. He hung with his head outside, phoning for the cops to bring an ambulance.

I found a blanket at the foot of the bed and another stored away in a cedar chest in the bedroom. I came back and found Guffy had finished his call and was examining the lock on the window. There wasn't time to ask questions, and I hurried out through the door. Sheriff Lindley had turned Phylana over on her belly and was applying the Holger-Nielsen back pressure, arm lift method of artificial respiration. It's an easy method to apply, especially over the long haul, since it's not as exhausting for the operator as other methods.

He was at her head, reaching over it with both hands planted just below the shoulder blades. He'd press down, then lift her by grasping her arms just above the elbows.

I spread one blanket over her and then managed to push the other under her body as the sheriff lifted her. Finally we arranged her so that she was lying on one blanket.

When I finished I heard sirens, and very soon afterwards an ambulance pulled into the drive behind my car. Two uniformed cops came running around the house from a squad car in front.

One of the cops was Henderson, the officer I'd met at the Highland Heights police station that morning.

An interne brought a pulmotor from the ambulance and in a jiffy he'd fixed the mask over her nose and mouth and started a small battery-powered motor running. Then the sheriff leaned back and wiped the sweat off his brow.

The interne took a stethoscope and put it against the girl's back and side, listening. "A close squeak," he said. "Lucky you fellows found her in time."

Henderson moved over to the sheriff. "How'd you happen to come out here, sheriff?" he asked. "Still working on the Sydney case?"

The sheriff nodded and glanced past the cop toward Guffy, who was trying to look innocent. "There's been a second killing," said Lindley. "Guffy, over there, thinks it ties in."

The cop swung around. He must have known Guffy, because he frowned.

"We didn't expect to find anything like this," said Guffy, "or we'd have dropped in on you boys first."

I was enjoying this. It's cop courtesy, when an officer goes into a town to visit the local police—if he's on business—to take a local cop along. Even the sheriff does this, except when he's serving papers in civil suits.

"You never know what you're going to run into," said Henderson. "If you'd given us a buzz, we could have talked to this girl. Maybe we'd have been here a lot quicker."

"It almost wasn't quick enough," said the interne. He was using a hypodermic to shoot something into Phylana's backside.

The cop looked at me. "How come you're in on this?" he asked.

"He's one of my deputies," said the sheriff.

"He told me he was a newspaper reporter," said Henderson.

"Well, he is," said the sheriff.

"Make up your mind," said Henderson. He turned to his partner. "Better herd those folks around to the front of the house." Several people now had crowded around the garage, but they'd stayed a respectable distance away after they noticed the cops. Henderson's partner started to shoo them off, but two women insisted on staying.

"We're her neighbors," said one of them. "I'm Mrs. Blackett, and I live next door, west. This is Mrs. Kampf, she lives next door, east. We want to help if we can."

Guffy spoke to Henderson. "Might be a good idea to talk to them, don't you think, Henderson? They might have seen somebody around here this morning."

"Somebody? Say, what is this? I thought it was an accident."

"Could be. And it could be attempted murder," said Guffy. "The kitchen window was unlocked. Somebody could have climbed in that way."

Henderson signaled his partner, and the two women advanced toward us, their bosoms flopping underneath house dresses.

"Oh, dear! Isn't it awful?" said Mrs. Blackett. "Did the poor thing try to kill herself? I thought, when those two men were fighting over her last night, that something like this would come of it. The poor girl, she was very emotional."

"We don't know exactly what happened, ma'am," said Henderson. "Did you see Miss . . . uh . . . this woman last night?"

Mrs. Blackett looked at Guffy. "Well, not exactly."

"What do you mean 'not exactly'?" Henderson asked.

"Well I heard the back gate close. I was in the kitchen. Over there, you can see my kitchen window." She pointed to the house on the west. "I heard her back gate slam, and I said to myself, 'I'll bet Miss Kane's going up to Mr. Sherman's place for something.'" Again she lowered her voice almost to a whisper. "You know there was a lot of talk around here—not that I believed a word of it—that Miss Kane might have had something to do with it."

"Really?" said Guffy.

"Yes," said Mrs. Kampf. "I heard her go out the night before the murder. Not long afterwards a man came and pounded on her front door, then he came around to the back. He even called her name. He said 'This is Max.' She'd left the light burning in her house, and I guess he thought she was there."

"Did men call often?" said Guffy.

Mrs. Blackett's eyes enlarged knowingly. "Well, of course, we don't know. We don't like to spy—"

"But you, Mrs. Kampf, only heard the gate slam. You never saw anyone this morning?"

"No."

"What time was that?"

"Not long ago. Maybe an hour. I didn't notice the time exactly," said Mrs. Kampf.

"Did she leave a suicide note?" Mrs. Blackett wanted to know.

Guffy shook his head. "I think, ma'am, that somebody tried to kill Miss Kane, and if you saw anyone around here this morning, it may have been the murderer."

"Murder!" Mrs. Blackett gasped.

The interne stood up. "She's breathing naturally now," he said. "I think we'd better get her to the hospital."

"She's still unconscious," said the sheriff.

"Yes," said the interne, "that's what's strange about it. She should have revived before this. Could be there's some brain damage from lack of oxygen."

"Somebody gave her sleeping pills," Guffy said. "There was a box beside her bed. Also a glass that had contained milk. It was empty except for a little in the bottom. Anybody at the hospital that could examine that glass?"

"Sure," said the interne. "Bring it to the hospital."

"I'll look it over for prints," said Henderson quickly.

"Good idea," said Guffy. He was doing his best to make Henderson feel wanted.

Guffy went into the house and returned with the glass in a paper bag.

The interne and the ambulance driver went to their meat wagon and got a stretcher, one of the type that has wheels.

Together they lifted the sleeping girl onto it and pushed her over to the ambulance and loaded her into it.

The ambulance started up and backed out of the drive.

"Come on, Henderson," said Guffy. "Let's dust this glass and then we'll take it over to the hospital and see how well she was doped."

"I'll ride with Henderson," said Guffy, turning away from Mrs. Kampf. "Mike will go with you, sheriff."

Sheriff Lindley and I didn't go into the station. We waited outside and talked to Henderson's partner. I never did get his name. I didn't try to. The Highland Heights cops had thrown me in jail the night before, and I wasn't going to make heroes of them by using their names in my story.

Guffy and Henderson came out of the hospital together. They both got in the car with us, taking the back seat.

"Find anything?" the sheriff asked.

"Wiped clean," said Guffy. "If that doesn't prove it's murder, nothing else does."

"You can pick up a glass without leaving prints," said Henderson.

"You won't leave prints, but at least you'll leave a smudge," Guffy told him. Henderson didn't answer.

At the hospital we found the resident physician who had examined Phylana. "She's sleeping now," he said. "If she took sleeping pills, she didn't take enough to harm her. We decided, finally, she's better off sleeping."

"How long before we can talk to her, doc," said Guffy. "This is attempted murder, and maybe she can tell us who made the attempt."

"If you did awaken her now, she'd probably be too weak and too groggy to be of much help," said the doctor. "Why not let her sleep for an hour or so?"

"Because, doc," said Guffy, "time's important."

"Well, it wouldn't do much good to wake her for at least forty-five minutes."

"Who do we give this to for analysis?"

"There's a technician in the lab," said the doctor. "Is that the stuff someone gave her?"

"Yes," said Guffy. He reached into his pocket and pulled out the box of sleeping tablets. "This is what we found beside her bed. Probably the same stuff that was in the milk, but we want to know whether it was in the milk or not."

The doctor took the glass and sniffed. He shook his head. "Can't tell from the odor, of course, but I don't think it's the same."

"Why not?"

Doc was thoughtful. He opened the box and counted the pills. "These are barbiturates," he said. "Prescriptions are usually for twelve, and there are twelve in this box. Of course she may have had some on hand and put them in the same box, but I don't think her sleep is right for a barbiturate; she's a little too restless."

"What else? A Mickey Finn?" Guffy asked.

"We'll find out," said the doctor. Guffy gave him the glass and doc went off to have it analyzed.

We waited for a little while and Doc returned smiling. "Besides milk there were traces of scopolamine aminoxide, methapyrilene and salicylamide," he said.

"Sounds like aspirin and truth serum," I said.

Doc looked at me like a night club performer scowls at a heckler. "Truth serum is sodium pentothal and aspirin is acetylsalicylic add. The drugs I mentioned are ingredients of those new non-barbiturate sleeping pills. A patent medicine, but harmless if taken as directed. However, Miss Kane had an overdose. I judge she took the equivalent of about five tablets in her glass of milk."

Guffy whistled. "Quite a bit, huh?"

Doc nodded. "One or two is the normal dosage. Five aren't dangerous to most people, but I wouldn't advise it. We've been giving Miss Kane stimulants and we'll have her awake in about fifteen minutes. She'll have a jag, but coffee will bring her out of it." He went away.

It was a little after two o'clock when Guffy, the sheriff, Henderson and I got to see Phylana Kane.

She was propped up in a hospital bed, wearing one of those ungodly hospital nightgowns. Her eyes were droopy and she was pale, but she managed to throw a smile my way after she nodded at Sheriff Lindley. The sheriff introduced Guffy and Henderson, whom she knew by sight. "You had a close call, Miss," said Henderson. It was his territory and he took charge.

"That's what the nurse told me," she said. "Did someone really try to kill me?"

"Unless you tried it yourself." Henderson watched her closely.

"I didn't. I had no reason to kill myself," she said. "But I can't understand why anyone would want to kill me."

"Guffy and Sheriff Lindley think the attempt has a connection with the murder of Mr. Sydney," the officer said.

"I don't know how it could. I was only Sherm's secretary."

"Maybe you knew something?"

She shook her head. "Nothing connected with the murder."

"Someone put sleeping tablets in your milk, Miss Kane," said Guffy. "Do you know when it was done? Any visitors last night?"

"Only Mike," she said, looking at me. "Max Vickery was here . . . uh . . . briefly. He and Mike got in a fight."

Henderson scowled at me. "Vickery's dead, and she's had a narrow escape. How about it, reporter?"

"I didn't dope her milk," I said. "And I never saw Vickery alive after the last time he punched me. But something did happen last night that might shed a light on this. I thought I heard a noise at the back door. I opened it and saw somebody on the path leading up the hill toward Sydney's place. Then Phylana . . . uh, Miss Kane . . . saw a bottle of milk on the doorstep. I remarked at the time I hadn't heard a milk truck."

"Is that right, Miss Kane?" Henderson looked at her.

"Yes," she said. "That's the milk I had for breakfast."

"How'd the would-be murderer know when you'd drink it?"

"Maybe he was watching the house and saw the regular delivery," I said. "He could have swiped the milk, doped it and brought it back later. The murderer probably figured it wouldn't be used till today."

"Yeah, but how'd he know she used it today?"

Phylana said, "I know. The telephone call."

"What call?"

"The phone rang about eleven o'clock. I was still asleep; I'd had such a trying day yesterday. It woke me up. I answered the phone and heard a click, as if somebody had hung up. I went back to bed, but couldn't sleep, so I got up and dressed. It was about noon when I drank my milk. Soon afterwards I began to feel drowsy. I lay down on the bed and I heard the phone ring again, but I was just too tired and I didn't get up. That's the last I remember until the doctor woke me up."

Henderson looked at Guffy, who nodded. "That sounds like our boy," he said. "He knew you were still awake at eleven, so he tried an hour later. There were enough pills in the milk to keep you knocked out for several hours, so he finished off Vickery, then tried to call you again. When you didn't answer, he came out, turned on the gas and almost got away with murder."

"Vickery?" she asked. "Did you say Vickery?"

Guffy nodded solemnly. "Yes, Miss Kane. Somebody killed him this morning. He was shot the same way Sydney was."

She closed her eyes. Her tiny fists, lying outside the covers, clenched and unclenched. "Poor Max! He called me last night, after Mike . . . er . . . left." She opened her eyes and looked at me. "He said he was sorry for what happened, Mike, but he thought you had it coming for the way you mistreated Ella. I told him that it was all Ella's fault."

"He got a lot worse punishment for his misdeeds than I got," I said.

"Maybe he doped that milk," said Henderson.

"Oh, no. Max said he came here last night to tell me he was going to sign a contract with Arnoth to draw *Dream Man*. He wanted me to stay on as his secretary."

She turned over and hid her face in her pillow.

"Miss Kane," said Guffy softly. She turned her head. "The murderer thinks you know something. Maybe you don't know yourself what it is that is a threat to him, but something which was responsible for Sydney's death, and probably Vickery's death, is probably locked up in your mind. Think hard! Did anything happen Friday, or any other time this week that might have a bearing on the case?"

She blinked her eyes and did not speak for several moments. Her eyes were red, but no longer droopy. "Sherm said something Friday that struck me as odd," she said. "He said, 'To hell with the readers; they don't know what they want. To hell with Arnoth. To hell with you, Nora. To hell with everybody. This is my strip and I'm going to run it the way I want.'"

"He was talking to Miss Donovan at the time?" Guffy asked.

She nodded her head.

"What did Miss Donovan say?"

"She said, 'You can't help pleasing somebody no matter what you do, Sherm. So you can't damn everybody with your crazy ideas.'"

THIRTEEN

Phylana Kane hadn't added much to what we already knew. It seemed clear, as we went to the Highland Heights police station, that the murderer had planned to pin the other killings on Phylana by making her death appear to be suicide.

Henderson, who seemed to be showing more intelligence than I'd given him credit for at first, agreed and added that it might have fooled us if a forged note had been placed beside the body.

"Maybe and maybe not," said Guffy. "We're dealing with a smart killer. He knew that it takes skill to forge a note. Maybe he didn't have the time or the skill. Besides, he knew we'd compare it with Miss Kane's handwriting."

"You'd think an artist could do it," Henderson persisted.

"An artist would be just the person who'd know how hard it is to get by with a forgery," Guffy said. "And before I forget it, I told the boys at headquarters to pick up Gervais. There hasn't been any word, has there?" He looked at Henderson who shook his head.

"Maybe he's spending the afternoon with Arnoth," I said. "That's where he was last time. Personally, I think you're overlooking a few things if you try to pin this job on Gervais."

"He expected to get the comic strip," said Guffy, "and he killed Sydney. When Arnoth decided on Vickery instead, he killed Vickery. Open and shut."

"Arnoth's got the closest thing to an alibi in this case," I said. "Why don't you suspect him?"

"Mike," said Guffy, "stop batting your gums around. Why do you suspect the only person in the case that has an alibi?"

"Who'd be careful enough to have an alibi by six a.m. unless they expected to use it?" I said. "Arnoth arranged to have Gervais stay all night. Maybe Arnoth arranged to have Gervais picked up by the FBI. Of course, Gervais got up and left early, and Arnoth had no reason to expect that, but the fact that he did simply helped Arnoth's plans. Arnoth got up and left immediately after Gervais. The alibi isn't worth a hoot."

"The fact that Gervais got up early *is* suspicious to me," said Henderson.

"Okay, but how about the two women—Nora Donovan and Ella Aldwin?"

"Both of them showed up at the scene of the crime the next morning, for one thing," said Guffy. "I don't think they'd have risked it if they did the killing."

"Maybe that's what they wanted you to think," I said.

"Okay, supposing it was for effect," said Guffy. "Ella had a chance to kill Sydney the night before and didn't. And Miss Donovan didn't have a way to get to Sydney's place unless she used public transportation and risked being seen by witnesses."

"She could have borrowed a car," I suggested.

"Whose?"

"Anybody's. Vickery's maybe."

"And killed him for his kindness?"

"What we've got to crack," said Henderson, "is the motive."

I'd been thinking about motive quite a bit. I had a hazy notion since I saw the strips that I knew it. But I didn't know whom it applied to.

"If you ask me," I said, "we haven't eliminated anybody but Max Vickery and Phylana Kane."

"And Arnoth," said the sheriff.

"He must be able to swing votes," I said. "Otherwise you wouldn't be so damned hot trying to keep him off the suspect list."

"Okay," said the sheriff, "I'll throw in Miss Donovan as clear. She isn't even a voter in this county. Legal residence is in Florida."

"Then on your list, sheriff," I said, "there's Gervais, Ella Aldwin and her father, Dick Aldwin."

"With special emphasis on Gervais," said the sheriff,

"He's the *only* one on my list," said Guffy. He turned to the sheriff, "Let's go back to town and see if we can't dig him up."

"Suits me," said the sheriff. "It's a cinch he won't be here where we can tie the attempt on Miss Kane on him."

"Coming, Mike?" Guffy got to his feet and looked at me.

"Looks like I'll have to if I don't want to ride the Greyhound back to town."

We shook hands with Henderson, and Guffy said he'd keep in touch with him in case Henderson got more information out of Phylana later. Then we started out

As we got in the car, I had a bright idea. "I'd like to see the script for next week's series of strips, Clyde. Wonder if we can't commit a little burglary on Sydney's studio and find it?"

"I've got a key," said the sheriff, "and the legal right to look for evidence in a crime. It might not be a bad idea, Mike."

We circled and came up on the other side of the hill.

We drove up the driveway, and just as we made the left turn that brought us parallel with the south door of the house, Sheriff Lindley put on the brakes. A car was parked in the driveway ahead. Standing there, watching us, was Jet Gervais.

The sheriff set the brakes on the car, and he and Guffy sprang out so quickly that I was left seated alone in the car while they grabbed Gervais by each arm.

It was all so fast that Gervais was nearly scared out of his senses.

"Let go!" he said, twisting and squirming. "Take your dirty hands off me."

"In a pig's eye," said Guffy. "We've been looking for you all morning. You're coming in to town to answer a lot of questions, Gervais."

"I've already told you all I know," said Gervais.

"What are you doing here?" the sheriff asked.

By this time, I was out of the sheriff's car and standing by Guffy s side, taking it all in.

Gervais nodded his head toward the back seat of his car, a Rambler coach. "I came out to get some of my stuff," he said. A T square, a box of paints, a box which probably contained penholders and penpoints, and several cigar boxes with rubber bands around them were in the car.

"Getting ready to take a powder, hey?"

Gervais was angry now. "Is this an arrest?"

"No, we just want to talk to you."

"Then turn me loose. You don't have to hang onto my arms to talk to me."

The sheriff nodded to Guffy, who patted Gervais's pockets and waistband to make sure he wasn't carrying a gun. Then they turned him loose.

"All right," said Guffy. "Where have you been all morning?"

"At my hotel during the first part of the morning. I went to church, had dinner and then drove out here."

"How long you been here?"

"Since about one-thirty."

"Come now! You were here at twelve-thirty. You were here earlier than that—about ten o'clock, let's say."

"Okay, you know so much, you tell *me* what I've been doing today."

I could see Guffy signaling Sheriff Lindley with his eyes. "All right, Gervais," Guffy said. "You tell your story and we'll listen. Did you know that Max Vickery was slated to get the job as *Dream Man* cartoonist?"

Gervais nodded. "Arnoth told me yesterday. And I talked to Vickery over the phone. He offered to keep me on as assistant, even with a raise in pay. I told him I'd have to think it over."

"You expected to get the job, didn't you?"

Slowly Gervais nodded his head. "Yes, frankly, I did. Until I talked to Arnoth yesterday I thought I was in line for it. Arnoth told me—after you left, Lanson—that he wanted to use Vickery, and that he'd keep me on, doing something else—maybe a new feature, if I could develop one. He said Vickery had met his terms, but the contract wasn't signed."

"Know about the terms?" Guffy's eyes narrowed.

"I gathered that he'd get the same kind of a deal most new artists get when they take over somebody else's strip," Gervais said. "You see, a man's over a barrel when he doesn't have his own creation to sell. He really has no legal right. The syndicate owns the strip and there are a lot of damned fools who'd draw a strip for peanuts just for a start. Vickery wouldn't get anywhere near what Sherm got for drawing it. Arnoth would pay him a straight guarantee, maybe two hundred and fifty, maybe three hundred a week. It would be charged against royalties from *new business*. He wouldn't get anything from papers that bought the strip while Sherm drew it. Arnoth would take all that himself."

"Doesn't sound fair."

"Arnoth had a way of making you feel he was doing you a favor."

"Then you were out cold," said Guffy.

"No," Gervais said quickly. "I had a five-year contract with Arnoth. It became effective the moment Sherm stopped drawing the strip—for death or any other reason. Arnoth had to find work for me at the same salary, or better, in his organization."

"Is that the usual thing in this business?" the sheriff asked.

"All syndicates don't do it, but Arnoth and a few others do it with a man they think can do them some good later on. I've got no complaints. That contract was one reason why I kept working for Sherm instead of trying to develop a feature of my own. I always figured I'd have a chance at *Dream Man* some day."

"What about Miss Donovan and Miss Aldwin?" Guffy asked. "Were they out too?"

"I don't know about Ella," said Gervais, "but I talked to Nora yesterday, before I talked to Arnoth. She said Arnoth had told her he had plans for her, but she wasn't sure she wanted to do anything unless it was writing the *Dream Man* script. She didn't think she could handle another type of thing."

"Then Arnoth must have hinted that she'd be taken off *Dream Man?*" I asked.

"I don't know about that," said Gervais, "but when I talked to Vickery—"

"You talked to Vickery, huh? When was that?" Guffy asked.

"Last night. He called me at the hotel. He wanted me to know that he hadn't tried to cut me out. Arnoth hired him on the basis of a sports feature Vickery had submitted a couple of months ago. Vickery claimed he had no idea that Arnoth was going to put *Dream Man* in his lap."

"What did Vickery say about, Miss Donovan?"

"He said he was going to keep her on as a writer, but he thought maybe he'd try doing some of the stories himself."

"When was the last time you saw Phylana Kane, Gervais?"

Jet thought a moment. "Not since Friday, I guess."

"You sure? Weren't you over to see her this morning?"

"I told you, Friday was the last time I saw her. If you don't believe me, why don't you ask her?"

"I will," said Guffy. "Did you see Vickery today?"

"No. I haven't seen Vickery since the last meeting of the Society for Artists. I just told you though that I talked to him on the phone last night."

"You sure you didn't talk to him this morning—in person?"

"What are you trying to get at?"

"Did you know somebody tried to kill Phylana Kane?"

"No!" Gervais leaned against his car for support. "Is she . . . uh . . . all right?"

"Yes. She'll get over it."

Gervais eyes narrowed. "You think Vickery or I did it?"

"It couldn't have been Vickery."

"Vickery had been going around with her."

"Vickery is dead. He was shot this morning."

Gervais wiped his brow. "And you suspect me? Why?"

"I think you'd better come to the station with me," Guffy said. "We want a full statement about everything you've done since Friday afternoon. And that includes your *tête-a-tête* with the FBI."

Gervais nodded slowly. "Of course. I've nothing to hide. Mind if I park this junk at my hotel?"

He pointed to the stuff in his car.

"You'd better ride with us," Guffy said. "Mike will drive your car to the station and lock it. Your things will be safe."

"You're arresting me?"

"Just questioning you. I think you've been lying. I think you know who killed Sydney and Vickery and who tried to kill Miss Kane."

"I don't." Gervais was scared now. "I don't know anything. I want to see a lawyer."

"That's what they all say. Come on. Get into the sheriff's car."

"Listen—"

"You can talk when you get to the station. Better think over your story again and make it good this time." Guffy turned to me. "Drive his car to the station, Mike. See you later."

He shoved Gervais in his car, and I stood there and watched them drive off.

FOURTEEN

It was a little after two-thirty on Sunday afternoon, May 10. I was alone at the scene of a violent crime which had taken place less than thirty-two hours before.

I'd been operating on the theory, since I discovered Sherman S. Sydney's body yesterday morning, that the clue to the whole business was in the missing comic strips. Even if Gervais were lying, I didn't think he fitted into the picture in a way that a comic strip could solve.

I was alone, and since I had no inhibition against trespassing, or even non-felonious burglary, I felt that maybe some hint as to the meaning of the changed last frame in the July 4 strip would remain in Sherman Sydney's studio.

I went around to the side door of the garage. It was unlocked. I was glad that Gervais had been picked up because nobody had given Gervais a chance to lock the door.

Up the stairway I went, and found the studio door not only unlocked but wide-open. Somebody had scrubbed the blood spots from the composition floor. I presumed it had been done by Phylana. But the place looked messier than before. This was to be expected. Sheriff Lindley had said that some Creston specialists had been out from the police lab, and in addition Art Gervais had been here collecting his materials.

There were pencils, erasers and paint tubes on the floor.

Over in one corner were two filing cabinets. Neither had locks on them and I opened the first. It was filled with envelopes containing etcher's proofs of the strips. Each envelope was dated, and I noticed they ran back about seven years. Another drawer was devoted to tabloid-size Sunday pages, mostly black and white, but some in color.

Another drawer was labeled *Old Scripts.*

I turned to the second filing cabinet and looked for the labels in the slot on each drawer. *Current Scripts* was the top drawer. I opened it and found the script for June 29 to July 4 on top. I shuffled through these to the last script and read the last frame.

It ran like this:

4—Close-up of Glenda's reaction to her realization that Commando Green is to leave her life forever. Use expression No. 8, three-quarters' view with light coming from Glenda's left. Her head is slightly bowed, and a single tear courses down her right cheek. No balloons. We'll repeat this scene in frame one of Monday's strip, and let her bring the reader up to date with a balloon. Make it good, Sherm. I know this is a holiday strip but we've got to give holiday readers something besides firecrackers!

That was the picture that Art Gervais had ghosted for Sherman Sydney. The altered version, unghosted, had not followed Nora's script.

I looked for later copy but could find none. Possibly Nora intended to write it over the week end, or perhaps Monday morning. Somebody had said six strips took three days to draw. In that case, Wednesday morning would be the deadline for copy.

In the bottom drawer of the filing cabinets I found a small folder containing about a dozen snapshot pictures of Ella Aldwin in various poses, and wearing various expressions. These had been made by one of those Polaroid cameras which develop pictures immediately after they are taken. One of the shots showed Ella slapping a bust of Shakespeare on the cheek.

I stuck this photo in my pocket and went down the stairs. Fortunately, I found Gervais's car keys in the ignition. My watch said three-thirty, and my stomach told me I hadn't eaten for a long, long time. I drove down to the airport, parked and went into the Sky Lounge for a chicken dinner.

Afterwards I had another bright idea. I went around to where there were a number of shops. I went into an office and talked to a man named Wainwright. He wasn't very helpful at first, but after I got down to cases he remembered what I wanted to know.

When I came away from the airport I had everything figured out. I knew who had killed Sherm Sydney and why. First I drove to police headquarters, left the keys with Sergeant Russell and got him to call in a squad car, which drove me to Vickery's apartment, where I'd left my own car.

Then I drove back to police headquarters and asked Russell if I could talk to Lieutenant Guffy.

"He's busy," said the sergeant.

"Tell him I'm in the press room," I said.

"He'll probably be busy for a long time," said Russell. He didn't know that I knew what Guffy was busy with.

Jimmy Brandt, the *Globe's* police reporter did a double take as I came through the door. "Jeez," he said. "I thought you got canned." He was sitting at his desk, typing with two fingers.

"Temporarily suspended," I amended. "I'll probably go back to work Monday."

"What you doing here today if you're suspended?" he asked suspiciously. I wasn't supposed to work on Sunday, except at double time.

"I'm moonlighting," I said. I glanced at the electric clock on the wall. It was only a little past four-thirty. "You're on the job a little early, aren't you?"

"Russell tipped me off that Guffy and the sheriff just brought in Art Gervais for questioning in the Sydney and Vickery murders. I'm getting out a night lead for the bulldog in case the story doesn't bust before then."

"Think they'll wrap it up?"

"Russell thinks it's a cinch."

I sat down at my desk, pulled up the top allowing the typewriter to pop into position. I got some copy paper, pencil and carbon paper from a drawer.

Brandt watched me amusedly, "Writing a novel?"

"Maybe I'll settle for a novelette or a short story," I said.

Brandt finished his lead, and I made some notes on my copy paper. It was nice to be able to write a story leisurely, without Hank Newcomb yelling at me or calling me on the phone. It was almost a new experience not to be pressing a deadline.

I finished an outline of my story and wondered if Arnoth could sell it to fifty or sixty newspapers. It wasn't going to be a news story in the strictest sense. It was what you might call an interpretive yarn. A story that interpreted a murder in the whop and wham industry.

Brandt stopped typing and went to the john. I picked up the telephone and dialed Arnoth.

The syndicate head answered pleasantly, and when I told him I had everything in my pocket but the arrest, he chortled with joy, "They're questioning Art Gervais now," I said.

He stopped chortling and groaned. "Not Gervais! It mustn't be him. I've got to use him to draw the strip now that Vickery is . . . uh . . . unavailable."

He was so damned eager to work things out so they'd fit into his own little scheme of things that I decided to let him suffer. "Well, I'll see what I can do about it," I said.

"But we can't send out a story yet—not until an actual arrest is made," Arnoth cautioned. "You know a story doesn't have to get printed to be libelous. Some years back a story got on the wires and wasn't even printed, but a party collected damages because the telegraphers read it."

"I'll be very careful," I said, remembering that I would be a party in any lawsuit brought for libel. "I think I can prove the guilt of the person who killed Sydney."

"But you've told the police?"

"Not yet," I said.

Arnoth was silent for a few moments, then he said, "Mike, if you know who did this thing, and can prove it, is there any way you can keep the police out of it till . . . well for a few hours?"

"It's my duty—"

"I didn't ask you what your 'duty' was, Mike. Can you?"

"The murderer isn't where the cops can lay hands on him," I said. "But I don't want to get into a jam with the cops either.

I might be accused of obstructing justice or withholding evidence in a murder case."

"I've got a good lawyer."

"Even good ones lose when the law's plain," I said. "But I'll tell you what, Mr. Arnoth. My proof is good, but it's circumstantial. Nobody saw Sydney or Vickery murdered, but I can prove that only *one* person had a good motive to kill Sydney, and that Vickery's death was a direct result. I can make it stronger if I can get a confession. That's what I intend to do."

"You're going to meet the murderer?"

"Yes," I said. "The murderer is going to know that I know. He'll do something about it."

"It's a man then?"

"I was using 'he' because there's no word in the English language that means he-or-she, either one."

"Mike, if you could keep this thing from breaking before midnight, it would mean a lot more money for you."

"You trying to bribe me, Mr. Arnoth?"

"Of course not. But after midnight it'll be an afternoon story. There are only fourteen morning papers that I know will buy this story. There are about forty evening sheets. We'll lose some of the evening papers if it goes into a morning paper first."

I thought it over. "How much of a difference?"

"Well, we charge on the basis of circulation. The morning papers will average twenty or twenty-five dollars apiece; they've got the largest circulations. Afternoon papers will average about fifteen or twenty, but there are more of them. We'd pick up some P.M.'s even if the morning papers used the story first, but there might be a hundred dollars difference."

"Ain't worth it," I said, feeling like I lit cigars with hundred-dollar bills.

"Well, remember that if you can postpone the arrest, do it."

"If I try to postpone it," I said, "there may be another murder—mine. I'd rather lose a hundred dollars than my life."

Arnoth sighed. "Well, it's not very good business, but if you see it that way, go ahead." Not very good business for him, maybe. "I'll start to overhead the queries right away." Overhead in this case meant sending a telegraph query to the prospective client.

Brandt hadn't come back from the john, and I risked dialing Colonel Tanner's home. His housekeeper said he'd gone over to Mr. Aldwin's house. Before I could call there, Brandt came in.

"Nothing new on Gervais," he said. "Dammit, Mike, wouldn't you like to play leg man for me? Might help you get your job back."

"Nope," I said. "I want to work on my novel. Why don't you call Don Hillard. He'd like to grab a few bucks overtime."

"I tried, but I can't reach him."

"Well, if you want to check, I'll watch the shop."

"Thanks, Mike." Brandt disappeared through the door.

I dialed Aldwin's number and Ella answered. "This is Mike Lanson," I told her. "Colonel Tanner's housekeeper said he was at your place."

"Oh yes, Mike," she said, much sweeter than I'd ever heard her voice. "He's been trying to reach you all day. Where have you been keeping yourself?"

"Around," I said.

"Did you hear about that awful thing that happened to Max!"

"Yes," I said. "And Phylana Kane."

"Father won't even let me stay in my apartment," she said. "He's afraid someone might try to murder me."

"I think the case will be solved before long," I said. "The police are working on it. May I talk to Colonel Tanner now?"

"Yes, Mike. He and father have ironed everything out. I'll call the colonel and he'll tell you. Hang on."

I hung on and then Colonel Tanner's sonorous voice came over the wire, "Mike, you bastard, where have you been all day? I've been trying to reach you since ten o'clock this morning."

"Hither and yon, sir," I told him.

"Did you know there's been another murder? Of course you do. I wouldn't have you on my payroll if you didn't know what was going on."

"Am I on your payroll, colonel?"

"Of course you are. What happened yesterday was all a mistake. That business of firing you was Hank Newcomb's idea. I'll make his tailbone burn for that."

"Don't be hard on him, colonel."

"Well, he deserves it. You're on the payroll without loss of pay, and if you did any work last night or today, you'll get overtime, plus expenses."

There were a few expenses I'd like to chisel out of him: a new suit of clothes, a doctor bill for taping a cracked rib, gasoline and bus fares, and a few phone calls. But I said, "That's generous of you, colonel, but I don't want any overtime, and I don't want any expense money."

"What's that you say? I never have heard a reporter say a thing like that."

"Let's just say I'm on leave of absence, starting at noon yesterday and ending whatever time I get to work tomorrow," I told him.

"Mike, you've gone stark, raving mad."

"I just want to feel free for a few hours."

"Knowing your crafty little mind, I'll swear you've got some scheme up your sleeve. What are you bucking for, a raise?"

"I wouldn't object to that, colonel, providing it started tomorrow, but I don't want to be on the payroll till then."

"Mike, have you solved these murders? Are you selling out to somebody else? Has one of the radio stations got to you?"

"A radio station, sir!" I managed to get a note of horror into my voice. "How can you say such a thing!"

"Well, this runaround sounds damned fishy to me."

"You're saving a day-and-a-half pay, most of it overtime." I reminded him.

That got through to his heart, if he had one. "Hmm. Well, I don't like this idea, but I guess I owe you something. My treatment of you was shabby. But don't forget, I can get another reporter if you've stabbed me in the back."

"Sir, I don't like to have you suspicious of me. I'm doing nothing competitive. Nothing that will harm the *Gazette* or the *Globe.*"

"You'll give your word?"

"Yes, sir." I almost clicked my heels together and saluted.

"I believe you, Mike. I'll see you tomorrow. Try to get to work on time for a change."

"I will, sir. Good-bye, sir."

I hung up the phone.

FIFTEEN

I hoped that Jimmy Brandt would stay downstairs for a while. I still had another call to make.

I dialed the Hotel Creston. Nora Donovan wasn't in her room, so I left word for her to call.

Since time was running out, I decided to start writing. I could guess the answers to most of the questions that could be verified when I talked to Nora.

From my desk I took a sheet of carbon paper and stuck it between two sheets of copy paper. I stopped, got another carbon and added another sheet of copy paper. I had decided to cut the *Globe* in for free. Mr. Arnoth had to let me do that.

I started writing the story:

> An attempt of a man to control his own destiny today was given the responsibility for provoking the murders of two cartoonists and the attempted slaying of a pretty secretary.
>
> The dead are Sherman S. Sydney, 37, creator of the world-famous comic strip *Dream Man*, and Maxwell Vickery, 28, sports cartoonist for the Creston *Gazette* and its morning edition, the *Globe*. Recovering at the Highland Heights hospital, near Creston, is Miss Phylana Kane, Sydney's 25-year-old blond secretary.

Sydney, whose strip appears in about 150 U.S. and Canadian newspapers and is translated into several foreign languages and appears in other papers all over the world, and Vickery, who was named to become his successor, were shot by a .32 caliber pistol. Miss Kane was rendered unconscious by non-barbiturate sleeping pills put in her milk by the murderer, who then opened the gas jets in her small home in Highland Heights.

An arrest was made early tonight by Lieutenant Clyde Guffy of the Creston Police Department, and Lake County sheriff August Lindley. On first degree murder charges. . . .

I stopped typing for a moment, remembering that if I named someone before the actual arrest was made, I would be laying myself wide-open for a libel suit. I left a space to insert the name of the murderer, then went on with my story.

While philosophers have debated for centuries on the subject of free will and whether any man is master of his fate, developments in the Sydney case show that a comic strip artist, at least, cannot under *any* circumstances control his creation, his own destiny lies within the borders of his strip.

The chain of events began with Sydney's effort to live his own life and to bring a measure of comic strip happiness to the character of his creation, Commando Green, known to fifteen million readers as *Dream Man*.

The vital clue was a redrawn picture in the strip dated for release on Saturday, July 4. The killer apparently had been long aware that Sydney planned an insurrection, and a decision had been reached that Sydney would be killed, if necessary, to stop him. Perhaps a gun was purchased in an out-of-the-way pawnshop for this purpose.

Sydney, an extremely gifted cartoonist, was the victim of complex events, all of which worked in favor of the murderer.

It is not unusual, in the peculiar calling of comic strip production, for the artist, upon whom many others depend for a livelihood, to have very little control over his creation. The strip itself is owned by the syndicate, which as a matter of policy, has the right to accept or reject the material which Sydney submitted. There were also the editors of client papers, with all shades of tastes and beliefs, who could buy or not buy the strip. Finally there were readers, upon whose interest the success of the strip depended. In Sydney's case, even the story was beyond his control, since it was written by pretty auburn-haired Nora Donovan, to whom Sydney once was married. The divorce was to become final in three weeks.

Sydney himself was not a storyteller, and he relied upon his ex-wife's ability as a fiction writer for the red-blooded performances of Commando Green. Sydney's sole talent was his ability to draw, and nearly all of the work on the daily strip was done by an assistant, Arthur Gervais, 30. Sydney's influence on *Dream Man* was slight.

Although Sydney was, in a sense, a prisoner in the world of fantasy on top of his drawing board, he did not mind for a time. Over the years, he slowly began to identify himself with the swashbuckling hero of his strip. It might be said that he lived each adventure in his mind, traveling the world, bringing villains to brook, and winning the hearts and applause of luscious but fictitious heroines.

There was evidence of this in his own life. He surrounded himself with Miss Donovan, his writer, Miss Ella Aldwin, his assistant, and Miss Kane, his secretary. They were heroines, not only in his strip, but in his life. He was Commando Green, who won the hearts of fair ladies. Then one of these ladies, Miss Aldwin, became his fiancée.

There had been minor rebellions before Miss Aldwin appeared: He would make subtle changes in Miss Donovan's stories; when he got into situations from which he could not extract himself, he got help from Miss Kane.

Miss Donovan expected a certain amount of tinkering with the script. No one in the comic business is master of his creation—too many creative minds are involved.

But now, Sydney decided to find a wife for Commando Green, just as he intended to marry Miss Aldwin. The metamorphosis was complete— Sydney was Green.

Naturally it was unthinkable for Green to get married.

On the afternoon of May 8, a compromise was reached between Sydney and Miss Donovan. It was decided to delay the marriage that Sydney planned. That same afternoon, Sydney quarreled with Miss Aldwin. It was not a coincidence. Sydney had provoked the quarrel by showing extra attentions to Miss Kane in the presence of Miss Aldwin.

The fatal strip, dated July 4, had been drawn according to the compromise of the afternoon of May 8, and was to have been mailed by Gervais. But Sydney decided suddenly *not* to mail these strips. We can only guess his motive, but there seems only one guess. He had decided to make some sort of change.

Gervais thought at first he had lost the strips. There was an unexpected complication when Gervais was questioned by the FBI, according to his own admission, regarding the picturing of a security-wrapped missile in the strip. This was adequately explained, but it served in preventing Miss Donovan, who surmised that Sydney had the strips, from blocking the change. Miss Donovan, who flew here from Florida, had no car and public transportation from Creston to Highland Heights late at night was unsatisfactory for an unescorted woman.

An ad in the Creston *Globe* would have apprised anyone, including the murderer, that the strips were in Sydney's possession. However, we shall soon understand that the murderer already knew.

The picture meanwhile had been changed. Sydney had quarreled with his sweetheart; now he had decided to win her in a red-blooded, highly seasoned, swashbuckling romance. Since he identified himself with the strip, he started the strip moving along the lines that he visualized himself as following.

But at six in the morning Sydney was murdered. The murderer had not seen the strips, but had guessed, or heard from Sydney s own lips, that Sydney had started to control his own destiny via the comic strip. After the slaying, the murderer searched for the changed strip, but failed to find it because Sydney had put them in his own room in his residence. The murderer assumed they had been mailed, but with Sydney dead, the story could be guided back into proper channels. Besides, the strip involved was a holiday strip, not used by papers which do not publish on July 4.

Sydney was killed because he had moved into a situation, which, if developed, would lead *Dream Man* to the marriage altar. In the script prepared by Miss Donovan, *Dream Man* was to bring home the realization to Glenda Ovahead, the current heroine, that he was not the man for her. This was the standard gimmick for taking one heroine out of the story in order to pave the way for the introduction of a new love interest.

Sydney changed the drawing in the last frame of the July 4 strip to show Glenda, not heart-broken with sadness, but reacting with fury, slapping Commando Green as he tried to give her the air.

Slapping is a curious symbol, both in real life and in fiction. People are not really hurt by a slap; they are infuriated. In fiction it is used as a means of heightening conflict between the hero and heroine in order to promote a suspenseful romance, leading to marriage. The formula runs: remorse (for the girl); admiration of the girl's spirit (for the hero); love, marriage.

Because of Sydney's subtle changes, Sydney already had received letters suggesting that *Dream Man* take unto himself a wife. Now he had started movement of the plot toward an inevitable, even if corny, climax that even an inexperienced writer could develop. Green would be either yellow or a cad if he didn't conquer the heart of Glenda Ovahead.

Think what marriage would do to a swashbuckling adventurer like Commando Green. . . .

At this point my telephone rang. I stopped writing to answer it, and I heard the musical voice of Nora Donovan on the line. "Did you call me, Mike?"

"Yes, Nora. Did you know Sherm planned to let Glenda marry Commando Green?" What a hell of a question to ask in a murder case.

There was a long moment of dead silence showing its importance. Then, "Yes, Mike. That's why I flew here for the story conference. I finally dissuaded Sherm from letting it happen immediately. I told him we'd keep Glenda around, use her in succeeding stories, finally let them both fall in love. But I hoped by that time the readers would get sick of the insipid bitch and we could break it off with no harm done. You know Commando Green isn't the marrying kind." I'd guessed right.

"You didn't like Glenda, I take it?"

"I thought our hero deserved something better."

"A man's woman, like yourself?"

Nora laughed musically. "That's the nicest thing I've heard from a man in a long time, Mike. But I'm really not sure what type we'd choose for Commando Green's mate."

"I see. I'm writing a story and I wanted to check on it."

"A story? Is the case solved?"

"Not yet, but soon. The police are questioning Jet Gervais, by the way."

She gasped. "Not Jet!"

"He hasn't been arrested, and the cops may be wrong," I said gently. "Personally, I'm convinced that Jet didn't realize what Sydney was doing to the strip."

"Would that prove Jet wasn't guilty?"

"Yes, but not so a jury would understand it. The murderer knew that Sherman Sydney was Commando Green. What happened to Sherm in real life didn't matter; it was what happened to Commando Green in the comic strip. If Sherm had been able to separate fact from fancy, he wouldn't have been married."

"In other words, the killer didn't care what Sherm did in real life, as long as Sherm didn't try to bring it into the strip?"

"Exactly. Sherm was slightly schizoid."

"Who isn't?" said Nora. "All normal people have abnormal tendencies."

"In Sherm's case his normal abnormalities were abnormal," I said.

She was silent for a moment. "I think I see what you mean. But Sherm didn't have the ability to develop a good romance, even a first-grade story that readers would accept as possible."

"Could anyone else have helped him?"

"Phylana always thought she was a writer. She loused up several of my stories for him."

That then was why Phylana Kane was so interested in getting the strips mailed. That was why she visited Sherm Sydney the night he died. Perhaps she did not know what the change was that he made, or even that he made them, but she must have guessed after she found the strips, and urged him to follow the storyline toward marriage of Commando Green the night before.

"Mike?"

"Yes."

"What are you writing?"

"Arnoth wanted me to do an interpretive story on the murders—why, and all that, included what trapped the killer."

"I thought you said Gervais didn't—"

"He didn't. At least I don't think so."

"Someone else?"

"Yes, but I don't dare mention the name. No one will know until the arrest is made. Only the murderer knows I know."

"Tell me, will you, Mike?"

"When the time comes," I promised. I hung up.

Brandt came up the stairs. He'd been gone more than an hour. "They're still trying to make Gervais confess," he said.

"Is that so?"

"Yeah. He won't admit a thing. Sticks to his story that he hadn't seen Sydney since Friday and Vickery for several days. But they'll break him down. Come on, Mike. You've fooled around long enough. Let's go downstairs and get in on the kill."

"Sorry, chum. I'm no longer one of the working press."

Jimmy looked disdainfully at the pile of typewritten sheets beside my typewriter.

He swore. "I always thought you were a newspaperman, Mike. Any honest-to-God reporter couldn't be kept away from a spot where a murder story was breaking, but you sit here writing the Great American Novel."

"I don't work without pay."

Jimmy snorted his disgust. He picked up the phone and called Taylor, the night boss of the *Globe*. I heard him giving the details while I read over my story.

Murder to keep a comic strip character from getting married sounded weak as hell, if that were the only reason. Like I said, you had to look at what was underneath. That's why Guffy and Sheriff Lindley hadn't tumbled yet.

There was one more call to be made, a toll call to the Highland Heights hospital. I learned that Phylana Kane had left the hospital and had gone home. I tried her home and got no reply. I'd make the change in my story.

I cussed my luck and sorted the originals and carbons into three piles, each making a complete take. One I put into my desk, another I put in a basket for delivery to the *Globe* when the copy boy showed up. The original I put on the copy hook on top of my desk. Then I resumed writing on clean paper:

> Max Vickery's death resulted from the sports cartoonist's agreement to draw *Dream Man* for Arnoth Features.
>
> Vickery, a capable artist with a great deal of creative ability, was undertaking the work eagerly, and he sought to include some of Sydney's aides in his staff. He offered Miss Kane and Miss Donovan their former posts.
>
> The murderer was disturbed at this development.
>
> Vickery's temperament was even less submissive than Sydney's. He was aggressive and would stop at nothing to have his way.
>
> All along it had been assumed that Gervais would be Sydney's successor. Vickery had to be removed.
>
> The slayer believed that the factors that had kept suspicion from the true facts of Sydney's death would again apply in Vickery's death. But Phylana Kane's removal, if made to look like suicide, would serve a double purpose: remove a dangerous person and throw police off the track.

I stopped writing and listened. Someone was coming up the stairway. . . .

SIXTEEN

The sound of footsteps paused at the top of the stairs. I wondered if it was Brandt. But there was a tap of high heels in that sound— A woman was approaching.

Then she came in the doorway. It was Nora Donovan.

She wore a pretty red and white print dress and she carried a light spring coat over her right arm. She was pretty as ever.

"My curiosity got the best of me, Mike," she said. "I want to read the yarn you're doing for Arnoth."

"You know its unethical for a newspaperman to show his story before it gets into print," I said.

"Phooey to ethics," she said, and before I could stop her she took the story off the copy hook. She sat down at Jimmy Brandt's desk and started to read. I lit a cigarette.

When she finished, she put the story on top of the desk and looked at me. "You didn't name the murderer."

"Disappointed?" I asked. "No arrest has been made. It would be libelous if I named anyone."

"I don't think you know who killed Sherm."

I crushed out my cigarette in the brass ash tray on my desk. "Well, isn't it a good story anyhow?"

She shrugged. "Sherm controlled quite a bit of his destiny," she said.

"Not much. You made him successful by creating *Dream Man*. He couldn't have done it by himself. Arnoth ran his life with a contract; you wrote his stories; Phylana took care of his love life; and the readers yelled for more. What did the poor man ever do for himself, except incite his own murder?"

"You've been guessing, Mike."

"Not entirely," I said. "I talked to a fellow named Wainwright today."

"Wainwright? Who's he?" she looked blank.

"He runs a rent-a-car agency at the airport. He rented a car early Friday morning to someone who came out in the airport limousine from downtown. He also rented one about noon, or a little after, today."

"I don't see—"

"It robs you of the one thing that made the police overlook you as a suspect, Nora. You thought you had an alibi—no transportation to the scene of the crime. You knew the sheriff would check taxis and buses, but you also knew it would be pretty tough to check on a rented car, and that probably no one would think of renting a car to commit the murders, or rather murder and attempted murder. But Wainwright remembered you, Nora. You're too damned beautiful to forget easily. You can't explain renting the cars because you told the sheriff you were downtown."

She stood up and picked up her coat, from Brandt's desk. "You're a nice guy, Mike. It's a shame I'll have to kill you."

From the coat pocket she took a tiny .32 caliber automatic, almost exactly like mine, except that it was a pastel blue.

"Too many killings are going to be your undoing, sweetheart," I said. "You won't get away with another."

"They won't catch me, Mike, Sure, you've wrecked my plan, but I've been ready just in case something didn't jell. I've got my money in travelers checks, and I'll take off for Mexico the moment this last job is done. I can live the rest of my life down there on what I've got salted away."

"The police won't let you get far. You haven't got a car."

"I'll have yours," she said. "You'll drive me part of the way, then I'll kill you."

"You missed once. Phylana isn't dead. Maybe you'll miss now," I said. "Why didn't you wave to me last night when I saw you leaving Phylana's?"

"You recognized me?"

I hadn't, but I let her think so. I just laughed. It was not a hearty laugh. I wasn't feeling very brave right now.

"I had to kill Sherm, Mike," she said. "He wanted to marry off Commando Green. I couldn't write it as a domestic strip. I want to write adventure. It was pure corn out of travel books, but the readers liked it. I didn't want to write a fifth-rate soap opera."

"You couldn't," I said.

"No. I couldn't."

"And even if you had got a lot salted away, that income of nearly twenty thousand a year looked pretty good. You wanted to keep it coming in."

"I suppose that's the way I figured. Mostly I was out to stop Sherm from changing my creation. It really was mine, you know. I invented it; Sherm only drew it."

She picked up my story from where she'd put it on Brandt's desk. She tore it in halves, then crumpled each sheet and dropped it in the waste basket. Then she lit it with her cigarette lighter. As the flame licked the sides of the metal waste basket she said, "Give me your carbon copy, Mike."

"Carbon?"

"I know you must have made a carbon. Where is it?" I sighed and got the carbon from my drawer. She crumpled the sheets and dropped them one by one on the blaze as she kept the gun leveled at my belly. I was glad she didn't think of the possibility that I'd made two carbons. But I was beginning to think the other carbon wouldn't do me a hell of a lot of good.

The flame died out, and she took a ruler and stirred up the ashes. Then she said, "Get your hat. We're going out."

"What if I'd rather die here at my typewriter?"

"You may be dedicated to your job, Mike, but not that dedicated. But if you want it now, I'll oblige. I doubt if the cops would hear a shot downstairs. They're all talking about how poor old Jet is about ready to crack."

"What's the reason for wanting me to leave?" I asked, stalling. I hoped Brandt would come back. Brandt or anybody.

"It would look better if you drove your own car, Mike. Maybe I could get away, but I want a long head start, if possible."

I took a deep breath. She might get me past the offices and cops downstairs. I was in a fix. I hadn't expected things to turn out like this. Like a damned fool I'd tried to wrap up the case without telling all I knew to Guffy. Now I'd pay for it. I thought that I'd be reasonably safe in the police station, and that I could stall for awhile. Even 'till midnight, when I'd get more money for breaking the story for afternoon papers. But Nora was spoiling my plan, just like I spoiled hers.

"You won't get away with it," I said, starting to rise.

"Let's not talk about it, or if we do talk, let's be optimistic. If you're good, and want to go, I may take you to Mexico with me." I knew she was lying.

"What did you expect to gain by killing Sydney in the first place?" I asked, as I started toward the hat rack.

"I thought Gervais would draw it. I could handle Jet. He was halfway in love with me. He'd draw my stories just the way I told him to. Sherm never would listen to me."

"Then it was Sherm's fault, not yours, that the marriage broke up?"

"I detested Sherm. He'd never do what I wanted him to do."

"Why'd you kill Vickery?"

"He had his own ideas too. You'd think that both of them, Sherm and Vickery, were the creators of *Dream Man*. It was my idea. Commando Green was my ideal type of man."

I put on my hat. I took a great deal of care to get it straight. "You mean that about taking me to Mexico?" I asked, still stalling.

"We'll discuss it later. I don't want to kill you, Mike. Not unless I have to."

"I'll bet you don't dislike it as much as I do," I said.

The phone rang. I started toward it.

"Stay where you are," she snapped. I saw her trigger finger tighten and I stopped. She meant business all right.

"Let's go," she said. "Walk on my right. I'll keep my coat over my arm to hide the gun, but remember it's pointed at you, even if you don't see it. If you try anything, I'll pull the trigger. The cops may get me, but it won't help you. And I won't be any worse off if you're dead than if they catch me and you're alive."

"Sounds sensible," I said. I started toward the door.

She moved over to my left, so she'd be on my right, and nudged me with the gun. It felt pretty big for the size it was.

As we went, through the door, I realized that she got all her adventure material from travel books. Nobody that had ever had anything to do with firearms would have done what she did. You'd think that a writer of adventure yarns would have learned somewhere that when you've got somebody at gunpoint, never get too close to him.

Reflexes are a marvelous part of the human mechanism, but sometimes they lead you astray. A sudden movement triggers a reflex, and when you react with a reflex you're off guard.

I pretended to slip on the slick marble floor of the corridor and her gun arm moved instinctively to keep me from bumping into her. That fraction of a second was enough for me to use my left arm to knock the gun aside.

It took her by surprise. She pulled the trigger, of course, but it was too late. The bullet missed me and splatted into the woodwork of the wall. In another fraction of a second I'd grabbed her right wrist with both my hands and twisted till she dropped the gun.

She screamed to high heaven with pain, and sank to her knees.

Then she butted me with her head and it was my turn to yell. She hit my cracked rib.

Possibly the cops downstairs heard the report of the gun, maybe they didn't. That's the one fact I never checked on, but they heard us yelling. We were still yelling, I was trying to hold her as she scrambled to her feet, kicking and hitting at me with both feet and her left hand, when Sergeant Russell came up the stairs. He yelled, "What in the devils going on here?"

He grabbed me and swung me away from her.

"What are you tryin' to do to this lady? Rape her?" he bellowed.

His back was toward her, but looking past him, I saw Nora stooping to pick up her gun on the floor.

"Watch her, you fool!" I hollered at Russell.

He turned and saw her coming up with a gun. Then he did something that I didn't think was ever done, not even in a comic strip. He kicked a pretty girl in the jaw.

She went down like she'd been hit with an ax, and Russell grabbed the gun from her hand.

"In answer to your question, sergeant, I was trying to keep from getting killed," I said, holding my aching ribs.

More cops were coming up the stairway now. They got handcuffs on Nora and carried her downstairs. By that time I'd told Russell that she killed Sherman Sydney and Max Vickery. He wouldn't believe me, of course, so I had him get Guffy and Sheriff Lindley and I told them about her renting the car. And I told them that the motive was twenty thousand a year. That kind of motive they understood.

"Sherm was going to let Commando Green get married," I said. "Nora believed it would ruin the strip; she didn't want to write anything but adventure. Sherm felt that the readers were clamoring for his hero to get married, and he'd probably listened to Phylana Kane, who felt that she could get the inside track with Sherm if she turned into a writer and replaced Nora."

"We'll check on it, Mike," said Guffy. "Meanwhile, we'll have to get a statement from you. After Miss Donovan gets over her groggy feeling, we'll talk to her too."

"I've already got a statement," I said. "It's upstairs in the Out Basket in the Press Room. I'll have to copy it, because Arnoth's coming down here to get that statement pretty soon."

"You mean you're going to give me a newspaper story for a statement?"

"What's wrong with a newspaper story, Clyde? It's true."

"I've seen some of them that weren't," said Guffy.

He sent a cop up after the carbon I had intended to send to the *Globe,* and I borrowed Guffy's typewriter, some carbon paper and some police department stationery.

I wrote a new story, naming the murderer in the lead and mining the plot, but it was a damn good yarn, and my split on the syndication was three hundred and forty-three dollars.

KILL ME WITH KINDNESS

TWO COMPLETE NOVELS 35c

THE CASE OF THE
DEADLY DO-GOODER

KILL ME WITH KINDNESS

J. HARVEY BOND
Complete & Unabridged

Mike Lanson, crime reporter for the GAZETTE.

Lucrezia, also known as **Mabel (Luzy) McGuire**, a strip-tease artist whose career has been interrupted by the cops.

Clarence Proost, a professional reformer.

Mr. and Mrs. Manton Arkwright, a wealthy, middle-aged couple who are active in the Citizens' Anti-Vice League.

Brick Lorchetto, operator of the swank Hilltop gambling casino.

Jim Bomo, Lorchetto's henchman and bodyguard.

Cliff Ramcaster, county prosecutor who knows what is going on but is reluctant, for reasons, to act.

ONE

I climbed a dark stairway which led off the street to the second floor of an old store building on Jefferson Avenue near Sixty-eighth Street. At the top was a long, ill-lighted hall, lined with low-rent light housekeeping rooms.

As I looked around for apartment Number Three, a baby bawled in one of the rooms. I smelled onions and cabbage cooking.

Number Three was the second door from the front of the building, on my left as I came up the stairs. The name *Mabel McGuire* was crudely hand-lettered on a card in a holder on the doorframe. This was the babe I wanted to talk to. I'd tried to reach her by phone, but she wasn't listed. No phone.

Mabel McGuire was the off-stage name of a fourth-rate stripper the cops had hauled in from the Block Buster bar on West Tenth Street a week or two ago. I knocked on her door.

When the door opened, I hardly recognized her with her clothes on. Lucrezia—that was the name she appeared under—was fully dressed in a Gondola outfit, tight white pants, a loose-ly knit sweater. She had a towel wrapped around her head like a turban to hide her hairdo-in-the-making. But I knew her hair was jet black.

Her looks were nice. This was the kind of an assignment any reporter would feel was worth while. "Miss McGuire?" I asked.

"Yeah?" Her voice was low and husky. It told me that she liked the half of the human race that wore pants.

"I'm Mike Lanson of the *Gazette,*" I told her, edging forward so she couldn't slam the door. I didn't think she would but you never can tell.

"Migod, a reporter!" Her voice got a little shrill, but it still was pleasant. "I've had just about enough of reporters. Do you have to run a continued story about me?"

"Sorry, Miss McGuire," I said, "but reporters have livings to make. I'm not here on a story now. Just checking up on a few things. Can I come in?"

She hesitated, then stepped back. "All right. You're half in already. But I'd like to know first if you're really a reporter. For all I know, you're Jack the Ripper."

I grinned and pulled out my identification card. "I'm harmless," I said. "I'll talk to you here if you wish and if you don't care about nosy neighbors."

The door to Number Five was opening a crack.

"Come in. I'm eating breakfast."

I looked around the room as I entered. It was homey and pleasant. Much different than I expected. She had a pretty blue spread on her bed, blue drapes, and white furniture. Cheap, but neat. A table hear the hot plate had a coffee cup and a plate with a couple of pieces of toast on it. She sat down, and I sat across from her on a white kitchen chair.

"Coffee? Fetch a cup off the shelf and I'll give you some."

"No thanks," I said. "Just information."

"For free, I suppose. You want my life story? I was born Iowa. Learned to dance in Chicago, and came to Creston three years ago with a road show that went busted. You ruined my career when you printed my picture, and now I've got another job—"

"I—"

"My new job's not creative, like dancing, but I get paid. I prefer art. Dancing is an art, even without clothes. More without than with, because you're conditioned against nakedness and you've got to learn to control your timidity—"

"I understand, but—"

"Of course you understand. You're creative too. You're a writer. I write too. Poetry. Let me read you some—" She jumped up, went to a chest of drawers and pulled out a sheet of paper. She read as she returned to the table:

"Strippers are maidens who are seldom forlorn.
They dance before menfolk the way they were born.
On top of a bar, before lecherous eyes
They bump and they grind for amusement of guys—"

At that point I couldn't help laughing.

"It's not supposed to be funny," she said with a frown. "There's more—"

"Some other time, ma'am," I said. "Right now, I'm—"

"Would your paper print my poems?" She leaned forward almost dipping her right besweatered bosom in the coffee.

"Newspapers go more for prose," I said. She had dark blue eyes, high cheek bones, a straight, but pretty nose and firm, full lips.

"Edgar Guest wrote poetry for newspapers," she said.

"He was a special case," I told her.

"You don't like poetry because you're skinny," she said. "Skinny men are sad and cynical."

"Sometimes they're busy," I said, although I was very sorry I was working and sorrier still that I was conscientious. "Do you know a man named Clarence Proost?"

She opened her mouth to say something, then closed it again. Her eyes fixed mine for a moment. Then she picked up a piece of toast and nibbled on it. I got the idea she was stalling. "I know a lot of guys," she said finally. "Am I supposed to know him?"

I shrugged. "He's the executive director of the Citizens' Anti-Vice League, the outfit that signed the complaint on strip tease acts at the Block Buster Bar."

"What would I have to do with a guy like that, Mr. Lanson? Is that your name?"

"Mike, if you can't remember the last name," I said, nodding. "I thought maybe you might have seen the man talking to Leonard Audell, your boss, before the bar was raided."

"Gee, Mike, a lot of people talked to Lenny."

"Well, if you don't know Proost, I don't suppose you can help me," I said. I had to be tactful. Colonel Tanner had his suspicions about Proost, but they were only suspicions. Unless we found somebody willing to talk, we couldn't very well expose him as the kind of reformer who puts the squeeze on small-time operators.

"Sorry, I can't help you," she said. "But I'm sure glad you called. I hardly ever have company, living odd hours like I do. The women in this place are crumbs—and no men at all."

"I'm sad and skinny," I said. "I'm not good company."

As I rose from my chair, she looked up at me. "Don't take my cracks to heart and run off, honey. I like tall, skinny men. You'd make a good Gary Cooper if you were about thirty years older."

"Yup," I said. "But I've gotta go, because I'm working."

"You work every day?"

"I'm off one day a week. Next week it's Monday."

"Chee! Monday's my day off too. I work nights, you know. Doesn't leave a girl much time to run around."

"We'll have to get together Monday night."

"Shucks, I wasn't hinting. But it's a good idea."

"Okay. Pick you up at eight."

"I'll be waiting for you, honey. Can you find your way out?"

"Yup," I said, still trying to be Gary Cooper. "So long, Mabel."

"Don't call me Mabel. I hate that name. Call me Luzy, Mike."

"Okay, Luzy. S'long."

I went back to my car already anticipating Monday night. This was Wednesday. Five days.

I drove across town, stopping on the way to have lunch and to call Hank, so that he wouldn't think I was taking the day off. Hank Newcomb is my city editor, and I'll tell you more about him later.

My call on Luzy had been the fifth that morning concerning Clarence Proost. Everyone I'd talked to had praised him to the skies or remained noncommittal, but Colonel Tanner was convinced that Clarence Proost was a shakedown artist.

Colonel Gordon Curran Tanner, editor and publisher of the *Gazette* and its morning twin, the *Globe,* had been asked by Proost to wage war on sin and vice in Creston. Colonel Tanner does not approve of large-scale sin and vice, but he can take small amounts of it in his stride. And he is willing to let the police take care of the rest as long as they seem to be doing their duty.

But Proost was executive director of an organization called the Citizens' Anti-Vice League, of which a large group of prominent people were members. Most of the membership was sincere, a few fanatical, and others not so concerned. Perhaps some belonged for political or selfish reasons, but nevertheless the membership was imposing and when the newspapers of Creston were asked to help them crusade, the request could not be taken lightly.

Tanner had had reporters, including me, check up on the club's activities. During the past year, Proost had signed twenty-six complaints against small-time operators, charging them with operating at illegal hours, taking bets, operating slot machines, promoting strip-tease shows, and chiseling in any number of ways. It had also come to the Colonel's attention that several joints in Creston and on the outskirts of town which really operated on a large scale had not been bothered. This, plus some rumors that Proost could be had, had sent the Colonel in the direction of reforming the reformers. He had found that large sums had been subscribed to the Committee, which had expenses that were not large. While the books of the organization had been audited, the Colonel felt that Proost might have found ways to dip his hands into the treasury for one reason or another.

But I'd found out nothing thus far.

I drove up in front of a nice little ranch house in the University Hill section of town. It was the home of Manton Arkwright, a wealthy investor, who spent most of his leisure time being public spirited. He handled estates and things to make a living.

A young woman, very pretty, answered the door. Like the girl I'd seen before lunch, this one had black hair. But the one I was seeing now was older, about my age, although it's unsafe to judge a woman's age. Still there was a bloom of maturity that I liked in her face and manner and she was well poised and gracious. Classy's the word.

"Miss Arkwright?" I asked.

"Mrs. Arkwright," she said with a smile. "Mrs. Manton Arkwright."

I showed my surprise. I thought she was Manton Arkwright's daughter. He was in his fifties. This babe was at least 25 years younger. "I'm Mike Lanson of the *Gazette*," I said when I had recovered.

"Oh yes, Mr. Lanson," she said warmly. "Manton told me he expected you this afternoon, but I understood you'd be here later. He did too, I suppose, because he hasn't returned from downtown yet. He usually has lunch at his club. Won't you come in?"

It was almost one-thirty and I didn't think I'd have to wait long. Besides, it would be nice work waiting with this dame.

"Yes, I'll wait," I said.

I followed her into the house. It was modern in every way. She took me into a large living room told me to sit on the divan and went to a portable bar in the corner. "Can I fix you a drink?"

"A small one," I said. It was too soon after lunch to enjoy a drink, but I have no objections to a drink at any time. "Can I help you?"

"Goodness! Mixing drinks is about the only exercise I get. Bourbon or Scotch?"

I told her bourbon and water and she mixed the drinks. She came over and sat down beside me. She was dressed in slacks with a short-sleeved blouse. She was small and bosomy. Stacked like everything. "I hope you don't mind my costume," she said, noticing my gaze. "I didn't expect to receive you."

"I don't mind in the least," I said.

"Tell me about newspaper work. It must be so interesting."

"It's always new and different," I said.

She put her drink down on the coffee table and moved over close beside me. "You must meet all kinds of people. My life is so dull, most of the time."

"You don't look dull," I said.

"Thanks." She ran her fingers along my arm. "Do you have a city editor who swears at you? Do you make love to all the pretty girls? Do you get drunk every day?"

"You've been going to the movies," I said. My city editor swears at me, but he'd swear at his mother. I also made love, when I had the opportunity. But I seldom got drunk because I hate hangovers. "Movies exaggerate."

She snuggled close. "Make love to me," she said.

It was so startling and sudden that I didn't know what to think. I was scared. I'm not used to having women melt in my arms ten minutes after I meet them. But I had to be polite. I put my arm around her, pulled her close and gave her a friendly kiss.

I spilled my drink, which was still in my hand. Then I set it down and discovered that she was laughing. "Not that way," she said. "Like this!"

And I was suddenly engulfed in a woman's arms, smothered with kisses. I didn't fight it, of course, but I was certainly confused. And more than a little bit bothered.

"See! I knew the movies weren't exaggerating," she said.

I felt limp and embarrassed and incompetent, irrelevant and almost immaterial. "Do you do this to all your guests?"

"Just the ones I like," she said. "That's very nice, Mr. Lanson. I think we'll have to continue this some other time."

"Yes," I said. "With a little warning."

"You're cute. What's your first name?"

"Mike," I said. I'd told her before.

"Mine's Martha." She got up, brushed the spot where my drink had spilled, then looked out the window. "Here comes Manton now. Better rub the lipstick off your face. He won't notice, but I'm always afraid he will."

I used my handkerchief and tried to compose myself while she went to the door and threw herself into the arms of a portly gray-haired man who entered.

Now she turned around and pulled him by the arm toward me. "Manton," she said, "this is Mike Lanson, the reporter you expected. He just spilled his drink."

Manton Arkwright smiled as I rose and shook his hand. He was heavy-set and had a noticeable bay; he was not overly stout for a man of his age. He wore rimless glasses and the mustache on his upper lip was pure white.

"Clumsy of me," I said, pointing to the wet spot on the divan.

"Martha is sometimes distracting," he said. "Colonel Tanner gave me an inkling of the reason for your visit, Lanson. Finish your drink and we'll go into the study and talk."

There wasn't much left in the glass, but I started to work on it. Martha asked, "Do you want one too, dear?"

She ran her hands through his hair. A moment ago she'd been in my arms and it didn't seem to concern her.

Arkwright patted her hand. "Too soon after lunch, my dear," he said in a fatherly tone. "I expected to see the Colonel at the Plymouth Club today, but he didn't show up."

"Noon is a busy time on a newspaper," I said. "Sometimes he's tied up and can't make it."

"Don't tell me that the Colonel personally supervises everything at your place?"

I grinned. "No, not exactly. But he has his finger in most of the pies."

I finished my drink and Arkwright turned to Mrs. Arkwright. "We'll be in the study, Martha," he said.

Martha smiled. Turning to me, she said, "It was very pleasant meeting you, Mr. Lanson. I hope we'll see you again."

She moved off to a door on the right while Arkwright and I went into the study.

It was a large study, about a third the size of the living room, fitted with a long highly polished desk, tiers of bookcases and other furnishings. I sat in a chair facing the desk.

"Colonel Tanner told you," I said, "that we'd like to know something about this man Proost."

Arkwright nodded. "I have met him several times."

"He's asked, in behalf of the Citizens' Anti-Vice Committee that the *Gazette* support his crusade against county-wide corruption."

Arkwright sniffed. "I'll have to have a definition of corruption," he said. "It means many things to many people."

"Well," I said, "it's common knowledge that several gambling casinos are operating on the outskirts of town."

"There's gambling in town as well," said Arkwright. "Not that I approve of it, you understand, but I'm not particularly concerned if fools want to throw their money away."

"That's pretty close to Colonel Tanner's attitude too, sir," I said. "But the existence of these places shows laxity on the part of county officers."

"And what has this got to do with Mr. Proost?"

"I'm coming to that. When we go into a crusade, we want to know it's to correct something, and not simply a political or some other kind of gambit in behalf of selfish aims."

"Meaning?"

"To be perfectly frank, Mr. Arkwright, we've heard rumors that some people are dissatisfied with the way Proost carries out his reforms."

Arkwright studied the surface of the desk in front of him. "I said I knew Proost. I am also a member of the Citizens' Anti-Vice League. I've never questioned his sincerity. Perhaps these rumors about him are circulated by the hoodlums themselves."

"Then you'll go on record as saying you have faith in him?"

"As far as I know he's a zealous man," said Arkwright. "I don't know everything about him. I'm a member of the board of trustees of the League, but I'm too busy to watch its affairs or check on Proost personally. Perhaps Martha can tell you more. She's well acquainted with Mr. Proost. She goes to all of the meetings. Perhaps you'd better talk to her."

He rose suddenly, took three steps from his desk to the door and threw it open. Martha Arkwright was standing on the other side, twisting her fingers awkwardly.

"I was just coming in to ask Mr. Lanson if he'd like to have lunch with me," she said, somewhat flustered. "I haven't eaten yet."

It was obvious that she'd been eavesdropping, but Arkwright turned to me smiling graciously. "We'd be glad to have you," he added.

"No thanks," I said. "Newspaper reporters can't eat lunches in leisurely fashion. I've got a deadline to make."

"I'm so sorry," said Martha Arkwright, starting to turn away.

"Just a moment, dear," said Arkwright. "Mr. Lanson wants to know what kind of a man Mr. Proost is. I told him you knew him better than I."

"Mr. Proost is a splendid man," she said enthusiastically. "He's so dedicated to his work. He's immersed in it."

"Even a little overzealous sometimes, isn't he?" Arkwright asked.

"But that's nothing against him. Vice is zealous too and we must fight fire with fire." This from her?

"He's a paid investigator, isn't he, Mrs. Arkwright?"

"He's the executive director," she said. "Because he devotes full time to our activities, we pay him a small salary and his expenses. He's comfortably fixed besides. He had a small inheritance which Mr. Arkwright invests for him."

I nodded as if I believed every word of it. "Thanks," I said. "Colonel Tanner will be much relieved to hear you trust him."

"Of course we trust him," said Arkwright heartily. "Colonel Tanner is just too suspicious of people for his own good. But I suppose lots of unscrupulous scallywags do try to make a cat's paw of a newspaper."

"They do," I admitted. "Thanks for your cooperation."

Arkwright stood aside as I went through the door. He followed me to the front door, but before he opened it, he asked, "Proost is aiming at the Hilltop Club, isn't he?"

I nodded. "I think that's the main objective. He says the county officers are deliberately closing their eyes to what goes on there."

He still didn't open the door. "Tell Colonel Tanner not to rely solely on my word or Martha's recommendation," he said in a low voice as Martha moved back to the rear of the house. "It's been nice meeting you, Good day."

Before I knew it, I was outside and the door had closed behind me.

What in the devil was the idea of that last statement? Was Arkwright reversing himself, or simply asking Colonel Tanner to get confirmation?

The more I thought about it, the more I began to believe that maybe Arkwright was sending the boss a warning.

TWO

The Hilltop should have been at the top of a hill, and surprisingly, it was. Once the home was at the center of an estate, where thoroughbred horses were bred, fine liquor consumed and hired help underpaid. In more recent years the pastures had been converted to truck gardens and the old manor had been remodeled for less legal uses.

A tree-lined lane ran from a side road to the top of the hill. There a large parking lot had been built just outside the high, sturdy steel fence which surrounded the fine old house. There was only one gate in this fence, and beside it stood a courteous, uniformed attendant who assisted suckers from their high-priced cars.

My car was not high priced, except to me, but it was shiny and sporty looking, which will get by in places like these. I arrived at the Hilltop at 9 p.m., wearing my tailored suit and a three-dollar necktie, the best I had. If I didn't look like I was in the bucks, perhaps I could convince the gateman that I was a junior executive trying to crash the big leagues. The Hilltop was definitely big league.

This was not a poor man's rendezvous. Only the financially capable could spend much time here. Drinks were twice as expensive as anywhere else, and liquor was the cheapest thing to spend money on. People came here to spend. The fiction that one could win large sums upstairs in the gaming room came true on occasions so rare that it was a novelty. It was easy to lose a

great deal. But nobody expected to win. People were judged by
what they could lose without flinching. If they happened to win
even a small sum, there was the exhilaration of beating a professional gambler—temporarily.

Colonel Tanner had given me one hundred dollars expense
money, with orders to get by on twenty bucks if I could. The
rest was to flourish, to aid the impression that I had come here
to rub elbows with the upper income bracket.

I had duly reported my interviews with various friends and
foes of Clarence Proost. There was no evidence that Proost was
crooked, but plenty that he got around considerably. There were
even some clues that for one reason or another nobody wanted
to tell all he knew about Proost.

"Very well," the Colonel had said, "we'll stage our crusade,
but we'll do it our way. Proost will get no credit for this."

The term "we," as the Colonel used it, meant that I would do
the rough stuff and the *Gazette* would grab the credit.

There's no newspaper reporter alive who doesn't at one time
or another gather information without letting on that he is connected with the newspaper industry. It's considered ethical, but
I don't think it's sporting. But who ever said business was sporting? Newspapers have to use undercover tactics, just like busi-
nessmen when they steal the jump on a competitor.

I was here posing as an ambitious young man who was trying to impress somebody. And all the while, I was to gather in
evidence that there was gambling at the Hilltop, as if it weren't
common knowledge already.

The uniformed doorman halted me politely after I'd parked
my car and advanced toward the gate. I had had a feeling long
before I reached him that other eyes than his had been inspect-
ing me carefully from concealed spots in the house—possibly
that attic dormer above the doorway.

"Do you have a card?" he asked in a gently inquisitive voice.

"Sorry," I said, "I'm from out of town. I was told that I
might get a little action here."

The doorman looked sympathetic. "This is a private club, sir.
But if you step inside, we can post your name for membership."

He brushed against me. Did I feet his fingers gently touch me in various spots to feel for concealed weapons? Perhaps I was mistaken. He opened the door.

I entered a big hallway. At my left was a small, highly polished table. Behind it was a hawk-faced youth in a tuxedo, who looked up at me.

"This gentleman would like to join our club," said the doorman.

The youth smiled, even though it made his facial muscles ache to look pleasant. "The initiation fee is five dollars, sir," he said.

"And the monthly dues?" I asked.

"The bartender will collect it whenever you drop in," said the young man, no longer smiling.

I pulled out my billfold, taking care to expose the twenty-dollar bills that it contained. I gave him one. He gave me a card and fifteen dollars change without even asking my name.

"Show this card to the doorman whenever you come back," said the young man. "Otherwise, you'll have to pay the initiation fee again."

"Thank you," I said.

"The bar is in the room to the left and the dining room on the right," he said.

I looked around. The doorman was going outside again.

"I wanted some action," I said.

"The game room probably will open in a few minutes," said the youth.

I sauntered toward the bar, after pocketing the card. It would be photographed later and used with my story.

At the doorway, I stopped. There were only half a dozen people, four men and two women there. It didn't look like much of a crowd. I went up to the bar and ordered Scotch, just to prove I liked the finer things of life.

Just as the bartender delivered my drink, a hand touched my arm and a husky voice said, "Why don't you blow, newspaperman?"

I looked around and saw Mabel McGuire, alias Luzy, standing beside me. But now she was a far cry from the bepanted young gal with a towel wrapped around her head that I'd seen that morning. I only recognized her by her eyes.

She wore a low-cut, black and red dress. Her black hair rolled across her head in beautiful, graceful waves. She had just the right amount of make-up and she was lovely.

"Well, well," I said. "So this is your new job?"

"Didn't you hear me, wise guy? Get the hell out of here while you're all in one piece."

I knew I was dead as far as this story was concerned. I decided, however, to stick around and see what happened. I really didn't think that the management would do any more than kick me out, and I'd been booted before. "I'm sorry, my dear," I said, waving my glass and slopping the scotch around in senseless waste, "but I have only one life to give for my city room."

She shrugged. "Okay. I tried to warn you. Now I'll tell you what I was sent here to tell you. You're wanted upstairs."

"Ah! Who wants me?"

"Who do you think wants you?" she asked. "If you were smart you'd leave."

Then I saw a big husky hardnose coming through the doorway from the hallway. He wore a tuxedo, like the hawk-faced youth, and I sensed that he also wore a gun, but I didn't see it.

He came over to where I stood beside Luzy. "You comin'?"

"What have I got to lose but my handsome features?" I said, and started toward the stairway with Hardnose following me.

We went up the stairs together. At the top, I started toward a door with a peephole in it, but Hardnose grabbed my arm and shoved me in the other direction toward a door which said "No Admittance."

"I can't go in there," I said.

"You're special, Buster," said Hardnose. He opened the door and pushed me in.

"Who you pushin?" I asked, swinging around. Hardnose must not have expected resistance at this point, because when I gave him a push he went back through the door. His foot caught the edge of the carpet in the hallway and he sat down right on his fanny.

He roared and came to his feet. From somewhere a blackjack appeared in his hand.

"Hold it, Jim!" snapped a voice behind me.

I turned around and saw a man sitting behind a desk on the other side of the room.

"Sit down, Lanson," the man said, after Hardnose subsided and closed the door. "Don't be afraid of Jim. He's rough and ready, but he has a heart of gold."

"I can easily see that he has," I said, sitting down in a leather chair.

"I'm Brick Lorchetto," he said. The name Brick was easy to understand, because he had red hair. But the name was Italian, and he didn't look like an Italian to me. Maybe he wasn't. "I'm the proprietor of the Hilltop Club," he added.

"I'm a member," I said. "I'm entitled to rights and privileges."

"You're a lousy newspaper reporter," said Lorchetto. "You came out here to cause trouble."

"You've been causing me trouble," I said.

"Don't be funny. You want to run a big story about big gambling in the Hilltop Club. Do you see any going on?"

"No," I said, and I didn't expect to see any now. The *Gazette* business office would weep for weeks over that five bucks I spent to get in.

"There is none. No law violation of any kind. Anything you may have heard is poppycock. This is a private club, and our members consist of some of the most respectable people in the community. We serve liquor and meals, and sometimes we hold dances. There's no law against those things."

"Okay," I said, "I'll print that. Now can I go?"

"Not yet," said Brick.

"Kidnaping is against the law," I said.

"You're not being kidnaped," said Brick. "But I wouldn't advise you to leave. Jim is still angry and once out of my sight he might get out of hand. Better wait till he cools off."

"I get the message." I leaned back in the chair and waited. I didn't know what I was waiting for, but I waited. After about fifteen minutes, the door opened and two men came in. I recognized them both. The big, heavy-set, fortyish man was Sheriff August Lindley, and the young, tall man was Cliff Ramcaster, assistant county prosecutor.

"Hello, Brick," said Cliff. Then he saw me. "And Mike! What in God's green earth are you doing here?"

"I'm being held captive in a nonexistent gambling hell," I said.

"Always the funny man," said Brick. "I told him not to drink so much."

Cliff laughed. "Well, he's right on the spot for a big story. We're raiding you, Brick." He pulled a warrant from his pocket and slapped it down on the desk. "Suspicion of maintaining a gambling establishment."

Brick picked up the warrant. "Well, well," he said. "You don't say." He looked at the warrant. "I don't understand this legal gibberish, but you know I'd never break any laws, Cliff. Just like I know you wouldn't haul me in without evidence. You got it?"

"Not a shred," said Cliff. "But there's been a lot of talk around town and some pressure has been put on our office to investigate. In order to make it legal, I got a warrant and came out here to look around."

"Help yourself," said Brick.

I stood up. "I get the pitch," I said. "My story has blown up in my face. The place has been raided, no evidence of gambling found, and if I print a word I can be sued for defamation of character. Now can I go?"

"Sure," said Brick. "You can go, but don't you want to wait till the boys finish their search."

"I know what they'll find," I said. I walked out the door.

The downstairs was still quiet, except the group at the bar. But Luzy stood near the doorway with a jacket thrown over her shoulders.

I opened my mouth and grinned. "See, honey? All my teeth!"

"It isn't your fault," she said, "you tried hard. Mind if I bum a ride back to town with you?"

"The pleasure's mine," I said.

We got into my car and drove down the lane to the side road. Then we cut over to the highway. The evening was cool, but not too cool. It was a gentle spring night and she sat close to me. At Dunn Avenue, I slowed down and pulled into a filling station.

"Out of gas?" she asked in surprise. For a woman who had been all yak the first time I'd seen her, she had been strangely quiet tonight.

"I gotta call the office," I said.

"Oh. You're always working."

"After I phone, I'll not be working," I said.

She moved closer to me. I could feel the soft contours of her body against my arm. "That'll be nice," she said.

I hated to leave this spot, but duty called. I went into the station and dialed Colonel Tanner. He had instructed me to call as soon as I left the Hilltop. I saw by the clock on the wall that it was two minutes of eleven.

I told him all that had happened and the Colonel took the news noncommittally. "We'll keep working on it," he said, "but I think the Proost angle is a bigger yarn than the minor vice that goes on at the Hilltop."

"I'll get on the story first thing in the morning, sir."

"Yes—uh—but there's no need for you to come in until noon, Mike," he said. "We don't want to run up too much overtime on this story."

Again the term "we" had a special significance. I didn't mind overtime. But I didn't complain. I like to sleep late too.

I went back to my car full of anticipation. But the car was empty. I looked around at the filling station attendant who was wiping off my windshield.

"She said not to wait for her," he said. "She flagged a taxi."

I swore softly and got into my car. All of my plans were down the drain. A few minutes before she'd been cuddlesome and now she'd shied off like a frightened virgin. I got home about midnight, after putting up my car and stopping for a cup of coffee.

I didn't get to sleep late the next morning. About nine o'clock, Lieutenant Clyde Guffy of the Creston police department, criminal investigation division, woke me up by pounding on the door of my hotel room.

After I let him in, he told me that Clarence Proost had been shot dead. Murdered.

THREE

I sat on the edge of the bed in my pajamas and lit a cigarette. "Does Don Hilliard know about this?" I asked.

"If you mean your lame-brain assistant, I don't think he does. The body was found about forty minutes ago and I just heard about it myself."

"Nice of you to look me up the first thing," I said. "Now, if you don't mind—" I reached for the phone.

Guffy's arm shot out and put the phone back in its cradle. "Uh-uh. Not till I finish talking to you, newsboy."

Guffy's a nice man off duty and when he hasn't anything special on his mind, like he had now. He hates newspapers, which I suppose a lot of cops do in their own special way, but he liked me and we'd had some times together. But when he was on a case he was all cop and friendship didn't mean a thing.

"Finish talking," I said, dragging on my cigarette.

"I got word yesterday that you were asking all the places on Tenth Street about Proost," said Guffy. "I want a list of everybody you talked to and a little about what was said."

"I was told that Clarence Proost was a man of high character, a zealous reformer, and a goddam busybody," I said. I told him where I'd been, from Luzy's place to Arkwright's.

"And why all this interest in Proost?" he asked.

"Because he wanted the *Gazette's* cooperation in a crusade to expose lax law enforcement in the county," I told him. "Colonel Tanner was suspicious. He had heard that Proost was lining his pockets at the expense of the tinhorns and chiselers, and the *Gazette* believes that blackmail is a worse evil than shooting crap."

"I suppose I should applaud the sentiments," said Guffy, "but a chiseler is a chiseler, and I don't see much difference between them. But this is murder, and that's a hell of a lot of difference. Your questions yesterday made a lot of people nervous."

Guffy knew all this because he has the best cote of stool pigeons west of J. Edgar Hoover. Since he knew everything or he'd find out what I didn't know if I didn't tell him, I spilled my guts.

"So Lindley and Ramcaster were out there last night," he mused. "Naturally they didn't find anything."

"If I had thought there was one chance in a traiload that they'd find even a poker chip on the floor, I wouldn't have left so early. But Lindley and Ramcaster knew what went on in those upstairs rooms, before the tables and gear were packed away."

"Suspecting and proving are two different words, Mike," said Guffy. "Even when you know something, you've got to prove what you know in court. Sometimes a cop's word isn't good enough. There has to be another witness. And try to find one."

It sounded like a big job. The people who patronized the Hilltop had good reasons for not wanting it known that they gambled away more in an evening than some people make in a year. Even if these folks suddenly decided they wanted to clean up the county, they might be a little timid about talking. Brick Lorchetto might take a dim view of such testimony.

"If Ramcaster wanted to clean things up," I said, "he could call in a grand jury and make folks testify."

"And where would that put him except on the wrong side of the number eight ball?" asked Guffy. "Ramcaster and Lindley both are politicians. The people he'd force to give testimony are people with connections. Political and financial connections. Even if Ramcaster honestly wanted to clean up things, he'd have to work pretty slowly and carefully."

"But he doesn't want to," I said.

Guffy shrugged. He was something of a politician too.

"Well," I said, "this murder is going to raise a stink and I'll bet it reaches into every nose in the county."

"You think so?"

"Sure. Proost intended to finger Lorchetto in order to prove Ramcaster and Lindley were on the take. So Lorchetto fingered Proost. Or maybe Ramcaster did. Or Lindley."

"Or any one of twenty-six chiselers, tinhorns and brothel keepers Proost signed complaints against this year," he said.

I crushed out my cigarette and scratched my chest under my pajamas. "Jeez, I'm glad I'm not a cop," I said.

"Where's the girl who rode into town with you last night, Mike?" he asked suddenly.

I had intended to tell Guffy about Luzy, really I had, but I hadn't gotten to it yet. "Oh, the girl," I said. "For a cop that just found out about the killing, you know a hell of a lot."

"We notified the county prosecutor as soon as we heard about the killing," Guffy said. "He told us he saw you leave the Hilltop last night with Proost's girl friend—"

"Girl friend?" The ice-cold finger of something or other ran up my spine. I hadn't known the girl long enough to be jealous. Maybe it was suspicion.

"That babe you took home last night, the one that's known as Lucrezia McGuire; has been working with Proost for two years."

"She told me she didn't know Proost."

"She lied. We know a lot of things about Proost that we haven't been able to prove. I might add that the Colonel's suspicions about him aren't without basis. And he's been using this McGuire dame to shake down his suckers. She worked for four or five joints before she went to the Block Buster and several of them were raided on Proost's complaint. She was working at the Hilltop up till last night, and the Hilltop was next in Proost's little campaign."

If what Guffy had just said was true, I could understand why she denied knowing Proost. She might have gotten herself in a lot of trouble. "You're sure about this?"

"As sure as you were that dice are no strangers to the Hilltop," he said. "I can't prove it, but I know it's so."

"You think she killed Proost?"

"I didn't say that, but she's missing and my evil little mind is full of suspicions. You saw her last, Mike. Where'd you take her?"

"She ditched me at a filling station. I went to make a phone call—"

"What station?"

"I don't know. I didn't even notice what brand of gas it sells. But it was at Dunn Avenue on highway 182."

"That's close enough. We'll check it from there."

"The attendant said she hailed a taxi."

"We'll find the driver. You can go back to bed now, boy."

"Thanks, flatfoot. And if you find Luzy, ask her why she stood me up."

I didn't go back to bed after Guffy left. I wasn't sleepy any more. I got a bottle of bourbon off the shelf in my clothes closet and poured me a stiff drink. I'm not the kind of a man who waits till the sun is on the meridian before he takes a drink. I'll take one whenever I need one and I needed one now.

I was just starting to dress when the phone rang. I knew who was calling before I answered; it was Hank Newcomb, my city editor.

Hank is the kind of person who second-guesses his instincts. And he has the instincts of a werewolf.

"Sorry to disturb your rest, Sleeping Beauty," he said, "but we've got a murder and nobody can handle a murder case like you can. So get into your panties and come down."

He thought he was having a good time, because he just loves to cause a reporter discomfort. But I didn't want to spoil his fun, so I didn't tell him I'd been up for about half an hour.

"Okay, sweetheart. I'll be down in an hour."

"You can make it quicker than that."

"I have a full beard, milord. I must shave. I must also bathe because I stink. Furthermore, I must eat breakfast. If you can stand me unshaved, unbathed and unfed, I'll come down right now. I won't even put on my clothes."

"Okay, okay, but snap it up."

"Sure."

"Don't you want to know who's been murdered?"

"Not as long as it isn't you."

"Well, it's your old friend Clarence Proost. Somebody put a bullet into his chest last night. The Colonel thinks you know all the angles, which I doubt."

"Sir, are you calling Colonel Tanner a liar?"

"Don't try to make things out of what I say." Hank is very touchy about the Colonel because Hank is insecure. He never allowed humor to come within ten miles of the Colonel's name. Hank was almost a stranger to any kind of humor except the sadistic kind. "All I said was that you—aw, hell!" He slammed up the phone.

Exactly one hour after Hank's call, I walked into the city room. He looked up from his desk. "You sure as hell took your time."

I let it pass. I said an hour and it was an hour, but Hank is never satisfied. "I'm here," I said. "That's something."

"You'd better be here. Go to work."

I got the galley proofs and read what Don Hilliard had phoned in up to now. Don hadn't touched upon Proost's alleged shakedown racket because he didn't have anything to hang it on. But he quoted the cops as saying that the murder may have been a result of Proost's reform activities. If you considered Proost's ideas of reform, it amounted to the same thing.

Luzy wasn't mentioned. Apparently Guffy was keeping the lid on that angle. At least he hadn't told Don.

Proost had been shot in his apartment on West Forty-ninth Street between midnight and one a.m. The body had been found just before eight o'clock by a man named Ernie Stauffer, who worked as Proost's secretary. Proost used his apartment as an office and Stauffer, who had a key, found the body when he came to work.

Stauffer said Proost had a revolver which was usually in a drawer of his desk. It was missing and its .38 caliber matched the wound in Proost, although the autopsy report hadn't yet verified that it was a .38 slug. The only clue was given by a couple named Elgarth who lived in the apartment building. They had returned home late, about twelve-thirty, and they saw a woman wearing a black and red dress enter the apartment house ahead of them.

When I read this, I felt a little chill up and down my spine. Luzy had been wearing a black and red dress. But she'd also had a little jacket on. The news story said nothing about a jacket, but I'd check on that.

No one had heard any shots, but the apartment was supposedly soundproofed, although such claims aren't always strictly true.

The rest of the story was a rehash of Proost's activities as head of the Citizens' Anti-Vice League, as far as it was a part of the public record.

Hank was fretting and fussing long before I finished reading the galley proofs. "Well?" he asked.

"Any special angle you want me to cover?"

"The Colonel says you know all about this case and for you to get on it. But he said to talk to him before you release anything that doesn't come from the cops or county prosecutor."

The County Prosecutor was named Sherman, but he didn't handle criminal cases, unless they were something special. Cliff Ramcaster was in charge of that.

"Get something new on the killing for the suburban edition," Hank said.

"Okay," I said. It was a little after ten. I'd have about three hours, which was plenty of time. "If I get anything sooner, I'll call."

I was just starting for the door when Johnson, who has the desk next to mine, called, "Hey, Mike! Phone!"

Most of my work is done at the Press Room of Police Headquarters, but I have a little desk in the city room too, and Johnson and I share the same extension.

I went back to my desk and picked up the phone. "Mike Lanson speaking," I said.

A soft, husky voice came to my ear. "Mike, this is Luzy."

I stiffened tensely and looked down at Johnson. He was pecking out a story with two fingers on his decrepit typewriter. He seemed pretty engrossed, but he was a reporter and reporters have big ears.

I almost whispered: "Where in the devil are you?"

"Mike," said Luzy, disregarding my question, "I had to leave you last night. I'll explain it all later, but right now I've got to have your help."

Johnson stopped typing and studied his scrawled notes, trying to read his handwriting. I was sure he hadn't heard Luzy's voice over the phone. She wasn't talking loud.

"How?"

"Can I trust you, Mike?"

That was a hell of a thing to ask. For all I knew she'd committed murder. I wasn't going to compound a felony. Besides, it wasn't a question I could answer handily with Johnson close by.

"I'm working on a big story now," I said. "A fellow named Proost, a big shot, got murdered last night."

"You think I killed him, don't you, Mike."

"Where are you calling from? Maybe I'll have time to drop by."

"I'm using a phone in my room," she said. "And if I tell you where I am, will you keep it a secret until I talk to you?"

"If you promise to take my advice afterwards."

"If it means surrendering to the cops, I won't promise. Ramcaster would like to put me out of circulation too. He'd even frame me for murder."

Johnson got up and walked over to Hank's desk with his story. I heaved a sigh of relief.

Maybe it's because I figured that she was the best angle in the story, and I had to talk to her before the cops. Maybe it was because she was so damned beautiful. Anyhow, I said.

"Okay. You don't have to promise anything. We'll thresh it out when I see you. Now where are you?"

"You won't tell anyone? Not a soul?"

"Nary a soul," I said.

"I'm at the Hotel Creston. Room 1209. Ask for Maybelle Bruce."

"The Hotel Creston!" That was the best hotel in town.

"Sure. I figured they'd look for me in all the second and third-rate flea traps first, so I came here. But I'm not going to be safe for long. I've got to get out of town."

"Be seeing you, honey."

Ten minutes later I knocked on the door of room 1209.

The door opened and I stepped inside. She flung her arms around my neck.

FOUR

For a moment our lips met and pressed tightly, then she drew back. I pulled her back toward me but her hands pushed against my chest. When I started to fumble around, she drew away and said, "No, Mike, this isn't the time."

"It's gotta have a time?" I asked. "It's like a coffee break?"

"We've gotta figure out what to do!" she said. "Sit down and cool off."

I sat down, but I cool slow. She took a seat on the bed, facing the chair I was in. She was wearing a dark blue suit of some light material. She had on a red blouse. This gal went in for red. Proost's caller wore red and black last night. Then it suddenly struck me that this wasn't the dress she had on when I saw her last.

"You ran out on me last night," I said. "Not that it isn't your privilege, but if you'd stuck with me you wouldn't be up to your—uh—chest in trouble."

She looked toward the window which wasn't even a view from where she sat. "I'm sorry I stood you up, Mike," she said. "But Lorchetto knew I'd tipped you off. The bartender told him, and I thought I'd better leave quickly. Then he and Jim followed us."

"The hell he did," I said. "I didn't see him."

"He did, Mike. Honest. He drove past the filling station while you were inside. He and Jim Bomo."

"Bomo?"

"The fellow who took you upstairs."

315

"You sure he didn't find out you worked for Proost?"

Her blue eyes fixed on me. "He wouldn't care too much about that."

"No? He doesn't care what the executive director of the Citizens' Anti-Vice League learns about the casino upstairs, huh?"

"Lorchetto knows the right people. He doesn't have to worry about Proost."

"Meaning what?"

"Get smart, Mike. This town is organized. Lorchetto's okay as long as he does what he's told. Even Proost doesn't dare touch him."

"Maybe Proost is in the rackets too."

"Maybe he is." She sighed. "Look, Mike, this talk is getting us no place. I'm sorry I stood you up, so don't be peeved. I told that filling station man to tell you—"

"You worked for Proost. You were his girl."

"Don't talk like a lovesick adolescent, Mike. Whose girl I was doesn't matter. There are a lot of people right now that would like to lay hands on me."

"Cops mostly."

That crack about being a lovesick adolescent made me mad. Sure, I was a little whooped up about this babe, but mainly I was mad about the runaround. Call it male pride.

She laughed, came across the room and sat down on my lap. Then she kissed me again. "Do you fall for every girl that smooches with you, Mike?"

"You told me you didn't know Proost," I said stubbornly, realizing I was behaving like a kid.

"Am I supposed to bare my soul to every stranger who comes knocking at my bedchamber door?"

"Considering the intimacy of it, yes."

We both laughed and she rumpled my hair, gave me another kiss and got up. She went back and sat down on the bed. "I'm glad you got your sense of humor back," she said.

"It'll do till the fire department gets here," I said. "Okay. I see your point. And I've outgrown my childish ways. Now why don't you give me some straight answers. What happened last night?"

"Like I told you," she said, "Brick saw me at the filling station. Luckily a taxi came along. I flagged it and had it take me to my room. I told the driver to wait while I changed clothes, I did it in about ten minutes, then I had him take me to Proost's place."

"Why?"

"Because I had some things to settle with him."

"Okay, Go on. Did you kill Proost?"

She sighed. "I heard that he was dead on the radio this morning." She nodded toward the speaker above her bed.

"If you didn't kill him, why did you come here?"

"To hide from Brick Lorchetto." She didn't look at me and I knew it wasn't the whole truth. "Mike, I want to get out of town. Will you help me?"

"First, I've got to have an answer. Either yes or no. Did you kill Proost?"

"Supposing I did?"

"Then you'd better go to the cops," I said.

"Supposing I didn't?"

"Then you can go to the cops and tell them. They won't hold you if you're not guilty. But hiding out is going to make things worse for you—for both of us."

"You're really thinking of yourself," she said bitterly. "So if I killed Proost, you'll turn me in. And if I didn't kill him, you insist that I go to the cops and clear myself. Is that it?"

"The cops will find you sooner or later," I told her. "When they find you, you'll have to answer the question I just asked. *Did you kill him?*"

Her shoulders sagged and she looked down at the floor.

"Maybe."

"That's no answer. Either you did or you didn't."

"I can't answer it any other way, Mike. Maybe it's the only answer I can give."

My mind went back to the old movie melodramas where the innocent heroine struggled with the villain over the possession of a gun and the damned thing went off. "There was a gun," I said. "And you fought over it? And it went off?"

"There was no gun. I didn't shoot him."

"That's the way he died." I reached for the phone. I got an outside line and called Don Hillard at the Press Room of Police Headquarters.

"Who are you calling?" she asked.

"Another reporter."

"You certainly have cooled. Five minutes ago you were drooling over me. Now I'm just another news story."

"Nuts," I said.

Don's voice came over the wire. "Who's nuts?"

"Oh, Don," I said. "I wasn't talking to you. This is Mike. You got the autopsy report on Proost yet?"

"Sure nuff, pal. I just called Hank about it."

"How'd Proost die?"

"Jeez, Mike, nobody questioned that. He was shot, of course. Right in the chest."

"That's what Guffy said. I thought maybe he didn't have it straight."

"Well, there was just one other little thing, Mike."

"Yeah? What?"

"He had a bruise on his head, like somebody might have belted him one before the shooting, but the coroner said that had nothing to do with his death."

"Okay, Don. Thanks."

"Don't mention it. And say, Mike, Hank just called for you."

"If he calls again, tell him not to bother me when I'm working." I hung up. Luzy sat tensely in the chair. "Proost was shot. If you didn't shoot him, you didn't murder him."

She said nothing.

"Did you hit him over the head and then shoot him while he was unconscious?"

"No matter what I tell you, you're going to think the opposite," she said.

"I want to think that you're innocent. And if you are, nobody can prove you're guilty."

"It has been done," she said. "Besides, maybe I'm guilty."

"If you didn't shoot him—"

"Mike, you sound like a cracked record. You want me to call in the cops. The people who are after me will get me, cops or no cops, unless I get a thousand miles from here. I know what I'm talking about, Mike."

"Who's after you? Maybe the cops can handle them."

"Don't make me laugh," she said. "The people who are after me buy and sell cops and give them away at Christmas time. I don't know who they are. The reason they're successful is because they know how to keep their names out of things. But if I surrender, I know that they'll make sure that I won't tell what little I do know."

"What do you know, Luzy?"

She laughed mirthlessly. "Do you want to be murdered too, Mike?" She sighed. "Stop trying to find out what it doesn't do you any good to know. Help me get away from here. I'm not safe even in this hotel. Lorchetto has bellhops working for him. They steer suckers to the Hilltop. As soon as Brick spreads the word that I'm wanted, they'll tell him where I am."

"You can't leave town without the cops getting you," I told her, "They're watching the airport, the trains and the bus stations. You'd never get past the ticket windows. And I can't take you. Even if I did, the sheriff's force and the state police are checking the highways, even the back roads. The only thing is to surrender. I know a cop that isn't bought. He'll make sure that nothing happens to you."

She shook her head. "I can't explain, Mike, but I can't surrender. Help me!"

I looked at her. I couldn't believe she murdered Proost. Yet, murderers seldom look like murderers. That's because they're not a special breed. I knew she'd been at the scene before, during or after the crime, and still I didn't think she had anything to do with it. I knew she had lied to me, yet I thought she was telling the truth. I knew she was a double-crosser, yet I trusted her. Good Lord, I'm a sucker.

But biological chemistry makes suckers of us all. "All right," I said, "I'm a fool, but I'll help you. I can help you hide from these bad boys you think are after you. Maybe you can also get away from the cops, but I can't take you out of town now. You'll have to wait till tonight."

"I'll wait. Can you take me somewhere now?"

"Not now. How soon do you think Brick will start spreading the word about you?"

She shook her head. "He might be doing that right now."

"If you're safe now, you ought to be safe from him for another hour," I said. "First I've got to find out just where you stand with the cops."

"Hurry, Mike. Please hurry."

I left the hotel.

Reporters don't work the same way cops work. They can't. Two or three men, at most half a dozen, do the work of hundreds on the police force. Ninety percent of a reporter's skill comes from knowing where to go to get the right answers. And you know where to go because you know the order in which things happen. When the cops close in on a suspect, they try to find him in the usual spots. If not successful, they place their evidence in the hands of the legal talent of the city or county and get a warrant. Then they search the unusual spots.

I decided to learn if a warrant had been issued for Luzy. It would be based on purely circumstantial evidence, but the cops probably knew as much as I did about Luzy's visit to Proost, and that was enough to hold her on suspicion of murder.

The county attorney had a suite of offices in the county building. He had several assistants in charge of different phases of his work. Cliff Ramcaster usually handled criminal cases, with the help of one or more of the assistants. Sometimes the county prosecutor himself.

I walked to the county building, a distance of three blocks, from the hotel. Several secretaries were busy typing in the large outside room, but Ramcaster's office door was partly open and looking through it I saw Ramcaster at his desk.

He saw me and gestured with his hand. "Come in, Mike. I've been wanting to talk to you."

I stepped in the room, conscious immediately that someone else was there.

Seated in a chair near the desk, calmly smoking a cigarette, was Martha Arkwright, looking as fresh and as beautiful as she had looked the day before.

"Well, Michael!" she beamed, as if we were the oldest of friends.

"You know Mrs. Arkwright, I see," said Ramcaster, taking my hand in a limp shake.

"Michael was out to see us yesterday," Martha said. "He's quite exciting."

Ramcaster sat down. "If Martha said that, you must be," he said. "She's a connoisseur of interesting people."

"That why she's here?" I said, kidding of course. Ramcaster was my idea of a dud.

"I came up to sell Cliff some tickets to our church benefit next week," Martha said. "Can I sell you one?"

"Reporters never buy tickets. They give free publicity," I told her.

I dug in my pockets for a cigarette. I found one and stuck it in my mouth, then I searched for a match.

"Light?" Martha asked, holding out a match folder.

"Thanks," I said. I took the folder and lit my cigarette. I started to hand the folder back, when I noticed the name printed on the cover. It said, "Hilltop Club."

I handed the folder back to Martha.

"We'd love to have you drop in," Martha said. "I'd see that you had a good time."

Ramcaster laughed. "What is this attraction you have for young women, Mike?"

"Do I have one?"

"You certainly do. Martha is acting like a school girl. And yesterday I understand you ran off with one of Brick Lorchetto's beauties. A former strip teaser known as Lucrezia."

"Really!" said Martha.

"And now you come into my office with a faint smear of lipstick around your mouth."

"Huh?" I drew my handkerchief so fast that I could have made Wyatt Earp look like a stone statue. I rubbed it over my lips. A pink smear came off on it. "Must have been the strawberry pie I had during my coffee break," I said.

Martha Arkwright giggled. "I know we can hardly get along without you at the benefit," she said. She got to her feet. "Well, Cliff, I really must be going. I have a lot of tickets to sell. Thanks a lot."

"Any time, Martha," he said.

After she left, he turned to me. "Where is she, Mike?"

"Who are you talking about?"

"The McGuire woman."

"You think I'm hiding her?"

"You were with her last night."

"She left me about eleven o'clock," I said.

"You haven't seen her since?"

I lied without thinking. "No. The cops woke me up this morning looking for her."

"The cops think she murdered Clarence Proost," said Ramcaster. "If you're hiding her, you'd better stop it. Harboring a fugitive, compounding a felony, and lots of things can get you into trouble, Mike."

"Has a warrant been issued yet?"

"One doesn't have to be if she committed murder, Mike. But we're going to issue one, just in case she leaves town."

"Well, why don't you go out and take another look in my hotel room," I said.

"We would, if we thought she was there." He laughed quietly. "Where did you get the lipstick, Mike?"

"I told you it was strawberry pie. And it's none of your business besides."

"Okay, okay." He played with his fingers like Ed Sullivan. "Well, what can I do for you, Mike?"

I'd already learned what I came to learn, that a warrant was being issued and the cops suspected Luzy of murdering Proost, but I had to stall.

"I wondered why you came out to the Hilltop last night," I said. "Isn't it unusual for the county prosecutor to take part in a raid?"

"Unusual, but not unprecedented," he said. "I went because Proost was trying to tell folks I was on the take for alleged illegal gambling at that place. I thought you knew all about that raid, Mike. Didn't Colonel Tanner brief you?"

"Why should he? He didn't know you were going to raid it."

Ramcaster laughed. "He suggested it."

"The devil you say!"

"Colonel Tanner is nobody's fool, Mike," Ramcaster said. "He figured Proost had some little game up his sleeve. It's my guess too that Proost was up to no good when he tried to get the *Gazette* as an ally. Tanner couldn't back out of it gracefully, and so he suggested we stage a quiet little raid on the Hilltop. He even got Brick Lorchetto to go along with the idea. Brick, of course, was agreeable. He didn't mind if his place got a clean bill of health. We proved there was no evidence of gambling and Colonel Tanner could wash his hands of the whole deal without making some of his friends, who, frequented the Hilltop, mad about it."

I could hardly believe it. Yet I knew that Colonel Tanner was a deep man and he did things in devious ways. He was much more anxious to expose Proost than he was to close down a joint such as Lorchetto operated.

"Colonel Tanner didn't tell me. I guess I've wasted time by coming here," I said. "By the way, is the McGuire warrant that you told me about for publication?"

He thought a moment, then said, "Go ahead and use it," he said. "She knows by now that we're looking for her. Otherwise she would have gone home. If everybody knows about it, it may make it harder for her to hide." He paused. "Unless you're hiding her."

I pulled some copy paper out of my pocket and got busy making notes. I seldom make notes of things I'm sure to remember, but I didn't want to answer that crack he made.

"Another thing," I said, "didn't you know there was gambling at the Hilltop before this?"

"Did you see any evidence of gambling out there, Mike?"

"No-o, but—"

"Neither did I. No officer has and no one else has come forward to sign a complaint."

"But Colonel Tanner and you made sure there would be no evidence by tipping off Lorchetto."

"You don't think I've been bought off, do you?" he said sarcastically. "The tipping off of Lorchetto was the Colonel's idea, not mine. I don't know what his angle was, but I can guess that he didn't want to have anything to do with Proost. If we had found evidence of a little friendly penny ante game at the Hilltop, we might have had to bring into court a few prominent Citizens' whose only crime was a desire to relax among friends. And Proost would have made big capital of it. You've got to remember, Mike, that the Hilltop is a private club. We've got too many things to do besides worrying about a friendly poker or dice game among people who can well afford to play poker and shoot craps. It's not like a public casino. The Hilltop isn't Monte Carlo."

I felt that he was minimizing the Hilltop's reason for being. "Thanks for putting me straight, Cliff," I said. "Our readers will be glad to know why the Hilltop has been left alone."

He didn't like that. "Be careful what you print."

I grinned. "If I did that, I'd probably be fired for not turning in any copy. I've got a hunch that there's a connection between the Hilltop and Proost's murder."

"When you find it, let me know," said Ramcaster. "But about the only connection you'll find is that one of Lorchetto's dice girls pulled the trigger."

I said good-by politely and left the office. There was a phone booth in the lobby of the county building and I used it to call Hank Newcomb.

FIVE

Hank was very pleased with what I gave him. An ex-striptease dancer being sought for the murder of a reform league leader made interesting reading, he said.

After I finished calling, I left the county building and started back toward the office to get my car. But I noticed a very big man loitering outside the door of the county building. He was a cop. Not one of the policemen I knew, but I'd been around enough cops to spot them anywhere.

I hadn't gone very far when I looked back and saw that he was following me. Instead of going back to the office, I cut across the street and started back in the direction I came. Flat-foot did the same thing.

And then I saw somebody else. This fellow had his hat pulled down trying to hide his face, but I knew that big nose and lantern jaw. They belonged to Jim Bomo, Brick Lorchetto's handyman. Bomo was following me too.

Neither Bomo or the flatfoot seemed to notice each other. They were so busy watching me that they paid no attention to anyone else.

A few doors down, in the middle of the block was the Essex theater, one of the first-run movie houses in Creston. As I came under the marquee, I saw the box office was opening to sell tickets, I walked down a short distance to a drugstore, went inside and entered a phone booth. I called the Hotel Creston and asked for Room 1209. Luzy answered.

"Golly, I'm glad you called. My God! I've been all jitters since you left."

"Well, we're moving now," I said. "Wait for ten minutes, then go down in the lobby and check out. Afterwards, wait in the side entrance, the one on Sixth Street, till I come along in my car to pick you up. Got it?"

"I got it. Is somebody following you?"

"Yes. Two somebodies, but I know how to get rid of them."

"Be sure you do, honey. Brick Lorchetto can play rough."

"I will. So long."

I went out of the drug store. On one side of the doorway Flatfoot was taking a great interest in a Geritol window display. On the other, Bomo was pretending to be interested in athletic supporters. I acted as if I hadn't noticed either one of them and sauntered slowly toward the marquee of the Essex theater.

I stopped to look at the posters advertising a new science-fiction movie. Out of the corner of my eye, I noticed that neither of my shadows had moved.

I edged into the lobby, behind the ticket booth, then walked rapidly up to the doorman. I flashed my press card and said, "Mike Lanson of the *Gazette*. Is the manager in?"

The doorman bowed politely and waved me through. "He's in his office downstairs."

Both of the men outside would be waiting for me to buy a ticket, not realizing that reporters can almost always get in a moviehouse on their press cards, especially when they pretend to have business with the manager. By the time either one of them wised up, I was leaving by the alley exit.

I made it to the office, got my car and drove around to the Sixth Street entrance of the Hotel Creston.

As I drove up to the side door I saw a blonde standing in the doorway. Not until she reached the car did I recognize her as Luzy, who had had black hair when I left her.

"What in the devil—"

"Get my bag, you lummox," she said, pointing to the side entrance of the hotel. A big brown-leather valise was sitting there.

I was in a state of shock, I guess, or maybe I have the id of a gentleman. Anyhow, I got the bag. It must have weighed fifty pounds, but I'm a strong gentleman and I carried it to the back of my car, unlocked the trunk, and stuffed it inside.

Then I got in the car beside Luzy. "I thought strippers didn't wear much," I said.

"Hunh?" She must have thought she'd forgotten to dress, because she started to run her hands over her figure. "I got everything on!"

"I mean the suit case. It weighed a ton."

"Oh, that!" she said. "It's full of manuscripts. My poetry."

I started up the car and we drove off. I watched the rear-view mirror, but I saw no sign of anybody following. "What did you do to your hair?" I asked.

"I used some of that spray stuff," she said. "I had the bellhop get some for me. I figured everybody would be looking for a black-haired dame. Everybody on Brick's payroll anyhow."

"I thought you said the bellhops were working for him."

"My God!" she said. "I didn't think of that!"

We rode in silence. It wasn't Brick I was worrying so much about. It was the cops.

Finally, I said, "Since I'm sticking my neck out, I ought to have a few answers."

"Why don't you get off that jag?"

"It's more important than you think. Besides, I've got an overdeveloped curiosity. I'm a reporter."

"You're not going to print what I could tell you. Where are you taking me, Mike?"

"To my hotel."

"That's cozy. I thought you were too busy to take me out of town."

"I'm going to hide you there," I said. "The cops already have searched my room. I doubt if they'll come back."

"It's not cops that I'm worried about. If it was only cops, I'd hire a lawyer."

"Tell me what happened last night."

"I already did. I went to see Proost and left him."

"Did you slug him by any chance while you were there?"

"What gives you that idea?"

"Somebody hit him over the head before he was shot."

"Mike," she said, "I told you maybe I killed Clarence. That's the only answer I'll give. You can beat me with a rubber hose and I won't change it. I've got good reasons."

"Okay," I said, "why did you kill him maybe?"

"Because I helped him with his dirty racket," she said. "I didn't feel sorry about cheap crooks he forced money out of. But there were others. Nice folks. He blackmailed them."

"How?"

"Anybody can make a mistake once in awhile. Supposing a nice old guy wants to prove that he's younger than his years. So he dates up some cheap floozy who works with Proost—"

"Like you?"

"Shut up," she said. "Proost or somebody else is around with a camera. One that uses infra-red flash bulbs which takes pictures in the dark and which nobody can see flash. You can see what happens."

"The guy should have thought of things before he got mixed up in the mess."

"I suppose so."

"If you didn't like working for Proost, why did you?"

She was silent for a moment. Then she said, "Mike, I had to. You see, I've got a brother. He's on parole for stealing a car. Since then he jumped parole and Proost knows where he is. If I don't do as Proost says, he'll turn in my brother."

"So he was blackmailing you too." If the cops found out that about Luzy, it would supply the motive for Proost's murder.

"Yes. My God, Mike, I feel lower than anything that crawls."

I drew up in front of the Waltham Hotel. I gave her the key to my room. "Go up to room 615," I said. "Nobody will ask you questions and I'll keep your suitcase in my car. You eaten yet?"

She shook her head.

"Better grab some lunch at the coffee shop. It's still early and not many people will be in there. Then go up to my room."

"You're not coming in?"

I shook my head. "I've got work to do. I'll see you soon after five o'clock."

"Then what? After five, I mean?"

"It depends on what happens before five."

"Mike, you're not going to turn me in to the cops?"

"I promised I wouldn't," I said. But I knew the cops would get her. Maybe I could persuade her to surrender. "Maybe I can find a good lawyer."

"And a good bodyguard who'll stay in jail with me?"

"Nobody's going to touch you in jail."

"Mike, you don't know what kind of people you're dealing with."

"I don't think they're magicians. But don't worry until you have to. I'm going to try to do something before five o'clock."

"You're sweet." She leaned over and planted a kiss on my cheek. Then she hopped off.

Remembering what had happened at Ramcaster's office, I pulled out my handkerchief and scrubbed my face. No lipstick came off this time.

Then I gunned my car down the street and headed back to town. I watched my rear-view mirror, but as far as I could find out, nobody was following me.

When I turned off Bradley Trafficway, I stopped in a filling station and called Don Hilliard. He was just going out to lunch. "Nothing new," he told me. "But Manton Arkwright called. He left a number for you to call."

"Okay," I said. I took the number, a downtown exchange.

A voice that used broad A's told me I was connected with the Plymouth Club. I identified myself and presently I had Arkwright on the line. "I'd like to talk to you, Lanson," he said.

"All right," I said, expecting him to talk.

"Not over the telephone. Can I see you now?"

I hesitated. As one of Proost's associates in the Citizens' Anti-Vice League, he might be able to offer something, but I wasn't sure it would be of much value for the next edition. Still, a statement from him might pacify Hank till I got something with meat on it.

"Yes, sir," I said.

"Have you had lunch?"

"Why no," I said, warming up a little. "Not yet."

"Why not join me at the Plymouth Club as my guest," he said. "How soon can I expect you?"

"In fifteen minutes," I said.

The Plymouth Club was the most exclusive, the most expensive, and the most stuffy social organization in Creston. It occupied a large three-story building right in the heart of town on Main Avenue. I don't believe an income tax bracket was a requirement for membership, but I doubted if any of the members were under the fifty percent classification. Not only that, but they were all 'eminently respectable.'

I'd been there once as a guest of an important corporation lawyer and the thing that impressed me most was that members didn't smoke ordinary cigarettes, but they got a brand stamped with the Plymouth Club name in packages that had the club crest on the outside. They were ritzy, but a lousy smoke.

It took me fourteen minutes to get to the door, where I was admitted by a uniformed man, who looked me over to see if anything was crawling on me, but when I gave my name he softened a little and let me in.

"Mr. Arkwright is in the library, sir," he said.

I looked blank and he added. "Second door on the right."

As I walked toward it, I heard the click of billiard balls on the left and saw some green covered billiard tables there. Next time Hank Newcomb accused me of loafing in pool halls, I'd tell him I'd been at the Plymouth Club.

I also heard another unmistakable sound. The clink of poker chips. I grinned inwardly as I told myself that this was a private club, just like Brick Lorchetto's Hilltop, except that the members had a tougher time getting in and they weren't quite so flashy.

But I didn't see any harm in a friendly game. Even here, where the stakes were probably much too rich even for some of the Hilltop patrons. But it was a friendly game, played with skill and for fun. Men who lost could afford their losses. And probably they were so nearly even in skill that they wound up about even over a long period of time.

Gambling *per se* wasn't wrong. Everyone gambles. I've bet on every major sporting event and often I've put two bucks up on a horse if I thought my hunches were right. If I won, I gloated; if I lost, I called it entertainment. I didn't expect to get rich at it, and I could afford my losses. Where gambling becomes wrong is when it ceases to be entertainment, or becomes a waste of time. Or when it cultivates crime, corruption and the things I felt were associated with Lorchetto's place.

Arkwright was sitting in a big red plush chair talking to a gentleman whose back was toward me. He spotted me coming in the door. Smiled and said something to his companion.

The latter got up, turned and faced me. I felt like somebody had pushed the panic button.

Manton Arkwright's pal was Colonel Gordon Curran Tanner, my boss.

Colonel Tanner was in his early fifties, a man whose hair was graying, but who was still big and strong and prime. His eyes were concealed by shaggy brows. Sometimes he wore glasses, but not when he was meeting people. He didn't want to weaken his biggest weapon—the ability to look right through a person.

Once he'd been in the oil business. During the war he'd been with the O.S.S., which is no pussyfoot organization. He came to Creston after the war, made a pile speculating in real estate and bought the tottering newspapers, the *Globe* and the *Gazette* and welded them into something financially strong.

He looked at me with a sober face as if it was the most natural thing in the world for me to meet him there. It was, I guess, because he was a member.

We said some inane things and then the Colonel remarked, "Mike is very busy today, Manton, and since I'm paying his salary, let's go into the dining room. We can talk while we eat."

That was very like the Colonel who watched the nickels and dimes like he didn't know where his next hundred thousand was coming from. We ordered drinks. The Colonel took a Bobby Burns, which is a Scotch version of a Manhattan with a dash of

Benedictine. Arkwright ordered a Blue Blazer. Since they were
ordering Scotch and I didn't want to appear plebeian, I ordered
a highball, Scotch and soda, although I prefer Bourbon.

After we got our drinks, the Colonel turned his cold gray
eyes on me and said, "Mike, I know you're surprised, but I had
Manton arrange this in order to talk to you privately. I was
afraid to call the press room lest Don recognize my voice."

I nodded. "I understand, sir."

"Now just for the record, I want you to tell Manton truthfully how many times I've ever asked you to leave a news story
out of the paper."

I thought for a moment, and then said, "Never, sir."

He continued staring at me and said, "Qualify it, Mike. I
want Manton to know the truth."

"Never, as long as it was legitimate news, not libelous, and
fit to print," I said.

"Surely, in the case of an advertiser—" Arkwright began.

"We've printed news to which advertisers have objected,"
said the Colonel. "I'll admit we have played down stories that
might reflect on some of them, but we don't hush up things that
are of public interest."

Arkwright heaved a big sigh. "It might be different if you
were in the middle, Colonel," he said.

"I *am* in the middle, Manton," said the Colonel. "Look, if
this thing comes to light and I print it, I'll be accused of being
vindictive. If, by some chance I let you persuade me not to print
it, the people who count will know about it and I'll be accused
of squelching something that puts me in a bad light."

I didn't know what they were talking about, but it was my boss
and to me he was right as long as I got my paycheck every week.

"But Colonel," said Arkwright, "think of my reputation!"

"Your reputation be damned. Nothing could hurt you, Manton. You are the best example of solid respectability I've ever
known and I've been around in my time."

"Nice of you to say so." Arkwright sipped his drink. "I don't
approve of vice, even petty vice. I've lived a life of unimpeach-
able honesty. I've handled estates for widows and dependents

without misappropriating a penny. And now I suddenly am finding it difficult to explain my motives."

The waiter came and took our orders. After he went away, Colonel Tanner said, "Manton believes the Hilltop Club episode is likely to crop up as a motive for the murder of Clarence Proost."

I wondered, and not idly, what a man like Manton Arkwright, who handled, widows' estates without misappropriating a penny, might have to do with a gambling joint like the Hilltop.

The Colonel answered my question as he continued. "You see the old Prentice homestead, which is now the Hilltop, once belonged to me. I gave it to my third wife as part of her divorce settlement."

Now certain things were beginning to take shape.

"I leased it to Lorchetto several years ago," Arkwright explained. "I thought it was a legitimate deal, and it seemed to be, at first. He had a sort of country club there without a golf course. Swimming, dining and dancing, private parties and so on. I never belonged, of course. Martha and I don't go in for that sort of thing and the Hilltop was patronized by a flashy, sporty crowd. Then I began to hear rumors that the club wasn't as private as it pretended to be and that Lorchetto was operating various gambling games upstairs. I questioned him about it and of course he denied everything. I couldn't evict him without proof and naturally I set out to get it. I asked Proost to help me." He sighed.

"Proost knew all about it," Colonel Tanner went on. "But he hadn't made a move because he saw that it was going to be a regular gold mine. Ramcaster knew about it too. And Proost knew that Ramcaster knew."

"I don't know if Ramcaster was accepting bribes or not," Arkwright said quickly.

"No," said Colonel Tanner, "but Proost knew. You can bet your bottom dollar on that. And somehow, Proost also stumbled onto the fact that I'd owned the place and now the title was in my divorced wife's name." He paused.

The waiter brought in our orders and set them before us. After he had served us, he retired discretely and the Colonel resumed:

"Proost had four angles, no less. He threatened Brick with raids, threatened Ramcaster and Manton with exposure. Then he came to me and suggested that I join in the crusade against gambling, knowing what a spot it would put me on."

I grinned. "So that's why you sent me out to find out what I could about Proost."

"And you didn't turn up anything," said the Colonel "Everyone concerned had his own personal reasons for keeping quiet."

Arkwright turned to me, his eyes were almost pleading. "The police are certain to find out about this. They know all about your movements, Lanson, and they already suspect that the Hilltop club is somehow involved in Proost's murder—"

"They don't suspect you of that," I said.

"No," said Arkwright, smiling. "But they'll investigate this woman—it's in the early edition of your paper." I realized. that Hank must have wedged a bulletin on Luzy into the noon edition. "She worked for Lorchetto and the police do things thoroughly. They'll check on Lorchetto. I know his reputation isn't too good. And they'll find out who owns the place, who handled the lease, and so on. Once my clients hear of it—" He threw up his hands in a gesture.

"Your mistake was leasing the club to Lorchetto in the first place," said the Colonel. "Especially if you knew about him."

"I didn't know about him at the time," said Arkwright. "Proost tipped me off later that he'd been involved in some very nasty affairs, including a shooting in Cincinnati."

The Colonel thought for a moment. "Manton wants you to soft pedal his connection, Mike. I told him that we couldn't if the police brought it into the case. I don't know why they should, but they might. So let's play it this way: if the police mention it, we'll have to print it. We don't have to play it up, but we'll have to run it. If the police ignore it, as they probably will, we have no reason for dragging Manton Arkwright's good name into the case."

"And you have my deepest gratitude," said Arkwright. "I have really done nothing wrong, gentleman. After all, there's a very thin line in most cases between a good name and a bad one. Every man is the sum total of his acts. Over the years, if you have been trustworthy and honest, people regard you as righteous. But one false step can upset your reputation, even though you may still be a good man within. Dessert anyone?"

The Colonel, who was beginning to develop a little weight in the cummerbund region, said he didn't want any. I didn't have time and Arkwright said he didn't want any either. He paid our check and we left the club.

SIX

The Colonel had taxied to the Plymouth Club and I offered to drive him back to the *Gazette* office in my car. It was only fair, because I got an expense allowance on my car from the office.

It wasn't far, but the Colonel made the most of it. He put me on the grill immediately after we started from the club.

"You're not hiding that woman, are you, Mike?"

I wondered how he had learned about it, but Colonel had pipelines everywhere. Guffy might have told him. For all Guffy's hatred of newspapers, he had a warm spot for the Colonel, in some matters, as long as the Colonel didn't try to tell the cops how to run their business.

"Why should I stick my neck out?" I asked evasively.

"You're young, for one thing," he said. "When a man's young a pretty woman can make him do things. But if you are hiding her, Mike, I'd get out from under very quickly. This thing is more than a mere murder case. I've been expecting trouble for a long time."

"You mean the rackets?"

"I mean the rackets." He nodded vigorously. "I know that they exist in every city. You'll always find men who disregard the law for their own personal ends. But in Creston, the rackets are too well hidden to be the ordinary kind that the police can handle. I've got reason to believe that Proost was well up in the organization, that he may have been near, or actually at the top."

"I thought he was a reformer."

"What better spot would there be for a man to run things than to pose as a reformer? He could use the police to enforce discipline, and hypocrisy to hide his identity."

"He didn't live very high." Proost's apartment had been in a rather high-priced section and Arkwright had said he had money of his own, but he hadn't lived on the scale that gangsters reputedly live.

"That isn't evidence. Income tax problems might crop up. One thing gangsters and racketeers have learned is that it's very hard to try to fool Uncle Sam."

Colonel Tanner had given me something to think about and now he continued. "I hope you'll forgive me for the bad time I gave you at the Hilltop Club last night."

So now he was going to confess that the raid was his idea. "Cliff Ramcaster gave me an inkling on that raid," I said.

"Ah! Then I suppose I'd better 'come clean' as the police say. My idea was to give the Hilltop a clean bill of health in order to smoke out Proost. I wanted to find out what his game was. But apparently I upset his organization so much that it provoked his murder."

I whistled softly.

"One more thing, Mike," said the Colonel. "I may be in the clear on this, but I think I'll tell the police my story anyhow. So don't be surprised if you hear that I was among the visitors that Proost had last night."

"You?"

He laughed. "But I didn't murder him. I called on Proost about nine and I left before ten. Two or three hours before he was murdered. I wanted to give him to understand that my newspapers are not cat's paws for anybody. No matter how high-sounding their motives pretend to be."

"I suppose I'm to use this in my story, if it comes out?"

"By all means. Use the same discretion on me, that I asked for Manton Arkwright, but don't protect me."

So much has been said about newspapers not printing all the facts, suppressing stories and so on, that I thought it was a pity that more people couldn't have heard the Colonel. There may be editors, nowadays especially, who do censor for advertisers, for personal reasons, or because of pressure groups. But Colonel Tanner was an old-time newspaperman in theory if not actually old from a standpoint of service. He actually leaned over backwards to be honest. It's difficult, if not impossible, to erase all bias from news. But I think Colonel Tanner came close to it. He thumped hard-headedly, even foolishly on his own sacred cows when he voiced the editorial policy, but he didn't let his policies interfere with the news.

We walked into the city room together.

Hank Newcomb's teeth would have itched with nervous tension, had he known that I'd lunched with Colonel Tanner at the Plymouth Club. As it was, they almost withered at the roots to see Colonel Tanner and I walk into the city room chummylike.

"Keep Mike informed of any and all new developments in the Proost case," Tanner said.

"I understand, sir," said Hank. He made it sound nice, but I knew he was thinking sarcastic thoughts.

"He's on a special assignment in connection with the case," the Colonel said. "Don Hilliard is capable enough to take care of the police angle."

"Yes, sir," said Hank, winning an academy award for concealing his thoughts. "Mind letting me in on the secret, Mike?" He directed the question at me.

"He minds," said the Colonel, turning on his heel and departing for his ivory tower.

Hank waited until he knew the Colonel was safely out of earshot "How do you like that?" he said. "He goes over my head and doesn't even tell me what it's all about. I thought I was in charge of the city room."

"He's in charge of you, sweetheart," I said.

"Don't get too damned chipmonk," he said. "I can still give you a hard time, Rover Boy."

"Don't disillusion me, Hank. You've always been my ideal for fairness and consideration of others."

"Don't rub it in," said Hank. "By the way, somebody's been trying to get hold of you. He left a number." He picked up a sheet of copypaper on which he'd scrawled a phone number, WYoming 7-3477. An easy number to remember. Seven, three and four make seven. Two more sevens and Wyoming has seven letters. After I fixed the number in my mind, I crumpled up the paper and threw it into the wastebasket

"Don't do that," said Hank. "You might forget it."

"I'm a human elephant," I said. "I never forget. Did this guy leave his name?"

"No. Just the number. Probably one of your pool hall pals."

Hank wasn't feeling very well, or I'd have mentioned the Plymouth Club. Maybe it didn't have pool or snooker tables, but it had billiards, which is snobby pool.

I went to the phone I shared with Anderson and dialed the number. A gruff voice answered, "Hello."

"Mike Lanson of the *Gazette*," I said. "Somebody there want to talk to me?"

"I did, Newsboy."

I waited. "So?"

"Want to make a deal?"

"What are you talking about?" I asked.

"You know what I'm talking about. You get the stuff from the girl, and I'll pay a good price for it."

"What stuff? What girl?"

"Don't act so damned ignorant. You know what's going on. You're the best friend she's got now, Lover Boy. She'll give you the stuff if you get her out of town before the cops nail her."

He was talking about Luzy. But that was about all I'd figured out up to now. I tried to stall. "Who is this?"

"Wouldn't you like to know?"

"How do I know who to deliver the stuff to, unless I know whom to call?"

"I'll call you later."

"When?"

"You name the time and the place. I'll call you."

"Maybe I don't want to go along with this."

"You will. You'll want to see the sun rise tomorrow," he said. The way he said it made me feel cool in the backbone.

I was trying to figure out if I'd heard the voice before. I wondered if it was Brick Lorchetto, or maybe Jim Bomo, but I couldn't be sure. Maybe I'm a human elephant, but my memory is visual rather than auditory. I don't remember pitch and sounds very well. I'm a hell of a poor singer. I can talk to a guy and a half-hour later I can quote what he said, almost word-for-word, but I still don't remember the tone or quality of his voice, except whether he was a bass or a tenor. This guy was a husky baritone.

"Call me at five-thirty here at the office," I said. "If I'm not here, I'll leave word where to reach me."

"If you don't, I can find you," said the voice.

"I can always call you at this number."

"Take my advice, Bub. Don't." He hung up.

I went back to the city desk. "Anything important?" Hank asked. He never liked to have anything going on that he didn't know about, which was unfortunate because he didn't know about a lot of things and it nearly drove him crazy. Or maybe that was the trouble with him.

"A life and death matter," I said. It was the truth, but he didn't believe me.

"Run along and earn your salary," said Hank.

I could think of an answer to that too, considering how much I felt myself underpaid, but I decided that I'd run my spurs into him enough for one noon hour, so I departed.

There were several people I wanted to see. Most of them were people I should have seen in the morning, but I'd been pretty busy and hadn't gotten around to it.

My first stop was at Sheriff Lindley's office. He was a big man. Even in Texas or Alaska he would have been called big. He was at least six-five and he weighed, to make a bad guess, 275 pounds. He was over forty and a politician. I found him in his office filling up one side of a desk on which he was writing things which made no particular difference to me.

"Hello, Mike," he said, putting aside his pen. "Damned reports. Always got to be writing one. What's itching under your armpits today?"

"I'm doing a little checking on the murder case," I said casually.

"Oh. That." He relaxed a little. "The police are handling it. I don't have anything to do with it, so long as it's in the city. If you ask me, Proost asked for it."

"Yeah," I said. "I thought there might have been some sort of a hookup with your call at the Hilltop last night."

Sheriff Lindley shrugged. "You know how those things are, Mike. I get a warrant. I gotta serve it. No skin off my nose if some rich bastard wants to shoot craps in a gyp joint like Brick runs."

"Proost sort of hinted that the county officers were fixed," I said. "He claimed Brick should have been shut down months ago."

Sheriff Lindley stopped relaxing. A gleam of anger burned in his eyes. "If he said that, he's a liar," he said, "I never took a dime off Brick Lorchetto."

"I didn't think you did," I said. I really didn't know. Basically Sheriff Lindley was honest. But he was also a good politician . . . He'd overlook things if he thought you could hand him a parcel of votes. Maybe Brick Lorchetto worked it that way. "You knew what was going on though."

"Sure. I knew. Everybody knew. But proving it is something else and in order to make an arrest stick, you've gotta prove it. Why, Brick coulda sued my pants off if I arrested him and he proved it was false. Sure, Proost came around to me a couple of times and said I oughta raid the place. I said that if he'd sign a complaint, I'd raid. But I'm not stickin' my neck out."

"Who signed the complaint last night?" I asked.

The sheriff shrugged, "You ought to know that and if you don't know, I ain't sayin'. I don't ask questions anyhow. Ramcaster got everything fixed up, then he handed me the warrant and said, 'Let's go, Gus.' So we went. We didn't find anything, but like I said, it's no hair off my tail."

"Were you on good terms with Proost?"

"Sure. I was a member of his club. The Citizen's Anti-Vice League. I figured it would give me some votes."

"How much did you pay to belong?" I asked quietly.

"Proost told me a membership was a hundred dollars. He said that if I belonged he wouldn't raise hell about my not raiding the Hilltop and some other joints in the county."

I grinned. To Sheriff Lindley it was an innocent and benevolent smile. "You haven't got a new angle on the murder, huh?"

"Not so much as a red hot suspect. I told the boys to watch the highways, just in case that McGuire tomato tried to leave town, but I don't reckon she has. If she did, she left last night. My boys would have spotted her today."

"You've got a pretty good bunch of deputies, sheriff," I said, getting up. "Thanks for your time."

"My time's always available to voters, son."

I stopped at a drug store before I went to my car. I spent a dime of Colonel Tanner's expense money to call Manton Arkwright's home, which was a UNiversity exchange: UNiversity 4-3400. Arkwright wasn't at home, but Martha answered.

"Well, Mike!" she said warmly. "I'm seeing a lot of you lately. Why don't you come out?"

She wasn't seeing me now, because this wasn't television. "Sorry," I said. "I'm busy. I wanted a little information about the Citizens' Anti-Vice League. I thought Mr. Arkwright could help me."

"He doesn't know as much about it as I do, Mike. Maybe I can help you. What do you want to know?"

"What are the dues?"

"Oh. Are you planning on joining. Then we'll see a lot of each other."

"No, I haven't time to join things. I just wanted to know what it cost to belong."

"Ten dollars a year," she said.

"Did you have just one kind of membership? Weren't there contributing memberships where some people paid more?"

She hesitated while she thought about it. "No-o. Not memberships. But some people contributed small amounts sometimes. But there really wasn't much expense to the organization. Just Mr. Proost's salary and expenses and the salary of his secretary—Mr. Stauffer. The dues took care of almost everything."

"How many members did you have?"

"Two thousand I think," she said.

Two thousand times ten made twenty thousand. And Sheriff Lindley had paid ten times ten dollars.

"Thanks, Martha," I said.

"Come over sometime," she said.

After I left the phone, I wondered if I shouldn't tell Sheriff Lindley that ninety dollars of his dues went into Proost's pocket.

Proost really had a racket.

I made one more call to the telephone company repair service. But before I made it, I checked the Hilltop Club's number, which was GReenwood 5-4506. Not WYoming 7-3477.

"This is Brick Lorchetto," I said. "My telephone seems to be out of order. Can you send a man out to look at my line?"

"Certainly, sir. What seems to be the matter?"

"It cuts out when I'm making a call," I said. "I think it has to do with the overhead line which comes into my place. That's the Hilltop Club, north of town, you know."

"What's your number, sir?"

"GReenwood 5-4506," I said. "Can you get on it right away? This is a business phone."

"Yes, sir. We'll send someone out right away."

I hung up and went back to my car. Lorchetto would see linemen working around his place and get gray hairs wondering if his phone line was being tapped. If he had anything to do with Proost's murder, he'd sweat blood.

Having laid the egg of my little plot, I drove out on the highway toward the Hilltop to see it hatch. I suppose I was a damned fool for thinking I was so smart. Maybe I'll learn someday.

There was a single car, a Buick convertible, parked at the Hilltop Club's blacktop parking area, and two cars behind the building, a Ford and a Dodge. The place looked like everyone was asleep. No doorman, no sign of life.

I knocked. An eye appeared in the peephole in the door. "We ain't open," said a voice. It was Jim Bomo. It was harsh, but not the voice I'd heard over the phone. Bomo could have disguised his voice, I suppose, but I didn't think he had any talent except in applied violence.

"I want to see Brick," I said.

Somebody inside said something and Bomo turned away from the peephole. I heard him say, "It's that snoop of a reporter."

"Let him in."

Bomo growled and opened the door. The place was dark and had a musty smell. Bomo motioned toward the room to the right, where the bar was located.

I found Brick behind the bar with a tall glass in his hand. "Hello, Lanson," he said. "I didn't expect you back so soon. But you're early. We don't open till six, and not much goes on here before nine."

"I'm just checking up," I said.

"You won't find any news here," said Brick. "Drink?"

"Don't mind. Bourbon and water."

He scraped some ice cubes out of a bin, put them in a glass and poured whiskey over them. He filled the glass with water from a pitcher. "I got a bartender's union card, so it's okay," he said, grinning as he handed me the glass.

I raised the glass. "Lucky days," I said.

"Let us hope," said Brick. "What you checking on, news-boy?"

"I got a phone call this morning," I said. "I didn't remember your voice clearly enough to know if it was you."

"Was it?"

"Can't say for sure," I said, sipping the drink. "Whoever it was, wanted to make a deal."

Lorchetto's eyes narrowed. "What kind of deal?"

"I didn't like the sound of it," I said.

"About the girl?"

"What makes you say that?" I asked.

"Listen, Scoop," said Brick, "a lot of people know you've got the girl hidden away somewhere. God knows why you're hiding her. She's trouble all the way. She eats boys like you."

"Thanks, I'll watch myself," I said.

"She hasn't got a friend in this town now that Proost is dead. And she probably killed him. But she remembers what an easy mark you were last night, so after she shoots Proost, she calls you up. She puts a sigh in her voice and says, 'Come on over and get me, dearie.' And you run like a slobbering school boy. She can't do anything for you, Scoop. And you'll wind up behind the eight ball, take it from me."

I looked at him, and grinned. "For a man who doesn't know what he's talking about, you sure say a lot."

I took my glass and paced back and forth. At the end of the bar, I stopped and looked out the window. I'd been worried when I drove in, because there hadn't been any phone company truck out there. I wondered if they'd foul things up and not show at all. But now the truck was stopped out there by the line that ran up the lane to the club house.

"What can you do for me, Brick?" I asked.

Brick laughed. "Now that's the kind of talk I like," he said. "Where's the girl?"

"I don't have her," I said.

"But somebody wants to make a deal."

"He doesn't know any more than you do," I said. "And I'm not so sure it wasn't you. I told the cops about it." I looked toward the window. "Is that the phone company out there, or are the cops putting a tap on your line?"

Brick came around the bar like he was trying out for the Olympics. He went to the window and looked out "Jim!" he called. "Go out there and find out what the hell goes."

"Yah!" Jim Bomo went out the door.

"So it was you," I said.

Brick looked at me like I gave him a headache. "Do you know why Proost was killed?"

I studied a moment. "Was it because he was unpopular?"

"Don't be funny. Proost had the sweetest little racket this side of nowhere. He was bleeding everybody. He tried to bleed me, but I've got constipated arteries. That's why he pulled those shenanigans on Colonel Tanner, and all the rest. He wanted the Colonel to pay off for not raiding this joint. He put the

bee on old man Arkwright for the same reason. Then he tried
to squeeze Ramcaster, because we contribute to his campaign
fund—he's running for County Prosecutor next time. But that's
pin money for Proost. He's got a file that would choke a whale.
He knows where everybody keeps his skeleton. And it's no wonder he got killed. Anybody else would have been shot ten times
five years ago."

"The cops didn't say anything about a file."

"The file wasn't there when the cops were called. Your little
girl friend has it all. And somebody wants it."

"Meaning you?"

"Believe me, paper boy, I wouldn't mind having it. Yes, I'll
even make a deal with you."

SEVEN

I finished my drink without answering. "Want more?" he asked.

I shook my head.

"You got something coming for that five bucks you spent to join the club last night," he said.

"I didn't get much for it, that's a fact," I said, "but it wasn't my money."

Brick laughed. "What kind of a story did Luzy give you pal?" he asked.

I gave him an innocent stare. "What gives you the idea I talked to her?"

He snorted in disgust. "Come now, newshound!"

"You ought to know where she is. You're her boss," I said. "How does it happen that you hired her, if you knew she worked for Clarence Proost?"

"Sometimes it's better to know your enemies," said Brick. The way he said it told me that this wasn't the right answer.

"Could it be that you felt that Proost couldn't hurt you?" I asked. "You knew all about the raid, didn't you? You knew it was coming."

Brick laughed. But before he could answer, Bomo admitted himself with a key. "Them guys working on the phone line say they're from the telephone company, boss. They said you reported phone trouble."

"That's a lie." Brick picked up a phone behind the bar. He dialed a number while I watched. He didn't realize that he was calling a number that was easy to memorize: UNiversity 4-3400. He waited a moment, then: "Hello, honey? How you makin' out? Oh, no special reason, honey. Somebody said the phone wasn't workin' and I was just tryin' it out . . . no, I wasn't checking up on you. . . . What the hell? Maybe I should check up!" He slammed the phone back in its cradle. "Women!" he said.

He went to the window and looked out. "Wire tappin' is illegal!" he said.

"Just shows how lax our law enforcement agencies are," I told him.

He turned on his heel and gave me a stare.

"All right, funny man," he said. "Let's talk turkey. Where's Luzy McGuire?"

I shrugged. "That's what the cops want to know."

"And if the cops find her and learn that you've hidden her, you'll be in the cell next door."

"Maybe she's in his room, boss," said Jim.

Brick looked at me. Then he shook his head. "That's the first place the cops would look," he said.

"They already did," I told him.

"She was at the Hotel Creston," Brick went on. "A bellhop tipped me off. She dyed her hair blonde and went out the side door a little before noon today. She got in a convertible—a red Ford convertible. That's your car, chum."

He had me there. I didn't answer.

"Jim," said Brick Lorchetto, "maybe you ought to persuade this guy a little. Work him over nice. Don't put any marks where they show. He's a nice-lookin' young fellow and we don't want to spoil him for the girls."

"Yah," said Jim, and he moved toward me.

"Wait a minute," I said. "Let's talk this over."

"Where is she?" asked Brick.

"I don't know!"

Jim Bomo swung, hard. His fist ran into my belly up to his wrist and I felt like I'd been kicked by a bear.

"Where is she?" Brick yelled.

I groaned.

Bomo slapped my face on both sides with the back of his hand. "Where is she?"

I couldn't talk. I was gasping for breath.

Once more Bomo's fist sank into my belly.

I collapsed on the floor.

The next thing I remembered was that Brick was bathing my face with a towel and somebody was pounding on the door.

"Open up! Open up, Lorchetto!"

I wanted to cheer, but my insides were still all mixed up. That was the voice of Lieutenant Clyde Guffy.

"He's coming out of it," said Lorchetto. "On your feet, Scoop! Come on, stand up!" He pulled me to my feet. Surprisingly, I was able to stay that way, although I was swaying a little. "Open the door, Jim."

Jim opened the door and Guffy came in. He stopped as he looked through the double doors into the bar, where I stood with Lorchetto steadying me with his hand.

"I hope I'm not interrupting anything private," he said.

"I'm sure glad to see you," I said.

"I'll bet you are," said Guffy. "I should have let you get out of your own messes, but I couldn't stand to think of getting somebody worse in the Press Room." He turned to Brick. "Now what the hell has been going on?"

"You're putting a tap on my telephone," said Brick.

"Why don't you sue me?" said Guffy. He turned to me, "You all right, Mike?"

"Sure," I said.

"You want to prefer charges against these goons?"

"You can't do anything to us," said Jim Bomo. "This ain't inside the city limits."

"I got authority anywhere in the county," said Guffy. "Shut up. How about it, Mike?"

"We didn't hurt him," said Brick. "Just roughed him up a little."

"Ain't a mark on him," said Bomo, a little proudly, I thought.

"I don't want to put anything on them," I said. "Maybe they can do me a favor sometime."

"These fellows never did favors for anybody, not even themselves," said Guffy. "If you're smart, you'll stay clear of them."

"I guess I'll go," I said, starting for the door. "Thanks for nothing." I went out the door with Guffy following me.

Guffy walked beside me till I reached my car, which was parked next to a police car. "Got anything to tell me, Mike?"

"What should I tell you?"

"Where's that McGuire woman?"

I sighed. "Okay, Guffy. Get out your rubber hose. This seems to be my lucky day."

"Go on back to town," said Guffy. "If you've got her, we'll find her. You ain't smart enough to hide her long."

My watch said three o'clock and I hadn't finished what I'd set out to do, namely discover who might have had a better motive than Luzy to kill Clarence Proost.

I drove back to town. Guffy followed me, then made a pretense of heading for Police Headquarters when I turned on East Twenty-fifth Street. He wasn't fooling me. It had been pretty obvious that he had been following me, possibly since I left the Plymouth Club at noon. His appearance at the Hilltop Club wasn't coincidental. And glad I was of that. I suppose he got worried about the things that might be happening to me. Now that I considered everything, it had been foolish of me to go there. But I figured the phone linemen would put Brick Lorchetto in such a twit that he'd do something that would tell me things. And I wasn't sure that he hadn't done something that told me a lot.

I stopped in front of a rooming house on East Twenty-fifth Street. It was the address that the noon edition of the *Gazette* had listed as the residence of Ernie Stauffer, Proost's Secretary. He was in Proost's racket, that much I was sure. Those missing records might be in his possession, although it seemed strange that the police hadn't found them if they were.

The rooming house was large, rambling and old fashioned. It might have been considered something fifty years ago, but it was run down, needed painting and looked like it was falling apart at the seams now.

I went up on the front porch and pushed a doorbell button and waited.

Nobody answered.

I tried again. Still no one answered. I tried the door and found it locked.

While I was trying to decide what to do next, an old Plymouth, at least ten years old, turned into the driveway and came to a halt at one end of the porch. At the wheel was something that looked young and blonde and quite easy to rest a man's eyes on.

She opened the door and got out. She stood there looking at me as I went to the porch steps.

"Aunt Lou isn't here," she said, "but if it's about a room, I'm afraid were full."

"I'm not here about a room," I said. I jerked my head toward the house. "It's about one of your roomers. I came to talk to him, but I'm afraid he's not home."

She reached into the car and got a book, then she turned around and came toward me. "Are you from the police?" She reached the steps. "It's Ernie Stauffer you want to see, isn't it?"

"I came to see Stauffer," I said, "but I'm not a cop. I'm Mike Lanson of the *Gazette.*"

It's funny how some people react to a reporter. Those who are used to reporters accept them as human beings. People who lead ordinary lives that don't lead to headlines, are apt to decide the minute they see one that he's either a devil or a plumed knight who battles in the cause of righteousness. This girl wasn't used to reporters. She looked at me in awe, but I couldn't tell whether I tipped the beam toward Gilead or Gehenna.

"I'm Linda Norwick," she said. "I'm Mrs. Bagley's niece. Did you try the door? Maybe Mr. Stauffer's taking a nap?"

"Door's locked," I said.

She came up the steps. She handed me the book and started fumbling in her purse. The book was a shorthand manual.

"Ernie—Mr. Stauffer was here when I left to go to class," she said. "I'm studying stenography at the Business College. I have a one-thirty class every afternoon, and I left here just before one. He was in his room then."

"He could have gone out," I said.

She fitted the key in the lock. "I don't think so. He had a pretty rugged morning. The police had him downtown all morning, talking to him about the murder. That's why you're here, isn't it? About Mr. Proost's murder?"

"Yes," I said, nodding.

She opened the door. "Come on in. I'll see if Mr. Stauffer's here. No one thinks he had anything to do with the murder, do they?"

"What makes you ask that?"

"I don't know. Mr. Stauffer's a peculiar man. Oh, he's nice enough, but he always seems to have a chip on his shoulder. But I shouldn't say that. Aunt Lou doesn't like to have me talk about the other roomers."

She was very businesslike. She had brown eyes and blonde hair, an unusual combination and I thought her hair was natural, too. Anyhow, it wasn't dark at the roots. "Did he mention anything about the murder."

"No." She shook her head, then turned toward the stairway that ran steeply upward from the reception hallway. "I'll see if Ernie's in his room. You can come along too, if you wish."

I followed her up the stairway, noting her shapely legs. At the top of the stairs, she turned toward the front of the house. She stopped at the door on the left of the hallway, one of the two front rooms, and knocked on the door.

"Ernie? Mr. Stauffer? There's a reporter here to see you." There was no answer.

She turned to me. "He's a pretty sound sleeper. Aunt Lou has to wake him in the morning sometimes." She twisted the knob on the door and opened it.

She stood there a moment looking. Then she audibly gasped.

I looked over her shoulder. Ernie Stauffer was taking a nap all right. He was sleeping soundly. He was dead.

The body was on the floor just beyond the door. He was face upward, in his shirt sleeves. The white front of his shirt had a big red stain right over the heart. There was a little dark hole in the middle of the stain, unmistakably left by a bullet.

I took Linda's arm and pulled her gently back and closed the door. She kept staring at the panels for a moment, then she said, "What'll we do?"

"You go downstairs," I said. "I'll call the cops."

She pointed toward a little table beside the railing that guarded the stairway. "There's a phone."

As she started down the stairway, I went to the telephone, an extension. I started to dial, when I noticed the number stamped in the center of the dial. The number was WYoming 7-3477. The number I'd called to contact the gruff-voiced man.

"Miss Norwick!" I called.

She turned her white face up at me from the stairway.

"I think Mr. Stauffer called me about one o'clock this afternoon. Would you know if he did or not?"

She shook her head. "I don't know about it."

"What kind of voice did he have?"

"Sort of harsh. A gruff voice," she said.

"Thanks." She went down the stairs as I dialed the police station. The cop on duty told me to stick around and not to touch anything.

Then I dialed the Hotel Waltham and asked the girl on the switchboard to dial my room, 615.

Nobody answered that phone either. I had three guesses. Either Luzy wasn't answering, or she wasn't there, or she had been picked up by the cops.

EIGHT

I was talking to Hank Newcomb, giving him the details of the murder, when Lieutenant Clyde Guffy arrived at the rooming house. I promised Hank I'd call him back by three-thirty with all the latest developments.

I turned to Guffy. "I thought you'd be camping outside," I said. "You've had guys following me all day."

"Don't be silly, son. The only time you've been followed by cops today was when I heard you were going to the Hilltop."

There wasn't time to make an issue of it, nor remind him of the big beefy guy I'd seen watching my movements. The guy that looked like a cop. Guffy expected me to lead him to Luzy. Hell, if he was smart, he'd pay my hotel room a second visit.

Guffy went into Ernie Stauffer's room. He didn't tell me to stay outside, so I followed. He looked down at the body. "Messy, ain't it?" he said.

I'd seen worse, but I said, "All murders are messy."

"You're telling me!" He motioned for me to stand near the door, while he went around on tiptoe, looking for anything that might be interesting. He paused over the metal wastebasket, reached down and picked it up. Then he came over to where I was standing. He held the basket out for me to see. In the bottom were black ashes of brunt paper. "Sometimes were lucky enough to be able to read stuff like that," he said. "I'll let the genius department work on it." The genius department was Guffy's name for the lab boys.

He looked around a little more, then motioned for me to go back out of the room. He followed me out. "One thing I know for sure, Mike. You didn't kill this guy. I know every move you've made since you ate lunch at the Plymouth Club."

"You said you weren't having me tailed," I said.

"I told you I didn't have you tailed," he said. "There are ways of knowing what you're up to without having a dumb cop follow you around."

I wanted to ask him if the big beefy guy was a new kind of radar, but I didn't. We had a murder to work on.

"Did you know Stauffer called me about one o'clock or a few minutes after?"

He closed the door to the room. "No. What did he want?"

"What do you think he wanted?"

"I'll ask the questions, Mike. You give me straight answers for a change." Guffy isn't the type you fool around with.

"He wanted to know where the girl is," I said. "Same as you want to know. Same as Brick Lorchetto wants to know. Same as Colonel Tanner wants to know."

"If you want that girl alive, Mike, you'd better not tell any-body but me."

"How about Ramcaster? He'd like to know too."

Guffy didn't say anything. He took me by the arm and we went down the stairway together. Linda Norwick was in the living room staring out the window.

Guffy had our stories by the time more cops arrived. After that things went through their normal course. Apparently Ernie Stauffer had been dead at least an hour, since about two o'clock. Cops checked the neighborhood, but nobody remembered seeing any callers—not any special callers, anyhow. It seems as though the whole neighborhood had been swarming with door-to-door canvassers, peddlers and everything else that clutters up a neigh-borhood on weekdays. The family next door said their doorbell had rung four times since one-thirty, and they supposed the same people had also stopped at Mrs. Bagley's rooming house.

Mrs. Bagley, a tall hatchet-faced woman, came in right after I'd called Hank a second time. She'd been downtown shopping all day and hadn't seen Ernie Stauffer since breakfast that morning.

The only development that I considered worthwhile, was Guffy's observation that Stauffer had been killed by a bullet about the same size as the one that had killed his boss, Proost.

"Which means," said Guffy, fixing me with his round little blue eyes, "that if that McGuire woman killed Proost, she also killed Stauffer. I'd rather keep a rattlesnake for a pet."

It was nearly four o'clock by then and it was too late now for the afternoon paper, although my working hours extended to five. I made my last call to Hank and then I checked through to Brandt, the *Globe's* police reporter who would take over where I left off.

Then I told Guffy I was leaving. He nodded. "I guess we don't want anything more out of you on this, Mike. Not unless you want to hand over that dame."

"Guffy," I said, "I haven't the slightest idea where she is." And that was the truth this time.

I got into my car and drove back downtown. My faith in Luzy had been considerably shaken. A few hours ago, I could have sworn she was innocent. I weathered Ramcaster, Colonel Tanner, Lorchetto and Guffy when they insisted she had killed Proost. But the fact that she hadn't been in my hotel room—or hadn't answered the phone—was a pretty big strike for her time at bat. Of course, she might have been in my room, not answering the phone. But if she had killed Stauffer, she certainly would have had to leave it.

The Press Room at Police Headquarters was empty. Don Hilliard, whose quitting time is four p.m. because he starts at seven in the morning, had gone and Jimmy Brandt was elsewhere, probably working on the Stauffer killing.

I picked up a fresh copy of the home final, which was on my desk, and started to read the story of the latest developments in the case to see how badly Hank Newcomb and rewrite had loused it. It hadn't been wrecked completely although I never could understand why a rewrite man and an editor always believed they knew more about a story than a reporter on the scene. I'm ready to swear before a grand jury that ninety-nine percent of the mistakes and all the bad reporting I get blamed for is someone else's fault. Well, maybe ninety percent of the bad reporting.

The phone rang. Two lines run into the press room. One is a direct line to the *Gazette,* which at this time of day was known as the *Globe.* The other line was routed through the police department switchboard. Lest the taxpayers holler, let it go on record that the *Gazette* paid these phone bills, also a modest rental on the Press Room.

The phone that rang was the one that went through the police switchboard.

I picked it up. "Lanson speaking."

A woman's voice answered. "Mr. Lanson, I've got something important to tell you. Is anyone listening?"

I'd never caught the cops monitoring Press Room calls, but that was no sign that they didn't. I said, "I'd rather not talk over the telephone, if it's something private and personal. Who is this?"

"That's just the point," she said. "It has quite a bit to do with certain things you are interested in. Can I meet you somewhere?"

I'd been trying to figure out who it was on the other end of the line. So far I hadn't succeeded. "Yes," I said. "This isn't Luzy McGuire, is it?" I knew it wasn't, and I hoped that if she admitted she wasn't the cops would lose interest, if they were listening.

"No," she said softly. "And I should be mad at you for not recognizing my voice. But of course you only met me yesterday—"

"Martha!" I said.

"Of course, honey. Can you come out? I think we have some unfinished business and Manton won't be home till after dinner."

I hesitated. For some reason, I didn't want to get involved with Martha Arkwright. There was a little detail that hadn't passed unnoticed at the Hilltop Club during the early afternoon. Brick Lorchetto had dialed UNiversity 4-3400, which was the same number I had dialed before going to the Hilltop. That number was Manton Arkwright's.

Lorchetto had talked to a woman on what might be called intimate terms. That woman, I was positive, was Martha Arkwright.

"Well, I—"

"Mike, if you don't, I'm coming down to see you."

"I'll be over," I said. "Right away."

I called Hank and told him I was going out, but I'd keep in touch. I hoped I'd be able to.

So far as I could tell nobody followed me. Guffy had said I wasn't being followed, but I was sure he lied. Somebody that looked like a cop had been on my tail at least once. And Guffy had turned up opportunely at the Hilltop. Besides, Guffy said he had known every minute where I was.

Martha Arkwright had changed to a print dress. As she opened the door, she fixed her bedroom eyes on me and invited me in. We went through the same ritual as on the previous day as she poured a drink and sat down beside me on the divan. This time I put the drink down on an end-table so that I wouldn't spill it.

"You wanted to see me—"

She laughed, "Must you be all business?" she asked.

"Well," I said, "after all—"

She moved closer to me. "After all, what?"

I was getting too bothered to think what.

"Mike," she said softly, "I want you to do something for me."

I'm not always a sucker for women but she was getting a little too obvious. Maybe it was Brick Lorchetto's phone call that kept me from making a mess of things.

"Why don't you ask Lorchetto?" I asked.

She moved away from me quickly. "What do you mean?"

"He's a good friend of yours, isn't he? You carry matchfolders with Hilltop's name on them and Brick calls you up to check on you—"

"How did you know?" she demanded furiously.

"I'm a reporter," I said. "It's my business to know things."

"You've seen what Clarence Proost had—" She stopped suddenly.

"He was blackmailing you?" I asked.

"No," she said stiffly. "But he knew that I saw a few men that Manton wouldn't approve of. Mike, you must understand."

I thought I did. "Sure, I understand."

"That's why I asked you out here. Where's Luzy McGuire?"

"Why does everyone ask that question?"

"Because you're obvious. Mike, I don't want her arrested, if she means something to you. It's just that I don't want her to talk. She can ruin my husband."

This was a switch. "And you too?"

"I don't think she has anything on me," she said. "But Proost was blackmailing Manton, Mike. He had some evidence he was holding over my husband's head. Probably you realize that I don't love Manton. He's much too old and we have nothing in common. But I do respect him and I don't want to see him hurt."

More than likely she respected his wealth.

"How do you know that Proost had something on your husband?"

"He came here to see Manton." She was moving closer to me. "I—I eavesdropped."

I smiled. "I don't think you or your husband need worry. I had lunch with him today and he's unduly alarmed about something nobody will blame him for. He told me that Proost wanted money to keep silent about leasing the Hilltop to Lorchetto. That's not damaging. It won't hurt him much anyhow. He didn't know what Lorchetto was going to do there."

She shook her head. Then she sipped her drink. "I think there's something more to it than that," she said. "Mike, you're not telling me the truth. Please don't lie to me."

"That's the truth," I said.

"I mean about this McGuire woman. You know where she is?"

"I swear I don't. I wish I could help you, but I can't."

"You'd better help me." Her face lost its soft expression. It was hard. "Ramcaster says you've got Luzy McGuire hidden away. He says he can make it tough on you, Mike, if he finds you've been hiding her. And I can see that he does."

I could get hard too. "Ramcaster is another of your boy friends, I suppose?"

Her eyes flashed for a second, then she threw the rest of her drink in my face. "Get out, you louse! Get out before I call the cops and have you arrested for attempted rape."

I found my hat and went to the door, brushing the liquor off my coat with a handkerchief. Just as I opened the door she called to me:

"One thing you ought to know, Mike," she said. "I heard on the radio that a man named Ernie Stauffer was killed. Next time you see the McGuire woman, ask her if her real name isn't Stauffer."

I turned and faced her. "Her husband?"

Martha Arkwright laughed. "Husbands bother you, don't they? No, dearie. Ernie Stauffer was her brother."

He was the parole jumper that she'd been helping Proost to protect.

NINE

I called Hank from a saloon a few minutes after five, which was my checking out time. I've never been conscientious about hours, since I figured most of the time I turned in more than a day's work no matter how long it took. But today I'd worked a few minutes over time because the nature of this story was that it involved my own personal life.

Hank hadn't heard from me since four o'clock and he accused me of loafing in a saloon. How he knew I was in one, I'll never know because I hadn't told him. I had a beer glass in my hand; maybe he smelled beer over the phone. Hank has senses that normal people don't have. Or he's a lucky guesser. I told him that the saloon was the nearest phone to where I happened to be digging up information.

"What information?" he said.

"That Proost was blackmailing Arkwright," I said, "but we can't print that yet till we clear it with Colonel Tanner." Hank growled and told me to go home and sleep off my drunk.

I called my hotel after talking to Hank, but room 615 didn't answer. There was a problem of getting to her. Even though Guffy said I wasn't being tailed, I felt sure that I was and I didn't want to lead the cops to Luzy. I halfway hoped that she hadn't answered because she wasn't there. I was sick of my bargain with her anyhow. She was up to her neck in this murder case, no matter what I'd believed at first. The best thing seemed to be to try to get her out of town, but that was dangerous.

I couldn't say, however, that Luzy wasn't attractive. She still did lots of things to my body chemistry. I tried to tell myself that she knew how to cause chemical reactions, that it was her stock in trade. But my body kept reacting anyhow.

I finished my beer and left the saloon. Then I had an illuminating thought. Luzy had the key to my room at the Waltham. If she had left the hotel, surely she would have dropped my key in the slot at the desk provided for keys of departing guests.

All I had to do to find out if she was still in my room—and not answering the phone—was to ask the clerk: "Did I, perchance, leave my key there this morning." If he got by the perchance without swallowing his bridgework, he'd look and I'd know if Luzy was in. If the key wasn't there, I surely wouldn't be in much worse fix than I was now.

I drove to the Waltham, parked my car in the garage, near the hotel. I told the attendant I'd need it later. I didn't know for sure that I would, but if I had to get Luzy out of town I'd need it. Providing a cop wasn't watching the car.

As I entered the hotel, I saw a big beefy detective sergeant who I'd seen, but whose name I couldn't recall, seated in a leather chair with his eyes on the elevator. He was making sure he wouldn't miss me.

He didn't stop me though, when I went over to the desk and asked for my mail. The clerk looked at me over the top of his glasses and handed me a pack of envelopes from the pigeon hole under 615.

"And my key, please."

As if he did it every night, the clerk gave me my key, which was under the pack of letters.

Somebody tapped me on the shoulder. I turned and saw Sylvester Hammond, the house dick, standing behind me. Sylvester is an ex-cop, who took the job at the Waltham because it was easier. He was about 45, big and beefy, and good-natured.

"The sarge wants to talk to you, Mike," he said.

He took me over to the plain-clothes man whom he introduced as Sergeant Campbell.

"Lieutenant Guffy told me to ask you to take me up to your room for a drink," said the sergeant

"Good old Guffy," I said, "always looking out for his friends."

"Let's go," said Campbell.

"I haven't invited you yet," I said. "What's more, I don't think I will."

"Sergeant Campbell is a good fellow, Mike," said Sylvester.

"I'm sure he is," I said. "But does he have a warrant?"

"You don't need a warrant to have a sociable drink," said Campbell.

"Let's not play games, Sergeant," I said. "You want to see who's in my room. Guffy came up to my room this morning to look inside and God knows how many cops Sylvester has let in my room while I've been working. You've all had your look, so I'm going to take my room off the Cook's tour."

Campbell didn't seem to be bothered. "Guffy said you might object," he said. "And he told me to remind you that you are in no position to get him down on you. Things could be made pretty tough for you, Lanson."

Nobody realized that better than I did. But I felt sure that Luzy wasn't in the room. "Okay," I said. "I may have a shot of bourbon upstairs."

Sylvester grinned with relief. "I told you Mike would cooperate, Sarge. He's a right guy, even if he is a reporter."

"I suppose so," said Sergeant Campbell noncommittally.

We took the elevator up to the sixth floor. We walked around the corner to my room and I inserted the key in the door, hoping that Luzy wasn't there, and feeling pretty sure she wasn't.

I opened the door, stepped inside and turned on the light. My empty bottle of bourbon was on the dresser beside an empty glass. I put my mail down on the writing desk and turned to the Sergeant. "Gee, Sarge," I said, "I forgot. I drank all my bourbon this morning."

He went across the room and picked up the glass. He looked at it. "You wear lipstick, Mike?"

"No," I said.

"There's lipstick on this glass."

"I guess I didn't wash it thoroughly the last time I had a girlfriend up here."

Sylvester made a clicking noise with his tongue. The Waltham says it's a respectable hotel.

Without asking permission, Sergeant Campbell looked into my clothes closet, into the bathroom and behind the shower curtains, and even looked under the bed.

"You won't find a bottle there," I said. "I know how much liquor I keep and that's my last bottle on the dresser."

"I'm a real lush," said Sergeant Campbell.

"You'd better look in the flush box of the toilet then," I said.

"You could order a bottle from Room Service," Sylvester suggested.

"No thanks," said the sergeant. "I guess Guffy was wrong about you, Mike." He motioned for Sylvester to follow.

He wasn't fooling me. He knew from the lipstick on my water glass that Luzy had been here.

"S'long, Mike," said Sylvester, a little relieved.

"Come back again," I said. "Almost anytime."

Sergeant Campbell looked disappointed as he went out the door followed by the house dick.

I sat down on my bed feeling almost happy about everything. There had been times today when I was almost sure I would wind up in the clink.

After I rested a moment, I went over to my writing desk and sorted out the mail. There were three bills and an envelope, Hotel Waltham stationary, addressed to Mike Lanson.

I knew it was from Luzy before I opened it.

Inside was a sheet of paper on which was written:

Mike Lanson works in daytime, and his Luzy works at night,
Such harmony you never saw, because they seldom fight.
But love is left without a time, and that's her chief complaint.
Because when Luzy's ready to, her darling Mikie ain't.

Beneath the doggerel verse she had written:

*My poetry's dynamite, Mike. Be careful when you read it, if
something happens to me.*

I didn't get the drift at first Maybe you'll think I'm dumb,
but I didn't. My mind was full of all sorts of things, least of
which was doggerel written by a creative stripteaser. The fact
that this little message was a pretty vital part of the puzzle I was
trying to solve didn't occur to me until later.

I crumpled the sheet of paper into a ball and tossed it into
my wastebasket.

It was getting along toward six o'clock and I was hungry. I
went to my dresser, pulled out a clean shirt and laid it out on
the bed. Then somebody knocked at the door.

"Who's there?" I asked;

There was no answer. I figured it must be Luzy, so I went to
the door and opened it.

It was a surprise party.

Jim Bomo was standing there and behind him was Brick
Lorchetto.

Bomo reached out, gave me a push and walked right into the
room.

"Why don't you come in?" I said, standing with my hind end
against the writing desk.

Brick closed the door. "We're returning your social call of
this afternoon," he said.

"How nice." I pointed to the empty bottle of bourbon.
"Sorry I can't offer you a drink."

"We ain't that social," said Bomo.

"Maybe it's the kind of visit somebody paid Ernie Stauffer
today," I said. "And Clarence Proost last night."

Brick didn't say anything. He opened the bathroom door and
went inside. I heard him rustle the shower curtains.

"A cop was just here," I told him when he came out. "He
went through the same motions. I told him there wasn't a bottle
of liquor in the room."

Brick opened the closet door. Then he turned to me. "Where
is she, Mike?"

"Aren't you going to look under the bed? The cop looked there too."

"I'm not as dumb as cops," said Brick. "Where's Luzy?"

He came over to stand beside Jim Bomo.

"Your questions are monotonous as hell," I said. "I told you this afternoon I didn't know where she is. What goes with you guys anyhow? Yesterday I hadn't even met the girl. Now everybody seems to think we're living together."

"I saw the way she tried to steer you out of the Hilltop last night," said Bomo. "And we followed you when you took her back to town. Luzy ain't got another friend in Creston, besides you."

"And she couldn't have dropped out of sight like this without help," said Brick. "And I know a bellhop who says you helped."

"What's she got that you want?" I asked, but I already knew. "You're not dumb."

I didn't know what to say, so I said nothing.

Brick took a step toward me and slapped me across the cheek. "Start talking," he said.

My cheek stung. A blow like that can make you madder than a punch in the belly. And my belly still hurt from where Bomo worked on it that afternoon.

"He won't talk," said Bomo. "Shall I work him over?"

Brick shook his head. "Mike's a sensible guy. He's afraid we're going to hurt this good-looking girl-friend of his. Is that it, Mike?"

I said nothing. It seemed like the best way to stall.

"We won't hurt her. Not if she plays ball with us," Brick went on. "We might even help her get out of town."

"If you could do her any good," I said, "she'd have come to you instead of me."

Brick grinned. "So she did come to you! You admit it!"

I pressed my lips tightly together. I'd said too much.

"Talk, Mike," said Brick. "This is your last chance. We can be pretty rough, you know."

My belly throbbed. I didn't know if I could take another punch or not. I tightened my muscles and they hurt.

"Okay, Jim," Brick said, stepping back behind Bomo. "Give him a little treatment. Just enough to make him understand that were not fooling."

Bomo took a step toward me.

I was still standing back against the writing desk. Involuntarily I pushed back, half sitting on the surface of the desk.

Bomo doubled his fist.

Then I lifted both legs and kicked him in the belly.

I kicked as hard as I could. I tried to make like a mule. Bomo stopped. His eyes bulged and he staggered back, clapping both hands to his middle.

He bumped into Brick and together they struck the wall. Bomo slid to the floor, gasping and groaning, while Brick stood there a second, with slitted eyes, half angry because I hadn't taken what he expected to dish out.

Then he came after me.

Brick was a big man, but I wasn't afraid of him. Even before he moved, I was going after him.

But his fist shot out first.

It was aimed at my chin but I turned and it grazed the side of my neck. I whipped out a right for his face.

That was a mistake, because his right was coming toward me. It hit my cheek and I staggered back.

Brick came after me and I got tangled up with the writing desk, tipping it over on the floor.

It struck Brick's legs and he howled.

By that time I got my balance and I swung at him. It caught him on the shoulder. He swung back, but now I knew what I was doing. One thing a reporter learns to do early, is duck.

I ducked and punched. He blocked and punched. Neither us was getting anywhere.

On the floor beside the bathroom door, Jim Bomo was trying to catch his breath and halfway succeeding. I caught a glimpse of him struggling to rise, and I knew that unless I could handle Brick Lorchetto in short order I'd have two men on my frame.

I don't remember the blow-by-blow sequence, but I was yelling and slugging and Brick was swearing and grunting.

Then the door of my room swung open and Sylvester Hammond, the house dick, stood there hardly believing what he saw.

"There's been a complaint about noise—"

But he didn't finish. Bomo was on his feet now and his hand was snaking inside his coat.

Sylvester had been a cop and he knew what that meant. Sylvester's hand moved like a cobra striking, and out of a shoulder holster came a little snub-nosed gun.

There was a loud bang and Jim Bomo dropped his weapon as his throat exploded with a howl that could have been heard clear down in the lobby.

"All right," said Sylvester to Brick and me, "stand up against the wall or I'll use this thing again."

All the fight had gone out of Brick Lorchetto as he backed up against the wall. I was already there.

TEN

Jim Bomo's arm was dripping blood and he was yelling that he was bleeding to death.

"Tend to him, Mike," Sylvester said, "but don't get between me and this other guy."

Jim held out his arm. The bullet had plowed through the upper part of his wrist, but it hadn't penetrated the spot where the artery was. I took a couple of my handkerchiefs from the dresser drawer and tied up the wound. "He'll be all right," I said.

I expected Sylvester to use the phone, but he didn't budge. In a minute I knew why. Through the doorway came Sergeant Campbell and with him was Luzy.

"The complaint came from 613, next door," said Campbell. "I found her there."

Luzy looked at me, half tearfully. "I heard them come upstairs, Mike. They stood outside my door and talked. So I had to do something—I called the desk."

"You call the wagon, Campbell?" asked Sylvester.

Campbell nodded. "I used the phone in the girl's room. Guffy says to bring them all in. The whole caboodle."

Sylvester cringed. "Do you mind taking them out the back door?" he asked, "You know, some of the guests are awfully stuffy about things like this."

"Okay, Syl. We'll do anything you say. I don't think I could have gotten along without you."

"You can't take me to jail," said Brick. "I haven't done anything."

"The hell you haven't," I said. "I'll sign a complaint for something."

Campbell frisked him, but Brick was clean. Brick let Bomo do his heavy fighting.

Two squad cars picked us up in the alley behind the hotel Brick and Lorchetto were loaded into one, Luzy and I into the other.

Luzy told me that she figured that the cops or someone would search my room and didn't want to be caught there. So after finishing off my bourbon, she had arranged to occupy room 613, under the pretense that she was my cousin from Milwaukee and wanted to surprise me. Campbell hadn't taken Sylvester into his secrets or Sylvester could have told him the girl they were after was in room 613. Sometimes cops aren't talkative enough.

Luzy said she'd left a note for me at the desk. I told her I got it but didn't understand it. "I knew somebody would probably follow you," she said.

"They have been following me all day," I said. "When I found Ernie Stauffer's body, Guffy—"

"Ernie Stauffer!" The name came almost as a gasp. "Mike, Ernie was my brother!"

Her face wore a strained look for an instant, then her head was on my shoulder and she was weeping. Her grief came like an explosion and it vanished like the wind. Before we reached the police station she was wiping her eyes.

I said nothing. There's little that can be said at a time like this. For grief is personal, it's something that one person can't share for another. It cannot be explained, and it cannot be lightened except by the bearer.

Luzy had aided Proost to prevent her brother from going back to prison. That Stauffer hadn't reformed a great deal could be guessed by his phone call to me early in the afternoon. No doubt Stauffer hoped to get his hands on certain incriminating documents that he thought Luzy had in her possession. Now that he was dead, Luzy forgot her brother's instability, his life-long acts, and everything except that he had good points known only to herself.

She looked at me and struggled with a smile. "I'm sorry," she said.

"You needn't be," I said. "Crying probably did you a lot of good."

"My real name's Stauffer," she said. "I ran away and got married when I was sixteen to a man named McGuire. We broke up six weeks later."

One thing this gal didn't have was a shortage of trouble.

"You're nice," she said.

"Why shouldn't I be?" I said. "You gave me quite a help today, by getting Sylvester up to my room."

"I heard Brick and Jim in the hallway and I knew what to expect," she said. "But I guess I landed us both in jail. That's going to be tough on me. Nobody's going to let me stay there."

"Who's going to get you out? Ramcaster?"

She shook her head. "I told you, I don't know who's behind things in this town."

"Guffy will protect you," I said.

"Nothing will ever straighten out for me."

Guffy was still at headquarters. He'd finished up his part of investigating the Stauffer case, but hadn't had time for dinner when he learned about Luzy's capture. "We ought to get some answers now," he said.

Over Brick's objections, he and his pal Jim Bomo were booked on charges of disturbing the peace and resisting arrest. Although Sylvester wasn't a member of the police force he had authority to make arrests.

There was a warrant out for Luzy, of course, and there was no trouble about getting her under lock and key.

"You've been giving us a lot of trouble, young lady," Guffy told her.

"You've got troubles?" she said. "What kind of stuff do you think I've had for a steady diet lately?"

"If it weren't for you, two men would be alive that aren't alive now," Guffy said quietly.

Luzy looked at Guffy for a moment, then hung her head and burst into tears. "I know," she said. "I'm directly responsible. Book me for murder."

"Did you kill Clarence Proost?" Guffy asked. "Remember, if you confess, we can use it—"

"I killed him—maybe," she said.

"I want a direct answer, yes or no."

"I can't say yes or no," she said. "All I can say is maybe." She daubed her eyes with a handkerchief.

The door opened and Cliff Ramcaster came in. His eyes swept the group. Then they rested on Luzy McGuire and stayed there. He forgot about Brick Lorchetto, Jim Bomo and me. He was interested in only one person. Luzy McGuire.

"Well, Luzy," he said.

She glared at him.

"Lock her up and charge her with murder," said Ramcaster. "We've got an ironclad case against her."

"How about Mike?" Guffy asked. "It looks as if he's been helping her stay on the loose."

"She was on the loose for a long time before she met Mike. Was he hiding her?"

"Of course he was." I'd always considered Guffy my friend, but now he was trying to put me behind bars. "We can't prove it, exactly. She wasn't caught in his room, and there's no evidence that Mike's been with her or knew where she was since you issued a warrant for her arrest, but—"

Ramcaster winked at me. "Might as well let Mike go," he said. "Colonel Tanner will breathe fire if we hold him and I guess Mike was in his own room."

"He was disturbing the peace," Guffy said. "Besides he's been causing us a lot of trouble today. I'd like to get him out of circulation for a day or two. Maybe we could make headway on these murders if he wasn't around to raise a dust cloud."

"Not a chance," said Ramcaster. "You can't even prove he was interfering." He studied awhile and then said, "Put a peace

disturbance charge against Bomo and Lorchetto. They'll probably make bond in an hour, but we can't let them get away with
what they were trying to do."

"Maybe you can tell me what they were trying to do," said
Guffy.

Ramcaster said, "They intended to make mincemeat of Mike
Lanson. That's okay with me. He gets under my skin sometimes.
But they aren't subtle. Besides, Mike can write it up in the paper.
It would look sad as hell to have him say that two men entered
his hotel room and raised a rumpus and we turned 'em loose."

"A lot of people are going to look sad when this is over," I
said.

Guffy snorted, and turned to Campbell. "Any luggage in the
girl's room?"

"Only her purse. We got it."

Lorchetto, Bomo and Luzy were taken their separate ways
and Ramcaster turned to me.

"I'll buy you a drink," the assistant county prosecutor said.

"You'd put poison in it," I said.

I still had a lot of Colonel Tanner's expense money in my
pocket and since the *Gazette* was more or less responsible for my
predicament, I spent some of it for taxi fare.

I didn't expect to be followed now that Luzy was in jail, but
I took precautions anyway.

But apparently no one was behind me and I had the cab stop
at the hotel garage, where I'd left my car.

I went in, opened the trunk and took out the bag that Luzy
had brought from the hotel that morning. It was heavy as the
devil and I wondered how a gal like Luzy could have toted it
around the way she must have.

She hadn't taken a bag to Proost's place. She got the bag
there. Also its contents. I already had guessed that much and if
I needed any evidence to support my guesswork, I had it in the
form of gold initials "C.P." on a flap of the bag. This bag contained what everyone was hunting. It also contained evidence of
murder, but it was an intangible sort of evidence that I would
have to use some sort of magic to materialize.

But I didn't know that much yet. I wasn't even sure that the bag would hold what I guessed it did.

I carried it up to the hotel, through the lobby and up to my room. I had my key in my pocket this time and I didn't have to bother the desk clerk who was busy reading.

I locked and bolted my door and pulled down the shades. As I suspected, the suitcase was locked. Luzy had the key in her purse or on her person somewhere. But it's no trick to pick the lock of a suitcase. Everyone has done it.

The suitcase was filled with a profusion of manila envelopes. On each one was written a name. I looked through several and I had a sense of awe. This man Proost was unprincipled, utterly unscrupulous and as amoral as a cancer cell. The only thing I couldn't understand was how he lived so long.

He had carefully filed, documented records of every misdeed he could lay his hands on. He had a full report, plus affidavits, on Lieutenant Guffy's expulsion from the police force ten years ago—a political move as a result of newspaper heat being applied to a crooked municipal administration. Guffy later was put back on the force, because the only thing he'd been guilty of was obeying orders. He had lists of building code violations in real estate developments handled by Colonel Tanner. He had long lists of infractions by almost every bar in town; And there were envelopes that hinted that Ramcaster and Sheriff Lindley had not always been ethical.

With a file like this, a man could run Creston or ruin quite a number of its prominent, influential citizens. No wonder so many people had been in a fever to find Luzy McGuire, and no wonder she had tried to hide. I didn't know for sure if she was safe in jail. She wouldn't be for long, I knew. But Guffy, in spite of everything, was one cop I could trust. She'd be safe for a little while—long enough for me to take the poison out of a dead man's legacy and destroy a million dollars worth of blackmail material.

But here another problem presented itself. The victims must know that the evidence against them had been destroyed. The mere announcement by me that I'd done so, wasn't enough.

There would always be doubt and uncertainty unless I had proof that this had been done.

I looked through this material again. One envelope I had expected to find was missing.

Manton Arkwright had told me that he'd been in trouble over his handling of the Hilltop Club. Martha Arkwright also had hinted that her husband was being blackmailed. But in the Hilltop Club envelope there was no mention of Arkwright's name. Manton Arkwright was not named anywhere that I could find.

This discrepancy opened up the most sinister kind of theory. I began to wonder if perhaps Manton Arkwright had lied. If he had lied, there might be reason to doubt his veneer of honesty. And once you doubted on that score, you began to wonder about a lot of things.

But who was I to challenge Manton Arkwright? A newspaper has power, and a reporter backed by his newspaper has a certain amount of protection and privilege, guaranteed by the Constitution of the United States as freedom of the press. But there were limits to this power. I could only deal with public matters. Individuals still have the right of privacy and reporters learn early the difference between private and public matters.

Colonel Tanner would not approve of me probing into Arkwright's private life to expose him as not quite the man he appeared to be in public. And up to this moment, I had not suspected Manton Arkwright of being in league with criminals. But the fact that he had escaped Proost's attention while being rather close to the man was in itself suspicious.

Unless Luzy or someone else had eliminated Proost's record of Manton Arkwright's mistakes, such as leasing property for a gambling casino.

You can see how hazy my evidence was. I couldn't prove any of the suspicions I had. If I called Colonel Tanner and told him what I'd found, he would say that now that we'd proved that Proost was the number one racketeer of Creston, let's print it and let the cops solve the murders.

Colonel Tanner would be likely to say, "Whoever murdered him did the city a service. Let's pay our debt of gratitude by keeping our noses out of it. Besides, it's the duty of the police force to solve the crime. Not ours."

I don't say the Colonel is right, but he had a point. On the other hand, it's a newspaper's duty to learn and print the truth. If we kept our noses out of the case, Luzy McGuire would be charged with the murder and she might well be convicted. No matter how much Luzy was involved in Proost's racket, or what kind of a woman she was, no innocent person should suffer for a crime he did not commit.

If I called Guffy into the case, he'd have to know the contents of the envelopes. He'd learn the dirt on everybody. Maybe some of the people named deserved exposure, maybe they didn't, but I went along with the Colonel on one point. Proost was a dirty so-and-so and it would be playing his game to let the cops in on the secrets on which he was collecting.

If Proost's murderer was to be caught, I'd have to do it and I stood as much chance as an Army private has of accusing a General of unmilitary conduct.

I had to have help from the *Gazette*. Since the Colonel would veto my operation, I had only one choice: Hank Newcomb.

My city editor was a frustrated, insecure soul. He had risen from a reporter to city editor, but he had never been very much of a reporter. He was too much awed by big names and prominent men. He had forgotten how incapable he was because in his post as boss of the city room, he was Colonel Tanner's prophet and hatchetman. He thought he was the last word in journalism and nothing tickled his vanity more than to catch a reporter in a bit of stupidity that even the best are apt to exhibit in moments of unguarded haste.

Yes, Hank was a vain soul. And if you tickled his vanity in the ribs, he could be had.

If I could make Hank feel that he would become a journalistic hero in Creston by solving a front page murder, he'd do my dirty work.

I put the envelopes back in the suitcase, used my nail file to lock it, and then picked up the phone and dialed Hank Newcomb.

He exhibited modest surprise that I should call him outside office hours.

"I know it sounds funny, Hank," I said, "but this isn't costing the *Gazette* a white nickel in overtime."

He softened right away. "What is it, Mike?"

"I'm up to my ears in this Proost story," I said. "But I've run up against a problem that's too big for me to handle."

"Maybe I can help you," he said. He was so nice, I felt sorry about making a sucker out of him.

"Could you, Hank? I think I could solve this case if I could figure it out. But it's so damned complicated."

"Where are you, Mike? I'll be right over."

I told him I was in my room at the hotel, and to please hurry.

ELEVEN

Hank was in my room in fifteen minutes, which was pretty fast traveling, even when you considered that he lived on the same side of town that I lived on.

I pointed to the suitcase, with its initials "C.P."

"Where in the hell did you get that?" he asked.

I gave him a play-by-play account of my dealings with Luzy. I told him the truth, knowing that I was in the clear.

"I can't be charged with harboring a fugitive because she wasn't a fugitive until after I left her this morning and I didn't see her again until the cops arrested her," I told him.

"But she might be the murderer, Mike! You should have told me—"

"She told me enough to convince me that she wasn't," I said. "I still think she's innocent, but to clear her, we've got to make it pretty rough on a lot of people."

I didn't let on that I'd opened the suitcase, because I knew he'd smell a rat. I told him that Luzy had hinted what was in it and the fact that I'd had some run-ins with a lot of people over something Luzy had tried to take from Proost's home made me believe her. "That suitcase has enough blackmail evidence in it to turn the whole town on end," I said.

Hank looked at it and licked the drool off his lips. Greed is inherent in every man. I'd felt it when I looked over that mess of dirt. I felt like I was handling something that people would pay thousands, maybe a million dollars to lay their hands on. But I

remembered what had happened to Clarence Proost and Ernie
Stauffer and I had decided that after all there was no work like
a reporter's job. I didn't make as much as a crook makes, but I
had more fun and fewer worries.

"Boy! Think of the headlines," said Hank.

And I realized that in spite of his failings, Hank was a newspaperman at heart. Scandal sold papers and papers that sold
were attributes of a good city editor. I guess that's the difference
between a career man and a money-grubber. A career man takes
pride in his job, even if it's lousy. You don't even have to have
talent. You just have to have the feeling.

"Well," he said, "what do you think we ought to do?"

"I have a hunch that one envelope is missing," I said.

"How do you know?" He was a little suspicious that I'd peeked,
but he could see that the suitcase was locked and being an intellectual snob he didn't think I had brains enough to pick a lock.

"It stands to reason," I said. "Last night somebody murdered
Proost to get one of those envelopes. Therefore the envelope
isn't there."

"If it isn't there, we don't know who murdered him," he said.

"But we do," I said. "Luzy knows who killed Proost."

"Did she tell you?"

"Yes." As a matter of fact, she had. She hadn't told me in
so many words, but something she said might have given me
the clue. "She hasn't given me the whole story yet, Hank, but I
think I can reconstruct the events.

"She went to Proost's house about midnight. I'm not sure
why, but I think she'd decided to break with him. There was an
argument, but Luzy was firm about it. Whatever hold Proost
had on her was no longer any good. She was calling the deal off.
He could throw her in jail or do whatever he had in mind, but
from now on she was going to try to play it straight."

I paused and lit a cigarette, watching Hank. He was drinking
it all in. It was a story he could print, providing it checked out.
I was guessing at most of it though.

"About twelve-thirty a car pulled up in front of the apartment house and the murderer got out. A few minutes later there

was a knocking on the door of Proost's apartment, or more likely, the murderer identified himself downstairs through the tube
and was admitted.

"Luzy hid, not wishing to be caught in Proost's apartment,
or possibly because Proost wanted it that way. At any rate the
murderer came in and demanded whatever it was that he wanted
from Proost. It might have been anything illegal or scandalous,
but it was certainly something that he was willing to kill to get.
Proost refused to hand it over, but the murderer wasn't taking
no for an answer. The murderer may have been confronted with
a gun held by Proost, or the gun might have made its appearance
in some other manner. But the murderer attempted to get the
evidence at gunpoint and Proost underestimated the murderer's
willingness to use it. The result was a dead Proost, with Luzy in
the next room as a witness."

"Why didn't she call the cops? She could have told the cops
the whole story now and cleared herself," Hank said.

"Luzy's a funny kid, Hank. She considers that she is responsible for Proost's murder. Possible that evidence was something
she helped manufacture. Anyhow, Luzy is afraid to talk. She says
maybe she killed Proost. Now when would you say 'maybe' you
killed somebody?"

"If I didn't know for sure whether I did," said Hank.

"Or if you were afraid to tell the truth, or if you were pro-
tecting somebody. Let's say voluntary or involuntary protection
of the real murderer."

"Okay. Let's say it."

"Luzy all along has been more afraid of what racketeers
would do to her than afraid of the cops. She hid out from racketeers and she said that even in jail racketeers would get her. That
doesn't sound like petty crime, does it, Hank?"

Hank whistled softly. "It's the biggest underworld organization this town has ever had."

I nodded. "And Luzy McGuire can tumble it down into a heap."

"How?"

I shrugged. "I don't know the answer, Hank, but I feel sure
that she's the weak link in the setup."

"Let's open the suitcase," Hank said. "We can find out."

I shook my head. "Racketeers aren't pushovers, Hank," I said. "They operate by taking advantage of legal loopholes, as well as bribery, corruption and so on. Why the first thing that would happen in court, the racketeer's lawyer would hint that we tampered with the evidence. That we framed his client."

"But two of us, Mike—"

"Two newspapermen, who'd send a man to a chair to get a big story."

"You don't think a jury would swallow that!"

"Lawyers have made juries swallow bigger lies, Hank. We can't take that chance. We've got to open this suitcase in the presence of someone so solid in the community, that his reputation will never be doubted. Someone like Manton Arkwright."

Hank thought it over. I could see by his eyes that his opinion of 'prominent citizens' had the upper hand.

"Mike," he said, "I believe you hit the right answer. I was going to suggest Colonel Tanner, but he's a newspaperman too. Let's call Arkwright. Let me call him, because I know how to handle big men like Arkwright."

"Fine," I said. I wanted him to do the talking. "He'll agree to it. He's public spirited and we can rely on him all the way."

Hank, picked up the phone and called Arkwright. I gathered that Arkwright was quite interested in the suitcase and wanted us to bring it over immediately. He complimented Hank on his foresight. Hank hung up the phone very pleased with himself.

"He said he would treat everything in the suitcase in confidence," he said.

"Let's get going," I said. For all I knew, Manton Arkwright would be waiting for us with a loaded gun.

I wasn't sure he had killed anybody, but it could be that he had. And a person who had already killed twice, wouldn't hesitate if the occasion arose where his safety depended on adding a couple of more corpses to his score.

We rode over to Arkwright's home on University Hill in Hank's Dodge.

TWELVE

A flashy Buick convertible was half hidden in the shadows of Arkwright's driveway and there were lights in the front room casting a gleam on the lawn through the picture window.

Hank stopped his car in front. We got out and I waited for him to unlock the trunk and get the bag. I offered to carry it, but Hank wanted to be the man who broke this case and he wasn't going to give me a chance to crab his act.

We went up to the front door and used a brass knocker. Arkwright himself opened the door to admit us. I looked around for Martha Arkwright, but she wasn't visible.

"Let's go into my study, gentlemen," Arkwright said. "We won't be disturbed there."

There we seated ourselves. Arkwright behind his desk, Hank facing him on my left and I on the right, with the suitcase between us.

Hank nodded his head toward the suitcase. "We believe, Mr. Arkwright, that we have the records of Proost's blackmailing activities in Creston."

Arkwright looked at it, over the top of his desk. "Most remarkable, Newcomb! How did you come by it?"

"It's a rather long story," Hank said. "I suppose you heard that Miss McGuire was arrested this afternoon?"

Arkwright nodded solemnly. "There was something on the news broadcast about it. I suppose that solves the murder of Mr. Proost, the poor, misguided soul."

"We're not sure that it does," said Hank. "Mike here has believed in her innocence from the start. While I've kept what you might call an open mind, Mike believes the contents of the suitcase might throw additional light on the case."

The reason Hank's mind was open was because it was totally unoccupied, I thought.

Arkwright raised his brows. "Why not turn it over to the police?"

Hank gave me a knowing glance and went on. "Because, sir, we believe that the contents of this bag might injure innocent reputations."

Arkwright cleared his throat. "It has been my experience, Newcomb, that where there's smoke, there's fire. People who live respectable lives, don't leave themselves open to blackmail."

I felt that it was time for me to say something. "And it's been my experience, sir, that people who haven't made mistakes haven't done anything good either."

I expected a reaction from Arkwright on that, but he smiled instead. "I daresay you're right, Lanson. Some things I've done would seem pretty foolish if the world knew about them. No, I don't pretend to be a hypocrite, but I do say that major transgressions are seldom the indulgence of honest men and women."

Hank felt the ball getting away from him. He interrupted, "In any case, sir, the main thing is the solution of a murder and to prevent Miss McGuire from suffering for it if she is innocent. In order to do that, we feel that we should look into this suitcase. We felt that the contents should be examined by someone of repute, who could be entrusted with such a delicate matter. We thought of you at once."

Arkwright smiled broadly. "It's nice of you to think of me in that way. I feel complimented. But what am I to do? Will I know murder evidence if I see it?"

This troubled Hank. He had assumed all along that the murder evidence would be unmistakable, like a gun with bloody fingerprints on it. The idea that it might take brains to figure it out disturbed him.

"Well, we thought that something—"

"I think it's a matter for the police," said Arkwright. "I'm sure they're more able to recognize murder evidence than I am."

I got into the act again, in order to bring the conversation back into the proper channels. "We'd like to do that, sir. But we want it arranged that some responsible, trustworthy person is present so that anything damaging to an innocent victim can be turned over to the rightful person."

"What if there is evidence of crimes?"

"In that case no one should have an objection to the police taking action," I said. "But you know as well as I know, Mr. Arkwright, that all policemen are not honest. I know the crooks are in the minority. But crooked cops appear too often to be regarded as rare beasts. What we want to guard against is further blackmail."

Arkwright studied the top of his desk. "I believe Proost's murder has been solved," he said "The police think so. The radio quoted Mr. Ramcaster as saying so. If we were so inclined to perform a good deed, I'd say let's destroy the suitcase and its contents now. Immediately, and forget about it."

Hank fidgeted in his chair. He wasn't sure it ought to be done.

"I'm not sure we should do a thing like that."

"Let's look at it another way, Newcomb," Arkwright went on. "Supposing there were papers in that valise that were damaging to your boss, Colonel Tanner?"

He didn't have to go any farther. I could see a wild look growing in Hank's eyes. He hadn't thought about that possibility, yet he knew as I knew, that Colonel Tanner had been a hell raiser in his lifetime.

"How about you, Mr. Arkwright," I said softly. "Could there be anything about you in that suitcase?"

"I'm sure that beyond acting as agent in renting the Hilltop property to some gamblers, Mr. Proost could have nothing on me." He spoke with a great deal of conviction.

"Yes," I said, "but you were worried about that today when I had lunch with you."

"Naturally I don't want my connection exposed," he said, "But I acted in good faith. Colonel Tanner assured me that I'd hardly be accused of being in league with these gamblers."

"And you have an alibi for the time when Mr. Proost and Mr. Stauffer were murdered?"

His eyes glinted with a look that seemed alien to his kindly countenance. But he recovered quickly. "I've been over that with the police, Lanson," he said curtly. "Because of my connection with Proost they asked, in a routine way, for my alibi. I was at home last night, and in bed, sound asleep as a result of a sleeping pill, at the time Proost was murdered. My wife Martha will support me in this. I was home all afternoon today. I received several telephone calls in my study."

"I apologize for my question, Mr. Arkwright," I said. "But I have a feeling that the police are not working in the right direction and I wanted to check out every angle."

"The trouble with you, Lanson," said Arkwright, "is that because you had a little luck on a couple of murder cases, you think you're the second coming of Sherlock Holmes. Believe me, boy, the solving of murders is a job for the police, not newspaper reporters."

"The point is well taken, sir. But you understand of course that in a matter such as the contents of this bag, we don't feel that the police should stick their noses in it."

"You mean we ought to destroy evidence?"

He was twisting my words. "No," I said. "I mean to protect innocent people. Supposing we called in someone else, so the responsibility wouldn't be entirely yours. Someone like Colonel Tanner, who could go through the contents of this bag and decide definitely what items could not possibly do anything toward solving this, or other crimes in the city."

"Why are you so eager to open that bag, Lanson?"

"Because, Mr. Arkwright, it will show that you murdered Clarence Proost."

Silence descended like a cloud. I could hear Hank breathing heavily. Arkwright tapped the top of his desk with his fingers. Then he said, "I suppose Miss McGuire told you this."

"No," I said. *I looked in the bag!*

Arkwright grew tense, then relaxed. He leaned back in his

chair and fixed his cold gray eyes on me. "You shouldn't have done that Lanson."

If Arkwright had killed Proost, he had also killed Stauffer and he would kill again. Yet I wasn't afraid. That was because I'd brought Hank Newcomb along. I can joke about his stupidity, but Hank was husky and big and he would have an instinct of self-preservation. Two against one is pretty good odds and Arkwright didn't have a gun in his hand.

But now Hank bleated, "You didn't tell me that, Mike."

"I know, Hank. I'm sorry, but I had to sucker you in on this."

"No matter," said Arkwright. "I don't think Mike looked. Isn't the suitcase locked?"

"I picked the lock and locked it again," I said.

"You lie," said Arkwright. "Because you know there's not a damned thing in there that incriminates me!"

"How do you know?" I asked.

"There couldn't be," he said.

"How about the Hilltop?"

"That couldn't possibly be a motive for murder," he said.

"Naturally not, Mr. Arkwright," I said, "because you're the top man in this town. Proost was working for you. So were Brick Lorchetto and Jim Bomo and all the other hoods and grifters in this town. You had your finger in every brothel, every slick operation, dope, big-time stealing and everything that went on. You protected yourself through Proost, you didn't have to pay off to operate, you threatened."

"There's nothing to prove it in that bag," said Arkwright. "Young man, you'll eat those words."

"Except for one little mistake you made, Mr. Arkwright," I said. "You were involved in the Hilltop, yet your name is not mentioned in the papers for Lorchetto, or the Hilltop, which shows a great deal about its operation that only you and the proprietor could know. You were also involved in real estate deals with Colonel Tanner, yet your name isn't mentioned there. Why shouldn't it be mentioned, unless you were a sacred cow of some sort and couldn't be touched. The reason Mr. Arkwright, was because you were the man behind the whole dadblamed racket."

"Pure speculation," said Arkwright, but not very convincingly.

"Okay," I said. "You suggested turning this stuff over to the police. You felt safe, because you thought we wouldn't dare as long as something about Colonel Tanner was in that bag. But I'm going to show you something. . . ."

I got up, took a step over to the desk and picked up Arkwright's phone. Before I could touch the dial, he reached out with his left hand and caught mine. "What are you going to do, Lanson?"

"Call the cops," I said. "You thought we were hell-bent to persuade you to handle the papers in the suitcase, but you didn't want to appear too eager. But you're wrong, Arkwright. The cops are going to look inside that bag and I'll bet they find your handwriting in lots of places."

"You needn't call the cops," said Arkwright. "Call Ramcaster. He'll handle the case anyhow."

"The cops first," I said. "Ramcaster's your boy."

I pulled my hand away from his and started to dial POlice 1-1111.

I had gotten to the first number one when a voice said, "Okay, Lanson. Relax."

I turned around and looked over my shoulder. Standing in the doorway through which Newcomb and I had just entered was Brick Lorchetto. What bothered me most was the automatic pistol in his hand.

I should have known the car in the driveway wasn't Arkwright's. It was too flashy for the old man.

"Put down the phone, Lanson," Brick said patiently, moving the gun to show that he meant it.

In Proost's files I'd noted some information about Brick which indicated that he'd been arrested, but never convicted, on suspicion of murder. Brick once had been a gangland executioner. I put the phone back in its cradle.

Turning around so that I could face Lorchetto, I caught a glimpse of Hank. He hadn't said much when I started laying my cards down in front of Arkwright. He hadn't known what it was all about. But he saw the gun and he knew now. He was scared.

I didn't blame Hank. I didn't feel too comfortable myself. The pleasant little two to one odds I'd set up against Arkwright were all shot to hell. I could have brought along two more guys and they wouldn't have helped matters any because Brick held the old equalizer in his fist.

"I don't know how much you know, Lanson," said Arkwright, "but I'm convinced you know too much for your own good."

I didn't say anything, but I had a hunch that my wisdom would outlive me. And very soon.

"What's he trying to do, boss?" asked Brick. "Pin Proost's murder on you?"

"Yes," said Arkwright. "But that's not the only bad steer he's had. I didn't kill Proost, but he knows too much about the organization."

"If he'd kept his nose out of things and let the cops handle it, he wouldn't be in all this trouble," said Brick. "They've got the guilty party. That black-haired Queen of Stool Pigeons."

Arkwright sighed. "That's true. Curiosity is more dangerous than space travel. I'm afraid, Lanson, that you have entirely the wrong idea of me. You think that I'm a racketeer, whereas I'm a man of very high principles. I give liberally to charities. I live decently and quietly and I have civic pride. But I am also a business man. I realize that there are different standards among different people. To certain human beings brothels, gambling, narcotics and so on are a way of life. No amount of policing can eliminate these things, so it is necessary to control them from within. That is what I do, Lanson. I control from within. Vice in Creston is on a limited scale. It is hidden and orderly, so that it does not offend the decent folks."

"And you collect a good living from it," I added.

"I do because I'm entitled to. Very few men could keep it so well controlled." He spoke with conviction. I actually think he believed that he was doing a necessary thing. "Naturally there is a risk and a certain stigma attached to such a calling and my

fees are high, because I run risks of being discovered. You are
the first to suspect my connection, Lanson. No one knew it,
save a couple of trusted lieutenants— Clarence Proost and Brick
Lorchetto."

"How about Ramcaster?" I asked.

Brick laughed hoarsely. "That clown! All he wanted to do was
line his pockets. He didn't care where the money came from."

"Wasn't Proost getting a little out of hand?" I asked.

"Proost, let us say, was ambitious. I was aware that he was
not a man to turn one's back on, but I always felt that I could
handle him. But when he began to needle Colonel Tanner, I
thought it might be wise to discipline him. But—" he held up
his hand as I started to interrupt "—but I didn't kill him. And
you and Jim didn't kill him either, did you, Brick?"

"Uh-uh," said Brick. "He was alive and feelin' sorry when
Brick and me left him a little after eleven the night he got killed."

"I think that Proost decided that as long as we were lining
Ramcaster's pockets, he would remove the lining," Arkwright
went on. "He visited Colonel Tanner on his own, but after I
heard about it, I thought it might work out very nicely. For a
long time, I'd hoped to get something on Tanner. There was a
possibility that he might overstep his legal limits in a crusade
and that we might be able to use his mistakes to our advantage."

I nodded. Crusading editors sometimes do get in hot water.
"Just what was Proost's position in your organization?"

"You exhibit more than ordinary curiosity, Lanson. Aren't
you wondering why I talk so freely?"

"Not from pure talkativeness," I said.

Arkwright smiled. "It's not often that I have a chance to pa-
rade my achievements," he said. "And those who hear of them
seldom repeat them."

I could hear Hank gulp behind me. "You're going to k-k-kill
us?" he asked.

"That's the idea, Buster," said Lorchetto.

"But not here, unless necessary," said Arkwright. "We don't
want to soil the carpeting."

THIRTEEN

Hank groaned and I thought he was going to be sick. But he took it better than I expected. He didn't even faint.

"Any way we can get you to change your mind?" I asked. I wasn't any braver than Hank, in case I sound like it. I was scared to the holes in my socks and my insides were churning like I'd swallowed an electric mixer.

"If there were a way out of this, I'd be the first to approve of it," said Arkwright. He was actually talking in a fatherly tone. This guy was nuts. He figured he was the patriarch of Creston, who dished out life and death, pleasure and pain, to anybody he fancied needed these inconveniences. "I detest violence. As I said before, I'm a businessman. Violence isn't good business. When someone is killed, it causes a public reaction to find the murderer. We had nothing to do with the deaths of Proost and that rat Stauffer. And we know that if two newspapermen are killed there will be a great deal of fuss raised over it. But perhaps we can arrange your demise so that it will appear to be an accident. Mr. Newcomb might have a wreck in his car."

"Supposing we talk things over," I said. "Maybe we can come up with a good idea."

"I'm afraid not, my boy," said Arkwright. "It's a pity, too. But I don't trust you, Lanson. You're a great deal like me. We're dedicated to our missions in life. You'd stop at nothing to gather in a headline, while I—"

"You'd cut your mother's heart out for a fast buck," I said.

395

Arkwright flushed. "That was unkind of you, Lanson. I've handled widow's estates without misappropriating a penny."

"You used the money to set up joints like the Hilltop, or furnish parlors of your brothels," I said.

"At least the widows got good returns on their investments," said Arkwright. "They might have starved if the money were wasted in speculation or in unsound investments."

I don't think he had a point, but I'm not a moralist and I couldn't say. Personally, I'd set it down as action and reaction. You can't have too much ugliness without bringing a little beauty into the world too, and vice versa.

"Were wasting time, boss," said Brick. "When things like this gotta be done, you oughta get 'em over with."

Arkwright nodded. "I suppose so. Take them someplace." That was all he said. I wondered how many times he'd said it before.

Apparently this wasn't an ordinary situation though, because Brick objected, "All alone? Don't be outa your head, boss."

"Why not? You can handle two unarmed men, can't you?"

"Not when you've got to fix things up to look like an accident. I've got to have help."

"Well, call one of your boys."

"The only one I trust in a spot like this is Bomo. He's still in jail. The cops have a crazy idea about that gun of his."

"You don't expect me to help you, do you? You know I get sick to my stomach."

"Better you get sick, than get the chair," said Brick. "If they manage somehow to grab my gun—and they could with three of us in a car—"

"He certainly doesn't want you to mess up the carpet," I said.

I heard Hank groan and say, "My God, Mike!"

"Shut up, and sit down," said Brick. I was still standing in front of the desk. I didn't want to sit down because I figured that once Lorchetto moved that gun out of line, I'd have a better chance to get to him if I was on my feet. But I wasn't anxious to try it, yet. If I could only stir up something between Arkwright and Lorchetto. I had to keep this argument going.

"I was only trying to help," I said.

"Let him try," said Arkwright. "Who knows, he might come up with a solution."

"Any solution he comes up with is going to be bad," said Lorchetto.

"Try this one on for size," I said to him. "Why don't you shoot Mr. Arkwright and take this bag—" I gestured toward the bag between Hank's chair and the one I'd been sitting in. "Then you can go in business for yourself. You can be Mr. Prominent Citizen and eat lunch in the Plymouth Club while some crazy hood brings in the cash for you."

"Now, Lanson, don't be ridiculous," said Arkwright.

"All the dope on that shooting in Cincinnati is in that suit-case, Brick," I said casually.

I watched Lorchetto stare at the bag. I turned my head slightly and saw that Arkwright was no longer concerned with his role as public benefactor. He hated my guts.

"Yeah-h-h!" said Lorchetto, drawing out the word.

I was measuring the distance between myself and Lorchetto. It wasn't over six or seven feet, but it looked too far to go unless . . .

The gun moved just a little as Lorchetto made up his mind.

Arkwright was watching, and he went into action. He jerked open a drawer of his desk.

Lorchetto knew what Arkwright was after and that made up his mind. Lorchetto's automatic swept toward Arkwright and blasted.

And I sprang.

With my left hand I grabbed his wrist and brought my right hand down in a chopping blow on his forearm. He howled and his fingers opened. The gun dropped with the reflex.

Hank was scared, but he wasn't paralyzed. Almost before the weapon hit the floor, he was scrambling after it. Let it never be said again that I despise city editors. For in that instant I forgot all the humiliations I'd ever suffered at Hank's hands. I loved the bastard.

Brick wasn't any push-over. He was swinging his left hand trying to knock me silly, but I was hanging onto his right arm with my left hand and punching him in the belly with my right fist.

Hank stood up and brought the barrel of the pistol down on Brick's head. Brick dropped to the floor like a piece of dirty laundry.

Arkwright was moaning and groaning behind his desk. He'd fallen out of his chair as the bullet struck him in the shoulder and he was sure he was killed.

Hank went around the desk and stood over him.

"I'm dying," said Arkwright. "Call a doctor!"

Hank must have still regarded Arkwright as a 'prominent citizen' because he started to reach for the phone.

"To hell with the doctor," I said. "You watch 'em, I'm calling the cops."

"You'll do nothing of the kind," said a voice from the doorway.

I turned and saw Martha Arkwright, dressed in a pink lacy gown and looking as pretty as a picture even though her hair was in curlers. The only ugly thing about her was that .38 she held in her hand.

"Drop the gun, Mister," she said to Newcomb.

Hank hesitated. She blasted and a bullet went into the wall about two feet away from Hank. He dropped Brick's gun.

She looked at me. "Move back, Sweetie Pie," she said. "Go on the other side of the room, against the wall. And take that fat tub of lard with you."

"His name is Hank Newcomb, Martha," I said.

Hank had his hands over his head and he was shaking. "Pleased to meetcha," he said, and he moved with me back to the wall on the other side of the room.

Martha Arkwright moved across the room. She stepped daintily over Brick Lorchetto who was still sleeping from Hank's heavy blow on his head. "I hope he's not hurt," she said, looking down at Brick.

Then she went to the edge of the desk and peered down at her husband.

"Martha, dear, I'm dying," said Arkwright.

"I should be so lucky," she said.

She stood at the end of the desk, still keeping the gun pointed in the general direction of Hank and me. "Well, boys," she said, "we had quite a party, didn't we?"

"I'm not much of a party man myself," I said.

She laughed like it was a joke. "Let's see if we can figure a way out of this thing. Supposing you tell me everything."

"Your husband," I said, "is a racketeer. He's the big wheel in this town. He runs everything. Lorchetto was his hatchet man, and so was the late Mr. Proost, although he operated in a little different fashion."

"I know all about that," said Martha Arkwright. "Manton didn't know I knew, but I often listened in on his little chats down here in the study. And I have ways of learning things that he doesn't know about."

I remembered that I'd seen her at Ramcaster's office. "From Mr. Ramcaster, I assume?"

She laughed. "Wouldn't you like to know?"

She sat down at the edge of the desk. "The big problem is what to do with you," she said. "I know what to do with the other two."

"I can suggest something," I said. "Call the cops and they'll do it for you."

She turned the idea over in her mind a minute. "You know, that might be the answer." She looked down at her husband, who apparently had decided that he wasn't dying after all. "How does it sound to you, Honey Lamb?"

"Martha, for God's sake! Don't you realize that everything you have comes from me? If I went to jail, what would become of you?"

"I don't imagine the trial would take it all, and just think of the fun I'd have on what's left," she said.

Brick stirred, and Martha stepped back so that she could cover him with the gun as well as myself and Hank. Apparently she'd forgotten about the weapon that Hank had dropped which lay on the floor about four feet from Arkwright. He hadn't noticed it yet either, and I wondered what would happen when he did. Apparently she couldn't see very much of Arkwright from where she stood.

I started weighing my chances if they began to trade shots. "I think I'll call Cliffie," she said. This would be Cliff Ramcaster. "He'd just love to bag the big bad gangster boss and his right-hand gunman."

She took a step toward the desk and started to pick up the phone, then hesitated. She looked down at the suitcase that was parked between the two chairs. "What's this?" she asked.

"That's what you've been looking for," I said. "It's Proost's files."

She turned at me and her eyes weren't pretty now. "You know?" she asked.

She was between Lorchetto and me now. I was thinking about Lorchetto, but he wasn't thinking about me. His thoughts were on the gun. He had a stake in this business too. Maybe his stake wasn't his life, as I was sure mine was, but he knew he would lose his liberty if things didn't take a sudden turn.

"You'd better watch him," I said, nodding my head toward Brick, who had pushed himself up on his arms.

She turned and Brick saw her turn. A look of desperation crept into his eyes and he lunged forward at her.

She swung the gun, and missed.

But I was on my way. She must have heard me, either that or it occurred to her that I was in good health and far more dangerous than her groggy opponent on the floor. She turned around and squeezed the trigger.

The distance between us wasn't more than ten feet at the most. You've seen movies and TV plays where gunslingers of the West fire from the hip. Even Private Eyes fire their guns from almost any position, excepting the correct way to shoot a pistol.

Cops know how to fire a pistol, because they are taught how. Very few other people know that it's far different from pointing your finger as the movie gunslingers do.

If you don't believe me, try it. Pick a target as large as a man and point your finger from the hip, without looking at your finger, and then line up your finger with the target and see how far you're off. You'll hit once in awhile at ten feet, but not often enough to make a sure thing gamble of it. And history books are full of true accounts of men who have survived such shots in battle *at point-blank range*. Even a twenty-five percent record of misses is rugged when your life depends on it.

When Martha shot at Hank, I figured she had intended to hit him. But her bullet went two feet wide at a distance of about fifteen feet. This time her bullet struck my coat-sleeve.

And before she could fire again, I had knocked the gun aside. And then, damn it, I forgot that she was a lady—or a woman anyhow—and that she was pretty and sexy and desirable. I punched her in the jaw.

I grabbed the gun as she went down. Lorchetto was still trying to get up, but he was too dizzy to make it.

Then I heard Hank howl and I turned around in time to see Manton Arkwright trying to reach the gun on the other side of the desk. I fired a bullet into the carpet, making a big hole, I'm sorry to say, but nevertheless forcing Manton Arkwright to give up the idea.

Hank went over and picked up the gun while I kept watch over Lorchetto.

It was Hank who used the phone.

Instead of calling the cops, he dialed Colonel Tanner. "I don't trust anybody," he said. "But I trust him more than I do the cops."

The Colonel arrived in about half an hour, bringing with him Clyde Guffy and the big fellow that had been trailing me earlier in the day.

"I guess we'd better all go down to the station and wrap it up," said Guffy, his eyes still heavy with sleep. "But I wish to hell, Mike, you'd stay out of things or work on them at a decent hour."

"Guffy," I said, "I'm going to let you have all the credit for catching the murderer of Clarence Proost and Ernie Stauffer."

"She's in jail!" said Martha Arkwright, who had a black and blue jaw.

"The hell she is," I told her. "You're it!"

FOURTEEN

I was with Guffy in his office. Hank was there, mainly because I said that Hank was with me at the start of the business and he deserved to be in at the finish.

"All right," said Guffy. "You've been shooting off your mouth about things. Let's hear what you've got to support your story."

"Guffy," I said, "there's only one possible solution to the case. Martha Arkwright killed Proost. I suspected it when I went out to Arkwright's place tonight. I had to smoke her out somehow, but I guess I got in a lion's den by mistake."

"You can say that again," said Hank.

"Mike hasn't said anything yet," said Guffy. "All right, Mike. Stop hamming it up and give with the facts."

"You got Martha's gun?" I asked.

Guffy nodded.

"You checked it yet as the murder weapon?"

"The boys will check it tomorrow," said Guffy. "We can hold our prisoners till then."

"You'd better check it right now. Get somebody out of bed, if necessary. Arkwright can get a habeas corpus before you can wiggle your toes. That's the murder weapon, all right."

"How do you know?"

"Because Martha Arkwright was the girl that the Elgarth family saw going into the apartment house where Proost lives," I said. "They said it was a girl with a black and red dress. It threw

403

me at first because Luzy had been wearing a black and red gown that evening. But she went home and changed to a dark blue suit and red blouse before going to Proost's. Even a man can tell the difference between suits and dresses. Besides, Luzy was wearing a cape when she left me. If she didn't have on the cape, her gown was on the sensational side. Elgarth would have noticed its low cut as quickly as he'd have noticed its color."

"So it could have been any girl in a black and red dress," said Guffy.

"The Elgarths can identify Martha Arkwright," I said. "She's not the kind of a girl a person forgets easily."

Guffy nodded.

"What else do you need?"

"Motive," said Guffy.

"Okay," I said, "let's go back to the events preceding the murder. I'd been at the Hilltop Club. Arkwright had learned that afternoon that Proost was getting too big for his britches, but Ramcaster and Lorchetto, aided by the Colonel, stalled Proost's attempt to do a little wild-cat extortion. At Arkwright's orders, Brick and Jim Bomo drove in to see Proost. They followed us down the road and Luzy thought they were trailing her. I think Luzy knew what Proost was trying to do, even if Proost didn't take her into his confidence. Luzy was naturally frightened.

"But in spite of her fears, Brick had business with Proost. They started to make Proost see the light, but Proost turned a neat little trick. He scared Brick. He knew that Brick had formed a very close acquaintanceship with Martha Arkwright. Brick realized that Arkwright couldn't be fooled with. Arkwright could import some gunslingers to take care of Brick and all his gang. And he couldn't touch Proost because the evidence, probably a photograph, that could seal Brick's doom was in a safe place.

"Brick returned to the Hilltop a sadder and wiser man. Martha Arkwright had given her husband a sleeping pill that night in order to have a rendezvous with Brick. But Brick begged off, because he told Martha that Proost could make things hot for both of them.

"Martha drove over to Proost's house determined to get that evidence. She found Proost recovering from a blow on the head delivered by Luzy.

"There was a gun handy, where Luzy left it. She grabbed it and started to threaten Proost. He made a lunge for her and got shot."

"You don't know any of this is a fact," said Guffy.

"No, but it must have happened like that," I said.

"How about Stauffer?"

"Stauffer had the evidence," I said. "Martha killed Stauffer and got it. She knew Stauffer had it because the minute Proost was killed, Stauffer called Martha Arkwright and demanded payment. Possibly Stauffer was blackmailing her for Proost's killing too. He might have figured it out, because he knew more about Proost's affairs than anyone except Arkwright himself."

"So you think Proost was trying to muscle in on Arkwright? Why didn't Arkwright take care of him?"

"Arkwright moved slowly and he wasn't quite sure yet just what Proost was trying to do," I said. "Besides, Arkwright had a gangster's exalted opinion of himself. He figured he could handle Proost, just as he had handled others. He didn't know that Proost was attacking Arkwright's weak spot—Martha."

"Those burned papers in Stauffer's waste basket was the proof that Martha was unfaithful to Arkwright, huh?" Guffy asked.

"Possibly. Although Proost also had evidence that would have sent Stauffer to prison. I think Luzy mailed that to her brother the morning before he died."

Guffy thought it over. "We'll check out your theory, Mike. I'll buy some of it right now. But we'll have to get Luzy to talk. Maybe Brick or Bomo or even Luzy will talk. I don't expect Arkwright to say much."

"You'll stop shadowing me now?" I asked.

Guffy laughed. "Mike, I told you I wasn't shadowing you. That big bruiser with Colonel Tanner was a private detective that the Colonel hired to keep you out of trouble. But you ditched him every time you turned a corner and he was never on hand to help you."

"I'm sure glad you were once," I said, "but how'd you know my movements."

"Mike," said Guffy, "most of the cops in this town know you and your bright red car. The whole force knew where you were. Every time a cop saw you, he called the station."

I got red in the face. Hank, who had listened silently, now spoke, "You can sleep tomorrow, Mike. I'll write the story."

"Sure you don't need help?"

"Help? I was there, wasn't I?"

I went home and slept late. In the morning I read the *Globe's* account of the story. Hank had written it, and took a good deal of credit, but I didn't mind. Maybe I could do a little blackmailing myself, although I don't think Colonel Tanner was fooled.

I went to work at noon and during the afternoon I fed developments into the desk. Hank wasn't there. He'd gone to sleep about noon and they had carried him upstairs to a store room and stretched him out on the floor. He was a worn-out man.

Ramcaster was being investigated by cops, by the county prosecutor and by the Bar Association.

Arkwright had a superficial bullet wound and was under guard in the hospital. Meanwhile a series of charges involving extortion and rackets, had been filed against him.

Brick Lorchetto was to be returned to Cincinnati for trial on a murder charge. Bomo was wanted in California for a variety of things.

Martha Arkwright denied everything, but she had been identified by the Elgarths and the gun she had pointed at me, even missed me with, was the one that had been used to kill Proost and Stauffer. The motive was a little hazy, but Brick Lorchetto was singing his head off and he admitted his connections with Martha and that Proost had threatened to expose him.

Singularly, no one had actually seen Martha enter Mrs. Bagley's rooming house, but a car salesman had noted her Chrysler parked a block away. He'd jotted down the license number, expecting to check up on the owner and try to make a deal for a new car.

County Prosecutor Sherman, who took over the case since Ramcaster was suspended, was in the process of releasing Luzy on bail. He said that charges of some kind would be placed against her for helping Proost blackmail so many people, but since she had done this under duress she might get off lightly, possibly on a parole.

The Citizens' Anti-Vice League strangely enough, offered to supply her bail, because she had helped expose Proost.

Guffy found out that the ashes in Ernie Stauffer's wastebasket included some papers and a photograph. He hoped that he could use some parts of it in Martha's trial. Luzy admitted mailing the evidence of parole violation to her brother while she was in the Hotel Creston. She sent it special delivery and probably reached Stauffer just before he was murdered.

Minor hoods and grifters were fleeing the city, but they'd be back or others would take their places. One thing Manton Arkwright had said was right. Crime, vice and corruption would not be eliminated overnight, or by one defeat. These things would always exist in some degree, but the fact that they existed was proof that the law was there. Without laws, there would be no crime.

Luzy told Guffy why she said maybe she had killed Proost.

"I wanted to confuse Mike at first," she said, "but I really felt that I was involved in Proost's activities. He was killed because of these activities, therefore I was responsible. I'd tipped him off to Martha and Brick Lorchetto, you know. I suspected she might be the one who killed Proost, but I didn't know. But I did know that I'd put her in a position for blackmail."

Luzy had not known that Arkwright was the big racket boss that he was. Ramcaster had known it, having been tipped off by Martha. More people knew of Arkwright's secret life than Arkwright suspected.

There was just one other point. I asked Guffy:

"Why did Luzy take Proost's files?"

"We have to accept her word on that," he said. "Luzy said she went to Proost's place determined to break with him. She knew he had a gun and she got possession of it She used it as a club, knocking Proost out. Then she dug out the evidence Proost had of her brother's parole violation—which actually had forced her to do what Proost ordered her to do.

"Luzy told me about her decision at that point. She said, 'I saw all those envelopes, each one like a chain, holding someone to Proost. I thought that I ought to release them all. I didn't have time to destroy those papers there, so I loaded them into one of Proost's suitcases and took them all away with me. That night, after I was in the Hotel Creston, I put my brother's file in an envelope and sent it to him special delivery.'"

"Do you believe her, Guffy?" I asked.

Guffy nodded. "I always was a sucker for a pretty face. Do you believe her?"

"I always did," I said. "I never thought she murdered Proost. And I think she told the truth about those papers."

"Does that wind it up?" Guffy asked after he'd told me the last of these many things.

"If it doesn't I'll give you a ring." I looked at my watch. "Tomorrow, because it's quitting time now."

I went up to the Press Room and checked out with the desk. Hank was still sleeping but the desk said they were going to send him home very soon.

Afterwards I went downstairs, out the back door to the police department parking lot, where I am permitted to park my car as a personal favor.

Someone stood beside my car.

"Can I bum a ride, Mike?" It was Luzy.

"Anytime, honey. Where do you want to go?"

"Home," she said. "To 6810 Jefferson Avenue."

"Hop in."

We drove out into the rush hour traffic and soon we were headed north on Jefferson Avenue.

"I got off pretty easy, didn't I?" she said.

"You were lucky," I told her.

"I suppose you've got a low opinion of me."

"No," I said. "Everybody has a good side and a bad side. I've seen your good side and I like it."

"If you saw my good side, you probably saw my act. I show everything there."

I laughed. "You're creative. What was that gimmick about the poem you left at the hotel with my mail?"

"Oh, that. I was trying to tip you off as to what was in my suitcase in case I got caught. You have the bag in your car you know."

The bag now was in the custody of the court.

We drove in silence and then she said. "Did Martha Arkwright make any passes at you?"

"Stop acting like a teen-age kid," I said.

She laughed. "I had it coming, I guess. I'm sorry she was caught, Mike. Proost was in a dirty business. She did the city a favor by taking care of him."

"No murder is justified," I said.

"Probably not," she said, "but that was almost justified. And I wish I could help Martha."

"You shouldn't. She didn't come forward to help you when you were in trouble. She wanted you badly. She was afraid you knew too much about her."

"You tried to help me. I'll never forget it, Mike."

"You were good copy," I said.

"Was that the reason? Were you only thinking of your job?"

I shook my head. "Not all. I'm no Eagle Scout."

She was silent for a little while. "How'd you like that poem? The one I left at the hotel?"

"Beautiful sentiment," I said.

"You mean it was lousy."

"It reminded me of Liz Browning," I lied.

"Remember what it said? I'll bet you don't even remember it."

"It said something about me working in the daytime and you working at night and we never got together."

"That's right. But I don't work at night now. The Hilltop's closed. Neither of us are-working."

"Not till tomorrow morning," I said.

We drove on.

"Stop at the supermarket, honey," Luzy said. "I'll have to lay in some supplies for our breakfast."

IF WISHES WERE HEARSES

To
Jack Hean, Ll.B., for his help.

Mike Lanson
A reporter would make a good headline in a murder case—as a victim.

Freddie the Grape
This wino was a fruity character, about to be squashed to death.

Corrine Nimes
A luscious doll who loved her husband, but couldn't live with him.

Addison Sharp
As a lawyer he was quite familiar with other people's secrets.

Lieutenant Guffy
He liked to catch criminals and newspaper reporters who got in his way.

ONE
TUESDAY, 10:07 A.M.

If I hadn't known the lieutenant better I'd have thought he was drunk. His office at Police Headquarters reeked of alcohol. But Lieutenant Clyde Guffy is a conscientious cop and that is why I knew that the odor, mixed with non-alcoholic stenches, arose from the body of his unwashed guest.

"Know this bum, Mike?" the lieutenant asked by way of introduction.

He was a bum, this visitor. No word could describe him better. Unshaved face, clothes that were little more than rags, bloodshot eyes and hair that had flora and fauna enough to delight any biologist.

"I have moved in police circles for nigh onto six years, Guffy," I said, "and Freddie the Grape has been in jail almost as much as he's been out since I took over the *Gazette's* police run. But why, may I ask, does homicide interest itself in odd-balls from skid row?"

Guffy is not an easygoing cop; he was dedicated to his profession. But today he was in a delightfully whimsical mood—for him anyhow. His little round face was beaming with good humor and he showed dimples in his smile. Perhaps on this unusual day he even looked upon newspapermen in a charitable light.

"Freddie has moved into big time," said Guffy. "He has uncovered a plot to commit murder."

"Let me be the first to congratulate you, Freddie," I said to the scruffy, but rather average-built man.

"Din't wanna get in no trouble," Freddie croaked, blinking his eyes. "Jest an accident that I hear it."

"Tell Mike about it, Freddie," Guffy urged.

Freddie squinted at me. "He's a newspaper guy, ain't he?"

"One of the lousiest," said Guffy. "Mike Lanson holds nothing sacred and doesn't believe in secrets."

"Crap," said Freddie. "Only thing newspapers is good for is to keep you warm when you sleep in the park."

"Freddie is a believer in fundamental realities," said Guffy. "He'll never have anything in common with a crazy visionary like you, Mike."

"I wanna lie down," said Freddie, squirming uneasily.

"Do you mind waiting a moment till I brief Mike on your background?" Guffy asked, and without waiting for an answer he turned to me. "Freddie is a high-class wino, Mike. He drinks nothing but Manischewitz and Mogen David."

"I can't use that in the paper, Guffy. It's free advertising."

"More crap," said Freddie.

Guffy beamed like a man who has just taught an old dog a new trick. "Freddie, we suspect, is the man who broke into a wine store on Twelfth Street not long before midnight last night. One bottle of Mogen David was stolen. Freddie never steals more than he needs, which is more than I can say for some thieves."

"Put me in the tank," said Freddie. "I'm sicka dis crap."

Guffy paid no heed. "Afterwards, he walked down an alley to Lakeside Park and hid in some shrubbery to consume his ill-gotten refreshment. While so doing he overheard an interesting conversation nearby. Do you want to take it from there, Freddie?"

"Corrigan and dis guy I din't know," said Freddie. "Dis guy sez, 'Corrigan, I give you one thousand dollar if you do the job.' And then Corrigan sez, 'What? Me risk the hot squat for a measle grand. I din't make like no patsy.' So they talk around and pretty soon dis guy I didn't know sez, 'The way you do it, nobody tink it murder. There won't be no hot squat.' But Corrigan sez no, he din't wanna. Pretty soon they go way."

"Corrigan," explained Guffy, "is a stinko private dick. A couple of times we tried to revoke his license, but he squirmed out of it."

"Corrigan is a good guy. He gimme quarter almost regular. Once on Christmas, he gimme dollar. But he's crazy. For one thousand dollar, I would knock a guy off if it din't look like murder."

"Take my advice, Freddie," said Guffy in a kindly tone. "Just stick to stealing wine. We wouldn't want to strap you in a chair and cook you. You'd make the state prison smell like a winery."

"Crap," said Freddie. "Dis guy say nobody din't get caught."

"Is this for publication, Guffy?"

"How much can you print?"

"If you've got a confession signed by Freddie, we can print all of it," I said. "If you've got him charged with conspiracy to commit homicide, we can quote the police. But we can't mention this man Corrigan unless you bring him in to admit or deny it. If you're just going to sit there like laughing boy, I can't use any of it."

"I sent a couple of boys out to pick up Corrigan," said Guffy. He opened a drawer and pulled out a piece of paper. "Here's a carbon of Freddie's statement. He didn't sign this one, but we have two signed and witnessed copies in the files."

I took the paper. It was in Guffy's language, not Freddie's, but the facts were just as Freddie had recited them to me, although it didn't admit to burglarizing the wine store on Twelfth Street. Apparently Guffy had allowed Freddie a little latitude in exchange for information. It stated that Freddie had been picked up by policemen not far from the scene of the alleged conversation and that Freddie was intoxicated.

"Weird," I said, handing the paper back to Guffy. "Do you think somebody thought he could get a murder done for a thousand dollars? Didn't he know about inflation?"

"Freddie would have done it for a thousand."

"He would have botched the job."

"Nah," said Freddie. "Jus' lemme show you."

"How much experience have you had, Freddie? Did you ever kill anybody?"

"I tole you. I din't kill nobody. But I could learn."

"Don't try it," said Guffy. "There are occupational hazards."

"Whadda I get?" Freddie asked.

"For not killing somebody?"

"No. For signin' the paper. Do I go to jail? Or do you turn me loose?"

"We'll pass the buck to the judge," said Guffy.

"You said I din't get no burglary rap."

"No, but you could get thirty days for being drunk."

"Crap. You can't trust no cops."

The phone rang and Guffy reached out and picked it up.

He said, "Guffy speaking," and paused. I could hear an excited chirp but couldn't distinguish the words. "I'll be damned," said Guffy. "You call the coroner? Well, get on the ball. I'll be right out." He hung up the phone.

"Who died?" asked Freddie.

Guffy didn't answer. He pressed a button on his desk. Then he turned to me. "Get your hat, Mike. You may have a bigger story than you thought."

The door opened and a cop came in. "Put Freddie in the tank," said Guffy.

"Book him?"

"I'll attend to it later."

The cop took Freddie out of the room. Guffy put on his coat, while I stood there watching. "Well? Where's your hat?" he asked me.

"Hell, it's summer, Guffy. I don't need it. What in the hell has happened?"

"The boys I sent over to Corrigan's office found him dead," said Guffy.

"Maybe he took the thousand and the job backfired."

"And maybe the guy who offered the thousand figured Corrigan could do a little blackmailing," Guffy said.

I followed Guffy out of his office and to the parking lot behind Police Headquarters. A few seconds later we were on our way with the siren howling like murder.

And it was. Corrigan had been shot in the back.

TWO
WEDNESDAY MORNING

Andy Maunch, the copy boy, perched on the desk next to mine in the press room, while I read my second-day story on George Edward Corrigan's murder. Don Hilliard, my assistant on the police run, was off on Wednesdays and I was handling the beat alone, except for help that came from the office.

The follow on the murder sounded pretty good. I felt at home with the facts, I had everybody's initials right, and there is always room for a little hunching in a second-day story.

Nothing really new had developed overnight, but some of Guffy's boys were busy in Corrigan's office trying to turn up some evidence from Corrigan's files. I knew this would give several divorce defendants heartburn. It wasn't strictly legal procedure, but the cops do it and after it's done, it's done and nothing can be done about it. To be legal, the cops should have obtained a court order to go through the dead man's private files.

Corrigan had been shot in the back. The medical examiner said the bullet had glanced off a bone—the name of which only a doctor knows—and had played hell with the left ventricle of the victim's heart. It was a .38-calibre bullet, which can make a big hole after it's flattened by a bone. Death was so quick that Corrigan never knew what hit him.

The M.E. also decided that Corrigan had been dead about eight hours when his body was discovered. That would set the time of the shooting at about 2 a.m. The police report on Freddie the Grape said that he had been picked up in the vicinity of Lakeside Park at about midnight.

Apparently Corrigan and his buddy had gone to Corrigan's office, where the man who was trying to buy murder had decided that Corrigan, alive and unwilling to kill, was dangerous. My story quoted Guffy as saying that police were also investigating the possibility that a third party had shot Corrigan. I knew, the police knew, and most of the readers would guess, that there was no evidence of this kind to investigate.

Freddie the Grape's statement had been given a big play in yesterday afternoon's paper when the murder was fresh, and my second-day story rehashed it briefly. I had emphasized, maybe a little heavily, that Michael Lanson, the *Gazette's* number one police reporter, had witnessed Freddie's admission of the essential details of his allegations. Freddie was still in jail.

Corrigan, according to my story, had figured mostly in divorce cases. He had followed wayward husbands, spied on faithless wives. Occasionally the detective did other types of work, but he was not regarded by the cops as a man of untarnished virtue. This, of course, I didn't mention in the paper. His work hadn't brought me much copy; the *Gazette* rarely gave space to divorce actions, unless they were contested and important.

"You gonna read that thing all day?" Andy asked, getting restless as he waited for the copy.

"This yarn will live," I said. "It's immortal."

Andy scratched his nose. He knew I was exaggerating, but I did think it was a pretty good job and I always take the most pride in my stories in the first moments after they are written. Possibly my grammar and syntax could stand improvement. Maybe some commas were misplaced. Undoubtedly my spelling was not perfect. But copyreaders are paid to fix that junk and would be out of a job if reporters didn't make a few mistakes. It ain't everybody who can write.

I folded the copy and stuck it into an envelope, which I gave to Andy. "Guard it with your life," I said. "Don't let future generations be robbed of this literary treasure."

He tried to seem unimpressed. "Hank says to tell you to get the iron outa your pants. He wants a new lead for the suburban."

"His slightest wish is a requirement for my paycheck," I said. "Ask the big ape if he thinks I got this story sitting on my rear?"

"He thinks you fell into it," said Andy.

I started to pick up a chunk of type metal I use for a paper-weight. Andy got out of there quick, with my story in his hand. As he went through the door, he almost bumped into a red-faced gent just entering.

"'Scuse me," said Andy, who is polite even when he is running for his life.

"Watch it, you juvenile delinquent," snarled the gent, belching. He came through the door unsteadily, while Andy went on his way.

As he approached my desk, I detected the odor of a great many martinis, although it was only 9:30 in the morning. "You in charge here?" he asked.

I nodded. "In full charge," I said.

He held out his wrists. "Put the cuffs on me," he said.

It's not unusual for someone to surrender to a reporter. Almost every reporter has it happen to him if he's in business long enough. People do it for a number of reasons; mainly for publicity, but sometimes because they're afraid of the police.

"I left my cuffs at the pool hall last night," I said. "What crime have you committed." I knew the guy was more than average drunk.

"I am a blackmailer," he said. "They killed Corrigan and now they are coming for me. I want police protection."

"Wait a minute," I said. I reached for the phone.

There are two phones on my desk. One connects with the police operator, the other with the switchboard in the *Gazette* building four blocks away. In my haste, I got the wrong phone; the *Gazette* phone instead of the police phone.

The instant the operator answered, I knew I'd made a mistake, "Excuse it, please. I wanted the cops—"

"Mike," said the switchboard operator. "Hank wants you—" I hung up quickly. Hank Newcomb was my city editor and if I talked to him, no telling when I'd get to this more urgent business.

I started reaching for the other phone and the drunk looked hard at me. "You're not a policeman?" He swung around and looked at the frosted glass panel on the door. It said Press Room in letters four inches high. The door had been open when he came in and he hadn't seen it. He thought I was a cop.

"You're a reporter!" he said, and turned and started out of the room. I got to my feet and started after him, but he slammed the door. I fumbled to open it, and I heard him bounding down the stairs. By the time I got the door open he was outside, and by the time I was outside he was pulling out from the curb in a racy GM.

I tried to catch the license number, but he swung around the corner before I could focus on it.

I walked back into headquarters. A sandy-haired, red-faced man of about forty, tall but a little puffy around the middle, who drove a GM shouldn't be hard to get a line on.

Guffy was in the crime lab sorting out fussy little details that help cops to solve murders. He didn't hail me with delight, because usually I am a nuisance rather than a help to Guffy and his work. But when I told him what had happened he got interested right away. "Damn," he said, "if you hadn't fumbled the phone . . ."

"Guffy, I wish you'd stop being a perfectionist," I told him. "As it is, you've got a break. All you have to do is to run him down."

"Do you know how many GM's there are in town?"

I had no idea.

"Or how many tall, sandy-haired, puffy guys drive 'em?"

Again I was without idea. "You are a cop, Guffy, and cops are man-hunters. Get hunting."

"I got a better idea," he said. "The boys are wrestling with Corrigan's files right now. If this bird is mixed up with Corrigan, maybe we can get a quick line on him there."

Most of the time it's better to let the cops do your leg work for you, but it was still early in the morning and the suburban edition didn't roll till two. I might get the new lead I wanted by going with Guffy, so I rode over to Corrigan's office with him.

The office was in a four-story building at Ninth and Mohawk, not the most modern or busiest part of town. The building was old and it housed offices of small firms, a few professional people, and George Edward Corrigan's detective agency.

His quarters were on the second floor and consisted of a single room, lined with filing cabinets, an ancient Underwood typewriter, and an iron safe.

Two cops—Sergeant Russell and Virgil Lazarus, Detective, Second Class—both of Homicide, were busy arguing with a tall, dignified, white-haired gentleman. On the desk around which the three men stood, were folders apparently removed from Corrigan's files.

Their voices had carried down the hallway as we approached, but the argument stopped suddenly as we entered. The two cops grinned at Guffy. "Glad you came, Lieutenant. This guy claims we can't go through this stuff." Russell gestured toward the papers on the desk.

The white-haired gent gave Guffy a single glance, then he focused his eyes on me. I knew him and he knew me. It was Charles E. Hayten, one of the most prominent corporation lawyers in town. In addition to handling the legal work for several big firms, he owned stock in most of them. Hayten was the senior partner of the law firm of Hayten, Hartweig, Brusnik, Lyons and Jones. On one occasion, where I got to know him, he had defended a corporation president who got involved in legal technicalities in a bankruptcy case.

Hayten looked like the movie version of a Kentucky colonel, except that he had no goatee and didn't talk with a deep South accent. Nor did he carry mint juleps into the courtroom. I didn't know him well enough to know if he drank them in private.

"The police," said Hayten, "might have some rights here, in the investigation of a crime. But you, Lanson, are trespassing."

His pointed chin looked very determined and the expression was emphasized by piercing eyes on each side of his slender nose.

"Whoa," said Guffy. "Just who in the hell are you, mister?"

Hayten's mouth curled under his thin white mustache. "It makes no difference who I am," he said. "But for the record, I'm Charles E. Hayten, a lawyer, and I'm telling you that you can't go through these private files without a court order."

"Nuts," said Guffy. "We can and we will. Who are you to stop us? Was Corrigan your client?"

"No," said Hayten, "but I'm defending the interests of certain clients who may be mentioned in those files."

"How long do you think it'll take us to get a court order, Mr. Hayten?" Guffy asked. "We can get one in the time it takes us to fill out the forms and see a judge. You're interfering with a police investigation and you've got no right."

"Maybe his client's the one who done in Corrigan," said Russell.

"That's absurd," said Hayten.

"Well, if you ain't got nothin' to hide," said Lazarus, "you'd better co-operate."

"I'm warning you," said Hayten. "If you want trouble, you'll get it."

"What's all this about?" came a new voice from the door. It was a gruff voice, a harsh-sounding voice. I turned and saw a small, wiry looking man with thin hair standing there.

"My God, another shyster," said Russell. "They crawl outa the woodwork."

This gentleman I also knew, because it is a reporter's duty, especially that of a reporter who handles crime news, to know most of the lawyers in town. This was Addison Sharp.

"Hello, Addison," said Hayten.

"Hello, Charley," said Sharp. "Did I overhear some kind of argument about files?"

"You represent Corrigan?" Hayten asked his professional colleague,

"He does," said Guffy, and not very cheerfully. "Every time we tried to tie it onto Corrigan, Addison Sharp pulled the strings the other way."

"Tell them they're trespassing," said Hayten, sweeping his arm toward the three cops and me.

Sharp smiled. "That's not to the interest of my client, the late George Edward Corrigan," said the lawyer. "I believe he would want them to extend their best efforts to bring the slayer to justice."

"Those files have nothing to do with his murder," said Hayten.

"Maybe you have information we don't have," said Guffy. "We don't know."

"I'm sure the officers will be discreet," said Sharp. "The fact that a newspaper reporter is present isn't an indication that the *Gazette* will run a serial story on those files. How about it, Lanson?"

"You know the libel laws," I said. "Even truth isn't always a defense in a case like this. I'm just trying to see a murderer caught."

"You can't give them permission to touch anything," said Hayten. "These files are part of the estate. No part of the estate can be touched without a court order."

"Go haunt some corporation," said Sharp. "Go ahead boys. Just be sure that everything is put back where you found it."

Hayten shook his head, then he turned to me. "I'd like to talk to you privately, Lanson."

I hesitated. You get a sort of extra sense when you deal with people as a reporter. I knew without being told that Hayten was going to ask me to keep something out of the story on the murder. In ninety-nine cases out of one hundred, it would have nothing to do with the murder. But in ninety-eight cases out of the ninety-nine, it would make good reading. And in ninety-seven out of the ninety-eight, it would be news I wouldn't hear in any other way.

"I have a deadline to make, Mr. Hayten," I said. "But I can spare you a few minutes." My deadline was about four hours off, but he didn't know that.

Hayten looked at his watch. "Supposing you make your deadline and meet me at the office of the Nimes Chemical Fertilizer Company around ten-thirty?"

I pretended to consider it. "Sure," I said, after a short hesitation. "I think I can work it in. Where are the offices?"

"The eight-story building at Eighth and Willis," he said. "It's only three blocks from here."

He turned and left while Sharp held open the door for him. Afterwards Sharp came over to me. "Don't believe everything he tells you, Lanson. He's smooth."

I grinned back at him. "I always watch myself when I get alone with lawyers."

He thought it was a good joke. "We're not such a bad lot, Lanson. If it weren't for us, a lot of people would be in more trouble than they are." Sharp left.

I watched the cops going through the files, none of which were shown to me, I would have liked a look, since Corrigan did a great deal of divorce work. Finally I grew tired and called in my lead. It wasn't very hot, but I promised Hank to keep working in case something turned up for the suburban. The fact that officers were digging into the records of the late George Edward Corrigan over the protest of a prominent corporation attorney didn't look as if it would develop into anything earth-smashing.

For three generations, the Nimes Chemical Fertilizer Company had grown in size, but during those generations the location of their downtown offices had deteriorated. Eighth and Willis was only a couple of blocks from skid row now, and the red sandstone buildings that stood around it were blackened by soot and occupied by small factories, wholesalers and hole-in-the-wall stores.

But inside the building there was the ornate dignity of the early 1900's. Nothing had been changed, but everything had been excellently preserved. There were chandeliers, brass cuspidors, wooden frescoes, pillars and arches, even flowered carpeting on the floor.

There was a receptionist and a switchboard, the most modern thing in the room, but the receptionist wouldn't have gotten a whistle from a hermit on a deserted isle.

"Whom do you wish to see?" she asked.

"Mr. Charles Hayten asked me to meet him here," I told her.

"Mr. Hayten? Your name, please?"

"Mike Lanson of the *Gazette.*"

"Oh. A reporter?" She smiled and consulted a pad in front of her. "Mr. Hayten will see you in Mr. Calderson's office," she said. "It's through the arch, down the corridor to the end. A receptionist there will direct you."

I thanked her and set off on the safari. And that was what it was, for the building was half a block long, and I walked the length of it to a glass door on which was inscribed in gold letters: Executive Offices.

I opened the door into an anteroom governed by a woman cast from the same mold as the outside receptionist, except that this one was older. She was behind a fenced-in enclosure that divided the room into two halves, as if the three doorways beyond were sacred and holy and forbidden to the unclean. A single gate was in the fence, one with an old-fashioned trick lock, the mastery of which is one of the things a reporter learns early.

The three doors the receptionist guarded were labeled plainly, also in gold. The one on the left said: *Fenwick R. Calderson, President and General Manager.* The door on the right was lettered: *Harold C. Nimes, Jr., Vice-President, Production.* The center door, a little more ornate in its lintel, broader and heavier in construction, was labeled: *Harold C. Nimes, Chairman of the Board.*

"Yes?" asked the secretary coldly. A nameplate on her desk labeled her as Madeline Harkiss.

"I'm Mike Lanson of the *Gazette,*" I labeled myself. "Mr. Hayten asked me to meet him here. I understand he's in Mr. Calderson's office." I nodded toward the appropriate door.

"Oh, yes. If you have an appointment, he will see you," she said. "I'll ring." She picked up a phone, pressed a button at the base and waited. Someone apparently answered at the other end. I saw her lips move, but her voice was so low that I couldn't hear what she said.

She hung up the phone. "Mr. Hayten is waiting. Mr. Calderson said you could go in." She gestured toward the door and she started to get up to let me through the gate.

I reached over and worked the trick lock and entered. She seemed surprised. "Oh! You know how to open it!" I could see that my stature had increased in her eyes. In the business world it is little things like that which make lions out of men. "Most people don't know how to open it."

"I used to be a burglar," I said.

She shrank back and I think she believed me because she watched me as I entered Calderson's office.

Hayten and Calderson were seated across the room with their backs toward a huge, old-fashioned roll-top desk which had probably been purchased new in 1910. They faced me as I entered. Calderson impressed me immediately as a slow-moving, slow-thinking, huge and awkward individual, who probably owed his position to the fact that he'd been with the firm since boyhood and had been on time every day. His size was not due to fat, but to muscle. He probably played golf every sunshiny day, and attended gym classes in the evening.

Hayten rose soberly and said, "Thanks for being on time, Lanson. We always appreciate punctuality around here." He shook my hand with a warm, friendly grip. The he turned to his companion. "Fen, this is Lanson, Mike Lanson, the man I was telling you about. He's police reporter for the *Gazette*. Mike, this is Fenwick Calderson, general manager for Nimes."

"Glad to meet you, Lanson," Calderson bellowed, grasping my hand and squeezing it until I winced. "So you're a newspaper man! Excitement all the time. Must be a great life."

"It has its moments, Mr. Calderson," I said, wondering if he'd trade jobs. He probably didn't make less than twenty-five thousand a year, plus stock and options, and the only call he had to use his ingenuity was in making the cheap help happy.

"More interesting than selling fertilizer any way you look

at it. Sit down, Lanson. That chair over there." He rushed over to the nearby chair, lifted it like it was a sheet of paper, and brought it over to face the chairs he and Hayten had used. Then he sat down in his chair, which was beside the shiny brass cuspidor. Hayten seated himself and I plunked myself down and waited.

"We've a pretty big firm here, Mr. Lanson," said Calderson. "It's been run by the Nimes family since 1904, and it's bigger now than it's ever been. We sell fertilizer from coast to coast, from the citrus groves of Florida, to the potato growers of Idaho. We hold crop schools, give scholarships to farm boys so they can attend agricultural schools, and do all sorts of things."

"Make a good feature story for our Sunday magazine," I said.

"Oh, we been written up," said Calderson. "Even *Fortune* told about Nimes Chemical once. But that isn't why we asked you here. Is it, Charley?"

"No," said Hayten. "It was to keep something out of print."

Like I said, you can always hunch a thing like this before it happens.

"Well," I said, "if it's keeping something out of the paper, you'd better not tell me about it. My job is to put things in."

"You do, on occasion, keep confidences, don't you? I've heard that reporters will go to jail rather than tell some things."

"It's a sort of fine distinction between a confidence and a squelch," I said. "You tell me something that isn't likely to happen, but which I can print if it does happen, and all the tractors in the state couldn't drag it out of me before the right time. But if you want to suppress something, that's something else again. You get the idea, don't you?"

"I'm not sure I do. News has been suppressed."

"I'm not the man who suppresses it," I said. "Colonel Tanner is." Colonel Gordon C. Tanner was the editor and publisher of the *Gazette,* the afternoon paper, and the *Globe,* the morning paper. "If there's a good reason and if the news isn't the sort of thing that the community at large would be interested in, he often tones it down, and in a few cases he might forget it entirely."

"What sort of story would he forget?"

I shrugged. "It's hard to define. There's no set rule. Public interest is the main thing. The more the story would interest and affect people, the more reason there is for printing it. But there's no hard and fast rule. It depends on the circumstances."

"This story would reflect upon our corporation," said Calderson. "Nothing we've done is, ah, illegal or disreputable. But there would be talk."

I stole a glance at Hayten and saw him watching Calderson. I wondered if the business had anything to do with Hayten's visit to Corrigan's office an hour ago.

"As I said, it depends on the circumstances. The only way I know of to avoid publicity is to avoid doing anything that amounts to much—good or bad."

Calderson turned his head toward Hayten. "You're a lawyer, Charley. You're better with words than I. Maybe you can give him an inkle."

"Can you keep a divorce out of the paper?" Hayten asked.

"Yours?"

"I'm a widower. I might say that no member of this firm is either plaintiff or defendant in the divorce."

"Then why let it bother you?" I asked. I tried to keep a straight face. If they weren't parties in the divorce action they could be correspondents. "However, I will say that we don't monkey with divorces unless there's something unusual about them; an important person, or something that makes news."

"Nimes Chemical runs ads in your paper, Lanson," said Calderson.

"Okay," I said. "Thanks. Why don't you take up the matter with the advertising department?"

Hayten sighed deeply. "It's a tough spot," he said. "We can't tell you what we want, and you won't promise not to print it if we do. Maybe H.C. can talk to you. We seem to be going around in circles. See him. Fen."

Calderson rose slowly, and walked to the door connecting with the office of the chairman of the board. He gave me a glance, as he opened the door. Then he went through it, closing it behind him. I was left alone with Charley Hayten.

"The corporation isn't—wasn't involved with Corrigan, was it?" I asked.

Hayten, who had been deep in thought, was jerked back to reality. "Eh? No, no! Nothing like that." He stopped. "Listen, Mike, we, asked you here because we felt that you'd be helpful. H.C. is generous to people who are helpful."

I had a feeling of what he was leading up to. Let me explain quickly that payola is not unknown to reporters, or newspaper people in general. But most of them are honest—not from choice, but because they know that news can't be suppressed. If they don't print it, the news will get back to the newspaper brass in varied and sundry forms and the questions that are asked by editors or erring reporters can be as fatal as a congressional investigation. At least to careers. The only time a bribe is successful is in the case of little stuff—things that could have been suppressed by a simple request to the management—not news that people want to read, or which builds circulation or gains a reputation for a newspaper.

Even though it had been hinted that a divorce was involved, I wasn't kidding myself. I could keep a divorce quiet with the Colonel's knowledge simply by telling Hank Newcomb that it was of the ordinary variety. But divorces have a way of becoming big news. This one would, I was sure of that.

"I know Mr. Nimes is a generous man," I said. "I'd like to partake of his generosity, but believe me, Mr. Hayten, I'm too young to get drummed out of my trade. His generosity would have to keep me in sandwiches till Social Security took over."

The door opened and Calderson reappeared. He held the door partly open behind him and stood there, watching me intently. "Mr. Nimes would like to talk to you, Lanson," he said.

Hayten stood and I got to my feet. He led the way to the door and Calderson stepped back to allow me to enter.

The office of the chairman of the board was twice as large as Calderson's office and the furnishings were more luxurious, although they were all of the pre-war period. Pre-World War I.

There was a fireplace with shiny brass fixtures. The chandeliers had glass do-dads hanging down from them. There were

two big black tables in the room, made of mahogany, I supposed. One was used as a desk by Nimes, the other had 5 chairs
all around it, four on each side and one at the end. The room
was used as a conference room for the board, apparently. The
only thing modern was a fluorescent lamp on Nimes' desk.

Two men sat at the conference table, across from each other.
The one facing me on the far side of the table, was young, a
slender fellow about my age. Handsome and tall but nervous,
his face was red with anger. His companion, I knew, was H.C.
Nimes himself.

When H.C. Nimes turned his head toward me, he dominated
everything in sight. There are only a few men that can do this.
You know by looking at them that they are men who get things
done. Sometimes they aren't, but they make you feel that way.

He rose and extended his hand. A smile crossed his face.
"Mr. Lanson? Come in, please. I'm H.C. Nimes."

I grasped the hand, expecting a crushing grip, like Calderson's. But it was a soft, warm hand. The only crusher was Nimes
himself, I wasn't familiar with Nimes or his firm, but I recalled
faintly the stories I'd heard about the outfit. H.C.'s grandfather
started the business hauling barnyard manure in an old wagon.
Somewhere he'd learned that he could make more money and
produce more fertilizer with chemicals, and he had built a small
plant on the Wamego River, south of town. His son had gone
to college and learned more about crops and chemistry, and his
grandson, H.C. himself, had continued in that direction.

"I'm glad to know you, Mr. Nimes," I said like a small boy
reciting his company expressions. I told myself that I wouldn't
be afraid of him. Impressed maybe, but unafraid. I used a method that had served me well ever since I interviewed the governor
while he changed clothes in a hotel suite preparatory to making
a speech. Since then I had known that all men are mortal when
they have no pants on. I visualized Nimes without pants and
decided he too was of common clay.

"And this is Harry, my son," said Nimes, waving his hand
toward Junior as if the young man didn't count. The young man

on the far side of the table nodded curtly and I nodded back. He was too far away to shake hands.

"Sit down, gentlemen," said Nimes, moving to the chair at the head of the table.

On cue, Calderson took the chair on Nimes' right. Hayten seated himself on Calderson's right. Junior placed himself in the chair to the left of his father. In order to keep things balanced, I walked around the table and sat on Junior's left, leaving a vacant chair between us.

Nimes waited till the movement ceased, then he turned his gray eyes on me. He wore glasses, but his eyes burned through them. "Fen says you're a difficult man to deal with, Lanson. Doesn't anyone have the right of privacy any more? Can't we talk things over with a reporter?"

"Certainly," I said. "But a reporter's business is that of getting news, Mr. Nimes. Certain things are legitimate news. Hell and high water can't keep news from circulating. Dictators have tried it and failed. Individuals have tried it. But the news always pops out. You can bribe me, but another reporter will print it and I'll lose my job and my livelihood. What you're asking is that I do the impossible."

Nimes nodded his head as if I had a point, but I wasn't fooled. He wasn't conceding anything but a problem. "We have an opening here for an astute public relations man," he said. "The job pays ten thousand a year. With the proper cooperation and interest in our welfare, it's yours, Lanson."

My composure crumbled. My jaw dropped and my mouth hung open. A short time before this very morning, I'd listened to a secondhand account of a man offering a thousand dollars for murder. Now I was being offered ten thousand, and I didn't have to kill anybody. I wanted to say no, but my vocal chords wouldn't function. It would have been easy to say yes, but for once in my life my big mouth didn't flap.

"And there might be a bonus for accepting our offer," Nimes added.

Every day I read in headlines about billions of dollars, but it's remarkable how large a measly ten grand can look from the ground floor, I gulped a couple of times and finally got my voice back. "It—it's impossible," I said.

"Anything is possible," said Nimes, "including shutting up the press. Do you know whom you're dealing with?" He paused, before I could answer he went on. "I, personally, could buy out Colonel Tanner, lock, stock and printing presses. I could do everything to you for printing the story that he could do to you for not printing it."

I had been a little afraid of him, let's be honest, up to this moment. But now I wasn't. He'd lost his pants, figuratively speaking.

"Mr. Nimes," I said. "I've been threatened before. So many people have told me that they were so close to Colonel Tanner they could get my job that I decided that he's a bosom pal of everybody. A lot of others have threatened to sue me and the paper all the way to the poor house and over the hill beyond. I've had a couple of tough characters threaten my life and about a score of people have told me they'd bust my jaw. A couple have tried it. But there's nothing a newspaper likes better than a fight. There's nothing that brings up circulation like a battle. If you're going to try something, you'll get ten times as much publicity as you'd get if you had put the whole story right in my hands."

I shut my mouth, realizing that I'd poured a ten thousand dollar job down the drain. I didn't think I'd like the job anyhow.

"That's pretty tough talk, Lanson. I'm a fighter too," said Nimes.

"Dad," said Junior quietly, "you're beating your head against a wall. You can't gain anything by threats, and he's told you he couldn't profit by a bribe. Why don't you tell him everything?"

"Everything?" croaked Calderson. "My God, Harry! Don't you realize this business involves a fel—"

The crash of H.C. Nimes' palm on the table top drowned out the word; but I was almost certain Calderson said *felony*. Now the general manager paused, sheepishly.

"I'll do the talking, Fen," said H.C. Nimes. He turned to me. "The only lawyer here is Charles Hayten. My friend Fenwick Calderson gets excited at times."

Hayten cleared his throat. "Anything you print about what is said here will be denied, Lanson," he said. "Besides it's hearsay."

There was nothing for me to say. I was a tourist and besides I was trying to figure out a few things. Hayten had mentioned a divorce. Calderson had talked about something hurting business and had almost said felony, which seemed to be some sort of a dirty word to Nimes. The only felony I knew of that had an immediate urgency about it was the murder of a shady private dick named George Edward Corrigan. At this point, my guessing branched out in so many directions that I decided it wasn't worthwhile to explore the possibilities.

Junior was talking. "It really wasn't a matter of turpitude, dad. It was a simple mistake. No one was hurt. No one will suffer. No right-minded judge—"

"You can't speak for any judge, Harry," said his father. "And this conversation has gone far enough. Remember there's a reporter present and he has shown no inclination to co-operate with us."

"If this business was so harmless," I said, "why all the fuss?"

You'd have thought I'd asked them if they'd been smuggling dope. Nimes, colored until I was afraid he'd have a stroke. "We've wasted the morning," he said. "We'll find a way to shut up your filthy, yellow newspaper."

"Dad!" said Junior.

"A fight is our pleasure, Mr. Nimes," I said rising. "There's nothing I enjoy more." I put on my hat, which I'd been holding in my lap, and went to the door.

"A moment, please, Lanson!" Junior followed me to the door.

I paused, ready to open the door. "Yes?"

"Don't punish Corrine for my father's temper," he said.

"Please mention no names, Harry!" said Hayten.

"I won't deliberately punish anyone," I said. I went out the door. Miss Harkiss was sitting down in her chair. It was on odds-on bet that she had had her ear to the door. The look she gave me showed that in her list, I was at the bottom.

THREE
MIDDAY WEDNESDAY

I left the fertilizer company's offices full of righteous anger. While I had no illusions about my ability to withstand temptation, I take a great deal of pride in my guts. I'm not afraid of people who think they can bully me.

Certain things, such as ten thousand dollars, are attractive to me and I hadn't refused the bribe for any high-sounding reason. In spite of what Guffy told Freddie the Grape, I'm not all visionary. Sometimes I get teed off about right and wrong, but usually there's some other reason than flag-waving when I go to war. The reason that I'd turned down Nime's offer was because I couldn't accomplish the impossible. And I felt wronged because Nimes tried to scare me into doing what I couldn't do for money.

But once on the street again, my anger vanished. My emotions run high, but they lack endurance. The day was sunny and pleasant and just too nice to stay mad at anybody.

Glancing at my wrist watch, I noted that it was 11:30 a.m. I'd been in conference with the fertilizer moguls longer than I'd thought. I ought to eat lunch in order to clear the decks for the deadline. But there was a much more important matter that needed immediate attention.

As I told H. C. Nimes, being threatened was old stuff to me. But I knew he wasn't bluffing altogether. He'd try to get my job and try to make things tough for me. Therefore, I had to start building my defenses. The first move in this land of war is to let your boss know what is going on.

I looked around for a taxi, but the neighborhood wasn't the type that draws cruising taxis. I'd have better luck if I walked west to Sixth Street, which is a more respectable neighborhood.

As I approached Seventh and Willis, a ragged character stepped out of a doorway and came toward me. I guessed he was a panhandler who would hit me for a piece of silver. I kept my eyes front and didn't give him a glance.

"Hah. Din't think I'd member you, huh, dude?"

The voice, a sort of a strained yodel, reminded me of the bleat of Freddie the Grape. I gave him an involuntary glance from the corners of my eyes and stopped dead in my tracks.

It *was* Freddie.

"Great moon in the morning, Freddie," I exclaimed. "What you doing here?"

Freddie now became astonished. He remembered me and expected me to remember him, but he didn't think I'd be thunderstruck because he wasn't in jail, and he couldn't understand. Nobody was ever thunderstruck at things Freddie did.

He stood there in his bewilderment looking at me from his dirty, unshaved face. Slowly he gathered himself together and squinted his eyes as he said, "Oh, I dunno. Just loafin' aroun', I guess."

"Aren't you supposed to be in the tank? You didn't break jail, did you?"

He blinked. "Din't break jail."

"How'd you get out?"

"Habbish cabbish."

"What?"

"Cops lemme go. Habbish cabbish."

"Oh. You mean habeas corpus." I saw the possibility of a story. "A lawyer served a writ on the cops and the judge let you go, huh?"

Freddie's head bobbed. "Didn't think I got no frien's, huh?"

"Freddie, a charming man like you must have a host of friends." I put my hand in my pocket, pulled out a quarter and gave it to him. "Who was the lawyer?"

"Addison Sharp." He took the quarter. "Mr. Sharp, he say, 'Freddie, you get the hell away from the cops. You fine the man what was talkin' to Corrigan in the park and call me. You probably fine him aroun' Eight and Willis. Just lemme know!' You got two dimes and a nickel stead of a quarter, hunh?"

I fished around in my pocket and found two dimes and a nickel. I handed them to Freddie who seemed to be reluctant to put the quarter back in my out-stretched hand, but finally he did so.

"Gotta make a phone call," he explained. "Like I said, Mr. Sharp say to let him know."

"You found the guy?"

Freddie's head bobbed, and he grinned. Then he turned and started up Seventh Street in the direction of Busch Avenue.

"Hey! Wait a minute!" I called.

Freddie broke into a run.

I started after him, but a fruit peddler and his push cart wheeled out of an alley to block my path. He yelled as I almost crashed into his cart, and I dodged this way and that. By the time I circled the cart, Freddie was almost to the next corner of the short block.

Freddie gave a dismayed glance back over his shoulder and darted into the street. He had the advantage of a "Walk" signal. Just before I reached the corner, it changed to "Don't Walk."

I stopped by pure reflex because the *Gazette* recently had inaugurated a campaign to enforce the pedestrian traffic laws. The police department traffic division was issuing tickets to pedestrians who violated these signals which were at all heavily traveled intersections.

Across the street from me was Patrolman Eilings, an eager-beaver cop who liked to issue tickets. I saw Freddie reach the far curb, but I knew Eilings had his eye on me.

As I stopped, he grinned and called, "Nice stop, Lanson!" Freddie dodged behind the cop, turned his head, placed his thumb to his nose and wiggled his fingers derisively. "Stop that guy, Eilings!" I yelled.

A truck rolled by, drowning out my shout.

The traffic cop looked blank. He cupped his hand to his ear and yelled, "Huh?"

"Stop him!" I pointed at Freddie, who was by this time making tracks through pedestrians on the far side of the street.

Eilings turned and grabbed the nearest man, who happened to be some shipping clerk on his way to lunch. I heard the guy protest, and I decided that nothing helpful would come from this situation. I turned and walked rapidly away, leaving Eilings to fight it out with his victim.

I went west to Sixth Street and picked up a cab. Ten minutes later I entered the front door of the *Gazette* building and rode the elevator up to the editorial rooms on the third floor.

Hank Newcomb, who is fat and slob-like, looked up as I came-into the room. "Where you been?" he asked. "I've been calling all the pool halls."

"Never mind where I've been," I said. "I've got troubles."

"I'll say you have," said Hank, "The business office has been raising hell."

"Tell them to go peddle their want ads," I said.

"Nimes Chemical has canceled its advertising contract on account of you," Hank went on. "What in the hell business have you got, going around insulting advertisers?"

Hank always assumes that the reporter is wrong. He never gives a man credit for being right once in a while. That's because his job is too big for him. He feels insecure and he thinks everybody else is in a job that's too big.

"I think you'd better listen to me, Hank," I said. And I laid it on the line, just the way it happened in the fertilizer company's office.

He wore the same kind of expression a schoolboy would wear if his teacher asked him to work a problem in differential calculus. "You shouldn't have been so rough with old man Nimes, Mike," he said. "You should have thanked him and left the place tactfully." Hank is also the best second-guesser on the *Gazette's* payroll. He's never able to handle a situation himself, but he's always there ready to tell somebody else how to do it.

"All right, already," I said, "I didn't do what I was supposed to do, but it's done and Nimes is starting his campaign. Are you going to believe him and fire me, or are you going to get your hackles up and fight back, even if it costs us a two-column ad every two weeks?"

"Now, Mike," he said, "this thing has to be given thought. I—"

He was interrupted by his telephone. He picked up the receiver and placed it to his ear. "Yes? Oh yes, Colonel . . . Yes, Dwight told me . . . He's right here. I'll send him up."

He replaced the phone and turned to me. "Colonel Tanner wants to see you in his office," he said, with a worried look on his face. "For heaven's sake Mike, be diplomatic."

"I'll give him warning if I slug him in the snoot," I said.

Hank gasped at the heresy, and I went over to the elevators to ride upstairs to Colonel Tanner's office.

The editor and publisher of the *Gazette,* Colonel Gordon C. Tanner, occupied a suite in the front end of the building on the top floor. There are three rooms in the suite, and all traffic enters through the center door, where his secretary screens out the cranks.

Ruth Carpenter, the Colonel's gorgeous secretary, was typing a letter as I entered. "Hello, rosebud," I said.

She looked up and smiled prettily, which is one of her assets. "Welcome to the execution chamber, Mike," she replied.

Ruth was a dish. Dark-haired, curvaceous, she was one hundred and eight-proof whistle bait. I didn't think she could type worth a damn and probably was a hell of a secretary, but she was a status symbol. Only a few men in town could afford beautiful, inefficient secretaries. Colonel Tanner was one of them.

"God wants to see me," I said, jerking my head toward the door to the left, which was the lion's den.

"I know," she said. "The business office has complained that you've knocked a few dollars off our gross."

"How about lunch together after I get fired?" I asked.

"You don't even act worried," she said. "You're in trouble, Mike. As a confidential secretary, I ought to know."

"You didn't answer my question," I said. "I asked you to lunch."

"I'd better ask you to lunch. You need to save your money."

"Okay. You take me to lunch."

"I won't. Go in? Colonel Tanner's waiting."

I pushed through the door. Colonel Tanner was reading the current issue of *Editor & Publisher*. He lowered the magazine to his desk, and raised his steely blue eyes in my direction. Like Nimes, he could look pretty rugged on occasions like this.

"Well? What's your side of the story, Mike?" he demanded.

I stood at attention, like a soldier facing court-martial. He was in his early fifties, but looked younger. He was stiff and straight as a poker and his service in the O.S.S. during the unpleasantness in Europe some years ago made him military in everything he did.

"Nimes offered me ten thousand dollars to quash a story, sir," I said. "And when I turned him down, he threatened to get my job and fix it so I'd never get another."

Colonel Tanners mouth drew itself into a thin straight line. His eyes looked like the muzzles of anti-aircraft guns. "He can't threaten me that way!" he said.

While the Colonel has his faults, like all newspaper editors. I've never known him to let a reporter down. An insult to a reporter is an insult to him personally.

"What did he want to kill?"

"Didn't find out," I said. "I said he'd better not tell me anything he didn't want me to print."

Colonel Tanner nodded approvingly. "That's right. Never promise what you can't deliver, and asking a newspaper to keep silent is like telling the tide not to come in. If a reporter of mine ever promises anything and doesn't keep it, he's through working for me."

"Yessir."

"But," he went on, "you might have squeezed a little. Or am I wrong in thinking you sometimes might tell a little lie, or let somebody think just the opposite of what you intend to do?"

"I lie like hell, sir, but I don't make promises."

Colonel Tanner laughed. "Good. How much *did* you find out?"

"Well, this story involves somebody named Corrine. I learned from Junior—Nimes' son—that he thinks his father made some kind of a mistake. And there's a divorce in it somewhere."

Again the Colonel nodded. "Corrine would be Harry's—Junior's—wife. They were married a couple of months ago. It was an elopement, which is why our society columns didn't make a big fuss over it. She was married once before to one of the local playboys named Omar Leroy Swigert. That was an elopement too. She seems to prefer ladders to bridesmaids. They were married five days—she and Swigert, that is. That was longer than I would have stood him if I'd been the girl."

"Not so hot, huh?"

"Nice looking, but that's all you can say of him. He had squandered all the money he'd inherited. Most of it anyhow. Two previous wives walked off with big slices." Colonel Tanner had had three wives in his past, too, but I never mentioned it to him. "Swigert was an alcoholic, then an A.A., then an alcoholic, then a teetotaler. He fell off the wagon the last time on the day he married Corrine."

"Hayten," I mused. "That would make her Charles Hayten's daughter?"

"Correct," said the Colonel.

"Why would Hayten want any of these facts hushed if they're already known?" I asked. "Would there be something about her previous divorce that's jaded?"

"In every divorce case there's a little darkness," said the Colonel, who should know. "She got her divorce in Reno, alleging alcoholism."

"Beats me," I said slowly. Something in the back of my mind was nudging me, but I couldn't bring it out. There had been a similar case once, if I could only remember it. "Looks like they want to quash a story that everybody knows. You don't suppose it's tied in with the Corrigan case?"

The Colonel looked at me inquiringly. "You must have a reason to ask that?"

"Well, I met Hayten at Corrigan's office. He didn't want the cops to go through Corrigan's records. He said he was working for some unnamed clients, but maybe Corrigan knew where the body was buried in Hayten's daughter's divorce."

Colonel Tanner shook his head. "I think she was justified in everything she did. Her mistake was marrying Swigert on such short acquaintance. But there may be an angle there. Why don't you put a little work on it?"

"I will," I said, since it was the kind of suggestion that you don't ignore.

The boss reached for the *Editor & Publisher* as a signal that he was finished with me. I said good bye and left.

Ruthie was still typing inefficiently. "How about that lunch?" I asked her. "I've a job still."

She stopped typing and looked up at me in all her breathtaking beauty. "If you've got a job, you can feed yourself," she said.

"Okay, I'd rather make it a dinner date anyhow."

I could hear her typing raggedly while I waited for the elevator.

When I entered the city room, I found Hank Newcomb chewing his nails. "Wha-what happened?" he asked in a hoarse whisper which could have been heard at Police Headquarters four blocks down the street.

"The Colonel says that if the business office jerks stick their noses into the editorial room again, throw them out on their ears."

"Hu-huh?"

"He says he's sick of running manure ads in a family newspaper anyhow," I said, pouring it on. I went over to a phone desk leaving Hank to figure it out. I found Addison Sharp's number in the directory and dialed it. His secretary said he wasn't in, so I tried Corrigan's office. Sharp answered the phone.

"Oh, yes, Lanson," he said when I told him my name. "What can I do for you?" There are a lot of guys like Sharp who act like they'll do anything for a reporter, but when you sift it down, you find out that all they do is act friendly.

"I understand you sprung Freddie the Grape from jail," I said.

"You must mean Fred Gandy," said Sharp. "Yes. I got him out on a writ."

"How'd you do that?"

"He was being held without charge. He wasn't even booked," said Sharp.

Guffy had forgotten it, I supposed. Gandy was a key witness in a murder investigation and Guffy was going to look pretty bad when this got out.

"It's another example of the high handedness of our police," Sharp went on. "Fred Gandy is continually persecuted by them. Every time they find him on the street they take him to jail. The poor man can't even get a job, he's been so harassed. I'll probably file charges against the city over this. I'll let you know beforehand so you can give it a good play."

"He's quite a solid character, huh? I mean Freddie."

"He never hurt anyone in his life. Perhaps he does drink a little."

"I thought he broke into a store."

"There was no charge," said Sharp. "Gandy is just being persecuted."

"Okay, okay. You've made your point. He wasn't booked and you sprung him on a writ of habeas corpus. I suppose the guys who threw the Magna Charta into King John's lap knew what they were doing, but sometimes habeas corpus has turned loose a lot of bad guys."

I now remembered that Guffy had told the officer who took Freddie to jail to hold up the booking of Freddie until later.

"No one has been released by writs when proper legal steps were taken to hold them for trial," said Sharp.

"Not being a lawyer, I can't answer that one," I said. "But who asked you to spring Freddie?" I didn't think he'd go to bat alone for Freddie, who didn't have a quarter to his name.

"None of your business," said Sharp. "Is that all you want to know?"

"It's probably all I'll squeeze out of you," I said. "But you could save me a little work if you'd drop a hint as to what the cops found in Corrigan's files."

"Why don't you ask them? I'm not acquainted with the contents myself. That's why I'm here now. I'm looking over the estate."

"Hmm. Very funny," I said. "Well, thanks for nothing, Mr. Sharp."

"You're entirely welcome."

After I hung up the phone I stood by the desk thinking for a moment. Then the phone rang. I picked it up absently.

"Yes?"

"Is that you, Mike?" It was the switchboard operator.

"Yes, love girl, it's me."

"A man has been calling you. But he wouldn't wait or leave a number. He had a sort of funny voice and sounded drunk."

Instantly I thought of Freddie the Grape. "Why tell me now?"

"I thought you might know who it was and call him back."

"I don't," I said, "but if it's who I think it is, he won't have much to tell me and he'll want me to give him something. Forget it."

Hank yelled at me from across the room. "Are you going to stay here all day, Mike? We could have a bank robbery and a couple of murders and there's nobody at headquarters to tell us about it."

"Do you want a new lead on the Corrigan case?"

"Of course! I told you we'd need something new. You got anything?"

"Freddie the Grape has been sprung on a writ of habeas corpus," I said.

"Good Lord! And you just stand there drooping. Rewrite!" He bellowed the last word and a rewrite man jumped to attention. "Mike's got a story. Get it out of him."

I gave him the story of Freddie's release with a couple of paragraphs of quote from Sharp about the cops persecuting Freddie. I figured that would get under Guffy's hide enough so he'd cut loose with something I could use for a later new lead.

When I finished I saw Hank giving me the eye again. "Now are you going back to work?" he asked.

"Hank, what in the hell do you think I've been doing? Just because I'm not wearing overalls and haven't got a shovel in my hand, it's no sign I'm not working like a damned galley slave."

"But you're not at Headquarters," said Hank.

That was the way with Hank Newcomb. Nothing counted unless you were where you were supposed to work. If by some potluck I happened to win a Pulitzer Prize through a story I'd picked up in a pool hall or saloon, Hank would have said the prize committee was rigged.

"It just happens that I've got to go on a field trip to get some facts on a murder story, Hank. You've got four or five general assignment reporters here sitting on their thumbs—which you call working because they're in range of your eyes. Why don't you send one of them to the press room at Headquarters to pick up the routine stuff while I work a real yarn. Don's off today you know."

"Since when have you been telling me what to do?" Hank thundered.

"Since Colonel Tanner asked me to get to the bottom of something," I said.

Hank didn't reply to that. I saw him signaling for a general assignment man.

I walked out of the city room and went back to the morgue. A couple of librarians were elbow-deep in clippings and they looked as if they weren't pleased because I interrupted them.

"I want the files on a man named Swigert," I said to the nearest one, a woman.

"First name, or initials?" she asked.

"All the Swigerts, if you've got files on more than one of them. The one I want is supposed to be a playboy."

She got up slowly and went to a card index. She looked up the name, then walked along a corridor of filing cabinets until she found the one she wanted. She opened it, thumbed through some folders and pulled one out. She brought the contents to me in a large envelope.

The clippings were on Omar Leroy Swigert, son of a machine tool manufacturer, who had inherited a couple of million dollars on his twenty-first birthday. Swigert's age was given as thirty-eight in a clipping dated three years ago, when he was involved in a motor car accident and arrested for drunken driving. Other clippings were of other arrests for driving while intoxicated, and there were two from the society pages regarding weddings. He had been married first in 1943, and divorced in 1945 from his war bride. He was married again in 1951 and divorced a year later. Neither of the brides was named Hayten. If Swigert had been married to Corrine Hayten, she was his third wife.

I handed the file back to the librarian and left the office, wondering how Charles Hayten's daughter got mixed up with a man like Swigert. There's no accounting for taste sometimes. Colonel Tanner had said she was a nice young woman. Colonel Tanner sometimes was erratic in his judgements.

Again I searched the phone book. There was no number listed for H. C. Nimes, Jr. I called information and there was no listing with the telephone company. I went down the hall to the society editor's office. Flossie, the editor, a big, buxom woman with a voice which could have won a hog-calling contest, greeted me with, "What in the hell do you want?"

"Information," I told her, perching on top of the table she used for a desk.

"Have some of my little pets got themselves involved with the police?" she demanded.

"Not that I know of," I said. "Colonel Tanner told me that Junior Nimes married Charley Hayten's daughter recently."

"Yes. It was a quiet wedding though. She was a divorcee, you know."

"So I've heard. Do you happen to know where they're living?"

"Funny you should ask that. I just heard about it myself."

"Well, tell me and we'll both laugh."

"They've separated," said Flossie.

"You mean they're going to get a divorce?" I asked, remembering that Corrine Hayten left her first husband on their honeymoon.

"Honey, my sources can't read minds. Nobody but Junior and his bride knows what's going to happen. All I know is that Corrine went home to papa about a month after they were married. They'd been living in a little apartment on the East Side before then, but they gave up their lease and broke up house keeping."

"I'll be damned," I said.

"Why? Is it your fault?"

"No," I said, then asked suspiciously: "Is it somebody's fault? Like another man, maybe? Or another woman?"

"The grapevine didn't say," said Flossie.

"Thanks."

"Any time, sweetie."

I went back to the news room, stopping at the phone desk. The Greater Creston directory, which lay alongside the telephone directories, listed Charles Hayten's address as the Old South Road. This was outside the city limits, but not a great distance from the through highway running south of town. I could drive out there in half an hour, or make it by bus in an hour. I glanced at my watch. It was almost one o'clock. Thirty minutes out, thirty minutes back, and a half hour for the interview. That would make two-thirty, and the deadline for the home edition was three-thirty. I'd even have time for lunch.

"I'm going to be gone for a couple of hours," I told Hank.

"Where can we reach you?"

"You can't. There's no phone."

He gave a slow burn. "I hope, Mike, that putting out a newspaper isn't interfering with your activities?"

"It's one of the disadvantages of my career," I said. "But if you have any complaints take 'em to Colonel Tanner. Tell him that I've gone to check on the angle we discussed privately."

"Oh!" said Hank. Any time you mentioned the Colonel's name, Hank got on your side. "You'll have a new lead for the home edition?"

"I hope so."

I went out the door and could hear him yelling when I reached the elevators. Whenever he was mad he took it out on one of the younger reporters.

I got my red Ford convertible out of the office parking lot, and about twenty-five minutes later I turned off the main highway onto Old South Road. At one time this had been an important thoroughfare, but that was before the motor car. Now it was too full of sharp turns and loo narrow to be a lure for traffic. And for this reason a number of people had built nice homes along its wooded route.

Charles Hayten's place was easy to find. His name was on the mailbox and a blacktop drive led back through the trees toward the house, which was barely visible through the foliage from the road.

I went up the drive and parked my car outside the picket fence separating the driveway from the lawn. The place was one of those ranch-type dwellings which couldn't have been built for less than forty thousand. It was on top of a little hill, which sloped down toward the creek to the south. A dam had been thrown across the creek behind the house, forming an artificial pond, part of which I could see as I walked toward the front door.

The birds were chirping in the trees and there were flies buzzing around, and the whole place looked as peaceful as a painting. Somewhere I heard a door slam. I was quite certain it was not a door of the Hayten house, so I figured it must be a nearby house. I couldn't see very far through the trees, but I knew there were other houses nearby.

Faint chimes sounded when I pressed the doorbell button. No sound of movement came from within the house. The place was too quiet, it seemed. I had a presentiment that something was wrong, but I quickly told myself that the idea was crazy. I rang the bell again, but there was the same sort of stillness. I tried the door. It was locked.

I stepped back, undecided whether to go around the house or not, when I thought I saw movement through the trees off to my right. I walked over and saw a figure moving stealthily down a gravel walk leading to the pond.

It was a ragged figure which walked with an awkward gait. It was a moment or two before I recognized him: Freddie the Grape.

FOUR
WEDNESDAY AFTERNOON

A cannibal chief working in the kitchen of the Hotel Creston wouldn't have surprised me more. Not that the Hayten place was inaccessible, because it was less than a mile from the highway and a suburban bus line. But people like Freddie the Grape don't forsake their natural environment, which is skid row.

He walked down the path to within ten or fifteen paces of the pond, then halted and stood motionless. From where I stood, I could see that the pond had been fixed up for swimming purposes. A sort of pier had been built at the end of the gravel walk. A wooden building at the near end was the bath house, and there was a diving board at the other end.

Freddie was watching the pier, with his back toward me. He was unaware of my presence, but even if I had been standing directly in front of him, I doubt if he would have seen me. His eyes were concentrated on something else.

And now my eyes took in the sight and if I'd seen it first, I'd have been totally unaware of Freddie the Grape.

Climbing up the short ladder to the diving platform was a girl, her blonde hair glistening in the sunlight. She reached the top and stood there, fitting a rubber bathing cap over her head. The cap was the only item of clothing she had on.

Like Freddie the Grape, I was hypnotized.

She didn't know she had an audience and she took her time adjusting the cap. Then she stretched out her arms, turned her face up toward the clouds, drinking in the refreshing breeze, the quiet of the woods around her and the scent of flowers in the air. Then she half turned, exposing a profile that was perfect from top to bottom.

"Ung-ung-ung," said Freddie.

The girl turned and I caught the look of horror in her eyes as she saw the wino derelict advancing toward her.

"Go away!" she screamed. "Get out of here!"

Making strange sounds in the back of his throat, Freddie the Grape ran out on the pier toward the little platform where she stood. It was hardly large enough to be called a platform, since it only formed the base for the diving board. The little ladder from the pier to the end of the board was only about three feet high.

By this time, I had managed to rouse myself from the state of hypnotic immobility which had seized me when I first caught a glimpse of the unclothed beauty. I started down the gravel path toward the pier. As I did so, the girl, who undoubtedly was Corrine Nimes although I'd never seen her before, caught a glimpse of me and called out: "Harry! Help!"

At the same time, Freddie the Grape reached the diving board. He reached out his hands toward her legs, apparently in an attempt to grab her. She danced out of the way, ran to the end of the diving board and plunged gracefully into the pond.

A cry of distress came from Freddie's throat and he ran to the edge of the pier, looking out as she broke the surface, half tempted to jump into the water with all of his dirty ragged clothes on.

Corrine seemed to expect him to, and she swam out toward the center of the pond, with long easy strokes.

By this time I'd reached the pier. "All right, Freddie!" I called to the wino. "The party's over! You heard the lady. Beat it!"

Freddie turned quickly at the sound of my voice. He saw me approaching toward him and an expression of surprised panic crossed his face. He looked around, desperately seeking an avenue of escape. But I was at the end of the pier. The only place to go was into the water. Apparently Freddie the Grape would face anything in preference to the cleansing action of water. He turned and faced me. Or, it's barely possible, that I'm not as formidable as others Freddie had faced.

Formidable or not, I charged toward him like a herd of buffalo.

His hand went into his pocket and emerged with a gleaming something. I didn't need a second look. It was a switch blade, without which no tramp is complete.

"Yah," he gurgled pointing the knife at me. "Ngn! Ung!"

Strangely, I understood him. He intended to put a groove in my guts. I wasn't quite as eager to rescue the naked lady in distress, but my momentum made it impossible to stop.

The blade was pointed at me and Freddie braced himself for the moment when I'd be skewered.

I tried to dodge, but I lost my balance like an awkward oaf, tripped and did an outside loop over the edge of the pier, right into the water.

When I came spluttering to the surface, Freddie was running for the shore. Whatever he had in his mind before, now didn't seem to him to be worth fighting over and he was anxious to get out of this place.

"My hero!" said Corrine. She was swimming up behind me, where I was treading water in my soggy clothes. The water covered her, almost, but not too much to make me feel that my plunge into the pond had been without reward.

"Uh, Miss—er—Mrs. Nimes, I presume?" I said like Stanley.

"I don't know who you are, but you're welcome to swim here all you want," she said. "And I'll be glad to do anything else that's in your line. Do you sell magazines? Or vacuum sweepers? Or maybe you're working for the Gallup Poll?"

"I'm Mike Lanson of the *Gazette,*" I said.

"We take the paper, but I know a family in Canada that I send it to. Meanwhile, crawl out of this pond and go to the house to dry, while I put on some clothes. Dad has a bathrobe in his bedroom and there's a drier in the basement. There's also some bourbon, if you're so inclined. Even gin and Scotch. I'll join you in a few moments."

"Of course," I said. I kicked the water and grasped the ladder that ran up to the pier.

On the pier I looked around to see where Freddie had gone. But by this time he had disappeared into the woods that surrounded the house. Gone for good, maybe, and I wondered idly why he'd been here. Certainly he hadn't expected to find Corrine Nimes swimming in the raw.

My shoes squished and my clothes dripped as I walked the graveled path to the back door of the house. It was unlocked and inside was a very modern, all-steel kitchen. There was vinyl tile on the floor, and I reckoned a little water wouldn't hurt it. I stripped to the skin, depositing my clothes in a soggy pile. Then I found a towel in the bathroom and dried myself. Afterwards I located Charles Hayten's bedroom and put on a light-weight dressing gown.

As Corrine had said, there was a drier in the basement. Living in a hotel, I didn't know how to work the monster, but it wasn't hard to figure out. I wrung out my clothes before I put them in the machine, hoping that they would dry faster. I dropped my necktie into a wastebasket; feeling sad because it was almost new and I'd not eaten soup since I'd bought it. I didn't know how the drier would work on shoes, and I decided I couldn't have everything, so I put them on damp after shaking as much water from them as I could. Shoes are costly, but the suit was cheap, being one of those summer jobs that aren't supposed to need pressing. I hoped it wouldn't because I had to wear it back to town.

Then I went upstairs in search of the bourbon. I found it, fixed myself a shot and water and then found a mop. I was just sopping up the puddle left by my clothes on the kitchen floor when Corrine Nimes came in.

I've read a great deal of pro and con argument, and taken part in a little on the subject of women and clothes and whether the female figure looks more seductive in draping and other rigamarole or just as it came from the factory. I suppose it all boils down to personal taste. But when I saw Corrine Nimes fully dressed, the comparison wasn't valid because she wore slacks. She looked much better as I'd seen her first, although even in slacks she had breathtaking qualities.

And, for the record, while men without pants lose dignity, women are a different breed. Corrine had had dignity on that diving board.

"Did you find everything?" she asked cheerily as she came in.

I nodded toward the bourbon. "Everything," I told her.

"You needn't mop the floor," she said. "Don't do anything. Just sit and be a hero." She pointed to a stool in front of the breakfast bar.

"I wouldn't think of not cleaning up my mess, Mrs. Nimes," I said.

She was reaching for the bourbon, but stopped. "How did you know my name? The name on the mail box is Hayten."

"I told you, I'm from the *Gazette.*"

"Oh yes, that subscription. How much is it per year in advance?"

"I don't give a damn—oops, pardon me. I don't give a hoot about a subscription. I'm a reporter."

"Oh." There was a cold sound to her voice. She poured some bourbon in a glass and filled it with water from the kitchen tap. "Oh."

"I'm not that bad," I said.

"You don't know how bad it is," she said. "I suppose you want to ask me why I'm not living with my husband? Why I've separated so soon after my marriage?"

"Well, I had something like that in mind."

"Daddy said he was going to fix things with the newspapers."

"It wasn't because he didn't try."

"Oh. You're incorruptible?" She took a step toward me. She stood very close with half-closed eyes. This was going to be harder to refuse than a ten thousand dollar a year job.

"Not at the moment," I said. "Why did you leave your husband?"

"I haven't left him," she said. "We're living apart because . . . well, because there's something to be settled."

"Secrets are perishable materials," I said quietly.

She came very close and started fingering the lapels of the bathrobe I wore. "Try not to find out," she whispered.

Her face turned up toward mine. The next instant she was in my arms, her warm body pressed close to mine, her lips against mine, her fingers digging into my shoulders.

Things started to move and I didn't try to stop them. She was the one who stopped them.

Suddenly she stepped back, away from me. "A car!" she said. "Someone's driving in!"

I hadn't been listening, but now I heard the sound of a door slam.

She thrust the glass of bourbon and water into my hand and pushed me down on a stool as the back door opened.

Junior Nimes stood there looking at his wife who was entertaining a man dressed in a bathrobe.

For a moment he didn't speak. His face flushed and he ran his tongue over his lips. "I suppose there's a reasonable explanation," he said. "But I'm a poor guesser."

"Mr. Lanson fell in the pond," said Corrine. "He saved me from—"

"Drowning? He fell in and saved you?"

"No. It was worse than drowning, it was—"

"Worse than death? My God, am I supposed to believe everything?"

"Well, damn it. You don't have to be so smug. Mr. Lanson and I are having an affair. It's been going on for three minutes. Now are you satisfied?"

His eyes glittered with anger, and I carefully put the drink aside because in circumstances like this, one never knows what to expect. "Let me tell you what happened, Junior."

"That would be real peachy," said Junior. "But my name is Harry. Not Junior."

I was beginning to feel righteous indignation. After all, I hadn't hurt his wife. She'd given me a motherly kiss as a reward for saving her from a fate worse than whatever other fate was near at hand. I told him what happened and Junior listened, growing calmer by the moment.

"I guess you couldn't have made that up in the time you had," he said. "Where are your clothes?"

"In the drier downstairs," I said. "You want to see?"

For the first time he laughed. "I apologize for my attitude. But, well, I'm a bridegroom of two months and naturally—well, you can understand how I feel."

"I'll fix you a drink, Harry," said Corrine.

She got another glass and mixed a highball for Junior.

"Why aren't you and your bride living together?" I asked. I could see it wasn't because he didn't have affection for her. As for her affection for him—I wondered. That kiss wasn't a sure sign. It might have been bribery of sorts, or gratitude. Come to think of it, Ruthie's smooches, the few that I'd had, were of a much different variety. Corrine Nimes hadn't really run up the flag of surrender.

"You're a louse," said Junior bluntly.

"It can be argued either way," I said. "Did you ever wonder how much a louse might object if somebody, a cockroach maybe, called him a man?"

"You came here to get information out of my wife," said Junior.

Corrine shoved the drink in his hand. "Drink this and shut up. I didn't tell Mr. Lanson anything. And I'm the person who's in trouble."

Somebody had mentioned a felony today. I wondered what kind of felony. Murder maybe?

Junior said, "Thanks anyhow for coming to Corrine's aid. I'm sorry I called you a louse."

"I'm a louse and proud of it," I said. "It's my business to be lousy. But your business has me curious. Somebody's in trouble and the trouble is going to grow if you keep the lid on it. Give it air and it'll die. Everybody and everything isn't as bad as it seems. Good points can be found, maybe, if you look for them."

"Copybook stuff," said Junior. "We're wrong and nothing can change the facts. I'd like to tell you our troubles, Lanson, but I've given my word to dad—and to Corrine. Even though I agree that things are better if brought out in the open and settled, I can't do it."

"I don't think that at all," said Corrine. "I'm the one who would suffer the most."

"Are you two having marital difficulties?" I asked bluntly.

"Of course not," said Corrine.

"You're not living together," I persisted.

"It's not convenient right now," said Junior.

"Because it has something to do with the trouble you're in," I said. I waited for a denial, but none came. "It could be that you're not legally married."

Corrine got up from the stool she had perched herself on. "I think your clothes should be dry by now, Mr. Lanson." She went to the basement door and disappeared down the stairs.

Junior toyed with his drink while I finished mine.

"Things got a little out of hand at the meeting today, Lanson," he said, finally. "Dad was furious and canceled his advertising contract with your paper. But his furies die quickly. After this thing blows over—well, he may change his mind about you."

"Is it something that can blow over?"

"I think so."

"It isn't Corrigan's murder then?"

"Good heavens no! That hasn't anything to do with it."

"You object too much," I said. "I met Mr. Hayten at Corrigan's office. He was worried about something. Could it be that Corrigan was blackmailing you or your wife? That he had something incriminating in his files?"

"The papers?" Junior scoffed. "Don't be melodramatic."

"Somebody offered Corrigan money to kill somebody," I said. "I'd give a lot to know who had to be removed."

"If you're insinuating that I had anything to do with it—"

"I'm not. And a thousand dollars for murder sounds cheap for your dad, although I've heard that people who are rich don't spend their money lavishly. But what about the others? Calderson and the rest?"

"There are only two others, Lanson," said Junior. "And the whole idea is not only ridiculous but it's insulting."

"Harry!" Corrine's voice came from the doorway. Junior shook his head and resumed drinking as she entered with the clothes. She gave them to me. "They're not quite dry," she said. "But before you two get at each other's throats, I'd suggest that you wear them a little damp. You can use the bathroom to change."

I thanked her and left the kitchen.

FIVE
WEDNESDAY, 3:00 P.M.

As Corrine said, my clothes were almost dry. They looked as if I'd used them all year as pajamas, but they were all I had to wear until I got to town. After I'd dressed, I turned down another drink, offered by Junior, and started back to the city. I wondered if I'd really learned much. But I usually learn something every time I get mixed up with people.

Corrine Nimes was in difficulties because of a mistake. The mistake had something to do with her marriage to Junior, I could guess. Whether it had something to do with not living with him, I could not deduce. Something had been mentioned about a felony and a judge; legal complications, undoubtedly resulting from her first marriage. Once again I thought I almost knew something, but I wasn't sure.

A murder had been committed and somehow this had a bearing on the situation. Corrigan had been murdered. Someone had asked Corrigan to commit another murder. It followed that another murder was more than likely unless the man who plotted with Corrigan was caught.

Omar Leroy Swigert, Corrine's first husband, might talk. I'd have to see him, but first I had to change my clothing.

It was almost three o'clock. Hank Newcomb would be tearing his hair out in handfuls and he'd eat my shirttail out when I phoned him because I didn't have much in the way of a new lead for the home edition. Someday I was going to buy a dog and call it Hank because he'd be a genuine son of a bitch. Hank was only an imitation. He couldn't even be a good son of a bitch.

I detoured to the Waltham Hotel, where I made my home in Room 615. The Waltham is a residential establishment, housing only a few transients. Sometimes the management regarded me as something less than an asset, but since I paid my bills regularly and mentioned the hotel in the news occasionally, I was tolerated.

Edgar, the desk clerk, looked askance at my disreputable appearance when I asked for my key. "You seem to have had a misfortune," he said consolingly.

"Had a little accident," I told him.

"Too bad," he said. He looked relieved because I think he was wondering if I had decided to dress this way every day. He is not very inquisitive, a trait becoming to hotel clerks, and he asked no more questions. He handed me my key. "A man asked about you," he said.

"That's nice. Did you tell him I could be found at the *Gazette?*"

"Yes. He'd called the paper a couple of times. The last time they said you'd left for the afternoon."

I remembered that a call had come for me just before one o'clock. "Was he drunk?" I asked.

Edgar nodded. "Very. And obnoxious. I had to tell him he couldn't wait for you in the lobby."

"You sent him away?" If it was Freddie the Grape, he certainly would have. But it couldn't have been Freddie. I'd seen Freddie this afternoon. To reach the Hayten place he would have had to catch a bus before one o'clock.

"Oh no. He wanted to wait, and I suggested a room. He took a room on your floor. Number 602. He's probably there now."

"He must have wanted to see me pretty bad. What's his name?"

Edgar consulted the guest cards. "Omar Leroy Swigert," he announced.

"I guess I must live right," I said. I'd been wanting to see this guy, and now he'd come to see me, which would save a lot of time. I might even get a new angle on the Nimes case and find out if it was connected with the Corrigan murder. "I'll call on him after I get in some decent clothes."

I went up in the elevator. In my room on the sixth floor, I changed from the skin out. After which I called Hank Newcomb, who asked sarcastically if I'd been improving my pool game this afternoon. I told him that I had, which would make him wonder if I had or if I was being as sarcastic as he usually is. "Are there any new developments in the Corrigan case?" I asked.

"I've seen some dumb reporters in my day, but you've got 'em all beat," he said. "That's the story you're supposed to be working on."

"I am working on it," I said. "However, some breaks might come from the police. Their business is to investigate crimes. I've been away from the station and I wondered how things stood downtown."

"They're not even standing," Hank said. "They're lying down. Get on the ball."

Hank Newcomb believed that any reporter could jerk a new angle on an old story out of thin air. I never disillusioned him and if I didn't get a new angle, I always had a good excuse for not getting one. And when I did get one, Hank seemed to think that any idiot could have done it. Whatever he thought about my talents, he always made it uncomplimentary.

I checked my pockets and found I had money and the tools of ignorance—a pencil, press card and copy paper. Then I went to Room 602. It was around the L in the corridor, beyond the elevators. I knocked on the door, but there was no answer. Swigert had been drunk two hours ago, and was probably out by now. I didn't know if it was worthwhile to try to rouse him if he was blotto, but Hank wanted a new lead of some kind and for Hank's sake, I thought I'd try.

"Mr. Swigert?" I called, rapping again.

Still no answer. I tried the door. It was unlocked and I opened it a crack and peeked in. I saw Swigert lying on the bed, and I'd been right. He'd continued his drinking; there was a pint bottle on the night table beside the bed. Also a glass. Apparently

Swigert was a gentleman drunk who always used a glass unless one was not available.

I pushed the door open and stepped inside. The room reeked with whiskey fumes. I went over toward the bed. There didn't seem to be much point in trying to awaken him, because I doubted if I could get anything coherent out of him. But it was a challenge to try and I had a half hour before press time. Anything might happen.

Then, looking down at the face, I suddenly realized that I'd met the man before. Omar Leroy Swigert was the red-faced drunk who had staggered into the press room at Police Headquarters this morning and had mistaken me for a cop. His face wasn't so red now. It was sort of pale, which is a strange color for a drunk's face to be. I'd seen them all shades, from purple to green, but I'd never seen a white-faced drunk before.

His arm dangled off the bed and he wore no coat. I took hold of his arm and shook him gently. The body didn't seem to be limp, like drunks usually are. I'd heard the expression "stiff" used for being drunk and although I'd never encountered it, I supposed I hadn't seen quite all the different types of drunks. They're almost uncountable.

I shook him again. There was no response. But this wasn't the only strange thing I noticed now. For Swigert wasn't snoring; he wasn't even breathing. I reached down and took his wrist. I noted that his left shirt sleeve was open. The cuff link had come unfastened. I felt the wrist. It was cool. And there wasn't any pulse.

The guy was dead.

I stood up, went over to the phone and raised Edgar on the switchboard downstairs.

"What time did Swigert check in?" I asked.

Edgar took a second or two to look at the card. "It says here that he checked in at 12:30," he replied. "Is he there now?"

"He's here," I said. "He's dead."

"Dead?"

"Stone."

"He can't die here!"

"He was too drunk to know the rules," I said. "Call the cops."

SIX
WEDNESDAY, 4:00 P.M.

After I talked to Edgar, I hung up the phone and looked around the room. Another glass was on the dresser. The Waltham leaves two glasses wrapped in wax paper in each room every morning. The wax covering assures the guest that the glasses are free from germs, untouched by human hands or something.

Both the glasses in the room had been unwrapped and that meant both had probably been used since Swigert took the room at 12:30 p.m. I saw one paper wrapping on the floor, near where Swigert lay on the bed. The other was in the wastebasket near the dresser. I didn't touch them because the crime lab men might want to examine them for prints. They investigated everything, even swept the room with a vacuum cleaner in a case where there might be suspicion of murder.

Murder? I wondered what brought that to mind. There was no indication that Swigert had met a violent end. But two glasses usually meant two people and two people smelled of murder, now that one of them was dead.

Once more I looked at the dead man. He was a little stiff. Not in the sense that he was drunk, but stiff like *rigor mortis*. That meant he'd been dead about two hours. It was three now. If he'd been dead that long, then he died within thirty minutes after he checked in at 12:30. While I was traveling to the Hayten place.

Two glasses? Yet a natural death? Could be and also couldn't.

Maybe Swigert was the victim that Corrigan refused to kill in such a way that he wouldn't be caught. This didn't look like murder. Maybe that's why I thought it was. But how? Poison? Two glasses. I smelled without touching the glass on the night stand. Whiskey was all I smelled. The glass on the dresser had no odor. Maybe it had been washed. It looked like it, but I couldn't tell. The crime lab men would find the answers if I didn't monkey with things.

Why two glasses? Still the question throbbed in my mind.

Swigert could have used them both, of course; but it wasn't normal, even for a drunk, to dirty a second glass.

I looked around for signs of a visitor. There were none, save that extra glass on the dresser, and it wasn't proof.

The cops would be here soon so I decided there was nothing more I could do that they couldn't do better. I closed the door behind me. No use trying to preserve fingerprints on the knob. I'd already put my hand on it when I'd entered.

I called the *Gazette* from my room.

"Hank," I said, when he got on the line, "this is Mike."

"Ah!" he said. "I knew you'd do it, Mike."

"I've just turned up another dead man," I said.

"Does it have anything to do with the Corrigan case?" he asked. Hank has a one-track mind.

"Nothing direct," I told him.

"Then give me the indirect connection."

"There's nothing we can print without asking for trouble."

"What are we going to do for a new lead?"

"I've got a whole new story, Hank. New news is good news. Now listen. The stiff is Omar Leroy Swigert. Ever heard of him?"

"Swigert. Mm. The playboy, so-called, although he's not playing so hard any more. Wait a minute, wasn't he supposed to have married this Hayten babe, the one who is the daughter of the lawyer you had a meeting with today?"

"That's the one—and this broad is now married to Junior Nimes."

"There *is* a connection, Mike."

"Yes, but it's one we can't print without dangerous speculation, I've got to find a link, Hank. This Swigert may be it, but it'll take time to dig it up. He was a chronic alcoholic. Probably the reason Corrine Hayten left him on their honeymoon. But all that has to wait—"

"Deadlines can't wait," said Hank. "Hold it, while I give you a rewrite."

He switched me over to a rewrite and I told of finding the body, and how Swigert apparently had made a couple of calls to me at the *Gazette* but had failed to locate me because I was working on a murder case. "You might get that in the story," I told the rewrite. "There may be some connection later on. But don't dwell on it."

When I finished, Hank, who had been listening broke in. "It's only ten after three, Mike. Try to give us another call before three-thirty. I'll have somebody work it from the police end. You stay where you are."

"Okay," I said. I hung up.

I went down to the lobby in the elevator and got there just as the cops arrived.

Two of them came into the lobby and Edgar looked embarrassed. Sylvester Hammond, the house dick, greeted them and talked to them, having already been briefed on the case by Edgar. I could see that Sylvester was tossing my name around from the shifty glances he put in my direction. I think Sylvester suspected that I'd murdered Swigert, but when one of the cops waved at me and said, "Howdy, Mike," Sylvester sighed over his failure to pin it onto me real quick.

The cops went upstairs to make sure I hadn't been dreaming when I said I found a body, and pretty soon more cops came. The crime lab men and the deputy coroner and Doc Browne the medical examiner came in. Most of them knew me and said hello, but they were on a case and didn't linger to hear any new stories I might have been able tell them.

Finally Lieutenant Clyde Guffy came in with Sergeant Russell at his heels like a faithful, flea-bitten hound.

Guffy spotted me and his little round face grew solemn because he didn't like newspaper boys at the scene of a crime, when he was busy. He was afraid I'd louse things up, which I had on occasion, when I had to solve a case to make a deadline or something.

"Who in the hell do you think you are, Mike?" Guffy asked. "A poor man's Dracula, or something? You're always turning up corpses and things."

"I do it because I like to," I said. It didn't make any difference what I said because Guffy already had his opinion and nobody but the Police Commissioner could change it.

He snorted and beckoned to the Sarge. "Come on. Let's get in our licks before Mike gums up everything."

They went into the elevator. I waited.

A few minutes later, Sylvester Hammond came downstairs. He padded up to me like he'd just trapped a spy in a pay toilet in the men's john.

"Guffy wants to talk to you," he whispered. "He's in two-ten."

"Any report on the stiff yet?" I whispered back.

"He's dead," said Hammond hoarsely, as if maybe I hadn't been sure.

"I mean how'd he die?"

Hammond shook his head. "The medical examiner thinks it was acute alcoholism. He'll be sure after the post."

Hammond went with me to two-ten. It was a small room, and Guffy had put the desk in the center of the room and was seated behind it. I winked at Guffy and jerked my head toward Hammond, who was ahead of me and couldn't see the gesture. Guffy knew what I meant.

"I'll want to talk to Mike alone, Syl," said Guffy. "Do you mind waiting outside?"

"Guh-h-h, no. It's okay by me, Guffy. Only thing is, the hotel is pretty interested in getting a straight report on this thing."

"I'll let you know if Mike can shed any light on it," said Guffy.

"And if I did it, I'll make a statement clearing the hotel," I added.

Guffy gave me a dirty look and Hammond went out, closing the door.

"Take the load off," said Guffy, gesturing toward a chair across from him by the desk. I seated myself, and then he said: "Now?"

"Before you start beating me with a rubber hose, Clyde," I said, "I'd like to tell you a few things."

"You'll tell me not a few things, but every damned thing you know," said Guffy. "Or so help me, I'll put you in the tank. I mean it this time, Mike."

"I could protest, but it wouldn't do any good," I said. I proceeded to tell him everything that had happened since Swigert came into the press room about nine-thirty that morning.

Guffy listened. His face was a mask. I couldn't tell by looking at him what he was thinking. When I finished he said, "Can you remember the words Swigert used when he came into the station? His exact words?"

I thought for a moment. "He said: 'I am a blackmailer. They killed Corrigan and now they are coming for me. I want police protection.' That sort of ties it in with the Corrigan case, doesn't it?"

"It would, only this isn't murder," said Guffy.

"You're sure?"

"Not positive. Doc Browne thinks it's acute alcoholism. No sign of violence."

"Poison, maybe?"

"He'll find out, but I wouldn't put any bets on it," said Guffy. He thought for a moment. "Another funny thing happened, Mike. We got a tip that you were the murderer."

"Me?"

"Somebody called us anonymously and said that Mike Lanson was the name of the man who talked to Corrigan in the park."

"You're kidding!"

Guffy shook his head. "On the level, Mike. Could be a crank, or maybe somebody thought he saw you, or really did see you. We checked it out. The hotel says you were in last night. All evening. Of course you might have slipped out. It wouldn't be hard, but we figured maybe the man who talked to Corrigan was about your size and looked like you."

I remembered now that Junior Nimes and I were about the same size. When Corrine first saw me she had called out, *"Harry."* But the woods were full of tall men in this case. Calderson was big and tall. H. C. Nimes was tall too. Even Hayten was tall. For that matter, Swigert was above average height.

"Where were you today before you found the body, Mike?" Guffy asked.

I told him about my visit to Hayten's place. "Of course I might have killed Swigert before I left," I said. "What time did he die?"

"Between 12:30, and 1:30. We'll get all that from the medical report."

"Listen, Guffy, you don't suspect me, do you?"

He shook his head. "No. Not yet anyhow. Nothing connects you with Swigert. And as I said, we don't think this is murder. Corrigan was different. And Swigert connects with Corrigan. He said 'They killed Corrigan and now they're coming for me.' What did he mean by *they?* More than one person? Or did he use *they* meaning something else?"

"They means more than one," I said. "However, a drunk doesn't always say what he means." Guffy grunted, and I decided the time was right to ask him for some information: "Did you find anything in Corrigan's files?"

"Well, nothing except a lot of dirt. I don't think Corrigan kept everything in his files. A lot was in his head, or maybe he had a confederate. Sharp maybe." He paused. "There was a file on Swigert. Corrigan investigated Swigert on several occasions. About the worst thing we learned about him was that he liked gals other than the one he married. And of course he's been a chronic alcoholic since he was old enough to buy whiskey."

"And Doc thinks Swigert died from too much whiskey?"

"Yeah. Doc said Swigert drank so much he forgot to breathe."

"Doc likes to say things like that."

"He's pretty sure about this. He said it could be a heart attack induced by too much alcohol, or respiratory repression caused by the same thing. And Doc wouldn't go out on a limb if he wasn't sure."

"But you've got other ideas. Like murder."

"If you quote me—"

"I'm not quoting."

"Well, I always look at things in the worst light first. Then I know they're pretty apt to get better. If this is murder, it'll be a stinker. I hope it ain't."

"Two glasses," I said.

"Yeah. Even you noticed it. Well, one of the glasses had prints. The crime lab boys will find out they're Swigert's. I'll bet my paycheck on it. The other glass had no prints. It'd been washed out and wiped with a towel. No prints on the whiskey bottle. You ever hear of a drunk wiping off his fingerprints from a bottle and glass just before he passes out?"

"Nope," I said. "But I expect everything has been done at least once. This is the most unoriginal world I've ever been a reporter in."

"You're the most unfunny reporter I've ever known," said Guffy.

"What about the waxed paper? The stuff that the glasses were wrapped in?"

"Crime lab boys have it. They think there may be prints on both of them." Guffy sighed. "Now get the hell out of here. You've told me all you're going to tell me and now we're wasting time. This probably isn't a murder at all, and the Corrigan case is stalled. But you'll have to be at the inquest tomorrow. Tell your boss to let you off."

"Let me off? My God, Guffy, he'll send me to the inquest and fire me if I don't go. It's my job to be there. I'll even be paid for it."

"Beat it," said Guffy.

I departed.

SEVEN
THURSDAY MORNING

The business about two used glasses, one without fingerprints, gave me a good angle in the home edition and stock final that afternoon, and the morning *Globe* really beat its columns over it. The mystery death of Omar Leroy Swigert, the thrice divorced playboy, was much better news than a private eye named Corrigan, even though the evidence that Swigert had been murdered was very slim indeed.

In the *Globe's* story, written by Carl Brandt, my opposite number on the morning paper, I was quoted at length. He had called me on the phone, since he is a telephone reporter, and I'd cooperated by giving him all the information that the *Gazette* had already printed. He also gave the conclusion of the medical examiner which came too late for my story.

Doc Brown said Swigert had died of cardiac and respiratory repression caused by acute alcoholism. Although it was his studied opinion that Swigert was not murdered, there were some questionable details which the coroner would take up at the inquest at 10 a.m. on Thursday, the story said.

About half a column was given over to Swigert's obituary, which was picturesque but not to be envied. Born with an entire silver service in his mouth, Swigert was the only son of a wealthy industrialist. He had been kicked out of some of the best colleges in the country. The only thing he ever did was serve in the Army for four years, having been drafted at the beginning of World War II. Most of his service was spent in the guardhouse.

However, he was out of the guardhouse long enough to woo and wed a WAC, who divorced him as soon as he shed his uniform. She got a reported half-million dollars as a settlement. His next marital venture was with a night club singer who talked him into investing in an outfit producing television films, with her as a star. The company flopped and so did the marriage and the entire deal cost him at least a million.

Swigert's third marriage was to the former Miss Corrine Hayten, who was Society if anything, and probably ignorant of most of Swigert's shortcomings. This marriage had been legalized by a justice of peace in the adjoining county after a whirlwind romance lasting eight days. The bride left him after five days of the honeymoon and obtained a divorce in Reno, Nevada, two months later. The former Mrs. Swigert's recent marriage to Harold C. Nimes, Jr. was announced two months ago.

Swigert's age was given as forty-three, which made him at least twenty years older than Corrine Nimes.

I finished reading the account in the Waltham's coffee shop and was just getting up steam to go down to work, late as usual, when a deputy sheriff came in and slapped me with a subpoena to attend the inquest.

"Does the coroner really think I can help him figure this out?" I asked the deputy, whose name was Powell.

"I dunno, but you'd better be there, son," he said.

"According to the paper this guy drank himself to death," I said.

"The coroner said the cops want a couple of things on record," Deputy Powell told me. "They're tryin to make somethin' out of it. These cops are headline grabbers."

They weren't according to Guffy, but I let it pass. "What about the glass without any fingerprints?" I asked.

"Fingerprints aren't always left when somebody picks up a glass," said the deputy. "Swigert mighta had wet hands. Or maybe the glass was wet."

"Or maybe he wore gloves," I said.

Deputy Powell blinked and grunted a noncommittal answer since he couldn't figure out whether I was kidding or just crazy. He walked off.

I paid my check and went to the hotel garage to pick up my car. I didn't check in with Hank, because I was almost twenty minutes late and he gets mad at twenty seconds. From Police Headquarters I called the office and told Hank I'd been at work all the time, but the cops tied me up downstairs telling dirty stories. He ate me out for wasting time, not for being late. There's no pleasing that guy.

Don Hilliard, my assistant, was a little red-eyed from his day off. He pointed to an envelope in my typewriter. "That was here when I came in," he said.

I picked up the envelope and saw that it was on plain stationery and was addressed to Mr. Mike Lanson. The writing was slantwise, as if the guy was unsteady or couldn't see. I looked at the message, in the same cockeyed script: *Meet me at your hotel during your lunch hour. This is a matter of grave importance.— Omar Leroy Swigert.*

"Good Lord," I mumbled.

"Can't be that good," said Don. "What is it?"

"A note from a dead man," I said, passing the paper to Don. He read it, reread it, and handed it back.

"Maybe it's a gag," he said.

"If it's genuine, he must have left it here yesterday morning," I said, thinking out loud more than making a reply to Don. "I left the office between nine-thirty and a quarter of ten and didn't come back."

"Soft job you got," said Don. "You don't even come to work."

I let it pass. Don was young and he was easily influenced by Hank Newcomb's idea that a reporter is not working unless he is pounding a typewriter or talking over the phone to a rewrite man.

I got up and went down the hall to Guffy's office. The lieutenant was in and he read the note with a sour face. "So he went to the Waltham to see you and got murdered while he waited."

"You know he was looking for me at the Waltham," I said. "Edgar, the desk man, told you that. And you know he came here yesterday. He went into the press room. Maybe he actually mistook me for a cop, or maybe he really came to see me and lost his nerve."

"He asked you to arrest him, Remember? He mistook you for an officer." Guffy turned it over in his mind for a moment, then went on: "He's been blackmailing somebody, maybe his former wife. Something threw a scare into him and he decided jail was the safest place to be. Of course, the thing that scared him was Corrigan's murder."

"Can I use this, Guffy?" I asked.

Guffy suddenly grew rigid. "Damn you! I was just speculating. If you dare print one word of this, I'll—"

"Okay, okay. Don't get in a heat about it. And don't threaten me. I've had it from experts. You know I can't print guesses. You'd deny you had the brains to guess and—oh hell, I won't insult you."

"You're a nice boy," said Guffy, like he'd enjoy choking me.

"You say such friendly things," I told him. "What did Mrs. Nimes say when you told her that her ex-husband had died? Or did you tell her?"

"Nothing you can print, newsboy," said Guffy. "She said she was shocked, of course. She admitted they hadn't had much in common since the honeymoon, but she said it was a shame he had to die so young."

"Hell, he was over forty."

"I'm forty," said Guffy. "It's young."

"Did you talk to anybody else?"

"Mrs. Nimes' father, Charley Hayten, was there, and so was young Harry Nimes. They said about the same thing. They also said that Swigert was a chronic alcoholic. Is that news?"

"Not now and probably never was," I said. "Do you think he was murdered?"

Guffy tapped his fingers on the note, which lay on his desk in front of him. "This note is just another little piece of evidence that he was. First the two water glasses, then this. Trouble is, Doc Browne said liquor killed him. I suggested poison liquor and Doc—you know how he is—said anybody would be crazy to put poison in the whiskey when Swigert had drunk enough to kill him. And then Sergeant Russell puts the kibosh on the two glasses."

"How's that?"

"Well, he says that Swigert wanted a chaser and was too lazy to fill his whiskey glass with water, each time he wanted a drink, so he used two glasses. I asked him how Swigert made the water and the liquor come out even, but he said it could happen. But we still got something else."

"Fingerprints?"

He stared at me angrily, and I knew I'd guessed right. Fingerprints were about the only thing left.

"Damn it, Mike, don't print that. It's the only thing we've got that can be used to trap the killer—if Swigert was murdered and if we've got the right print."

"But I can use it later?"

"Sure you can. When we match that print, you'll be the first to know."

"Guffy, you have my solemn promise not to print a word about fingerprints. Where'd you find it? Inside the whiskey bottle?"

He did a slow burn. "Well, I know one thing, Mike. When you give a promise not to print something, I can trust you. You know that waxed paper used to wrap the glasses?"

"Yeah. One on the floor, one in the wastebasket."

"The one on the floor had several prints. One set was Swigert's. The others belonged to different people. Possibly the chambermaid and the person who wrapped the glasses. We found these prints on the other wrapper, the one in the wastebasket. But there was another pair of prints and a couple of smudges on the wrapper in the wastebasket. We don't know about 'em yet. Maybe they belong to somebody else who handled the glasses before they got to Room 602. Or they could be another link in the chain that proves this was murder."

"Chee, Mr. Holmes. You're wonderful."

"Elementary, my dear Watson," said Guffy. "Now why do you suppose Swigert wanted to talk to you after he ran away from you in the press room yesterday? Why didn't he go on and find a cop and get thrown in jail, like he said he wanted? Why did he change his mind?"

I shrugged. "Know any way to get answers from a dead man?"

"I think he lost his nerve. Or maybe he got a better idea. Maybe he thought blackmail wasn't such a bad racket after all; that he'd threaten his ex-wife, or whoever he was blackmailing, to tell a reporter and get a nice lump settlement. Then he could get out of town, far from a nasty murderer who was trying to hire a private eye to do his killing. But while waiting for you he drinks too much whiskey and dies."

"Or was killed in some subtle way that doesn't look like murder," I added. "I thought Swigert was a rich playboy. Why'd he dabble in blackmail if he had money?"

"He wasn't so rich any more. His first two wives took generous helpings from whatever Swigert's old man left him," said Guffy. "And even so, maybe he was sore at his third wife and wanted to torment her a little."

"The girl and her husband are in trouble," I said. "I told you about the meeting I had with the whole corporation. They mentioned felony. What kind of a felony would it be, Guffy?"

The cop shook his head. "There are so many that I can't count 'em. Almost anything you do to harm a person or appropriate his property illegally is a felony. That's a general statement, of course. But laws are made to protect people and their property."

"Is a wife property?" I asked.

"Well back when men didn't have laboratories and space travel, a woman was property, just like a cow or a horse. But laws have been passed until it's started to look as if a man belongs to a woman nowadays. Wife stealing isn't a felony any more. You can sue a man for alienating your wife's affections, but you can't put him in jail unless he kidnaps her. Then it's a crime against the wife, not the husband."

"If somebody hadn't mentioned the word felony, you might figure there was an alienation of affections suit wrapped up in this case."

Guffy looked at his watch. "It's almost nine, Mike. Let's grab a cup of coffee and then go to the inquest."

"I would," I said innocently, "except that Hank wants a new lead on Corrigan for the bulldog. I've got to find a cop and get one."

"That's easy," said Guffy. "Did I tell you that Corrigan's files threw no light on his murder?"

"You did," I said. "We had it yesterday."

"All right, try this angle: ballistics definitely established that Corrigan was killed by a bullet from his own gun."

"Well, we sort of guessed it since you found his gun with one bullet discharged, but it's better than nothing and shows the cops have been working themselves to death. I'll call Hank on it after we have coffee. If I called him too soon, he'd think I got the story easy."

Guffy sighed. "Wonder what reporters did before phones and ballistics."

All of these things accomplished, Guffy and I reached the municipal court room, where the inquest was scheduled to be held at ten minutes of ten. Coroner Snow already was there, and so was Doc Leonard Browne, who had been the medical examiner in the case. Doc, who was a pathologist at Charity Hospital, was an old friend of mine.

Edgar, the hotel clerk, Hammond the house detective, and a bell boy represented the Waltham, and also present was Charles Hayten, former father-in-law of the deceased.

Hayten shifted uneasily when I nodded at him, but he rose and came over to where I stood talking to Guffy. "I want to thank you, Mike, for what you did yesterday. Corrine told me."

"You mean finding the body?" Guffy asked pleasantly, although he knew what Hayten meant.

"No," said Hayten. "Lanson saved my daughter from something unpleasant. I reported the incident to the sheriff's office myself."

"Oh, that," said Guffy. Hayten bristled, and the officer continued. "We've been looking for Freddie the Grape, but we haven't found him in his usual haunts. Give him time though. We'll pick him up full of wine."

"I've sworn out a complaint against this man Fred Gandy," Hayten told Guffy. "And I'll see to it that he is prosecuted. A person like that shouldn't be allowed to run loose."

"He's not loose very often," said Guffy. "I expect he spends as much time in the tank as he does out of it." I sensed that Guffy didn't believe that Gandy would have really harmed Corrine Hayten, but I wasn't at all sure of it. I'd been there.

The coroner stepped up to the judge's bench and seated himself. He rapped with a gavel, bringing the session to order.

In a nasal voice, Coroner Snow explained that this was an inquiry into the death of Omar Leroy Swigert, and that it was not a court and was not intended to do more than to ascertain the facts of the man's death. If the facts pointed to a felony, officers would be charged with bringing guilty parties to justice, or the results would be open to the inclusion of further evidence, if and when such evidence was found.

Then a jury, consisting of City Hall hangers on, was sworn and the proceedings were started. In more important cases a deputy from the county prosecutor's office usually was present to ask questions. The fact that the coroner conducted the questioning indicated that in his mind, at least, the death was not felonious.

Except for a couple of points, nothing of any consequence was brought out at the inquest. I testified as to the discovery of the body, and I introduced the note that I'd shown Guffy. Doc Browne, who performed the autopsy on Swigert, said that death had resulted from acute alcoholism.

"That's not a common cause of death, is it, doctor?" Coroner Snow asked.

"Not common," Doc said with a shake of his head.

Doc was a seedy-looking man for the profession he was in. Most doctors are neat and dapper. Doc's white hair was uncombed. He wore ill-fitting clothes. But he was always in good humor. Years ago he had broken his health by overwork, catering to a large practice. He gave this up and took a job at the hospital with the remark that he'd rather enjoy life than fight death. However, he still fought death in the laboratory.

"But people do drink themselves to death?" asked the coroner.

"Yes," Doc agreed. "But usually they're killed by complications from overdrinking, rather than the liquor itself. Alcohol in small amounts is actually beneficial. It's a food, it goes into the blood stream without digestion, and it contains calories. It is good for diseases such as hypertension, heart trouble, and so on. It's better than tranquilizers."

"But still it's a poison?"

"Not nearly as deadly as some medicines we take," said Doc. "You've got alcohol in your system right now, even if you haven't taken a drink for months, or never had one. Carrie Nation, when she smashed bars in Wichita, carried around one-third of one percent of her body weight in demon alcohol, and she was a teetotaler."

There was laughter and the stern-faced coroner rapped his gavel. "How does it cause death—as in the case of Mr. Swigert?"

"Through cardiac and respiratory depression," said Doc. "You see, alcohol is a depressant, even if it does make you feel high. Your body can handle a certain amount of it without any trouble, but as you begin to drink more of it, your system gets overloaded and the alcohol content of the blood rises. At first you lose your inhibitions. You say and do things you wouldn't do if you were sober. Then your nerves are affected. Your reflexes don't function. Breathing is a reflex and your heart acts by reflex. A man can get enough alcohol into his system so that he actually *forgets* to breathe and keep his heart functioning. That's what happened to Swigert."

"How much does it take?" the coroner inquired.

"Depends on how fast it's taken in," Doc said. "Alcohol can be tolerated, if taken over a period of time, in pretty large amounts. But ever so often a damned fool bets he can drink a pint of whiskey without pausing for a breath. He collects the bet but dies. That same man, or almost any normal person could consume a pint over a period of an hour without dying. He might get pretty drunk, but he'd live to see another sunrise if he didn't drive a car. Had he drunk that much in sixty seconds, instead of sixty minutes, he'd have died."

"In other words you eliminate the alcohol."

"Yes. Kidneys and sweat glands eliminate up to fifteen percent of the alcohol consumed. The rest is oxidized by the lungs and the liver."

"Is there any way of telling how much Swigert drank?"

"Officer Guffy testified that there was a bottle of whiskey on the dresser. It was down about eight ounces. However, we know that Swigert was drunk when he arrived at the hotel and that he went into the bar at the hotel. It seems like a very small amount of liquor to kill a man, but we've got to remember that Swigert was already drunk. And there are some people who can't eliminate as much as fifteen percent of what they drink. Sometimes it's as low as one percent. Usually a person passes out after a certain point, but some people don't, and these factors vary with circumstances in the same individual. Most alcoholics, strangely enough, have a lower tolerance for alcohol than the temperate man."

"There's no way of telling if the amount of alcohol, in the form of whiskey, Swigert would have to drink to die from its effects?"

"All I know, sir, is that the alcoholic content of Swigert's blood was well over one-half of one percent, which is an extremely dangerous level for normal people."

"You said something about a third of one percent earlier, doctor—"

"I was speaking of alcohol in the body in relation to the body weight. You mustn't confuse that with the alcoholic content of the blood."

"Thank you, doctor," said the coroner.

This concluded the testimony. The jury returned a verdict that Omar Leroy Swigert came to his death as a result of cardiac and respiratory repression, resulting from acute alcoholism.

I called the office. Hank was disappointed in the verdict I think he expected a verdict that would open the case for a murder headline, but Hank had to take what the records showed.

I myself wasn't so easily satisfied. I was hoping to add to the record. Doc had left the City Hall and so had Guffy when

I finished phoning and I took a cab over to Charity Hospital. Doc was only a few minutes ahead of me and I found him in his lab in the basement of the hospital, filling his pipe. He had removed his coat and had put on a laboratory apron.

"Hi, Mike," he said in surprise. "Didn't think I'd see you again today. Sorry I didn't get to talk to you at the inquest, but I guess we can make up for it now, eh?"

"Yep," I said, seating myself on a stool near his desk. "You performed the P.M. on Swigert, didn't you, Doc?"

"Take it easy, pal," said Doc. "Don't be in such a hurry and you'll live longer. Sit down and talk around to whatever you've got to say, don't dive head-first into it I'm likely to think I'm just a business acquaintance of yours, instead of a friend."

"Okay, Doc," I said, "How you doin'? Fine? That's fine. Now did you?"

He laughed. "Okay, heads I lose. Yep. And I said all I know on the subject of alcoholism today at the inquest. By the way, if those congenital idiots down at the *Gazette* use my name, be sure they spell my name with an *e*. Capital *B-r-o-w-n-e*. Get it?"

"I got it," I said.

"And speaking of alcohol," he went on, "I've got a bottle of Old Fitz over there on the shelf. Want to see if you can stand a shot?"

"Well, as long as it's in the interest of science," I said.

Doc got the bottle and dug up a couple of beakers for us to drink out of. I hated to think of what the beakers might have contained at one time or another, but Doc didn't seem to be squeamish and we fixed up a couple of shots.

"Now," he said, smacking his lips. "We have taken care of the niceties. What's on your mind?"

"Murder," I said.

"Naturally. It's uppermost in the mind of every reporter. Murder, sex, and pictures of animals. That's all you see in the paper, if you disregard the sports and society sections, and society is sex once removed."

"Swigert's murder," I amended.

"You think somebody put a funnel in his mouth and poured whiskey into him?"

"No," I said. "Hypodermic."

Doc had the beaker halfway to his lips when I spoke and he was so surprised that he forgot to open his mouth to drink and the liquor slopped all over his chin. "Good Lord, yes!" he exclaimed.

"How much would it take?" I asked.

"Not much," Doc said, "considering that he was already pickled and apparently had just taken another jolt or two. Maybe he passed out and somebody shot him in the arm with a hypodermic filled, with alcohol—or even whiskey! It could be, if he passed out, that even beer could have killed him!"

"Well," I said, "what are we waiting for?"

"What do you mean?"

"Let's not speculate about it. Let's find out."

Doc shook his head. "Like I said, Mike. It doesn't pay to rush. Let's finish our drink first. The body isn't going any place."

EIGHT
THURSDAY, 1:00 P.M.

The mortal remains of Omar Leroy Swigert had been removed from the County Morgue and taken to the Mitchell Undertaking Parlors, on the East Side.

Doc said it was customary in cases like this to eat first, in case he didn't feel like it later. We stopped at a drive-in restaurant, where Doc consumed a bowl of chili while he lectured on the atrocious eating habits of Americans. I ate a hamburger, which certainly isn't atrocious, but when I ordered pie Doc got more angry than ever because I was young enough to eat pie without increasing my girth.

"You'll be sorry when you're my age," he said, burping.

"I'll probably look back on it and be glad I did it when I could," I said.

We drove on to our destination. The undertaker, named Mitchell, frowned when he looked at Doc's credentials from the coroner's office.

"I hope there won't be any more notoriety," he said. "It's not very pleasant in our business."

He didn't ask for my credentials and I didn't tell him I was a reporter. But Doc, tactless as usual, mentioned it, and the undertaker turned whiter than he already was, which was about the color of whitewash.

There was nothing that Mitchell could do about it, however, and I've found that undertakers are always ready to accept the inevitable. That's their business.

He escorted us to the embalming room, in the rear of his place of business, where Swigert was laid out on a table and covered with a sheet.

I recalled that Swigert's left arm had been dangling beside the bed when I discovered him and that the cuff link on his sleeve was unfastened. "Try the left arm first," I said.

Doc peeled back the sheet. Swigert looked much more peaceful and serene than on the two previous occasions when I'd seen him, once in life, once in death. His face was relaxed and his arms were folded over his chest.

He was dignified, even without pants and other clothing. Doc looked at the left arm. He found the little hole made by the hypodermic needle almost at once. Whatever scab had been there had been washed away by the undertaker, but the hole could be seen.

"You were right, Mike," said Doc.

"Can you prove he was given alcohol intravenously?" I asked.

"Not alcohol," Doc said, "but whiskey. That we can prove, because whiskey isn't pure alcohol. It has other stuff in it. We could have found it before, if we'd been looking for it, but not in the blood now. The embalmer's art has taken care of it. However, there must have been a little seepage when the needle was withdrawn. It'll be tough, but I think we can show what happened."

"Then it is murder?" asked the undertaker, almost in a whisper.

"That's for the jury and lawyers to decide," said Doc. He looked at me. "I guess you saved me from letting somebody get away with murder, Mike. Thanks."

"I don't think the murderer thanks you," I said. I glanced around the room and saw a wall phone. "Can I use the phone?"

"Help yourself," said the undertaker.

Before I could reach the instrument, Doc was already dialing the coroner's office, setting the wheels in motion for a full-fledged murder investigation.

After Doc had finished, I called Hank, who was overjoyed to hear that we had a second murder. Nothing had developed in the Corrigan case, but a wealthy playboy's murder is by far a better story than the slaying of a private investigator.

"Think you can tie it up with the Corrigan job, Mike?" Hank asked.

"I'm working on it," I said.

"Can you get me a quote that it ties?"

"Don't be silly. The cops aren't even here yet."

"Listen, Mike, we've got to have this yarn before 3:30, when the home edition rolls. Step on it."

Hank always believed the world turned on his deadlines.

The clock said a couple of minutes before one as I hung up the phone. The cops wouldn't know for sure that they had a murder until Doc determined positively that an injection of whiskey had been made in Swigert's arm. That would take an hour probably. After that, the cops would have to sort out all they knew about the case, then start over on their investigation. I couldn't see very much chance of a turn in the case before 3:30, unless I did a little managing. Guffy, of course, took a dim view of my monkeying with a murder case, but Guffy was not the person who gave me orders. I was ordered to get a story.

And there was another motivating force that told me to get busy. In spite of the fact that the *Gazette* and the *Globe* are owned by the same stockholders and bossed by the same editor, there was rivalry between them. It wasn't good-natured, fun-loving rivalry; it was professional business. Reporters who broke stories got raises, promotions and bonuses. I didn't want Carl Brandt, my opposite number on the *Globe,* to ride the gravy train with a break that I might get with a little promoting of my own.

If a big break didn't come before 3:30, you could bet that a certain be-sainted reporter named Mike Lanson would try to stall the solution one way or another until the last edition of the *Globe* went to press. And Carl would be trying to stall it if the developments moved past his deadline. In situations like these, murderers can live forever. Therefore I would try to solve, but failing, I would try to prevent solution of the case after 3:30.

"This fellow hit the vein right on the nose," said Doc, bending over Swigert's body again. "Say, Mitch. I have to have some of this tissue. I don't want to foul up your job."

"Take what you need," said the undertaker. "He'll be wearing sleeves."

As Doc opened the bag he got from his car, I asked, "What about that vein, Doc. Does it show the fellow knew how to handle a hypodermic?"

Doc snorted. "Takes no special skill to handle a hypodermic needle. Just like putting a toothpick into wet macaroni."

In spite of Doc's opinion on the matter, I didn't think I'd be able to use a hypodermic successfully the first time I tried. Maybe it didn't take skill, but you had to know how to use one. "Where'd a person get a needle?"

"Any drug store," said Doc. "There's no law against selling 'em. You don't even have to buy a hypo if you've got a needle. Hopheads make 'em out of eyedroppers and adhesive tape. But this wasn't a makeshift job. No chicken tracks."

The scratchy marks and scars left by makeshift hypos probably wouldn't have shown as such on the body of a dead man, but Doc could have told by the jagged incision.

"Maybe the killer was a diabetic and already had a needle," I suggested.

"Could be. We don't know that."

"Any way to learn if certain people are diabetics?"

"Ask 'em."

"You're a doctor. Can't you find out?"

"No. Professional ethics."

"Baloney," I said. "You're a lab doctor. You don't have patients."

"I still got ethics," said Doc.

"You're letting a murderer get away with something."

Doc gave me a glance, like he was hurt deeply inside.

"Damn it, Mike, why don't you let the cops solve murders? You stick to your newspaper work."

"I am sticking to it. Don't you realize if we fail to round up a murderer in the next two and a half hours, another reporter will profit by my sweat, blood and tears?"

"Beat it, Mike. I don't need you. The crime lab men won't need you when they get here. If the police want you, they can find you." He paused, allowing his good-humor to get the upper hand for a moment. "Thanks again, Mike, for letting me correct my mistakes."

"Forget it," I said. "I got a story, and that's all that matters. But since you're such a lovable, ethical old bastard, I'll leave you to dilly-dally with the dead and I'll have to go out and find out about hypodermics and things. So-long, and thanks to you too, Mr. Mitchell."

The undertaker nodded his head soberly and solemnly. "You are entirely welcome, Mr. Lanson. Remember me in time of distress."

"I'll do better than that," I said, "I'll put your name in the paper."

"My initials are V. E." he said. "The V. E. Mitchell Mortuary. Service with a tear."

It was five past-one when I caught a cab and told the driver to take me downtown. I was positive the Swigert and Corrigan murders were linked somewhere, with Corrine Nimes in the middle. I didn't expect to get much help from H. C. Nimes, or any of his henchmen, but there is always a way to learn things.

Nimes was not talking and nobody under him dared talk. Corrigan and Swigert, who seemed to represent the other side of the story, were dead and couldn't talk. But Sharp, who had been Corrigan's lawyer, was alive and able to talk and somewhere in the city was a little niche in which Freddie the Grape was hiding. Of the two, Sharp was the most available. I told the taxi driver to take me to Ninth and Mohawk where both Corrigan and Sharp had offices.

Sharp's office was not chrome-plated and pastel-colored as some lawyers' offices are, but it was adequate and not as frowsy as I had expected. A secretary with a beautiful figure and an ugly face sat at a typewriter in the anteroom. She looked up from her work as I entered. Seeing that I was young, she smiled.

When I told her my name and that I was a reporter I was granted immediate audience with Addison Sharp, who was seated in front of a littered desk sucking an orange.

His private office was not as immaculate as the reception room and was more like I expected it to be. He put the orange pulp in the wastebasket and extended his hand which I shook.

"Expected to see you long before this, Lanson," he said. "What's wrong with your newspaper? Is it decadent or something?"

I always play along with people when they are good-natured, so I said, "Good reporters are always lazy." This was a First Commandment once spouted in the writings of a great editor named William Allen White of Emporia, Kansas, who got his picture on a postage stamp, probably because he knew what made reporters tick.

"You're lazy, all right, but whether you're good or not, is a matter which I'll leave to the jury," he said.

"And where do you think my paper is deficient and decadent?" I asked.

"I am sitting atop some of the juiciest tid-bits ever to be turned up since the scandal magazines breathed their last," he said. "You haven't asked to print them."

"Pish-posh, Mr. Sharp. We're a family newspaper."

"A family paper? With a sex story or a rape on every front page?"

"That is family reading. On the inside pages we print Sunday sermons for sinners. And you know damned well if I asked for these tid-bits, you'd say no."

"Well, if that's not what you want, I'm puzzled," he said.

"You were Mr. Corrigan's lawyer, Mr. Sharp?"

"That is a matter of record. I told you that yesterday morning."

"Did you also represent Mr. Swigert?"

He hesitated a moment "In a few matters. Do you have something in mind?"

"Well, Mr. Swigert died, owing a bill for the room he occupied at the Waltham," I told him. It seemed like a good thing to have in mind, even if I didn't know for sure if it were true. Then I continued: "I stay at the Waltham and being a good friend of the management, I told them that I knew Swigert's lawyer—or thought I did—and that I'd ask you about settling the bill."

Sharp's face took on a smug expression, "Does a hotel like the Waltham give a man a room without an advance payment when he has no luggage, excepting a pint of whiskey?"

"There was a slip-up," I said lamely.

"Well, the management of any business should know that you collect a bill owed by a deceased person through probate court, not through his lawyer." He paused for a moment, then laughed at his little joke. "What's the real reason, Lanson?"

"There's a suspicion that Swigert was blackmailing Nimes, or his son," I said. "I wanted to get the low-down. I can't ask Swigert, so I'm doing the next best thing."

Sharp drew in his breath and let it out slowly. "That of course is slander, against a dead man who can't defend himself. Who says so?"

"You're Swigert's lawyer?"

"I said I represented him in a couple of matters."

"In his divorce? The last one I mean."

"I advised him not to contest it."

"You can save me a great deal of trouble, Mr. Sharp," I said.

"In what way?"

"I could phone some stringer in Reno and have him get all the necessary facts in the divorce suit brought by Corrine Swigert against Omar Leroy Swigert. But you could give them to me and save me the trouble."

He thought for a moment. "Briefly, she divorced him because he was a chronic alcoholic. She charged that he got drunk immediately after their wedding ceremony and stayed drunk for five days, or longer. She left after five days of it."

"Was the marriage consummated?"

"I wasn't with them," said Sharp, "but no allegations were made to the contrary and it wouldn't affect the legality of their marriage."

"Was there anything about the marriage that might have resulted in blackmail?"

He shook his head.

"You're positive?"

"Absolutely. I'm as sure as I am of sitting here that the marriage was perfectly legal."

"How about the divorce?"

"As far as I know, it was granted. You can check your correspondent in Reno, if you wish. I'm sure the court there has handled enough divorces to do it properly."

"Damn it, Mr. Sharp," I said, "I've been getting the runaround somewhere in this case and I can't figure out where. But certain things are apparent. Two murders have been committed and they were connected somehow. I don't think Corrigan and Swigert were chummy—"

"I'm certain they weren't," said Sharp. "Corrigan turned up some evidence that helped Swigert's first two wives get divorces and large settlements."

"What about the third?"

"Corrine Hayten didn't need a detective to get that one." He did a double-take. "Did you say *two* murders?"

"Swigert was murdered too, Mr. Sharp."

Up to this point Sharp had been relaxed and affable. Now there was a change in his composure. He leaned forward. His face, rather handsome in composure, was now ruffled and strained. His eyes narrowed and he said, "Is this a newspaper idea? Where did you pick up this information?"

"A representative of the coroner's office has just found evidence of murder," I said. "Whiskey was injected in Swigert's bloodstream."

"Murder!" He said it as if he didn't believe it. He clasped and unclasped his fingers on the desk in front of him. His brow creased and finally he shook his head. "A gun, a knife or a blunt instrument I can believe—but a hypodermic full of whiskey!"

"A little fancy, but effective," I said. "Our murderer apparently was conformist on Corrigan, nonconformist on Swigert. Whether it means anything, I can't say, but I never was a hearty subscriber to the *modus operandi* theory." Not too long ago I was a believer in the principle that nothing much new ever happened. Now I realized that in this advanced age new things are being done every day.

"Well, it sounds like a wild guess," said he. "How can such a thing be proved in court?"

"Doc Browne thinks he can prove it."

"Well, coming secondhand from, a newspaper reporter, this report needs substantiation. I'll have to find out for myself."

"Okay. Meanwhile, we were talking about blackmail. Can you think of any other reason Swigert might have been killed?"

He sighed. "I suppose a few things ought to be cleared and I should take it up with the police. But up to now, the small details in my possession didn't seem important. But if Swigert really was murdered . . ." His voice trailed off. His clenched fist struck the desk. "Swigert believed he was the man that Corrigan was asked to kill."

"Care to tell me about it?"

"I might, at that. Some of it you can print. Most of it's dangerous and a little bit is dynamite. But that's your paper's I worry. It goes back to when Swigert married Miss Hayten. The divorce was a blow to his pride, but it hurt most when she married young Nimes. Swigert thought he was the better man—older, more experienced. They had the same backgrounds, give or take a million or two, but there was a difference, and of course Swigert would fare badly in anyone's comparison but his own.

"A week or so after young Harry Nimes married Miss Hayten, Swigert came to me contending he had grounds for a lawsuit against the bridegroom. I can't reveal what it was, but I'm sure it wasn't a motive for Swigert's murder and that Corrigan wasn't involved. I promised to investigate. I talked to Miss Hayten—Mrs. Nimes, I mean. Talked to her husband and to her father, who acted in the capacity of counsel. The idea was utterly absurd and about two weeks ago I told Swigert that the case would be tossed out of court on the first defense motion to dismiss if I filed it. He left me in a huff."

"Have you seen him since?"

The lawyer creased his brows in thought. "I don't recall that I have. I talked to him on the phone, however. The morning after Corrigan was killed . . . yesterday, wasn't it? Lord, it seems ages ago . . . yesterday morning he called me and said Harry Nimes had tried to hire Corrigan to murder him. He sounded drunk and I assumed it was the whiskey speaking. I told him to go sober up."

"Did you tell the police about the call?" I asked.

"You know an unfounded accusation like that can only result in trouble," said Sharp. "There was no reason to believe that Omar Swigert was murdered and I can hardly believe it now. However, I was curious and I obtained Fred Gandy's release from jail. He was the best witness available because he was the only man who had seen Corrigan's friend in the park. Gandy told me the man was tall. No other description. I told Gandy to go over to Eighth and Willis and watch men who went in out of the Nimes building. One of them might be the man he saw in the park. I had very little hopes of a positive identification and I only partly believed Swigert's accusation. I didn't tell Gandy that Swigert suspected Harry Nimes—Gandy wouldn't know young Nimes anyhow. I just wondered if an identification could be made."

"Did he make one?"

Sharp gave me a faint smile. "Yes. He identified you as the man who talked to Corrigan."

"Me?" I was dumbfounded.

Sharp nodded. "I didn't take it seriously, Mike. I told him to watch and see if someone else didn't look like the man. He called several times." Sharp laughed. "He thought I was paying him to put the finger on somebody, I suppose. I gave him a couple of dollars and promised him another five if he did the job. He was anxious to get the five, although he hasn't dropped in to collect it yet."

I thought it over. That could have been the reason, of course, but on the other hand . . . "You know that Harry Nimes and I are pretty much alike physically, don't you?" I said. "We're both tall and slender. Of course we don't resemble each other in the face, but as you say there were only a few park lights and Freddie couldn't have seen the face of the man very clearly."

Sharp shrugged. "Eyewitness identifications are never very good, Mike," said Sharp. "Every lawyer knows that."

"Do you happen to know why Freddie went to Hayten's place after his vigil at Eighth and Willis?"

Sharp acted surprised. "No. Was he there?"

"The reason he hasn't collected that fiver, Mr. Sharp, is that the sheriff and the police are looking for him. He threw a pretty bad scare into Mrs. Nimes yesterday afternoon."

"Lordy! I didn't know that. He must be hiding south of town."

"None of this has been given to the police, you say," I asked him.

Sharp looked sheepish. "Well, I did call them anonymously and I told them that you might be the man in the park who talked to Corrigan. But, Mike, I didn't mean anything personal by it."

I shrugged. "Guffy told me. The cops didn't give it a second thought." Cops always got anonymous tips in murder cases. Few ever amounted to anything.

"Well, I'm glad you weren't the man."

"I wasn't. Were you?"

Sharp looked shocked. "Lord, Mike! Would I kill a couple of clients. I need them! Seriously, though, I'd swear by all that's holy that I never tried to buy Swigert's murder, or anybody's murder."

It was convincing and I believed him. "I'll buy it," I said. "Nothing personal in my question either. Do you think Swigert's proposed lawsuit was an attempt to obtain money—a sort of legal blackmail, as it were?"

"Blackmail, is a rough word, Lanson. And as for the lawsuit, Swigert couldn't have collected a lead nickel. Not even for nuisance value."

Somebody was trying to get money somewhere. The whole case smelled of blackmail. "Then, if it didn't amount to anything, why didn't you at least wise-up the cops?"

"Until today, I knew of nothing that connected Corrigan's murder with Swigert."

"But Swigert told you that he might be a victim and you believed him enough to spring Freddie the Grape from jail and use him as stakeout."

"I only had a drunk's word for it," said Sharp. "And Swigert had asked me to do something. I really didn't think there was anything to it. That's why I made my phone call to the police anonymously. How much of this are you going to print?"

"Damned little," I said. "As far as I'm concerned it's a plate of red herring. However, I'm going to quote you as saying that Swigert feared for his life and that he believed that the man in the park was trying to hire someone to kill him."

Sharp sighed. "I'd prefer you didn't quote me, Mike. It wasn't a legal confidence, of course. But it would look bad because I didn't report it to police."

"Report it now," I said. "Omit the part about Freddie till the cops ask you. You can say you didn't take Swigert seriously. The cops wouldn't have believed him either."

"Sure," said Sharp. He picked up the phone.

I left after the call, feeling that I had ammunition to use against Nimes.

NINE
THURSDAY, 2:30 P. M.

You could always tell what time it was by the state of my city editor's mental balance. In the morning he was just stupid. At noon he started to go crazy. He reached his peak of insanity at 3:30 every afternoon when the home edition went to press. Then he returned to his normal state of stupidity.

He was approaching stark-raving madness when I entered the office. He looked up at me as if I were persecuting him. "All right. What have you got?"

"Nothing much," I said. "I just dropped by to find out if the cops have turned up anything interesting on Swigert yet."

Hank drew his chubby little palm slowly down the right side of his face, which already was smeared with ink from his typewriter ribbon which he must have changed between editions. When his fingers reached his jawbone, he exploded like he'd touched off some kind of detonator.

"Why didn't I get a job in the post office selling stamps? Why did I have to get into the goddamn newspaper business? Hellsamighty, Mike, you're a reporter. Remember? You're supposed to get the news. You don't come *here* to find it!"

"How many top stories am I supposed to turn in every day?" I asked. "I get you a new murder and you ain't satisfied. I've been off trying to dig up more facts, and you expect me to be at the cop house getting information that Don Hilliard is supposed to get."

"Go 'way," said Hank. "I've got the home edition on my neck."

"Okay," I said. "Maybe the Colonel will like to listen." I started to move away.

"Wait a minute!" Hank was always sensitive to the mention of Colonel Tanner's name. "If you've got something, what is it?"

"I've just been talking to a lawyer," I said. "Addison Sharp, who has represented both Corrigan and Swigert. On the morning Corrigan's body was found, Swigert called Sharp in a blue foop and said that Junior Nimes was the fellow who tried to hire Corrigan's gun."

"Well? You know we can't print that unless we get something to hang it on. Did you ask Nimes about it?"

"Supposing I did. Do you think he'd admit it?"

"Did you tell the police?"

"All right, supposing I did that. The cops would get a denial too, at first. If Nimes really did, and the cops sweat it out of him, it won't be until after several hours of grilling. So, the *Globe* gets the story."

"Oh," said Hank. It began to dawn on him that maybe I was a smart reporter after all. It was also to Hank's advantage for big stories to break first in the *Gazette*, even though both papers were under the same management. "Of course we don't want to obstruct justice or the investigation of a crime."

"Of course not," I said, glad that I was getting through to him. "However, a thing like this is pretty explosive. It's frozen dynamite. If we were to cast suspicion of murder on a reputable citizen we might get into all kinds of trouble. Yes, indeed."

Hank reached for the phone. "Gimme Colonel Tanner," he said to the operator. He waited and I could hear the Colonel's voice answering, even though I was four or five feet from Hank. "Colonel," said Hank, "Mike has run into an interesting angle in the Swigert case . . . no, I'm afraid not, Colonel. We don't dare print it yet. We'd better have our lawyers go over it—"

He stopped while the Colonel's voice chirped. Hank held the receiver a foot away from his head to prevent the blast from reducing his eardrums to lace curtains.

"I know, Colonel . . . Yes, Colonel . . . You see it makes Junior Nimes—that's H. C. Nimes, Junior—a big suspect in the case . . . There's nothing to hang it on, sir. I'd better let Mike talk to you . . ." Chirp, chirp. "Yes, sir, I'll send him up immediately."

Hank replaced the phone and looked up at me with the insane light still burning in his eyes. "Go," he said weakly, "and may God have mercy on your soul."

On the top floor, outside the Colonel's office, I found Ruthie, as pleasingly beautiful as ever, plunking at her typewriter. She looked up and winked back at me as I gave her the eye. "He's expecting you, Mike. Go right in."

"If I should return alive," I said, "will you have dinner with me this evening?"

"Don't you ever think of anything but eating?"

"Yes," I said, "but how am I going to get around to it unless I offer some bait?"

"Colonel Tanner," she said, "is impatient. Don't keep him waiting."

"I'm impatient too. But you keep me waiting." I went in, however, because this sort of thing doesn't make for progress with a lady.

Colonel Tanner sat behind a desk a size larger than a ping-pong table reading some clips from a morgue file. His eyes, glaring from behind dark-rimmed spectacles, brought me down to earth like guided missiles.

"How did the police overlook the murder, Mike?" he demanded. "Don't they know their job?"

"The murderer was very clever, Colonel," I said. "You can hardly blame the medical examiner."

"When a newspaper makes an error we get hell from everybody," he declared. "I like to dish it out once in a while. What's new in the case? Hank says you've struck oil, or something."

"I had an interesting talk with Addison Sharp," I said.

"That shyster! What kind of a line did he hand you?"

"Sharp said a lot of things, and I got the impression he was in this thing up to his little pointed head. But the one thing that impressed me was a phone call Sharp got from Swigert the morning after Corrigan was murdered. Sharp said that Swigert was scared and claimed that it was Nimes who had been in the park with Corrigan, trying to buy Corrigan's gun or hypodermic needle, whatever Corrigan was to kill with. And Swigert believed that he was the intended victim."

"Why didn't Sharp tell the police?"

"He said he thought Swigert was drunk. He has reported it since."

"Well, he should have told the police sooner," said the Colonel.

"We don't always do what we should do," I said. I didn't want to tell the Colonel to his face that he was second-guessing, which is a habit of all newspaper editors who by trade must second-guess everything that happens. "Supposing you got drunk and came to me—"

"Mike, I'm a temperate man!" he said.

"Beg pardon, sir," I said. "I was carried away by my theory and it was hypothetical anyhow, sir. Supposing I got drunk and came to you and said, 'The guy in the park talking to Corrigan was Hank Newcomb and he was trying to get Corrigan to kill me.' Would you believe me?"

"Of course not. Mr. Newcomb is a responsible young man. Law abiding, efficient, trustworthy—"

"Yeah. He's practically an Eagle Scout," I said. I could have told the Colonel a few things, but this was a time to live and let live. "Sharp had his office in the same building with Corrigan. He must have known—he did know in fact—that Corrigan had enemies. He had no reason to love the Nimeses, but you don't go to the police and say prominent citizens are bidding for murderers on the open market unless you've got more than a drunk's word for it. Sharp might have gotten around to it later, especially after he learned that Swigert was murdered. Until I told Sharp, he didn't know that Swigert died for any reason than the one given by the medical examiner in his first report."

"Mmm." The Colonel plucked at his heavy eyebrows. "Why would Nimes want to get Swigert rubbed? Certainly Nimes had no reason to be jealous of the man his wife left so suddenly."

"Sharp said that Swigert had some sort of a grievance against Nimes. He tried to bring a damage suit or something against Nimes. But Sharp investigated it and found insufficient grounds for an action. Maybe Swigert did have something on somebody—the girl or Junior Nimes. Remember that Swigert admitted to me in the police station that he was blackmailing somebody and the Nimes crowd inadvertently dropped the word *felony*."

"You've told all this to the police?"

"They know everything that's happened up to now," I said. "I was in Sharp's office when he told them about Swigert phoning him the day of the second murder."

Colonel Tanner sat silent for a moment. "Well, it's our duty to keep public officials on the job. We want this thing wrapped up. If not this afternoon, something should be done in time for the morning paper. You go back to the police headquarters and let it be known in no uncertain terms that the public demands action; that a murderer should be brought to justice. And tell them to get somebody in jail before the *Globe* goes to press!"

"Yessir," I said.

He looked at his watch. "It's 2:30 now. Probably they won't get much done in time for the *Gazette's* home edition, so Brandt will have to handle it. Stop by Miss Carpenter's desk on your way out and dictate all the facts to her. Have her type them up and send them down to Taylor, the night editor. He can pass them along to Brandt, so that he'll be able to follow through after the final edition of the *Gazette.*"

I died a little, because I'd hatched out nearly every important development in the case and Brandt probably would reap all the rewards if he broke the story of the murderer's arrest But the Colonel had the power of life and death over me and you don't argue with that kind of power.

"Yessir," I said again.

Ruthie was still typing as I emerged. "You survived, I see. Or didn't you?"

I leaned over and gave her a brotherly kiss, although my thoughts weren't along that line. She giggled and pushed me away. "Stop it! Colonel Tanner might come out of his office."

"He said to give you some dictation. Will you sit on my lap, in the tradition of big business, or shall I sit on yours?"

"Don't be ridic. What is it? A confession?" She picked up her notebook.

I took the elevator down and went directly to the morgue, which is the newspaper's library. I asked for the file on the Ridgewater case.

The Ridgewater case had occurred about six years ago, when I first started working for the *Gazette*. It had made an impression on my young inexperienced mind, because first things always are remembered.

Mrs. Ridgewater was a social climber who was married to a junior executive who didn't seem to be going anywhere. She had her sights set on bigger things and she looked around for a go-getter type husband who was headed for the top of the heap. She found him at length and he was willing. She packed her bag and hied off to Reno to get a quickie divorce so that she could nail the go-getter before someone else got him. She got the divorce, came home and married the man destined for great things.

Almost immediately the ex-husband showed signs of life. He swore out a complaint against his wife alleging bigamy. She was tried before a jury and was convicted. Her dream of being a social big-wig went down the drain.

The point was not that the divorce was illegal. It was legal but the law doesn't like detours. It sets down certain rules to be followed and there are no short cuts. The catch was the term in domicile, which loosely translated means legal residence. There is a vast difference between legal residence and simple residence.

In Nevada, a person must establish legal residence to obtain a divorce. Six weeks in domicile is long enough in Nevada, but in our state one year is required. There are half a dozen other states which permit divorces after three months or less. Our state holds that a person who packs his or her bag, goes to Nevada, gets a divorce, and then returns to his home state has not established a legal residence there. There must be a bona fide residence in Nevada—a reason for going there other than to get a quick divorce. Mrs. Ridgewater, in the eyes of the law of our state, was only a tourist. She was not in domicile in Nevada.

The clippings I examined brought out that a similar decision was upheld by the United States Supreme Court on an appeal from North Carolina, and that there had been decisions in several other states that bore out the point. I realized that there might be a lot of unreported bigamy in this country. But bigamy is a crime that doesn't often come to the attention of authorities unless there is a complaint, or unless something else brings it to light. In our state, for example, there had been another case of a man, an itinerant skilled worker, who went from town to town. In each town he got himself a wife, then left her without the formality of a divorce. Everything was okay until the man was killed on the job and the workmen's compensation commission looked into the matter. A number of wives were discovered, but only the first one collected. Two of the other wives knew he had been married before, but thought there had been a divorce.

As far as I was concerned, Corrine Nimes had committed bigamy unintentionally. But that was no defense for her and it was ample cause for blackmail. I wondered vaguely why Corrine had not been advised by her father, Charles Hayten, so that she could have avoided the trap. But there is the tradition of the shoemaker's family going without shoes, and I suppose lawyers sometimes neglect to give legal advice to their families.

Laws and court rulings make curious ground rules in many situations. But there must be sharply defined regulations to have an orderly society. Nevada was entitled to make its own laws on marriage and divorce. Other states have the same privilege. Other states recognized Nevada divorces, and Nevada recognizes divorces in other states. But no state likes to have state boundaries used as a means of getting around laws.

Well, I had discovered evidence of blackmail. Now I began to wonder how murder resulted from it. The weight of evidence now rested definitely on Corrine and Junior Nimes. However, my time for solving the case was limited. It couldn't be done today, and I didn't want Brandt to do it tonight.

The murderer had a reprieve.

TEN
THURSDAY, 3:30 P.M.

This was a case where I started out by trying in every conceivable way to be a public-spirited citizen and to let the cops do their duty without interfering. But once you get into a story like this, there's an urge to uncover things, discover reasons, and worry and probe until you find answers to all of the perplexing little questions.

There was no particular time, from the moment I heard Freddie the Grape talking to Lieutenant Guffy, that I was conscious of a desire to solve the case myself. Yet when I left the office of Colonel Tanner I knew that I was irrevocably committed to pursuing the killer, or killers, until I found him or them. And when that moment came I'd be sorry and asking myself why in the hell I hadn't let the cops do what they were paid for.

But I knew why. I was doing it myself. Why does a car salesman pursue a prospect? Why does a construction firm bid for a new contract? It was business, of course. I'm a reporter. The bigger news I break, the more valuable I am to my employer and the more sought-after I become in the trade. Ernie Pyle had to start somewhere. I don't know if he was ever a police reporter or not, but most good ones were at one time or another. The police and sports runs seem to produce better newspaper men than any other specialized type of reporting.

Three courses, at least, were open to me when I went out of the *Gazette* building. I could turn back and amend my report, which Ruthie was typing, and the case would be thrown wide open for Carl Brandt, another reporter, to solve. Brandt was a telephone man, while I used my legs, and he might not solve it. In that case, I'd have a second chance and Colonel Tanner would remember how I thought of the paper above my personal ambition to score a news beat and I'd get a pat on the head.

But Carl was ambitious and beats have been scored by telephone. It was a big chance to take.

My second choice also was to behave in an honorable way. I could march boldly down to the police station and report to some fatherly cop that Corrine Nimes was a bigamist and probably blackmail was a motive for her ex-husband's murder. I'd get another pat on the head, and Brandt would phone me the story after the cops had put the cuffs on Junior, or whoever had actually killed Swigert to protect the golden-haired Corrine from a dirty low-down extortionist.

The third choice was to double-cross everybody. I'd lure the murderer into a trap and sit on him till the cops came to put the cuffs on him. Although it looked good in a dream, it involved a degree of danger. This guy had created two new graves in local cemeteries and there'd be no hesitation about opening a third for me. And if I was successful the cops would be mad as hell. Not that I minded the wrath, which I'd weathered before, but cops have a funny way of reading the law into their wrath and putting people they get mad at in jail. Interfering with justice, aiding and abetting a fugitive, withholding evidence, and a lot of other things might enter into the case and it was cluttered enough as it stood.

Perhaps there might be a sort of compromise, in which I would be able to co-operate with Lieutenant Guffy and his minions, win everlasting praise from Colonel Tanner, *and* solve the case myself. And suddenly the idea came. I'd even co-operate with the murderer, whoever he or she was.

It would be a relatively simple plan. I'd offer myself as bait for a trap. When the murderer came slinking to add me to the notches on his hypodermic, Guffy would step out from his hiding place and put the cuffs on him. This also looked good in a dream world, but there would be ramifications. The principle objection was that Guffy would want to let me set the trap as soon as possible. That, most likely, would be before the final edition of the *Globe*. Again the story would break under Carl Brandt's by-line.

I entered police headquarters and sensed the tenseness that always makes cops different people when something big is about to break. For a few seconds I was afraid maybe Guffy had solved the case and my little dreams were shot to hell. But I told myself it wasn't possible unless the killer had walked into the station and confessed. I didn't think he had done that.

But something was going on. I could always tell, no matter how hard the cops tried to hide it. The taut-lipped business was always a cue. All over the place, uniform cops and plainclothes detectives were huddled in twos and threes talking in low voices. There were men going in and out of offices, and phones were being answered with alacrity.

Don Hilliard, also scenting big news, was hovering on the fringes and learning nothing. He saw me come in and drifted over to me, "They've got Junior Nimes and Hayten in Guffy's office," he said. "They had Sharp over here for a while, but he's gone."

I left Don downstairs to pick up what he could and went up to Guffy's office. A young cop was lounging near the door, ostensibly sneaking a cigarette, but actually there to scare off intruders, especially reporters. I started to go in Guffy's office, and he stopped me.

"Guffy's busy," he said.

"I got an angle," I said.

"Guffy don't need your angles," he said.

"Who's with him?"

"None of your business. Listen, Mike, we go along with you whenever we can. We bend over backwards seeing that you get news as fast as it develops. But Swigert's been murdered. See? We're talking to people who might know something about it. As soon as Guffy learns anything definite, he'll tell you."

That sort of simplified things for me. I went downstairs and got a cab, which took me to Eighth and Willis.

I found my way without help to the anteroom of the executive offices. Miss Madeline Harkiss looked up at me coldly, as if she didn't know whether she should remember me or not.

"Yes?"

I opened my mouth to say I wanted to see Nimes. Then I stopped.

She would ask me if I had an appointment and when I said no, she would have her defenses lined up. The best attack would be surprise.

"Thank you. I'll go right in. You needn't show me," I had the door of the trick gate open and I was stepping through.

She showed surprising agility for a dame who sat in front of a typewriter all day. She slid out of her chair and got between me and the door before I had taken a step.

"You can't see Mr. Nimes without an appointment."

I took a step toward her, seized her arm to pull her gently out of the way, but she took a backward step, against the door, and brought her palm smack against the side of my face. Then she screamed.

"Help! Mr. Calderson! *Help!*"

I tried to pull her aside, but she kicked my shins and started pounding me with her fists till I had to raise my arms to protect myself.

Calderson's door was flung open and I stepped back.

"What's the meaning of this?" he demanded. "So it's you, Lanson! What do you want?"

"I've business with Mr. Nimes," I said. "She's trying to keep me out."

"That's why we hired her," said Calderson. "To keep unwelcome visitors from bothering H. C."

Nimes' door opened suddenly and Miss Harkiss, who was still pressing her body against it fell heavily back and would have landed on the floor, but for the fact that Nimes caught her in his arms. At the same time, the outer door of the anteroom opened and several eager white-collar workers appeared there.

They halted, staring at the boss holding Miss Harkiss in his arms, she training her dress-covered armament on them. I wouldn't have blamed them if they had ducked.

Nimes suddenly realized he was in a rather awkward pose, and he released his hold. Apparently Miss Harkiss thought it was going to last forever because she had not endeavored to restore her balance. She slipped and bumped to the floor.

Immediately she burst into tears.

Nimes got red in the face and he took his embarrassment out on the three or four young men in the doorway. "Go back to your work!" he shouted. "And close that door!"

They vanished like a burst bubble and the door closed immediately.

"I'm sorry, Miss Harkiss," said Nimes, leaning over to help his secretary.

She got to her feet, sniffling. "Oh it—it's all right, Mr. Nimes." She pointed at me. "He tried to burst into your office."

Nimes glowered at me. "He is a newspaper reporter, Miss Harkiss. He learned his manners from the Russians."

Calderson, who had been standing as if paralyzed, his mouth open and his face pale at the apparent sacrilege I had committed by disturbing H. C., now stepped forward and grabbed my coat collar from behind with one hand and the seat of my pants with the other. He was about to give me the bum's rush out of there, but the outside door was closed and he couldn't do it without releasing me, or throwing me through the door. I think he was tempted, but he turned his head toward Nimes.

"What shall I do with him?" Calderson asked.

"Release him at once, Fen!" said Nimes gruffly.

"But—"

"I said turn him loose!"

It was an order from the chairman of the board and Calderson released his two-handed grip. I swung my elbow back and managed to connect with the pit of his stomach

"Ooof!" said Calderson, doubling slightly and putting his hands where I'd hit.

"Oh, I'm so sorry," I said. "Pardon me, Mr. Calderson."

He knew damned well it was intentional, but he couldn't talk. He just glared at me.

"What do you want, Lanson?" Nimes said, paying no attention to the discomfort of his general manager.

"To see you," I said. "I want to talk."

"You're looking at me and I don't think we have anything more to talk about."

"I wanted to talk to Mr. Hayten," I said, "but he's tied up at police headquarters. I wanted to ask him why he didn't advise his daughter on the matter of her divorce from Swigert."

Nimes' face hardened and for a moment he looked fearsome. But he had lost his opportunity to frighten me into silence because he had shown before that he was vulnerable. "Come into my office," he said, stepping back and holding open his door for me.

Miss Harkiss sobbed audibly and ran out of the anteroom through the door that led to the washroom. Calderson started to follow me through the door, but Nimes shook his head. "I'll talk to him alone, Fen."

Calderson growled. "I'll be in my office if you should need me," he said. He was hoping for a second chance to throw me out.

I went through the door and waited till Nimes closed it and strode across the room to his desk and sat down behind it. After he seated himself, I took the chair across from him.

"All right," said Nimes. "What do you want?"

"It's about Swigert," I said, uncertain just where to begin now that I had entered the lion's den. "He was blackmailing you, wasn't he?"

He sneered. "Why would he blackmail me? I've never had anything to do with him—and I've never done anything to be blackmailed for."

"Your son married his former wife. She wasn't legally divorced."

"My dear young man! Corrine's father is a lawyer. He says that a divorce granted in one state is legal in all others."

"If the divorced person is a resident of the state where he obtains the divorce."

"Corrine was a resident of Nevada at the time her divorce was granted."

"She lived there. At least it wasn't a Mexican divorce which can be obtained by proxy. But there have been court rulings concerning quickie divorces where a person goes to a state to get a divorce and for no other reason."

"It's a matter for a jury to decide," said Nimes. "What you say or what anyone else says has no bearing on the case. And if you dare print that my son is not legally married—"

"It's not a question of whether your son is legally married. I'm quite sure there was nothing wrong with the marriage. It's whether Corrine, his wife, was legally divorced when she married him. If she wasn't, she has committed bigamy."

He scowled. "Well, it doesn't make any difference now. Her husband is dead. She can be married all over again."

"Bigamy is a felony," I said. "You can't escape punishment simply because a witness dies. Her husband was a witness, not a party to it. And he didn't die. That's why I came to see you, Mr. Nimes. There have been two murders. Swigert said some things before his death that has cast suspicion on your son."

Nimes sat rigidly in his chair. "What did he say?"

"He said that your son was trying to hire George Edward Corrigan to kill him—to kill Swigert, I mean."

"That's an out-and-out lie. Did you hear Swigert say this?"

"No. Addison Sharp, Swigert's lawyer, told me."

"Thanks for telling me. I'll attend to Sharp."

"Since you offered me a job as public relations mail, Mr. Nimes, I've been thinking that you know a great deal more about Corrigan's death—and Swigert's, since the two are connected—than you've told the police."

"It's no concern of yours. If you suspect me of murder, tell the police. It's not your business to solve crimes."

"Is the job still open?"

"Not to you," said Nimes. He sat like a stone statue glaring at me. He didn't like me because I wasn't afraid of him. Finally he let out his breath slowly, instead of exploding as I expected. "There's no reason for us to act like a couple of alley cats, Lanson. I made a mistake the other day. Yes, Swigert had made some threats against us, claiming that Corrine had committed bigamy. I see no use to try to conceal it now, but I hope you'll use discretion when you print it in the paper.

"She wasn't aware of breaking any laws. She thought the divorce was legal. And it's no discredit to her father that he was not informed of the technicality. He's never been a divorce lawyer. He's a corporation lawyer. No lawyer can know everything. Even when he tries the most ordinary cases, he must research and study. A great many lawyers are probably unfamiliar with this kind of situation. After all, it's purely technical. No bigamy was intended—"

"It's a poor defense," I said, "but I'll grant that Corrine did it unintentionally."

"Nice of you," he said sarcastically. "After the marriage of my son to Corrine, Swigert said he was going to sue for an adjustment on the settlement involved in the divorce. Sharp, Swigert's attorney, talked it over with Charley Hayten, and decided not to take the case."

"Did Swigert demand blackmail from you?" I asked bluntly.

"I see you know a great deal more than we gave you credit for knowing," said Nimes slowly. "At the time he was threatening suit, Swigert demanded only the adjustment of the settlement. It seemed to me that he wasn't very logical in his demands. Later, a couple of weeks ago, Swigert came to Harry and threatened to have Corrine arrested for bigamy. He said Corrigan, this detective who was killed had evidence that Corrine was not a legal resident of Nevada when she obtained her divorce. Charley Hayten went to work on the case and decided that she was, in effect, a resident here, that her living in Nevada did not constitute legal residence. We paid Swigert five thousand dollars with the understanding he would obtain a quiet divorce from Corrine."

"Which would have established that she had married your son bigamously," I said. "Why didn't Corrine just get an annulment from Swigert in the first place?"

"Because there are no statutory grounds for annulment in our state," said Nimes. "Annulments are granted on common law grounds. Charley Hayten said that if property was involved it was best to get a divorce. Hayten of course didn't delve deeply into the divorce law, assuming that the lawyer she retained in Reno would advise her. Either he didn't know the law in our state, or neglected to tell her."

"He wouldn't kill the goose that laid golden fees," I said. "What sort of settlement did Corrine get."

"A small settlement. Some property that belonged to her, but which Swigert might claim."

Nimes seemed to be glad to talk now.

"The police know all this," he went on. "I told Harry to tell them everything when Lieutenant Guffy took him to the station for questioning. We tried to hide it, but you are right. Secrets are rare things in this world. Yes, it was blackmail, but my son did not kill Swigert or Corrigan. Our concern was over Corrine.

"We felt that if the truth came out about her divorce, she would be arrested for bigamy. You were invited to talk to us, in spite of our misgivings that we might be inviting a cannibal chief to lunch. But the press at the moment was our chief concern and we put our faith in the power of money. We believed you, like all men, had a price. I tried to buy you, but you weren't for sale."

"You were right, Mr. Nimes. All men do have a price. But the value isn't always expressed in money. Besides, what you asked me to do was impossible."

He thought it over and his head bobbed in agreement. "I guess you are right. We are only partly motivated by the dollar sign. Keeping Corrine out of prison was a big concern for Charley Hayten and my son. Since she was my son's wife, I naturally didn't want to see Harry's home wrecked by scandal. And, of course, Calderson didn't want to see Nimes Chemical suffer from a scandal that might sour our customers."

"You overestimated the possible damage," I said. "When you're losing, you play your cards tight to your belly so you won't lose much. Your son was on the right track when he said the mistake should be admitted and you all should take the medicine like a brave little board of directors. The public is just as quick to forgive as to condemn and a pretty girl like Corrine would have sympathy, since the mistake obviously was one that was made in innocence. I looked up the records of a similar case. An older woman, far less pretty than Corrine, was convicted. But she received a bench parole, never served a day in prison. The case has been forgotten."

"As Hayten said, when you go into court anything can happen. We couldn't be sure of what a jury would do, how long a judge would sentence on conviction, or what the public would reserve in its own judgement. Silence was the only thing that seemed really safe."

"You felt that way," I said. "It was your opinion. Hayten and Calderson were afraid to cross you, and your son was overruled. You make all the decisions here."

"I have to. I'm surrounded by incompetents."

"You think everyone is stupid who doesn't agree with you. You think I'm stupid right now."

"I think you're misguided, not stupid," said Nimes. "Besides, I'm the head of this business. Isn't the head of the firm the most qualified to make decisions?"

"The idea is old-fashioned, Mr. Nimes," I said. "But I sort of like the idea. It's refreshing in an era where no executive has faith in his own ideas. Every other executive I know calls a board meeting or shifts the deciding to some junior executive, or calls in a specialist—as you called me—in order to have a scapegoat in case something goes wrong. I like a man who has guts enough to decide things. But there's hell to pay if he's a stubborn ass like you are."

Nimes face grew red, but he took it. Nobody had ever talked to him like that before. At least not recently.

"I was trained for this business," he said. "My father and grandfather planned my future for me."

"Yes," I said, "that's what I hear. You took a great deal of chemistry in college so that you'd be able to improve your product. You took courses in agriculture, so you'd know what farmers were talking about. And you went to a business school, so you could learn how to manage a big firm." He forgot his anger. He nodded. "Yes, I did all those things."

"Did chemistry teach you, Mr. Nimes, how much alcohol injected into a man's bloodstream would kill him?"

The anger returned quickly. At first he looked at me as if he could not comprehend, then slowly his expression hardened as he realized that I had accused him to his face of Omar Swigert's murder. He sat there, like stone, uncertain what he should do about it. He wanted to kill me, but he knew it would be a big job.

Finally he exploded.

"Get out. *Get out!* I murdered no one, but if I ever see you again, I'll be tempted. Heaven knows, I'm tempted now."

"I must warn you, Mr. Nimes," I said, "anything you say from now on out is for publication."

"No. *No!* NO! You can't print that. Get out, before I lose control of myself."

I decided that nothing could be gained by staying. After all, you can be cocky for just so long and then you have to back it up with stuff.

ELEVEN
THURSDAY, 4:00 P.M.

The little room outside Nimes' office was empty. Miss Harkiss evidently was still in the powder room stifling her sobs. Or maybe she was taking a coffee break. As I pushed open the door leading outside, I heard Calderson's office door open.

I turned my head to see him motioning quickly for silence by raising his forefinger to his lips. I understood. He didn't want H.C. to know that he was fraternizing with the enemy.

I went out into the corridor and he joined me there. "I overheard. I eavesdropped," he whispered hoarsely.

"Glad to have you as a witness in case I'm murdered," I said. "Would you testify against H.C., Mr. Calderson? Aren't you afraid his proxies would haunt you after he went to the chair."

He looked as if he would have liked to turn green. "Please don't joke that way, Mr. Lanson," he said. "This is very serious. It's not like your game, the newspaper game. This is business."

"Newspapers are a serious business with me, Mr. Calderson," I said. "And don't forget that a lot of people make jokes about fertilizers. Something on your mind?"

"I want to tell you that if you can play this thing down in the paper, to not involve the Nimes company, I'd show my appreciation in a substantial way."

"I'm afraid I can't. But thanks for the bribe offer."

"If business falls off, I'll be blamed. H.C. will replace me as general manager; make me the scapegoat. Isn't there anyway out of this mess?"

"Depends just how guilty you are."

"Me?"

"I use the pronoun collectively. I mean you, H.C., Junior, Hayten and Mrs. Nimes."

"But you don't really think Harry murdered Mr. Swigert, do you?"

I thought a moment. "Junior has been mentioned as the man who talked to Corrigan in the park and Swigert was sure Junior was plotting to kill him."

"It's a lie," said Calderson. "Mr. Swigert said that to make trouble."

"We'll never know," I said. "Unless Fred Gandy can be sure it wasn't Junior who talked to Corrigan that night."

"You think this tramp might recognize the person?"

"I don't know. Freddie the Grape isn't very bright. Nor observant. And he was a little drunk on wine that night. But there's a slim chance that he didn't tell everything he knew to the police. That often happens, you know. If I could find him, maybe he'd talk to me and because we know a little more than we did when Freddie was in the hands of the police, we might be able to deduce something. But Freddie has disappeared. Either he's hiding for fear of punishment for what took place at Hayten's yesterday, or the murderer caught up to him and made sure Freddie doesn't tell all he knows."

"I hope the man's alive. The sheriff tried to find him at the place where he stayed sometimes. A cheap hotel at 879 Scanlon. But Gandy hadn't been there for several days."

"Well, if the cops and the sheriff can't find Freddie, I don't think I'd have any better luck. On the other hand, just as Freddie might be holding back from the cops, maybe the people that operate, the flophouse might tell things to me that they wouldn't tell the cops. I'll try."

We had reached the street door. The girl at the switchboard called, "Mr. Calderson!"

The general manager turned. "Yes?"

"Mr. Nimes said that you were to give Mr. Lanson every co-operation."

"Eh? Oh." He turned to me. "Goodness, H.C. knows I've been talking to you. Good-bye." He turned and loped back toward the executive offices, looking very weak, forlorn as a spy who had been caught with the fortification plans in his brief case.

It was past three-thirty, and my sole objective now was to keep the murderer from getting caught until after the last edition of the *Globe* had been rolled at 4 a.m. tomorrow. I was reasonably certain of doing this—not because I was especially clever, but because the cops were wasting time on Junior Nimes.

While Junior had a good chance of being guilty—better than most of the other suspects in the case—he also had a lawyer who was at his side and who wasn't going to let Junior say anything incriminating. The cops weren't far behind me. If Junior hadn't already told them that Corrine had committed unintentional bigamy, I was sure they'd find it out very soon. But Freddie the Grape was a question mark and until he was located, I was pretty certain that the case wouldn't be solved. Somewhere back in the dark recesses of my brain, I had a hunch that Freddie knew the second man at that meeting in the park.

It was only two blocks from Eighth and Willis to the flophouse at 879 Scanlon Street. The place didn't even have a name. Just a sign that said: *Beds Fifty Cents, Up.* The *up* might have meant that some beds were worth more than fifty cents, or that you had to climb a stairway to get to the beds.

At any rate, I climbed a wooden stairway which got smellier and smellier, as I went up.

At the top of the stairway was a room which served as a small lobby. There was a desk, a few chairs and a table.

Beyond the desk was a doorway. There were only two men in the lobby, both over fifty. The youngest of the two, who stood behind the desk and who apparently was the clerk, was wearing a dirty undershirt and suspenders. He had glasses perched on his nose and he was swatting flies with a newspaper.

The other man who wore clothes that made Freddie the Grape look like a dude, was working a crossword puzzle in a newspaper spread out on the table.

I walked over to the desk. The man swatting flies looked up at me. His eyes traveled over my clothing, which was pressed and fairly clean, and an expression of antagonism crept over his face. I was his enemy; I wasn't down and out.

He didn't say a word, but just stared. "Hello," I said.

The expression didn't soften. "Bed?" He didn't try to conceal the sarcasm.

"No. I'm looking for a man."

"He ain't here. Ain't nobody here. Nobody, 'cept Pops and me." He jerked his head, toward the man working the crossword. "Pops got rheumatism and don't go out till he gets hungry."

"You know Fred Gandy?"

"Nah." The answer came quick. "Don't know nobody."

"He's called Freddie the Grape. A wino, about forty, forty-five. Skinny as a rail—"

"Don't know nobody. People don't stay here reg'lar."

"You keep a register?"

"You a cop?"

"No," I said. I reached into my pocket and pulled out a dollar bill and laid it on the desk.

"What's that for?" he asked, picking it up.

"Information."

"Don't know him."

I put another dollar bill on the counter. This time I held onto it. He touched the end, gave a little pull. "This guy have red hair?"

"No, black, sort of gray around the edges, but not a great deal of hair on the very top. He had a funny way of talking. He always said *din't* for *didn't* or *don't.*"

"Oh, you mean Freddie," said the man, giving a tug on the bill.

"That's what I said." I released my hold on the bill.

"He ain't here."

"But he does stay here sometimes?"

"When it's cold or rainy. Sometimes. Other times he makes it free in the jail or the workhouse. He sorta likes the workhouse. Met lots of swells there."

"How long has it been since you've seen Freddie?"

"Week. Maybe longer. The last time it rained, when was that?"

"You haven't seen him in the last couple of days?"

"Nah." He folded the bill and put it in his trouser pocket. "All the cops in town been here lookin' for Freddie. I tell them the same thing. I tell you something more. You gimme two bucks, I treat you right."

"I've given you two bucks."

"That's what I mean. I give you more for the two bucks. Freddie don't double-cross no pal."

I gave him a blank look. "For two bucks you give me riddles?"

"Pops," said the clerk, "this dude—"

"Ain't no dude," said Pops. "He's a educated bastard."

"—He wants to hear about Freddie and you in the tank last Tuesday night."

Pop looked at me. "You a cop?"

"No cop," said the clerk.

"What did Freddie say in the tank?" I asked.

"He hears two guys in the park, Cops want to know what they say. Freddie tell 'em, because the cops got the goods on him. Cops want to know their name. Freddie tell 'em the name of Corrigan, because he is a dirty no-good private cop, who give Freddie a lead quarter once. But he don't tell who is the other, because this guy is an old cellmate of Freddie at the workhouse."

"Did he tell you?"

"Nah. If I don't know, I can't tell cops."

Pops squinted through the little pinhole made by his fingertips to decipher another definition. The clerk looked at me, proud of himself. "Cops don't know that, mister."

"Thanks," I said.

I reached the street and inhaled the fresh air. Then I started walking toward Sixth Street to find a taxi. As I walked, I thought. Freddie the Grape was the key. Freddie knew the man who talked to Corrigan. He could prove who it was.

The knowledge turned the whole case upside down. Only one person involved in this case had served time in the workhouse and that was Omar Leroy Swigert.

Up to now I'd been under the belief that someone had tried to hire Corrigan to kill Swigert. But Swigert had tried to hire Corrigan to kill someone else. Was it "they?" More than one? Or was it just one man, so big that he would be referred to by Swigert as a host of enemies? Or was it a corporation.

Whoever it was, Freddie could give a clue. And I had to keep Freddie from being caught till tomorrow morning.

He wasn't in his usual haunts. The last time he'd been seen was south of town. There were woods south of town.

And some empty barns. It would be hard to search everywhere for Freddie. I needed just one clue.

TWELVE
THURSDAY EVENING

It was 4:15 P.M. when I got back to Headquarters. Carl Brandt, a stocky black-haired fellow who was a good guy in spite of all the dirty tricks he pulled on me, was on the job and Don Hilliard, who came to work an hour ahead of me, had gone home.

After you've been around cops a while, you learn to read certain signs. The tenseness of a big case was still there, but there was more grimness in the air. The signs said it was a tough case, one that would not be broken overnight. These signs gave me a certain optimism that maybe I'd bring home the break in it after all.

"Thanks, pal, for getting things set up for me," said Carl.

"I'll expect the same from you in the morning," I told him.

"Hah! All you'll get is a follow. They've had young Nimes and his lawyer in Guffy's office since early this afternoon. If they didn't think they'd crack him, they'd have turned him loose before now."

And at that moment Guffy's office, door opened. Junior came out first, looking serious, tired and white-faced. Hayten, looking tense and nervous, followed. Then came Guffy.

Carl and I charged toward them. Hayten saw us and gestured with his hand. "Nothing now, boys! We haven't a thing to say."

"Is it true," I asked, "that Corrine Nimes failed to establish legal residence in Nevada before getting a divorce from Omar Swigert?"

Hayten's looks tried to kill me, but I'm used to dirty looks. "No comment," he said.

"What about it, Guffy?"

"The county prosecutor's office is making an investigation to determine if bigamy charges should be filed," said Guffy.

"What's your story, Mr. Nimes?" Carl asked Junior.

"I've nothing to say at this time," said Junior.

"Did you make a confession?" I asked because I was expected to ask something.

"Harry co-operated fully," said Hayten. "He had nothing to confess. That's all we can say now, boys. Please."

"There's a rumor that you were the man in the park who talked to Corrigan," Carl said to Junior. "Is it true?"

"It's a damned lie," said Junior.

"Please, Harry," said Hayten. "Let me do the talking."

"Was Omar Swigert blackmailing you?"

"No comment," said Hayten. "Please—"

"Was Mrs. Nimes illegally divorced from her husband?" I asked, feeling that this would worry Carl all night and keep him from learning things I didn't know.

"I told you, boys, we have nothing more to say," said Hayten, getting a little angry. "Now let us alone."

He almost pushed us aside as he pulled Junior out the station house door and to their car. Carl and I followed shooting more questions at them. Most of my questions were framed to get Carl all mixed up and I could see that he was listening to me more than to Hayten's replies which were nothing anyhow. Carl, by this time, must have known that I knew a few things he didn't know.

When at last Hayten and Junior drove away we went back into headquarters and found Guffy grinning in the doorway of his office. "No comment," said Guffy. And he ducked inside and closed the door.

We went to the press room and Carl sat down behind his typewriter. I couldn't tell whether he was worrying about my questions or trying to peal a lead for the bulldog off the ceiling.

Carl was the type who thought he could get inspiration from looking up at flyspecks.

I waited for a few minutes till I could see he was getting desperate, then I said: "As much as I dislike helping you, Carl, there's a little point that I'd like to clear up before I go home tonight."

He turned his head toward me so quickly that I wondered why a couple of neck vertebrae didn't snap. "Yeah? What?"

"Corrine Hayten's divorce from Swigert," I said. "Why don't we call Reno and find out about the grounds and the settlement and so on? If we don't get anything else that's new, it might be interesting."

His eyes brightened and I could see that he was ready to do anything because he didn't have a new angle for the bulldog.

"By God, you are a pal, Mike. What's happened to you? You got religion or something?"

"Just save something for me tomorrow," I said. "Besides, I probably would lose sleep not knowing something that even a copyboy could run down."

He didn't like to be compared to a copyboy, but being lazy he tried to think of reasons for not calling Reno. Or maybe he suspected I had an ulterior motive. Which maybe I had. "No," he said, "it's almost four-thirty. Too late for Reno to run it down today."

"Two hours time difference between here and Reno," I said. "It's only two-thirty out there."

"Yeah! How about that? Why do you want to know it, Mike?"

"It's like landing on the moon," I said. "You don't know whether anything good will come of it till you try it."

Carl picked up the phone and placed a call to the Reno *Courier*. He got the city editor on the line and they chatted awhile, and the city editor promised to overhead a report by telephone on the Swigert divorce. Carl gave him dates and so forth. He hung up the phone. "He'll have it in an hour."

"I guess I'll stick around."

Carl looked suspiciously at me. "You sick, maybe? Is that why you want to contribute free overtime to our big fat employer?"

"I've been late a couple of mornings and my conscience aches," I said,

"It'll be a stony day in Mudville when I believe you got a conscience."

"Blow," I said. "Go run your run."

He blew without buying and I suspect he was worried about the call to Reno. But he had to check the sheriff's office and a couple of other things and he couldn't hang around to find out why I was so eager. I hoped the call would come through while he was gone.

A cop came in with an armload of papers which the delivery boy had left downstairs. It was the stock final and I glanced at the story about the murder, just to see how much rewrite and the copy desk had loused it. They hadn't hurt it as much as I expected and I glanced at the other stuff on page one. Don Hilliard had turned in two or three sticks of type about minor police stuff and one, at the bottom of the third column on page one, caught my eye. It was headed: STORE ENTERED.

> *A highway market south of town on Route 81 was burglarized last night. Ed Kinsman, proprietor of the store at the Bagley Road intersection, said a small quantity of food and beverages was taken. A rear window was forced, according to the report made to the sheriff's office.*

I was willing to bet my typewriter that the beverage taken was a bottle of wine and that Freddie the Grape had committed the burglary. Bagley Road intersects Highway 81 about a mile south and a little west of the Hayten home on the old South Road.

When the time came, I'd find Freddie.

I looked out of the window and discovered it was raining. It was one of those late afternoon summer showers that never last long, so I turned to the comic page and read the funnies.

Finally, at 5:20 P.M., the phone rang.

"Hello," I said.

"Mr. Cyrus Pendler of Reno, Nevada, is calling Carl Brandt collect," the operator said. "Will you accept the call?"

"Okay," I said, "put him on."

"Go ahead," said the operator, and a sharp but rather pleasant voice with a western twang came over the wire.

"Hello? This is Cyrus Pendler, is this Mr. Brandt?"

"No," I said. "Brandt's out digging up dirt. This is the day man, Mike Lanson. Glad to know you, Mr. Pendler."

"Can you take this call?" Pendler asked. He sounded ten times more affable than Hank Newcomb. Even discounting the fact that the other field is always greener to the eye, I liked him better. Maybe all city editors are better guys at long distance.

"Sure thing," I said. "Both papers are under the same management here."

"Fine," said Pendler. "It's near deadline and I'd hate to call back. Ready?"

"Shoot," I told him, my pencil poised over a stack of copy paper.

He gave it to me briefly, another sign he knew his business. Hank Newcomb would have made a travelogue out of it.

Corrine Swigert alleged alcoholism in her complaint and obtained service on her husband through the secretary of state in our state, a procedure which had been legalized some years back. The divorce had not been contested, but a lawyer representing Swigert had been in court to work out the settlement. Corrine had offered proof of six weeks residence in Nevada, the legal period.

"What was the settlement?" I asked.

"Hold your breath, pal. It was five thousand shares of stock valued at one hundred and fifty thousand dollars."

I whistled. "Did you happen to find out what stock it was?"

"Yeah," he said. "I got it down here somewhere. Yeah. Here it is. The Nimes Chemical Fertilizer Company. Five thousand shares, valued at thirty dollars a share."

My heart went thump because I had almost everything. I even had a good idea of who the murderer was.

"Thanks, Pendler," I said, "I'll have my office send you a check."

I wrote out the information I'd received and stuck it in Brandt's typewriter. He'd find it but he wouldn't know how to put it together. Afterwards I got my hat, but before I started out the door, Lieutenant Guffy walked in.

"Just wanted to chew the fat," Guffy said. "Wondering if you've solved the case yet."

"I'm not trying to solve it," I said. And it was the truth. I was trying to keep it from being solved till the *Globe* had gone to bed. "You must've had a good talk with Junior and Charley."

"The usual," said Guffy. "When a man like Swigert gets killed we figure there's a dame in it somewhere. And the dame in this case looked like it might be the one Junior Nimes married."

"And you didn't strike oil?"

He shook his head. "No. Nimes had a loose alibi for yesterday afternoon, but if he'd had a good alibi, I'd have been suspicious. Junior said he went out a little after noon. He stopped at a drive-in for a hamburger for lunch.

"He couldn't remember which drive-in or what the carhop looked like. Said he was thinking of his troubles. He got to the plant a little before one, he said. Later in the afternoon—on the way back—he dropped in to see his wife. She's staying on the Old South Road with her father. He could have skipped lunch, of course, and doped up Swigert about twelve-thirty. But it didn't give him much time."

"Did he tell you why his wife was living with her father?"

"Yeah," said Guffy. "It's this trouble. As soon as Hayten decided to look up the law on this trouble—he's a corporation lawyer and divorce stuff is all Greek to him—well, as soon as he found out his daughter had committed technical bigamy, he thought he could have a talking point with the judge if they separated and took immediate steps to correct the situation. However, anything they did was likely to come to the attention of a newspaper reporter. You, Mike. They had to keep it out of the paper. That's why they called you in. That's why Corrine was living with her old man although she was practically a bride. They were trying to wriggle out of this bigamy situation."

I'd sort of figured all this out, but I was pleased that I'd guessed right. "Did Hayten have an alibi?" I asked.

"About as much as Junior had. He went out to lunch ahead of Junior. We found out that he ate where he usually ate, so that much is level. But he started back to the office about twelve-thirty and didn't get there till one-thirty. Claimed he did some shopping and stopped in a book store and browsed around. He could have done it, Mike. Only, when a man commits a planned murder with a hypodermic, he's smart enough to fix himself an alibi. So I think Hayten's clear. Halfway anyhow."

"Talked to H.C., yet? Or Calderson?"

"The old man said he'd come in tomorrow and we haven't a continental reason to suspect Calderson, except that he works with the others. Might as well suspect anybody in the corporation. The chief auditor or the boss's secretary. That secretary. Ever see such a hag?"

"They don't make 'em like that any more, thank God," I said, trying to imagine Madeline Harkiss with a hypodermic poised to commit murder on Omar Swigert. I pictured her as enjoying it. "Think a woman could have done it?"

"Anybody could have," said Guffy. "But it wasn't a woman who talked to Corrigan in the park. You know, Mike, a shooting and using a hypodermic needle is a crazy mixture. Of course the M.O. isn't something you can always figure to be the same—"

"You mean *modus operandi?* M. O."

"That's right. When a person commits a crime, he usually does the same thing in the same way. But in this case the killings seem to fit together. What scared Swigert after Corrigan got it? Why did he try to see you?"

I thought for a moment and had a hunch. "Why don't you look at them from the bottom? Turn 'em upside down."

"Speak plainly, Mike," said Guffy. "I'm only a fly-mug."

"Suppose Swigert was talking to Corrigan in the park."

THIRTEEN
THURSDAY, 8 P.M.

I drove out the highway, past the Old South Road and turned east on Bagley. The store was a short distance down the road, with a large parking area, graveled heavily, around it. A neon sign said *Wine & Beer,* and a painted sign over the door said *Groceries.* I knew I had the right place.

There were no other cars around. It was almost six and the proprietor was eating sardines out of a can as I entered. He stuck the can under the counter and licked off his fingers.

"Howdy, mister," he said.

"Howdy," I said. I sauntered back to the refrigerated bin filled with packaged meats and some dairy products.

"Anything special?" he asked.

"Gimme this," I said, reaching in and selecting a package of ham.

"Yessir. Anything else?"

"Yeah. A loaf of bread, a bottle of Coke."

"In the ice box at the end of the store," said the proprietor.

"And a small bottle of Manischewitz," I added.

"Over there on the shelf," he said.

I got the wine and put it on the counter. The proprietor added up the bill, which came to two eighty-five. I gave him three ones and he put the groceries in a sack.

"I see in the paper you had a burglar out this way last night," I said.

"Uh-huh. He busted in the rear window. Didn't get much though."

"You mean this was the place?"

"Yessir," said the man, proudly. "And my name was in the paper too. Ed Kinsman, it says. That's me, only my wife was mad because it didn't say Edward. But nobody calls me that. Either Ed or Eddie."

"Yeah. I read about it. Didn't get much, huh?"

"You read it? That little bitty piece in the paper? You know I wondered how many folks'd read it. Nope, the burglar didn't take much. Food maybe and a bottle of wine. I'm sure about the wine. Had three bottles of Mogen David on the shelf last night. Only two left this morning and mice don't drink the stuff."

"You got off lucky," I said, starting for the door.

"Yessir. He didn't find where I hide my cash. S'long."

About half a mile down the road I found what I was looking for. It was a fenced-in plot of ground, forty acres more or less, with a sign: *Nimes Chemical Fertilizer Company, Test Plot No. 8.* A gate, large enough for a truck, carried a smaller sign: *No Trespassing.*

I pulled up in front of the gate. There was a large, barn-like building about a hundred yards from the road. Apparently a storehouse of some sort. Built against it was a small toolshed and nearby an old style gasoline pump which had a glass reservoir.

The rain had stopped and the skies had cleared, so I flopped the top, because I wanted anyone who might be hiding in the barn to see me. I fixed myself a sandwich with two slices of bread and some of the ham, and opened the Coke. As I ate, I looked over the building. It was peculiarly constructed.

The ground floor was built of cement blocks and the upper story of wood. The roofing was some kind of tar paper, but it looked new. There were no windows in the shed or in the ground floor of the barn, but the second floor had a dormer just above the shed. The window was open.

There was no sign of life, but I suspected Freddie had taken refuge there during the recent rain. As added proof, I noted a barrel pulled over close to the shed. A man standing on top of the barrel could easily hoist himself onto the shed roof. And from that roof, he could reach the dormer of the peculiarly built barn. Even full of wine, Freddie the Grape could have done it.

I finished my lunch, tossed the Coke bottle into a ditch beside the road, then I rewrapped the ham and the bread and put them in the big sack with the wine. I got out of the car and dropped the sack over the fence and climbed over the gate, which was secured with a chain and a padlock.

I walked over to the gasoline pump, carefully avoiding a puddle of water and mud around it, and took the provisions from the sack, which I spread out on the concrete base for the pump. Then I put the bread, the wrapped meat and the wine bottle in plain view. If Freddie were in the loft of the barn, he could easily see the offering.

Calling to Freddie or pointing out that I'd brought him something would have done as little good as calling a rat or a squirrel. In fact, Freddie would have all of the instincts of these animals when it came to being suspicious of strangers bearing gifts. I just turned my back, and went back to the gate whistling. I climbed the gate, got in my car and drove eastward.

I was winning Freddie with kindness.

At the first road running north, I turned and drove to the Old South Road, then I turned west and presently came upon the entrance to the Hayten estate. Turning in the drive, I coasted to a stop by the gate of the picket fence around the house.

There was a tiny Simca parked in front of me, but no big car and I judged that neither Hayten nor Junior had returned from town. Telling myself that I was determined to defend my morals if she should be inclined to smooch again, which was a conceit that I wouldn't repeat aloud to anybody, I got out of the car.

The young woman that had cost Omar Swigert thirty thousand dollars for each day he was her husband, sat in a lawn chair on the other side of the picket fence. As I approached the gate, she stood up, smiling and looking like thirty million, give or take a few cents.

She wore a summer print dress, she was hatless and even without make-up she was as glamorous as a movie queen.

"I don't know if I should be pleased to see you or not," she said. "But you might as well sit down." She pointed to another chair next to hers.

"I won't stay long," I said, remaining standing.

She came toward me. "I talked to Fen Calderson," she said. "He told me you'd learned everything. I only hope that Harry didn't lie to the police today, now that everything will be in the papers tomorrow."

"You've nothing to worry about," I said quietly.

She raised her eyebrows. "Bigamy? Murder? Don't these qualify for big headlines, Mr. Lanson?"

"You haven't been charged with bigamy," I said. "Whether you are or not depends on the county prosecutor. We can't touch it until a warrant is issued."

"And then?"

"And then there'll be headlines," I said. "But why should you worry before that time? Even if you are charged, you must be indicted and tried. There may not be an indictment and if there is, you may be acquitted at the trial. In the event of conviction, I think there are extenuating circumstances which might bring a bench parole. Your sole crime was hasty marriage."

"Twice," she said.

"You regret the second one?"

She shook her head quickly. "No regrets. But if I'd waited, if I'd asked dad and had him check the law, this trouble would never have occurred. Aren't you going to sit down?"

"I'm afraid if I sat down, I'd stay too long."

"Is that to be avoided? What kind of a man are you, Mr. Lanson?" She smiled enticingly. "Am I unattractive?"

"You are not," I said. "But I know that playing the Lothario would get me nowhere."

"Oh dear," she said, "this is worse than being arrested for bigamy." She laughed. "No guts, huh?"

"I've been mixed up in your life for more than two days, Mrs. Nimes—"

"Corrine, my hero! Let's not be formal."

"Corrine. I've learned that you were the cause of two murders and you nearly wrecked a corporation that has existed for three generations. In other words, you're highly explosive."

"Ammonium nitrate," she said. "Did you know that stuff which my husband manufactures was used as an explosive during the war? Plain fertilizer?"

"I'll use the item for filler in the paper someday," I said.

"You are a peculiar man," she said. "I expected at least one pass." She turned her head from side to side. Then she laughed, "Of course! There's someone else waiting. Your girl—"

I hadn't thought of Ruthie for ten minutes, but now I thought of her and compared her with Corrine Nimes. Ruthie wasn't impulsive. She had better sense. She was not as glamorous, but she was every bit as pretty in her own way.

"I came to see you for a couple of answers, Mrs.—ah—Corrine."

"Oh? Then you'll have it solved. You'll know who killed poor Omar. But who really cares? He was no earthly use to anyone. He wasted his life. And he caused me a great deal of trouble. Why did you have to stir up so much hell over his dying?"

"I don't like to see murderers get away with it," I told her. "With a little encouragement, I'm afraid some people might try it on me. And besides, I make a living getting to the bottom of things."

"I'm not going to answer questions which will hurt Harry," she said. "I love my husband."

"That's why I'm not trying to be a Lothario," I said.

"I only wish I'd had sense when I met Omar. I knew he wasn't right for me. I knew he drank too much. But he was witty, handsome and a lot of fun. I didn't think of the rest of my life with him, only now. We were drunk, of course. And we decided it would be fun to elope. It's an old story, I suppose, but for some reason it seemed like a good idea then. I soon learned my mistake. Almost as soon as I got sober."

"Then you went to Reno, got a divorce and a settlement."

She backed up to the lawn chair and sat down. "How did you know about the settlement?"

"I have ways of learning many things," I said. "It's a trade secret. But I know. That's one of the questions I came to ask. What claim did Swigert have to that five thousand shares of Nimes stock?"

"None. None at all. My aunt in Rochester, Aunt Metabele, sent the stock as a wedding gift. I didn't get it until I'd reached Reno, but it was made out to Omar and me as joint tenants with right of survival. It was really my gift. She'd put his name on it because, well, most stocks are made out that way. It's cheaper income tax-wise, or something. Well, I knew about the stock. She'd called me on the phone when we were on our honeymoon in White Sulphur. That's why I didn't try for an annulment. I knew that property settlements should be made through a divorce court in this state, because there are no statutory grounds for annulment—only common law. Omar didn't object. He agreed to everything."

"And then when you married Junior, Swigert tried to get the stock?"

"He didn't have a chance. Even his lawyer admitted it."

"But why did he try?"

She shrugged. "I don't know. Unless he hated Harry."

"Did he hate Junior—Harry, I mean—enough to try to hire Corrigan to kill him?"

"Omar?" she leaned forward and frowned. "Don't you have it wrong? Wasn't it Harry who was supposed to be buying a murder?"

"No, Corrine," I said, "it was your first husband. The problem seems to be whether he was trying to get Junior killed, or someone else."

She furrowed her brows and studied the grass. "I don't think he wanted to kill Harry," she said. "Omar knew I wouldn't go back to him. And Harry had agreed to pay him—" She stopped suddenly.

"Go on, Corrine. Your husband was paying blackmail to Swigert, wasn't he?"

"I won't answer that. If the police found it out, they'd be sure Harry killed Omar."

"Not if I can prove that Swigert was the man who was talking to Corrigan about murder," I said. "And I can prove it. I am going to prove it tonight. And if Swigert was getting blackmail from your husband, it isn't likely that he'd want your husband murdered, is it?"

"No," she said slowly. "He'd want to kill anyone who tried to stop him from getting money. That could be H.C., or possibly—*my father!*" She looked at me with fear shining from her eyes in the deepening twilight. Then she shook her head. "No. It couldn't be that way. It wasn't Omar who wanted somebody killed. And you can't prove that it was. My father said the tramp was an unreliable witness."

"Your father has talked to Freddie?"

"Freddie? Was that his name? Yes. I don't know where father found him, but he talked to him yesterday. After the—uh—incident at the pool."

"And to make sure that Freddie would stay out of sight, your father told Freddie that the sheriff was looking for him."

"Father did sign a complaint."

"So no one would suspect your father was harboring him." Her eyes flashed angrily. "Please go, Mike. I'm in no mood to talk to you. Harry will be home soon and I must be cheerful and in good humor. He's so low that he needs a little pleasantness. You take it out of me."

"You can't tell me why Swigert changed his mind about the stock?" I asked. "Why was he willing to let it go to you uncontested as an alimony settlement, but then tried to get it back in the form of blackmail?"

"It must have been because he hated Harry," she said. "That's the only reason I can think of. If he wanted to have Harry killed, isn't that proof he hated Harry?"

"You don't murder somebody you're extorting money from unless he gets out of line," I said. "Did Junior—Harry—get out of line?"

"No. He paid some money and would have paid more. Go, please. Dad and Harry are coming up the drive!"

I heard the sound of a car.

"How's your father's diabetes?" I asked suddenly.

"Diabetes? Father? He doesn't have diabetes."

"Oh? I guess it's H.C. who's troubled with it. I must have them mixed."

"H.C. doesn't have anything wrong with him. He's too mean to get sick. It's Mr. Calderson who has diabetes."

"Calderson, huh?" A smile slowly crossed my face.

The smile or a note in my voice tipped her off. "I gave you a clue," she said. "I told you something I shouldn't have told."

"No," I said. "You told me something I didn't want to hear. If anybody but Calderson had had diabetes, or if he hadn't had it, I'd be happy. Now I'm not."

"I know," she said. "A hypodermic! You wanted to know who had a hypodermic or knew how to handle one! But that's not proof. Millions of people know. You can't accuse Fen Calderson!"

I walked over to the gate just as a big Cadillac drove up and stopped behind my car. Charles Hayten and Junior Nimes got out and came toward me.

Junior almost hurried to block me from my car. "What are you doing here, Lanson?"

"He came to see me, Harry," Corrine said, as she walked up to the gate.

Junior gave me an angry look.

"S'long," I said.

I walked over to my car and started to get in.

"Wait, Lanson," said Junior. He came toward me.

I waited, expecting him to throw a punch, but he didn't.

"What has Corrine been telling you?"

"Enough to clear you of complicity in either of the recent murders," I said. "Up to now, I wasn't sure, but tomorrow the cops will know that you didn't do it."

Some of the tenseness eased from Junior. "That's downright white of you. Especially since I've already convinced the police that I'm innocent."

"Maybe you think you did, Junior," I said. "But I'll bet Lieutenant Guffy is waiting at your office when you get down to work tomorrow." I slid behind the wheel of my car. "You see, Guffy doesn't know about the blackmail you were paying Swigert."

"He knows," said Junior. "He also knows why. He knows that Swigert threatened to have Corrine arrested for bigamy. I made a clean breast of it today, Mr. Lanson. But be careful what you print."

"I will. And your dad had nothing to do with keeping it out of the paper," I said. "It just happens that something in our laws says that a man or a woman is innocent, until proved guilty, even of bigamy. And we can't tell about it in the paper until charges are filed."

I pushed the starter button and drove off, before his anger got the best of him.

The sun was setting in the west as I drove up to the gate to the test plot on Bagley Road a few minutes later. It was about eight o'clock and in another half hour it would start to get dark.

I pulled the car off the road, locked it, and then climbed the fence.

The paper sack I'd left on the concrete base of the gasoline pump was gone. So was the bread, the ham and the bottle of wine. A set of muddy tracks ran from the edge of the puddle near the pump over to the barrel, and I could see more mud on the slanting barn roof just below the dormer.

"Freddie!" I called.

I waited for an answer, but none came.

I went over to the barrel, climbed to the top of it and called again. "I know you're there, Freddie, and I want to talk to you."

Still no answer.

I pulled myself up onto the roof of the shed and walked over to the edge of the barn roof. "Freddie, I'm not going to hurt you. I've nothing to do with the cops. I came out here to help you."

Utter silence.

I gave a run, for momentum, took a step on the barn roof, grasped the sill of the dormer window and pulled my head inside. The light was dim, but I saw enough to realize that I could be dead in two seconds.

Freddie was charging toward me holding a switch blade in his hand.

FOURTEEN
THURSDAY NIGHT

My best bet was to pull my head back out of the window and put distance between me and the switchblade, but when I get involved in a project something inside me keeps me going till it's finished. I'd come to see Freddie and I was going to see him.

I pushed myself through the window.

The knife slashed down and I rolled to one side. I heard it rip through the shoulder of my coat and felt a stinging sensation in my arm muscle. He'd scraped me a little. But the coat was tangled in the blade and before Freddie could get his weapon loose, I grabbed his right arm with my left hand and jerked as hard as I could.

I was lying flat and Freddie went rolling right over my back up against some sacks of ammonium nitrate fertilizer that were stacked just to the right of the window.

I wriggled through the window as Freddie came to his feet, still clinging to the knife, which had been torn loose from my coat when he did his somersault.

I rolled over and kicked at him. He slashed ineffectually with the knife, not trying to hit me, but to keep me from kicking him in the belly.

But I brought my legs around and came to my feet. "Freddie," I panted, "I didn't come here to hurt you. I brought you food and wine. I'm your friend—"

"Yah! Dirty cop-lover," said Freddie. "I cut your guts out."

He came toward me, jabbing the blade with each step. His walk was unsteady but determined and I knew that I could have been smarter than to give him a bottle of wine. Now he stood between me and the window through which I'd entered.

I backed toward the window on the opposite side. It was open too, but there was no shed on that side, only a sheer drop to the ground. A broken leg might be preferable to Freddie's knife, but a broken neck wasn't and if I went through that window, it would have to be head first. It wasn't big enough to do it any other way, not with Freddie bearing down on me.

"Listen to reason, Freddie!"

"I didn't ax you to come here," he said.

My foot kicked something. A bottle. I looked down. It was the remains of that bottle of Mogen David. Freddie halted.

The top was on, and the bottle didn't spill. I dropped to one knee, picked up the bottle and held it in my hand.

"Put it down," said Freddie.

"You think I'm crazy? One more step, and it goes out the window. It'll bust and you won't have any more wine, Freddie."

"I din't wanna hurt you," said Freddie. The hand holding the knife dropped to his side.

"Toss the knife on the floor, where I can reach it," I said, still holding the bottle ready to throw out of the window.

"Gimme the wine," said Freddie.

"Knife first. Hurry, before I count to three. One, two—" The knife clattered on the floor. I reached out and picked it up. I held it in my right hand as I left the bottle where the knife had fallen.

"Sit down, Freddie," I said.

He squatted cross-legged on the floor, uncapped the bottle and put it to his lips. He drank deeply. "Ah!" he said, wiping his lips on his sleeve.

"You're a pretty important man in Creston, Freddie," I said. "You can save a man's life if you'll tell the cops it was Swigert you saw talking to Corrigan in the park Monday night."

Freddie scratched his ear. "I ain no stoolie," he said.

"Swigert's dead, Freddie," I said.

His mouth dropped open. "He ain dead. I see him talk to Corrigan."

"Somebody killed Swigert yesterday. After I saw you. Or maybe just before. Do you know who Swigert was afraid of?"

"He is afraid of his ex-wife," he said. "I'll fix her."

"Take it easy, Freddie. What make you think Swigert was afraid of her?"

"He hate her. And her new husband and ever'body gang up on him. He tell me that."

I smiled inwardly. That was what Swigert meant by *they*. He was afraid that the people he was blackmailing would kill him. He thought they had killed Corrigan for not taking care of him.

"You sure nobody's name was mentioned in the park?"

He thought for a moment. "No. I din't know anybody who hate Leroy except his ex-wife and her folks. A screw at the work-house hate Leroy, but the screw hate ever'body."

"Well, I know who did it. And he's going to come looking for you. He knows where to find you, just like I found you. The best barn around here on a place where nobody lives, and near a country store that sells wine. Does Hayten know you're here?"

"The old Pops with white hair? Father of Leroy's wife?"

"Yes, that's Hayten."

"I see him in the woods. He point a pistol at me and so I din't use the switchblade. He say I go to jail, and I say I am here because Leroy told me. Then he ask if I mean Swigert. And I say yes. And he say maybe he not take me to jail, because Swigert is makin' trouble. But I hafta lie low for a few days. And if I come near his place, he will shoot me or Leroy's wife will shoot me. So I leave the country. Ony I don't know where to go and the barn looks good."

"You're sure it was Swigert who talked to Corrigan in the park?"

"Yah. I know Leroy. I was in the workhouse with him."

"All right. The cops and everybody think somebody asked Corrigan to kill Leroy—"

"Corrigan din't. It was his wife. Leroy's wife."

"No, Freddie. It wasn't a woman. It was someone else and Leroy was afraid of him too, only he figured that the wrong people killed Corrigan. That's why he drank a highball with his murderer the day he was killed. Now listen, it's getting dark outside. We've got to get out of here before the killer comes looking for you. We've got to keep him chasing us till tomorrow and by tomorrow we'll be ready to catch him."

"Maybe I should go see a cop?" Freddie was nervous.

"They'd put you in jail and they wouldn't believe you were being chased by a murderer, Freddie. The only way we can catch him is to make him come after us. But not tonight. I've got reasons for not wanting to catch him tonight. So we'll go to a nice hotel—"

"I gotta hotel on Scanlon."

"No fleebag, Freddie. The Waltham."

"Chee." The Waltham lacked being a first-class hotel, but to Freddie it was Buckingham Palace.

"Let's go." I shoved Freddie toward the window overlooking the toolshed. He turned, handed me the wine bottle.

"Din't let it drop."

I took it and he started to back out of the window.

There was a whip-crack outside, and glass clattered from the upper half of the dormer window. Freddie gave a yelp and dived back into the loft. In the glass was a little round hole, a bullet hole, surrounded by cracks.

Freddie groaned. "You hurt?" I asked. I went over and felt him for blood, but he wasn't bleeding. Just scared. Standing in the dark, I peered from the window. I saw a dark shadowy figure move toward the gasoline pump.

A gun flashed and a pistol cracked. It was not aimed at the loft, but at the reservoir of the gasoline pump. It shattered and gasoline sprayed into the mud puddle on the ground.

The man below moved out of sight and then returned carrying something. It looked like rags and for a couple of minutes I wondered where he got them. Then I realized that there must have been a pile of empty fertilizer sacks somewhere near the shed.

He dipped the sacks in the pools of gasoline.

When one was soaked, he tossed it onto the roof of the shed.

"He's going to set fire to the barn," I whispered to Freddie. "Any way to get out of here?"

Freddie looked helplessly toward the window on the far side. But once more I decided that this was not the right exit. I wouldn't have been so hurried, but now a broken leg would have been as bad as a broken neck, because the man outside had a gun.

I reached in my pocket and pulled out my cigarette lighter and struck the flame. Freddie gave an exclamation. "Put it out! This stuff burns!"

I doused the flame, immediately. I remembered now that ammonium nitrate does burn. Although it is perfectly safe as a fertilizer, it had been used as an explosive. And I recalled when I was a kid, back in 1949, that a shipload of the stuff had blown up in the Texas City harbor down on the gulf causing immense loss in lives and property. Something was said at the time about the stuff being stored in the hold of a ship, with poor ventilation. Just the situation that existed in this loft.

I moved around the edge of the loft until my foot found a stairway.

"Freddie!" I called. "Come here."

"Look!"

Light came through the window suddenly and I knew what Freddie was calling my attention to. The man in the courtyard had started a blaze going on the roof of the tool shed. The tar paper there would probably burn, aided by the gasoline soaked sacks. Whoever it was didn't want us out of here alive.

I wondered vaguely whether it was Freddie, or me, or both of us that he wanted dead.

Freddie stood in the middle of the loft, gazing at the flames as though he were hypnotized. I took a couple of steps, grabbed his arm and pulled him to the stairs.

There were no windows and no light below, and I risked striking my lighter again. There was a tractor and some farm machinery parked there.

"Come on!" I jerked Freddie to the tractor. "Can you run this thing?"

"Me? I din't even drive a car," said Freddie.

I went to the door and tried to open it. But it was locked. Overhead I heard the crackling of flames. Already it had started to get warm. In another minute or two the ammonium nitrate in the loft would catch fire and explode. A big loud bang and anything within a quarter of a mile would be seared.

From the road I heard sounds of a car starting. It didn't sound like mine. Undoubtedly the firebug had come in his own machine.

I climbed onto the tractor seat and pulled Freddie up beside me. There wasn't very much room, because the tractor wasn't built for carrying passengers, but we both managed to sit on the seat.

Once more I used the lighter and found what looked like the ignition and starter button. But the key was gone. There wasn't any time to fool around. I reached down under the ignition, grabbed the wires and pulled them out. I twisted them together and as they touched the starter whirred. I put the tractor in gear and the machine leaped forward.

It struck the door like a steam roller, smashing it. "Duck!" I yelled, putting my head down to escape a scraping from the ragged boards of the doors.

Then the tractor stalled.

I jumped down, pulling Freddie the Grape with me. We squeezed past the tractor into the refreshing night air. But it wasn't cool air. The heat of the fire scorched us.

Looking up, I saw the west side of the upper story of the barn in blaze and flames were being blown through the open window into the explosive-laden loft. In seconds, the stuff would go.

"Run!" I yelled.

I didn't try to pull Freddie with me now. It was every man for himself. But Freddie needed no urging. We reached the fence and I vaulted over the gate. Freddie came over on his belly, landing on all fours at the base of the fence.

My car was only a step away. If I could only reach it in time—

There was a *whoof,* a flash of light, and a tremendous crash.

The whole landscape was lit up, sparks and burning timbers showered around us. But nothing hit us.

I looked back and saw something that was only outclassed by an atom bomb explosion. A plume of smoke was hurtling into the moonlit sky, mushrooming out in a perfect imitation of shots I'd seen so often in the *Gazette.*

Then I realized the reason for the peculiar construction of the barn. It had been built that way to minimize the damage from just such an explosion. The sides and base were strong, the roof was of light construction. When a tremendous force pushed from the inside, the roof gave way first, sending the destructive blast skyward, instead of out across the fields and highway.

Freddie lay on the ground and groaned. "Come on, Freddie," I said, "you aren't hurt."

He sat up, felt himself and found to his joy that he wasn't. "Din't think I was," he said.

"Get in the car," I said, "we're going to that hotel room." When we reached the Waltham, I parked my car in the hotel garage and Freddie the Grape and I walked around the corner toward the hotel. Freddie looked like a tramp and I didn't look much better with my coat torn where Freddie's knife had jabbed me.

"Look familiar, Freddie?" I asked, nodding toward the hotel.

"Yah. I follow Leroy here. But I din't go into dis flea bag."

"Sharp give you two bucks to follow Swigert?"

"He say I get nother five later, but I din't see him later. But I din't tell him it was Leroy I see in the park."

"You didn't?"

"I call Mr. Sharp on the phone and say it is you. It is because you look like Leroy and I t'ink it not make no difference, but I din't wanna stool on no pal."

"What'd Sharp say?"

"He say I am nuts. But at this place, almost here—" he pointed to the sidewalk "—Leroy stop and see me. 'Why you follow me, Freddie?' he say. An' I say; 'Maybe you got two-bit for old pal?' And Leroy say, 'I gotta buck for you. You go out to see my ex-wife and give her a rough time? It sound like a good deal so I take the buck. When I see her I t'ink he din't haffa pay no buck."

"He told you where she lived?"

"Sure. I go there and see a great deal of her. Also you. I t'ink you are a cop-lover. I din't know you are a pal, then."

We went into the hotel. Edgar sneered from behind the hotel desk. "This is Cousin Fred from Illinois," I said. "He wants a room and a bath."

"I can see that you both need a bath," said Edgar. "What are you doing now? Hauling garbage?"

"Just tend to your desk clerking. Give Fred a room on the sixth floor."

"Sorry, we are full," said Edgar. "But I can recommend a good flophouse."

I disregarded the crack. "Is 602 occupied?"

Room 602, of course, was where Swigert was murdered. "Yes. A gentleman from Canton, Ohio, is sleeping there."

"He will soon move," I said, taking a step toward the elevator. "I am going to tell him that a murder was committed in that room yesterday."

"Wait!" said Edgar loudly.

I hadn't intended to bother the gentleman from Canton, and I waited.

"I see that we do have a room on the sixth floor," said Edgar. "A fifteen dollar a day suite—"

"You are mistaken," I said, "it is a five-dollar room. And if it isn't, the gentleman from Canton will get a full history of Room 602. However, since you searched so willingly and diligently, I'll give you a dollar reward for finding the five-dollar room for Uncle Fred."

"I thought he was your cousin."

"He's a cousin on my father's side, but he married an aunt on my mother's side, so he's both a cousin and an uncle."

Edgar sneered and pointed to the card on the desk. "Please sign the register. The room will be five dollars."

I gave Edgar the extra buck and signed for Freddie, because I wasn't sure he could write and because I was afraid he might use his right name. The cops have a way of learning where people are when there are warrants for them. I signed the name Fred Concord, Champaign, Illinois, which I didn't think Sylvester Hammond, the house dick would figure out before Freddie left tomorrow.

We went to the room and I waited there as Freddie looked at the luxury of it. "Take off your clothes," I said. "I'm throwing them away. I don't want you to leave for a bottle of wine," I said. "Also because your clothes are dirty and stink and I'm going to give you some clean ones. And you'll take a bath. Tomorrow I'll bring a razor and you'll shave."

"You can't do this to me!" wailed Freddie.

But I did, and I waited till I heard him in the shower before I left.

FIFTEEN
FRIDAY MORNING

I gave a bellhop two bits to take Freddie's old clothes downstairs and put them in an incinerator. Even the shoes. I had an old pair of casuals which were far better than Freddie's discards.

I left a call for 7:30, but much to my surprise I was awake and shaving before the phone rang. This was one morning when I could have gotten to work on time, but I take pride in my achievements and I didn't want to spoil my record of always being late.

Even before I knocked on the door of 608, which had been assigned to Freddie the Grape, I heard asthmatic snores from within. I knocked and the noises changed abruptly to a gurgle, a snort and the bleat of a goat.

"Who dere?"

"Me. Mike," I called softly, "Lemme in. I've clean clothes for you."

Freddie opened the door with a sheet wrapped around him.

Never in my life would I have suspected Freddie of modesty, and maybe he wasn't as a general rule. But I have noticed that men are a great deal like animals. Give them a little grooming, care and security, and they cease being curs and begin to act like champions. The reverse is true also, a thoroughbred can turn into a mongrel the moment he becomes rejected and insecure. But Freddie's bath, however hated, clean sheets and a night of sober sleep had been acceptance and security for Freddie, who was never the kind of person to prognosticate the future, or even ten minutes hence.

I entered carrying clean clothing.

I had brought my razor and while he shaved I called Hank Newcomb.

"You're not fooling me, Mike," said Hank, "I know you've never been to work on time and you're not at Police Headquarters now."

"It hurts, Hank," I said. "It hurts deep down inside to have you doubt me, to call me a liar."

"Is Don there?" he asked. He meant Don Hilliard of course.

"No," I said. "He's over at the sheriff's office checking on the fire."

"Humph." He was wondering how I knew about the fire. "Of course you could have read about the fire in the *Globe,* but that would mean you got up even earlier."

I knew I had to do something to convince him of the untruth. "Guffy's here," I said.

"Put him on," said Hank.

"Here, Guffy," I said in my normal tone. I paused for a moment, and then disguised my voice to a fair imitation of Guffy's Irish tenor, and said: "You worried about Mike, Mr. Newcomb? Well, you needn't. He's the finest reporter I've ever worked with. He came in whistling this morning and I says to meself—"

"Mike," said Hank, "it just happens that Lieutenant Clyde Guffy is right here in the office, standing beside my desk. He came over to ask me to keep you from meddling in police department affairs."

"Oh," I said, wondering what was worse than to be caught red-footed in a lie. "Why didn't you tell me?" I was burning because a stupid jerk like Hank Newcomb had put one over on me.

"Mike." It was the voice of the real Guffy on the wire now instead of Hank Newcomb. "Now listen to me. If you try to pull any capers on this case, like you've pulled in the past, so help me, I'll throw you to the grand jury and keep you there till they pin a good rap on you. Understand?"

"After all the things I've done for you, Clyde," I said.

"To me," said Guffy. "Not for me."

"Guffy," I said, "I'm doing something for you right now. I'm bringing in Freddie the Grape."

"Freddie? He and his wine-incrusted innards perished in the explosion on Bagley Road last night. He was hiding in a storage barn out there and—"

"Freddie is here with me. In the bathroom shaving," I said.

"Shaving? I might have believed you, Mike, if you hadn't said that. Now wipe the breakfast food off your chin and go down to headquarters and sit at your typewriter and write stories. Just stay out of my hair today and tonight I'll have a murderer for you."

"You'll probably beat a confession out of Madeline Harkiss," I said. "How de hell can I get stories sitting at my typewriter? Even a rewrite man has to use the telephone."

"Just stay out of my hair. And Hank Newcomb, your boss, says to get the lead out of your skinny ass and get behind that typewriter."

He hung up and I mused at the inconsistency of a world that believes that reporters and others who write manufacture things out of thin air. Maybe it looks like it sometimes, but even the lousiest of us, and I am in the group, does work at it.

There was a knock at the door just as Freddie finished putting on the new togs. He looked like a new man and if it hadn't been for his slightly receding chin, he might have been handsome. Even his eyes were less bloodshot this morning.

"Who is it?" I called, getting up from the bed, where I'd been sitting.

"Room service," said a voice.

"Who he?" asked Freddie.

"Breakfast," I said. Then it occurred to me that we hadn't ordered breakfast. "You didn't phone room service, did you?" I asked Freddie.

"Din't know him," said Freddie. "But if he got grub, let him in."

Speaking from a purely personal standpoint, my biggest fault is that I think I'm going to live forever. I never expect anything harmful to happen to me. That's why I opened the door.

Instead of seeing a waiter with a tray or cart full of food and steaming coffee, I looked at Addison Sharp. And he was holding a gun.

I tried to close the door, but he tried to rake my face with the gun. As I stepped back, he forced his way in, closing the door behind him.

"Wot you doin' with 'at cannon, Mr. Sharp?" asked Freddie the Grape innocently.

"He plans to do a little rubbing out," I said. "Me and you."

"Ngn! Ngn!" said Freddie, which was about as intelligent a remark as even I could think of.

"Sit down. Both of you. On the bed."

Freddie sat down and I sat beside him. Sharp stood facing us, holding the gun with his finger on the trigger.

"The gun will make a lot of noise," I said. "It's not silent like a needle. Besides, it's probably one that can be traced to you. You see, I don't carry a gun like Corrigan. You can't disarm me and use my own gun to shoot me."

"You know so damn much," said Sharp. "But you can't prove a damn thing!"

"I can prove you killed Swigert," I said. "One murder is enough to fry a man. You see, when I talked to you, you mentioned a pint bottle of whiskey in Swigert's hotel room. The paper said only that it was a bottle. No one but the cops, myself and the murderer knew it was pint-sized."

"It was only a guess," said Sharp.

"And when I called on you, you were sucking an orange. And it was right after lunch. Why would you be sucking an orange? To give yourself blood sugar. And why did you need it? Because you were diabetic. Being diabetic you knew how to handle a hypodermic, which isn't as easy as most people think."

"I'm not the only diabetic in the world," he said.

"Not even the only one in this murder," I said. "It threw me off when I learned Calderson had diabetes, but I dismissed him because I already had the goods on you and he had no motive to murder anybody—none big enough for him anyhow."

"He probably had more than I had—a big job to protect."

"But he didn't have the ego that makes a man think he's smart enough to kill and get away with it," I said. "You had ego and you were a pig. You saw a way to get your hands on a big share of a hundred and fifty thousand dollars worth of stock, or its cash equivalent, without anybody suspecting."

"This is interesting," said Sharp. "Go ahead, talk. I have a few things to do. But don't try any monkey business. Even though a gun makes noise, I'll take my chances and use it if I have to."

He reached into his pocket and took out a small box containing a hypodermic needle.

"You needled Swigert into claiming that stock as part of a property settlement in the divorce from Corrine Hayten. You knew he couldn't get it, but it was ammunition which would make Swigert a patsy if things went wrong. Then having laid the groundwork, you told Swigert that Corrine's divorce in Nevada could be held illegal in this state due to the fact that she had never been legally in residence there. Swigert demanded the stock as a price for not exposing Corrine as a bigamist."

"Harry Nimes paid off."

"But not enough," I said. "You were a pig. But the old man, H. C. Nimes, stepped in and Swigert was terrified at being tossed in jail for extortion. And he was more terrified when Corrigan came around and started roughing him up at Nimes' request. Freddie the Grape didn't hear all of that conversation, did he?"

"One of the reasons I had to spring him from jail," said Sharp. "I was afraid he had heard more than he actually did."

"Swigert must have told Corrigan about you, and Corrigan sensed a neat little blackmail setup. Swigert also sensed that you had been planning to make him the goat and he offered Corrigan a thousand dollars to get rid of you. Swigert wanted all the loot he got from Nimes. Corrigan refused, but he didn't give up the idea.

"After he left Swigert, Corrigan made a date with you. You may have been at home, but Corrigan made it clear that Swigert had been talking and you had to go into action. Corrigan underestimated you, because after Corrigan told you about Swigert wanting him to kill you, you pulled your gun and disarmed him. Then you shot Corrigan with his own gun."

"You're guessing," Sharp said.

"With this I am. We haven't come to Swigert's murder yet. I have proof and the police will get it if I'm not around, showing that you killed Swigert," I told him.

Sharp, still holding the gun in his right hand, had removed the syringe from its case and put a needle beside it. Now he took a bottle of clear liquid from his left-hand coat pocket and put it on the table. The bottle contained insulin. I was sure of that. I wondered how it would feel to die of insulin shock.

"Go on," he said. "I'd like to hear more before I do what has to be done."

I talked because it seemed to be saving my life.

"When Swigert heard of Corrigan's death, he couldn't decide who had done it. Whether it was Nimes, assassinating Corrigan for a double-cross, or you. But I don't think he really was afraid of you as much as he was of Nimes. But you were frightened yourself when you read about Freddie the Grape. You had to get Freddie out of jail.

"You knew that Swigert and Freddie had been in the workhouse together. You knew that Freddie surely would have known Swigert as well as he knew Corrigan. If Freddie hadn't told that to the police there might be other things Freddie hadn't told that would result in your arrest for murder. You sprung Freddie, then sent him to find Swigert, after you learned that Freddie didn't know you were mixed up in the case. Freddie called you with the phony tip, identifying me simply because I was the same build as Swigert and because he thought I was a cop-lover."

"I din't know you then," Freddie said apologetically, his eyes pleading with me to do something.

"Freddie," I asked, "did you tell Sharp that I'd gone to the Waltham?"

Freddie's head bobbed. "I tell him I follow you to the Waltham. It is after I see you on the street that Mr. Swigert come by. When Mr. Sharp ask where you are, I tell him where Mr. Swigert is. I din't wanna lie more than I haffa." "Freddie is honest," I said. I was running out of material to keep Sharp from whatever he had in mind. "Swigert had left a note in my typewriter telling me to meet me at the hotel. I wasn't around when he came back to the press room a second time and he probably looked up my address in the directory. Then he started out to see Nimes. He was afraid of Nimes, but by this time he had convinced himself that you were the man who Nimes ought to be mad at. But Nimes wouldn't see anyone without an appointment, so Swigert went to the hotel and started to call me.

"Meanwhile, you'd checked the hotel and found out that Swigert was registered and in Room 602. So you took your hypodermic and a pint of whiskey—which we may be able to trace—and went out on a mission of murder. The very way that Swigert planned to kill you. Corrigan had given you the information before you pulled the gun, while Corrigan thought he was cutting himself in on the Hayten's girl's stock certificates."

"And this proof? Where is it?"

"You left evidence all over the place after you killed Swigert. First you had a drink with him, but you were careful to rinse the glass and wipe your fingerprints off everything after you killed him. But you overlooked the waxed paper. Your prints are on the one in the waste basket. The cops will know. And surely somebody in the hotel saw you go in and come out. Nobody has associated you with the murder yet, but when they see your picture in the paper—"

"After you're dead, who's going to print my picture? Who's going to finger me to the cops?" Sharp asked.

"Din't talk about it," said Freddie.

"We'd rather have him talk, Freddie," I said. "I want to point out to Mr. Sharp that maybe he's still got a chance if he leaves us alone, or gives himself an extra high-voltage shot of insulin instead of going to the chair."

"We've had enough talk," said Sharp. He picked up the needle. "I'm sorry, boys, but I'm going to have to go to work."

He raised his gun to club me over the head. Then I heard a sharp click. Freddie's hand came out from under the pillow on the bed. He clutched his switch blade knife. I'd forgotten he had the knife, but he hadn't. He must have secreted it under his pillow when he removed his clothes the night before.

Sharp heard the click and saw the knife too late. He swung the gun down to shoot Freddie, but there was just an instant that spelled failure for Sharp. If he hadn't had the gun raised to club me, he might have ended Freddie's life with a bullet. The instant told the difference.

Freddie threw the knife.

Freddie missed.

The gun cracked and Freddie was flung back against the head of the bed and he slowly doubled up, writhing in pain.

But the interruption had been enough. I went into action even as the gun blasted. I sprang, seized the gun, and I threw a punch that had every last ounce of my strength in it.

Sharp went back, turning loose of the gun, but he jerked hard enough to make the weapon fall out of my hand.

He hit the wall, shook his head to clear the cobwebs as I charged in for another punch. He tried to dodge and as I swung he grabbed my arm and fell into a clinch.

I used my knee, landing in the groin. He groaned but hung on desperately.

He kicked and stamped and I had to break away, and then he reached out, picking up a bedside lamp from the table. He jerked it loose from the wall socket and threw it. The lamp hit me on the chest. It hurt, but it didn't slow me down.

And by now I had my fists working again, I slugged, one-two, block, one-two. Each of those one-twos landed, the ones in the belly, the twos on the jaw.

Addison Sharp went to sleep, sliding down the wall to the floor.

The door burst open and Sylvester Hammond came storming in, his pistol in his hand.

"Lanson!" he roared. "Throw up your hands! This is the last straw!"

I deliberately turned my back on Sylvester because I knew he didn't have guts enough to pull the trigger. I went over to the bed. Freddie looked up at me with bloodshot eyes. "Am I dead?" he asked.

His shirt was bloody, but the blood came only from a shoulder muscle.

"No," I said, "but you'll have to raise your wine bottles to your lips with your left hand till your right arm heals."

"I c'n drink wit' either hand," said Freddie proudly.

Guffy arrived within two minutes. He had called the hotel, learned about Fred Concord of Champaign, Illinois, and guessed the rest. Addison Sharp was carted off to jail and Freddie was taken to the hospital practically a hero and completely sober for the first day in many months.

I had a story for the bulldog, the suburban, the home and the stock final and I had a ten-point by-line in every edition. I even had a personal audience with Colonel Tanner, during which he presented me with a twenty-five dollar bonus and promised to take care of all the expenses, including the clothes I'd given to Freddie.

"I just had a call from H. C. Nimes," the Colonel said. "They're very interested in this Fred Gandy person. Want to give him a job as soon as he's out of the hospital. Know anything about him?"

"No," I said, "except that he has makings of champion. All he needs is a little care and kindness."

Colonel Tanner looked at me as if I were nuts, and I departed.

Ruthie was completely awed by my exploits and she gave me a look that would have melted the Sphinx. "How about dinner tonight?" I asked her.

"Mike," she said, "I've been thinking. Why should you spend the money that you risked your life to earn to take me to some expensive eating place? Why don't you come out to my apartment for dinner? I'll fix a nice meal of spaghetti and meatballs and afterwards we can watch TV and play games."

"Great," I said, overjoyed at the prospect of an evening alone with her in her apartment. "I like playing games better than TV."

"So does my Aunt Martha."

"I got an aunt in Des Moines that likes games too."

"Aunt Martha is visiting me. That's one reason I asked you out, Mike. I want her to meet a real reporter. She used to like Errol Flynn in the movies and—"

"You mean she's here? Visiting you? She'll be at this dinner with us tonight?"

"Of course, Mike, and you'll love her. She's just the very best sport and lots of fun and when she learns you like to play games, she'll adore you."

Those weren't the kind of games I had in mind. Some days you can't make anything. Not even a nickel.

ABOUT THE AUTHOR

Russell Robert Winterbotham (1904-1971) was born in Salina, Kansas, but spent most of his career in northwestern Ohio. Along with editing and writing for the NEA news service, he wrote genre fiction (science fiction, westerns, and crime fiction), as well as some storylines for the *Red Ryder* comic strip (and book adaptations) and the *Chris Welkin—Planeteer* comic strip.

COACHWHIP PUBLICATIONS
ALSO AVAILABLE

MURDER IN THE
FAMILY

NICE
PEOPLE
MURDER

Mary Hastings Bradley

COACHWHIP PUBLICATIONS
ALSO AVAILABLE

A SULTAN'S HAREM MYSTERY

Drink the Green Water
The Milkmaid's Millions

HUGH AUSTIN

COACHWHIPBOOKS.COM (PRINT)
COACHWHIP.COM (EPUB)

POISON CASE
NUMBER 10

MURDER CASE
NUMBER 33

FROM THE FILES OF
THE MICHAEL JOYCE AGENCY

LOUIS CORNELL

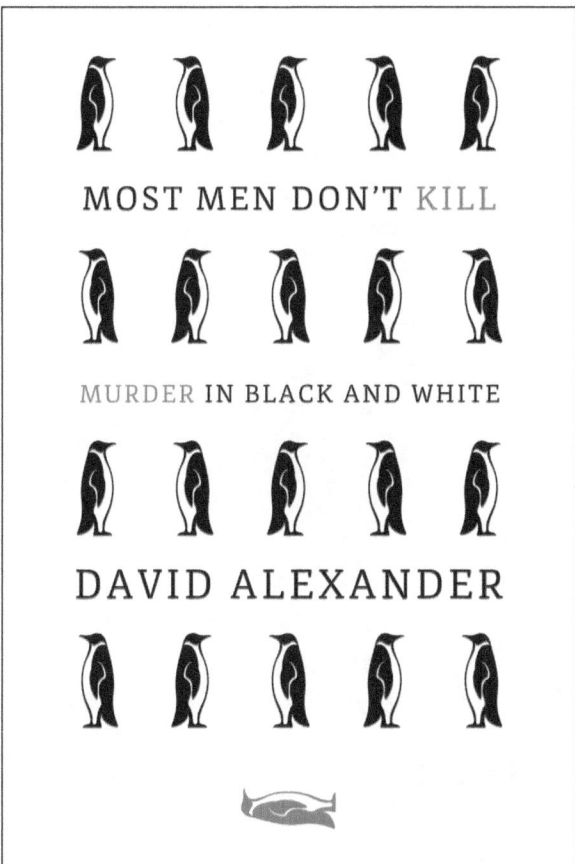

MOST MEN DON'T KILL

MURDER IN BLACK AND WHITE

DAVID ALEXANDER

COACHWHIP PUBLICATIONS
ALSO AVAILABLE

SCHOLAR TURNS DETECTIVE
IN TWO SOPHISTICATED MYSTERIES

MURDER IN THE ZOO
MURDER IN CHURCH

Babette Hughes

COACHWHIPBOOKS.COM (PRINT)
COACHWHIP.COM (EPUB)

www.ingramcontent.com/pod-product-compliance
Lightning Source LLC
Chambersburg PA
CBHW032254020726
47495CB00001B/101